"You said, 'I don't want to be like you and I'll never forgive you.' You're holding a pretty deep grudge. Who would that be, Leona? Who won't you forgive? Yourself? For what?"

"Go to hell, Owen," she managed coolly, but her emotions zigzagged from fear for her family to anger at him, and back to herself.

"Been there. It's not much fun." He leaned close. "You smell good in the morning. I'll pick you up tonight, and we'll have that dinner and talk."

Leona eased away; her senses were already humming and wanting to take those hard lips, to feel the heavy beat of his heart beneath her hand. Her blood simmered even now, when she feared and hated him. "I'm busy tonight."

"Cancel."

"I can't."

"You're afraid." His challenge hung in the morning air between them.

"No," she lied. *Of course she was afraid, of Owen, of opening, of what ran deep inside her that she couldn't turn off.*

FOR HER EYES ONLY

CAIT LONDON

AVON
An Imprint of HarperCollinsPublishers

This is a work of fiction. Names, characters, places, and incidents are drawn from the author's imagination or are used fictitiously and are not to be construed as real. Any resemblance to actual events, locales, organizations, or persons, living or dead, is entirely coincidental.

AVON BOOKS
An Imprint of HarperCollins*Publishers*
10 East 53rd Street
New York, New York 10022-5299

First Avon Books paperback printing: October 2008

Avon Trademark Reg. U.S. Pat. Off. and in Other Countries, Marca Registrada, Hecho en U.S.A.
HarperCollins® is a registered trademark of HarperCollins Publishers.

Printed in the U.S.A.

10 9 8 7 6 5 4 3 2 1

To My Readers

I hope you've enjoyed the Aisling Psychic Triplets as much as I have. For Her Eyes Only *concludes the stories begun with* At the Edge. *I'm sad to leave them. My thanks to Lucia Macro, Esi Sogah, and all others at Avon Books for their very fine work on my stories and covers. My thank you to my daughters for their patience. My thank you to you, my readers, for writing and encouraging me. You're the best!*

Prologue

"LEONA WILL NEVER FORGIVE ME."

Mist curled around Greer Aisling as she brooded about her daughter in the predawn hours. Beyond her northwest home, the Pacific Ocean's waves crashed against the shoreline.

As she stood in her garden, overlooking the ocean, she thought how much the black ocean swells suited her dark mood—and her fears for all of her daughters, who were asleep upstairs. But Greer held her rage deep within her, using every bit of her psychic ability to block her feelings from her intuitive daughters. The triplets were especially sensitive to her moods now, after all they had suffered these past months.

Her ten-year-old triplets, born three minutes apart, would never be the same now that they knew how very different they were. How being born of a world-famous psychic had marked their lives.

Greer's rage swerved as suddenly as the winds that shook the stunted branches in her oceanside garden. Studying the eerie silhouette of the trees in the gray light, she thought about how as a widowed, working mother, she had left her children in the care of a loving guardian and housekeeper, and friends. Greer had thought her daughters were well protected from the curiosity of the outer world, but her home had been invaded, her triplets taken by doctors and parapsychologists. "All in the name of research," she murmured darkly.

She had been accused of neglect and abuse, but that had been a ruse. Researchers at the Blair Institute of Parapsychology wanted to examine her daughters and had gotten the child-care authorities to cooperate. They actually took her daughters from her on trumped up charges, entering her home, shoving aside her daughters' caretakers with their false legal accusations, and took them from their home!

Greer swore to herself that she would destroy every one of them.

She had even changed her name from Bartel to protect her daughters. Now, despite her efforts, the triplets would be exposed to the world, newshounds sniffing at them for the rest of their lives.

Shivering against the mist's chill and the fierce anger within her, she inhaled the salt-scented air. The experience had made her daughters realize just how very different they were from other children, their childhood marred. And the tauma only made the extrasensory abilities the girls were born with even stronger. . . .

Though the sisters looked the same, with hair as dark red as Greer's and almost identical green eyes and pale skin, the triplets had very different personalities and psychic powers.

Claire, the youngest and an empath, had suffered the most during those two days of testing by researchers of the Blair Institute of Parapsychology; she'd absorbed too much from the people surrounding her. Their emotions, senses, and physical needs had battered her. As a result she would always have to lead a restricted, carefully sheltered life.

In contrast to Claire's calm, gentle personality, Tempest, the middle born, was impulsive, a rebel and a fighter. Her emotions easily read by others, Tempest was restless and more willing to take risks than her sisters. Whenever she left their home, Tempest wore gloves to protect her hands because any object she touched might be dangerous to her. Her ability to sense the history of anything she touched could be astounding. Unfortunately, Tempest also caught the emotions and thoughts of others who had come into contact with the object, which left her vulnerable to all kinds of evil.

Warmth slid up Greer's nape, a unique trickling sensation that told her one of her daughters was near. "Good morning, Leona. Can't you sleep?" Greer asked before she turned to the eldest triplet.

In the dim light, Leona's small face was pale and taut, her fists held at her side. Leona had always resented the extra senses that made Greer and her daughters so different, and the anger she'd withheld until now erupted. "I'm not going to be like you or grandmother," she stated fiercely. "I'm not going to be a freak."

Greer damned the researchers again, while carefully blocking her rage from her daughter's psychic antenna. "We can't help what we are, Leona. We have to learn to live with what we are."

"I don't. I won't. Grams doesn't want it, and I don't either. Look what it's done to her—she's gone crazy! Grams barely recognizes us now."

A streak of pain shot through Greer. Over six years ago, Stella Mornay's sanity had begun slipping. After her husband's fatal heart attack, her unwanted psychic gift went on overload with grief. In a sense, Greer had lost not only her father but her mother, too.

Greer could have used her mother's comfort now. In the aftermath of the trauma of recovering the triplets from researchers, Greer ached for her daughters. Her mother understood better than anyone how a psychic "gift" could be a lifelong burden and curse, and Greer wished she had her help now.

Greer wanted to hold and comfort Leona. Though still a child with an underdeveloped clairvoyant ability, Leona sometimes sensed disasters. As a precognitive, her mind caught visions of events before they actually happened. But Leona would not easily admit any of her insights; she attributed them to dreams that anyone might have. To resist what lived inside a mind, soul, and body was much more difficult than to accept it. But Leona was a fighter; she had and would continue to resist her psychic inheritance.

Greer moved closer to her daughter. Cupping Leona's face in her hands, she kissed her cheeks. "I'm sorry. But you're not to blame, Leona. You couldn't have stopped them."

Tears glittered in Leona's eyes, spilling in a silvery trail down her cheeks. Her thin, uneven tone rose above the crash of the ocean's waves. "I saw the bad men coming. I knew what would happen, but I didn't want to believe my dream."

"Maybe it was just a dream, nothing more. You couldn't have known, darling," Greer tried to soothe her daughter, knowing as she did that it was likely Leona had foreseen the kidnapping by the Blair Institute of Parapsychology researchers. If Leona trained and developed control, she could be the most powerful of the triplets. Her potential could equal Greer's, and she could probably even have more extrasensory abilities.

"You never should have left us," Leona stated, drawing away from Greer. She crossed her arms and scowled at her mother. "If you're such a psychic, why didn't you know they would come after us?"

Because Greer had believed she'd done everything possible to protect her exceptional children. Because she was a widow whose finances had run out, and she'd had to make a living. Because she'd been hired as a psychic and she had to take the job, even if it meant traveling to Canada, far from her daughters. Because her powers were weaker when she was away from the ocean . . .

"We can't always see everything, predict everything. I'm so sorry, Leona."

"I'll never forgive you, Mother," Leona stated fiercely. "And I will never be like you!"

One

___

Twenty-two years later

HER SENSES SEEMED TO SCURRY WITHIN HER LIKE A frightened mouse seeking a safe place.

Yet when Leona Chablis searched the shadows of her shop, she found no cause for uneasiness. Still, she struggled to free herself of the ominous feeling that danger waited for her. With determination, Leona put herself into her workday routine, just as she did every day, and prepared to open her shop.

She automatically straightened the necklaces on her shop's counter. The onyx beads glittered next to her pale hands, reminding her of drops of black blood. The display room of her Timeless Vintage clothing shop seemed eerily quiet, the September day bright beyond the tinted display windows.

At nine-thirty on what should be an ordinary Tuesday morning in Lexington, Kentucky, everything inside Leona seemed to stop and wait. She hated her sixth sense; it lingered inside her, ready to strike and toss glimpses of the future at her. For a lifetime, she'd fought her psychic inheritance. But now, just as "Bluegrass

Country's" racehorses circled the track, her sixth sense circled Leona . . . and it screamed *danger*.

Leona tried to wrap the reassuring safety of her present reality around her. In early September, the days were still hot, with fall's cooler temperatures seeping in during the evenings. Soon, the trees on the rolling hills beyond the city would begin flaming with color. Soon the restaurants would be filled with diners who, over open-faced sandwiches of "hot brown"—a mixture of turkey or ham and bacon covered in cheese and gravy—would choose their pick of the two-year-old horses. They'd talk of thoroughbreds, the various "horse farms" in the area, and the events held at Keeneland and at the famous Kentucky Horse Park, where racing champion Man O' War had been buried.

Leona turned to face her shop's large, seemingly cluttered showroom, which presented new elegant garments and accessories in simple, vintage-style designs. Timeless Vintage was a perfect boutique for discriminating tastes, for those moving in the "horsie" racing crowd. They needed elegant apparel for their boxes at the races, as well as for the social events that took place in the evening after the Kentucky Derby. Leona was always very careful to keep a regular client's purchases of designer evening-and-daywear listed. Her special care prevented the awkward situation of two clients turning up at an event with the same outfit.

Overhead, the slowly revolving ceiling fan stirred the soft fabrics of dresses, blouses, slacks, and skirts. Leona automatically adjusted the heavy curtains that concealed a doorway leading to the dressing and fitting rooms at the rear of the store. Beyond that was the tiny cubbyhole for storage, a rear entrance, and the narrow stairs that led up to her cluttered upstairs office.

In another half hour, Leona would unlock her shop's door. But for now, that feeling waited inside her, that uneasy stirring of her senses.

She knew an image in her mind was bound to become real when it was accompanied by icy prickles. The prickles would spear deep into her skin and enter her bloodstream. Her body would chill, then in a blinding flash of unreality, a scene would appear in Leona's mind. Sometimes her visions were small, everyday or natural occurrences. And sometimes, they were horrible, like a morning's image of a deathly car wreck that would occur at that evening's rush hour. Only brief contact could connect Leona to an image of another's future event.

Five years ago, she'd had that same uneasy sense of danger. The night before her husband left for his conference in Colorado, she'd had a vision of Joel dying in an avalanche. She hadn't stopped him from going—and Joel had been crushed to death in a snow avalanche.

Recently, her restless dreams came frequently, refusing to be locked away. Day or night, flashes of the future tumbled over each other, waiting to pop open in her mind.

She didn't want any part of her psychic inheritance from the ancient Celtic seer, Aisling. Leona's grandmother had killed herself because of this gift, this curse that had been handed down to the female descendants of her family along with red hair, green eyes, and pale skin.

Nights were the worst, when Leona was tired and worn and more vulnerable. Her dreams mixed with thoughts of her past and her family. Last night, that terrible sensation of being crushed she often experienced in dreams had awakened her into a cold sweat. "Since Joel died that way, it's only natural that I might have those dreams," she reasoned aloud.

Her denial was automatic and fierce; nonetheless, fear circled her, like a cat stalking a mouse and waiting to pounce.

On the other hand, Leona's mother, a powerful psychic, had said that there were "psychic vampires" among the "gifted." These psychic vampires could suck energy from others and cause the same crushing sensation.

Was the curse from centuries ago which she'd learned about only recently, the promise to end her family's bloodline, really true? Wrapped around an ancient brooch, the words of the curse had been translated by Greer months earlier: *He's sworn vengeance when the time is right . . . when he is strong enough. When his line has found the right descendant, one with enough power. . . .*

"You can have my so-called gift. I never asked to be a precognitive. Just leave us alone," Leona whispered desperately to the shadows. "Please don't hurt my family."

The curse had burned itself into her mind and slithered around her, waiting for a weak moment. It showed up in her dream last night. . . . *He* showed up. . . .

Leona hurriedly set herself in motion, anything to escape the overwhelming sense of danger. Her fingers trembled as she quickly checked the shop's cash register, although few shoppers used cash in her store. Her usual customers preferred credit cards and monthly billing.

Immersed in her daily routine, she scanned her eclectic stock of new clothing, straightening the scarves and glittering marcasite-and-gemstone jewelry on the glass countertop. She quickly adjusted the mirror her clients used to help them make their purchase decisions.

While mirrors were necessary for her clientele, Leona preferred to cover them. Because she had the same red hair and green eyes, her reflection was an unwanted reminder of Aisling and the ancient curse on her family.

She straightened the gloves inside the display case to one side of the counter. A long strand of dark gray pearls ran across the elbow-length dove-gray gloves. As she arranged the pearls, Leona looked up to see the mannequin's black, sightless eyes staring at her.

Pinned by "Jasmine's" stare, Leona shivered. The mannequin's eyes almost resembled those of the man in her nightmare: as bottomless as those in her enemy's cruel face as he cursed her ancestral bloodline. Thin braids framed his sharp face, his black hair whipping around as if he stood in a storm. . . .

Other than her dreams, she'd never actually seen a face like his, one with penetrating black soulless eyes. Yet he came in her nightmares to crush her breath from her body. . . .

He wanted revenge. From her dreams, she knew his name, and it was Borg.

With a gasp, Leona tore herself free from the sense that one day, she would see him in reality—or someone who looked exactly like him. A face like that, mesmerizing eyes burning at her, could never be forgotten. . . .

She forced herself back into reality and automatically checked the mannequin's clothing. The large floppy brim of Jasmine's hat shadowed her face, her hand stretched out artfully to show the drape of the surplice-styled dress. The luxurious charmeuse fabric suited the gray color—black stripes running down the skirt, the sleeves puffed and smocked. Tied to the side, the belt suited the style, as did the peep-toe platform heels. Jasmine's other hand fitted to her waist and held a tiny gold box-purse.

Leona adjusted the purse to show the tag, "Claire's Bags." She was very proud of her sister's exquisite handcrafting; Timeless Vintage was the exclusive seller of Claire's high-priced, handcrafted, one-of-a-kind handbags.

Leona crossed her arms, tilted her head, and studied the mannequin critically. Her outfit was perfect for fall's evening galas, but without the hat . . . perhaps just a large rhinestone barrette, maybe the feather design in the showcase.

Leona removed the hat to fluff and arrange Jasmine's wig. Then another chilling sensation circled and reached inside her. She forced it away and carefully arranged the mannequin's long beads. Just there, with her hand on Jasmine's cool hard chest, Leona braced herself against the bubble of her own rising fear.

It leaped in her again, this time much stronger, and seemed to crush the breath from her. She'd felt like that before, in her dreams and when she and her sisters had almost drowned. . . .

"Water or fog or mist," Leona understood her own weaknesses, her whisper uneven. "Okay, Jasmine, I admit it. Water terrifies me, even now." But there were no large bodies of water around here and no reason for her to feel this way now. Yet she felt just the same as when she and her sisters were in a sailboat accident at the age of three. They had been tossed into the ocean, and the trauma heightened their vulnerability. It was why the sisters couldn't live too close together. They would interfere with each other's lives. The accident also heightened their awareness to other extrasensory perception, especially when they were anywhere near a large body of water, which water could act as a psychic portal. Anyone who wanted to cast out their psychic net could possibly connect to one of the sisters when she was near a large body of water.

Leona's latest experience had occurred early one morning last fall. She'd delivered a client's hefty purchase to a thoroughbred farm nearby. Invited for a little walk around the gorgeous, groomed property, Leona had been suddenly gripped by the sight of a pond, mist rising from it. Her hostess had proudly explained that the pond was unusual on their "horse farm" because it wasn't man-made.

Small in comparison to the Great Lakes, or an ocean, or a mighty river like the Columbia, the pond's silvery surface had seemed to hold Leona. The mist was its extension; she'd almost felt it pressing into her chest, crushing her, sucking away her energy.

Startled by a shadow passing by her shop's display window, Leona was brought back to the present. By habit, her hand went to the silver brooch on her shoulder, the only jewelry on her plain white blouse. Crafted by her sister, Tempest, the brooch was a replica intended for good-luck protection and to unite her family.

The replica's Celtic swirls circled a wolf's head at the center. By contrast, angular Viking characters circled the real brooch.

Leona had once held the genuine ninth-century artifact. Borg's curse upon it had burned her skin as if it were marking her forever.

Now, her senses told her that she wasn't alone. Leona turned suddenly and met her own reflection in the shop's mirror.

In that heartbeat, Leona understood everything that she could be and everything she didn't want to be: potentially the most powerful descendant of the ancient Celtic seer, Aisling.

DNA had gifted Leona with Aisling's shade of dark red hair, though Leona's was smooth and in a cut that turned under at her shoulders. Her bangs framed earth-green eyes and skin as pale as the Celt seer's.

"If I could tear you from my blood, I would, Aisling. How I hate what you were, what my mother is, what I will *not* be. I will not go mad like Grams because I refuse to accept your so-called gifts."

Her silvery reflection stared back at Leona, the argument silent and effective, almost as if Aisling were actually speaking to her. *Look at yourself. You and your sisters and your mother and her mother before her, all resemble me. You think you can escape what you are? Ha! You can no more escape the visions of what would be, than I could. You have the power to be as strong or stronger than your mother, who has perfected her senses, who has studied her gifts and uses them.*

"I don't have to do the same. Why don't we just call it a day, Aisling? You go back where you came from, and I will try to live like any other woman—a normal woman."

The silent challenge came back swiftly, truthfully. *You have the gift of sight, to see what has not yet happened, and even more gifts, if you let them in. Deny it, deny me, if you will. Be careful, Leona. You've seen him in your nightmares. You know what he wants. He's coming, a descendant of Borg. He wants to kill you, or worse—he may take your mind. Once done, the bond that keeps your family strong will weaken and they, too, will suffer.*

"I refuse to live my life in fear. I'm safe here, as long as I stay away from natural large bodies of water," Leona stated boldly. But she knew fear, and it knew her; it had wrapped its tentacles around her before, and it would again.

An image flashed in the display glass, reminding her of one special man. A fit, tall, blond man with blue eyes, he'd come into her shop. Leona had immediately sensed his psychic energy.

She gripped the wolf's head brooch tightly as she remembered that day. The front door's tiny bell signaling customers had seemed oddly muffled and distant. At the rear of the shop, Leona had been busy with a woman shopping for an elegant hat to match her gloves. The man had nodded agreement to Leona's usual "Be with you in a minute."

The man had wandered slowly around the shop. He'd come to a display of Claire's Bags resting on a small display table. His smile had seemed too private, as if the handbags held a fond memory. He picked up one evening handbag and cradled it in both big broad hands.

Distracted by the way he studied the bag, as if it held something special, Leona handed another hat to her customer. But the hairs on her nape lifted slightly. From across the shop, he'd met her stare, and the filtered light caught his too-blue eyes, riveting her. His gaze had moved slowly to her silver brooch.

Leona had held her breath as those blue eyes lifted to meet hers again. The impact was almost physical, a silent storm swirling around her, as if there were feathers and beads inside her to shimmering in warning.

He'd smiled slightly, but his eyes held hers. He seemed to probe what she was, as if he knew *just what she was*.

Locked to the spot, Leona had tried to catch her breath. *She'd felt as if she'd been touched by something evil, the living warmth crushed out of her.*

Since that hot July day, when the earth had seemed to stop spinning, she'd suspected that man was the hunter, and she was his prey. Who was he? Had he taken just a tidbit of her psychic energy from her? Or had she given it?

The curse on the real brooch was too strong to deny. Nor could she deny its likeness to the one in her dreams, gleaming on the Viking chieftain's shoulder. She knew his name, Thorgood, the warrior who had taken the Celtic seer to wife and to love. With Aisling, he had created Leona's psychic bloodline. But by claiming the Celtic seer as his own, he had created a vile enemy. Was the blond stranger connected to this evil premise somehow?

Leona's hand trembled as she placed it flat against the mirror, willing the images to stop churning inside her.

Instead, beyond the silvery glass, they seemed to become real. In the smoke of a devastated Celt village, amid the terrified cries the image of the Viking chieftain with cold gray eyes came striding toward her.

"Thorgood, take me and let my people go. I am worth more than anything you will possess."

The sound of Leona's own uneven whisper cut through the image, and she stood in her display room again—in an ordinary, early-September day, just minutes from opening her boutique. She jerked her hand from the mirror to place it over her racing heart. Fear trickled icily over her and she knew—someone was coming to kill her and her family. . . . Thorgood's enemy wanted to possess the genuine artifact, the Viking chieftain's brooch, now in her mother's keeping.

The curse upon the brooch moved through Leona: *He's coming. The one. The descendant of an ancient line who wants to kill you and your family. He wants revenge. . . . Kill one, weaken the bond to the others, kill them, get the brooch, get the power. . . .*

Two

LEONA PUSHED HERSELF THROUGH HER MORNING ROUTINE and the sporadic flow of customers. But the eerie sense that she was being watched continued, and the curse on her family haunted her.

During a quiet moment in her office, Leona stared at her husband's picture. She tried to imprint Joel's face upon her mind so that he would stay with her in her dreams. Last night, her body had been aroused, just as if a lover had touched her. But Joel was not in her dreams last night; he'd been an integral part of her life, and now she felt like she was losing him forever.

She tried to inhale deeply and found that impossible. Her office's new shelving seemed too close and too cluttered, not a good sensation for Leona, who had claustrophobia. The limited space was uncomfortable; she hadn't expected the new shelves to occupy so much room. Her carpenter had said the additional extra inches were necessary to accommodate new plumbing. While Leona appreciated the tiny renovated bathroom, she missed the office space. Uneasy, as if another person were in the room and crowding her, Leona tried to work on the invoices on her desk but couldn't.

Restless, she got up, picking up the tote her sister

Claire had created. It was a special order for Rose Star-ling's daughter, Kerrylyn, who had placed first in *dressage*. Amid a winding trail of red silk flowers and horseshoes, Claire had stitched a girl dressed in a riding outfit on a horse.

Leona thought of her sister as she ran her thumb over Claire's delicate hand stitching. In May, Claire had been attacked without apparent cause. Tears burned Leona's eyes as she remembered the incidents. "I'm so sorry that happened to you, Claire Bear."

As she looked out of the second-story window onto the strip mall's parking lot and traffic passing on the street, Leona's hand went to her good-luck brooch. Her wrists were usually bare because bracelets of any kind caused her to remember the restraints she'd worn while at the Blair Institute of Parapsychology. She was only ten when she and her sisters had been unwilling subjects for medical research. Her claustrophobia had begun then.

Leona's emotions tumbled fiercely around her as she wrapped her arms around herself. The shadows that had settled firmly around her shifted when the door's tiny overhead bell tinkled, and a cheerful feminine voice sounded. "Leona? Where are you, honey? I brought lunch."

Leona smiled, welcoming the warmth of the shop's part-time seamstress and her good friend. Careful to choose friendships, Leona had been surprised at how easily Sue Ann Marshfield's easy, cheerful personality had suited her. Dinner, a movie, and girl talk with Sue Ann had often eased Leona's dark moments. The young homemaker and mother of two young children also enjoyed their friendship and dinner dates: Sue Ann had laughed as she explained to Leona how she badly needed the "breathers" from her family.

To escape her uneasiness Leona focused on girl talk over lunch with Sue Ann, the two of them sharing

Kentucky's customary sugared "sweet tea" with their meal. Sue Ann's soft Southern tone and her animated stories about her two young children calmed Leona's restless senses.

Three fittings had been scheduled for Sue Ann's busy fingers that afternoon. When finished, Sue Ann picked up the clothing to be altered and left at four o'clock. "I'll bring these back tomorrow. I'll start working on them the minute the kids hit the sack. You look tired, hon. Get some sleep tonight, okay? Take a long bubble bath, and you'll settle right down."

"Thanks. I'll do that." Leona thought of the wine she'd sip before, during, and after that bubble bath, just enough to take the edge off her tense nerves.

She was always very careful not to drink too much. Her grandmother had drunk heavily to escape her extrasensory perceptions; it hadn't worked.

After Sue Ann left the shop, Leona automatically waited on a few browsers and regular customers. During breaks, she refreshed her laptop's database with the day's purchases and called to check a late shipment of silk blouses.

She reached for the cell phone in her slacks pocket. There was no need for it to ring or vibrate; her sisters and her mother didn't need actual sound when psychic tingles served just as well. The tingle this time told Leona that her youngest sister was calling from Montana. "Hi, Claire."

Claire's soft, soothing tones reflected her empathic gift of bringing ease to others. Leona let herself flow into that easy, calming river her sister provided. Claire spoke of her new husband, Neil Olafson, of the camper he was building, and of the new Claire's Bags shipment she was sending to Leona. Then she asked, "Is everything all right?"

"I'm fine, but I miss Joel. It's been five years but I still dream of him. I—it's highly sexual—and now his face is blurring in my visions. I don't want to lose him. And I don't even want to talk about my other dreams."

"I know," Claire said softly.

As an empath and as a sister, Claire always understood. No matter how sharp or angry or frustrated Leona was, her sister remained calm. "The dreams are coming more rapidly now, aren't they?"

"They have since that man walked into this shop in July. Some of them are violent." Leona didn't want to remember the dream she'd had at daybreak. It was as if she were Aisling, her ancestor, awaiting the Viking raiders, their ships' sails the color of newly spilled blood. She understood the terror the raiders would bring to her people, but the violent images that came next had been even worse. Then the Viking chieftain, Thorgood, had taken Aisling for his own, and she'd made love with him.

Leona had made love with him. She had awakened in the aftermath, her body well sated as if the dream had been real. At that frantic, slippery twilight moment, she decided that it was time to take a real-life lover to help her erase the dreams. She wanted to exhaust herself body and soul, until nothing was left for her visions to invade.

"You have a plan, and it involves having sex, Leona Fiona," Claire playfully used Leona's childhood nickname. Her psychic connection had caught Leona's plan for relief.

Leona didn't deny the need Claire had picked up on. When on the telephone, the triplets often caught remnants of the others' emotions, and sometimes even what they were seeing, if the person or object made a strong enough impression. "I've decided to start dating again. Okay, I've dated infrequently—no sex involved—but this time, I want a brief, hot, exhausting, satisfying affair that goes absolutely nowhere. Don't worry. I'll be cautious and selective."

A newlywed, Claire laughed softly, and from her tone, she could have been wearing a blush. "Sex won't stop the dreams. It may enhance them, though."

Leona watched a tall man pause outside the tinted display windows, evidently considering coming in to browse.

Claire's sister-and-psychic connection quickly picked up the image in Leona's mind. "He's attractive, is he? The man outside your window?"

The man moved slightly, hidden by a window display. "I can't see that well. I'm at the back of the store, and the windows are tinted to protect against the sunlight's damage to fabrics. But he's tall and dark."

"And handsome?"

"Listen, if he spends money in here, I really don't care."

Claire laughed softly. "Try that hard-businesswoman act on someone else. You just saw a man who interested you. I felt the leap in your senses clear up here in Montana."

"I can't keep anything from you while we're on the line, can I? Thank goodness we can't live too close to each other, or you'd really be absorbing a lot of frustration. But, hey, you just got married, and you wouldn't have a problem relieving the pressure, would you?" While Leona kept her personal life private with outsiders, it was not possible with her family. It was not necessary either.

Her sisters understood her needs all too well. They also knew exactly how much she resented their psychic inheritance and their mother.

As if sensing the turn in Leona's thoughts, Claire said, "You resent Mom, and she can't help it, any more than her mother before her and so on. Aisling couldn't help it either. You could be the strongest of us all, Leona Fiona, if you ever decide to open that door fully and train yourself. Are you wearing your brooch? Promise me that you'll wear that brooch," Claire added urgently. "I'm wearing mine, and so is Tempest. It comforts me that we're connected in this way, when we have to live so far apart."

"No, it wouldn't be good for me to live close to you or Tempest and her husband. I'd pick up that newlywed pink cloud, then I'd really be on the make."

Leona smoothed the brooch with her fingertip. It was much lighter and less savage-looking than the original heavier four-inch-by-six-inch artifact—a wolf's head amid worn, angular Viking characters. On the outer band, empty indentations remained where once stones would have been set.

A very powerful seer and magician had sworn to end the line of Thorgood and Aisling, to take the brooch and to take the power. . . .

In her dreams, when she was Aisling, Leona had faced him. Borg's psychic power had sucked at her mind as his black eyes had stripped her body. "You will be mine," he promised, "sooner or later. Thorgood and his men can't protect you forever."

"Forever is a long time, Borg," she'd replied fiercely. "Your curses mean nothing."

But, with Claire and Tempest both recently attacked, Leona wasn't as certain as Aisling had been.

"You're thinking about the brooch again, aren't you? And the curse that goes with it?" Claire asked.

Leona struggled to block Claire, an empath too easily injured by dark savage emotions. "You asked if I was wearing the wolf's-head brooch?"

She looked down at her usual workday outfit. "Today I'm wearing it on a fitted white blouse with my black slacks. I wonder if Mother ever wears the real one."

"I doubt it. It would be too heavy for today's fabrics. But she might at times, trying to connect with whoever this 'right descendant' is. She's hoping this actual flesh-and-blood descendant of Borg will come after her—she says it feels like a 'him.' But she's been hunting him and says something is blocking her. She's said that those dreams you are having of being crushed are exactly what a psychic vampire can make you feel. They can suck away your energy and use it to build their own."

Leona picked up Claire's next suggestion before it was voiced: "Mother can't come here. She can't protect me every minute. Besides, she's strongest near the ocean, or a large body of water. Here, without that re-inforcement, she might be just human, after all. . . . That man outside the shop is moving toward the door, as if he's coming inside. Talk with you later."

"Leona, wait—"

"I refuse to live in fear. I have to go. That man is coming in the shop now." The man's body seemed to fill the doorway. His hand on the door handle, he seemed to hesitate, as if about to enter a foreign land. Leona smiled briefly. The man wasn't used to shopping for women's apparel.

Leona couldn't see his face, but a wedge of morning sunlight spread through those long legs.

"Mom isn't wrong about this danger, and you know it," Claire stated fiercely. "You have the same dreams as she does."

"Okay, I may. But we may both be interpreting them wrongly," Leona admitted reluctantly. "And sometimes seeing into the future is nothing but smoke and mirrors. The visions can be skewed and dead-end and meaning-less . . ."

The man glanced up at the bell, which had just tinkled, announcing his entrance. He carefully closed the door and placed his hands on his hips as he surveyed the displays.

This time when Leona spoke, her voice was low. "I know. Borg's descendant has already tried to have someone kill you and Tempest and he's failed in those attempts. Since you've both bonded with your husbands, logically I'm the weakest link in our family now, and I'm next on his list. I'll be careful."

Leona probed gently through her sister's humming silence but only saw happy little polka dots in her mind's eye, which changed their psychic connection in a heartbeat. "Um, Claire? Is there something I should know? You aren't trying to block me for some reason, are you?"

Claire's flustered, "Who me?" said she was doing exactly that. The polka dots abruptly evaporated. "But it's not a bad thing, Leona. I'd just prefer not to tell you, so stop probing. You're getting stronger, you know."

"I have to take care of this customer. Talk with you later. Bye." For the moment, Leona wasn't concerned about whatever her sister was trying to hide, the "not a bad thing." She was more interested in the man standing in front of her. Few men came into her women's clothing boutique, and the ones who did usually needed help. They seemed uneasy surrounded by so much femininity and, as an experienced salesperson, Leona always gave them time to adapt to the setting and browse a bit, before approaching them.

She smiled as she smoothed a pale lacy slip-dress; it was to be worn under a sheer, flowing, embroidered dress with a layered satin belt. Sue Ann had urged Leona to try it on "for fun." They'd ended the day laughing over how ill-suited the style was for Leona.

The outfit's wide-brimmed hat was perfect for a summer garden party and matched the dress perfectly. But fall's chill was on the way and Leona went to work with her marker, reducing the price of both. She hung the dress on the pegboard display near the counter, then placed the hat in a big tissue-lined box. As the man moved through her store, she gave him a more thorough once-over.

In a T-shirt that had seen better days, worn Western jeans, a belt and workman's boots, this man wasn't her usual browsing male. Leona guessed his height at about six-three without the boots. Long, lean, and angular, he'd make a perfect male model, "a clothes horse." The power apparent in his broad shoulders and muscular body would interest any woman.

Including Leona. The sexual tug she felt caused her to suck in her breath. Her nipples squeezed into tight nubs, and her lower body contracted as if he were already exploring it. An image flashed of him naked: lots of muscles, a hard, lean body, all wrapped up in nothing but that dark skin. The vision was so vivid that she gripped the counter; she could almost feel those muscles sliding next to her body, that thrust deep within her. Even now, her body was quickening, her pulse running hot . . .

On the street outside, a car honked, startling her. But her mind clung to the image, her body wanting more.

Leona quickly gripped the scissors she'd pulled out to remove a thread from a dress and pricked her fingers with the sharp tip. The slight pain was enough to help her refocus. Once she'd reclaimed her body's hunger and tucked it neatly away, she put the scissors back, bracing herself to discuss feminine fabrics and styles with a man with dust on his jeans and who looked as if he'd just ridden in off the range.

As she moved toward him with her usual, "May I

help you?" Leona's years of customer service told her that this man needed something special. Or else her damned psychic edge was quivering as it did when customers were deeply disturbed.

He didn't turn to her, but studied a display of Claire's Bags. "Mm. I need something for my sister."

Need, not want. The difference was striking. This man was no light shopper. He was obviously troubled, and he wanted to buy a gift for someone he loved.

As she faced his powerful back, Leona wanted to place her hand on those muscles, smooth them with her palms, then draw her nails down his burnished skin. It was an instinctive and primitive reaction, to mark a sexual partner, and one she hadn't experienced.

Lovemaking with Joel had been sweet and tender . . . not the hot, animalistic urge to take what she wanted.

Leona caught his masculine scent—dark, woodsy, soap—it seemed to flow into her with each breath.

He turned, his face in profile. His skin was dark, almost bronze, a vivid contrast to the cool vanilla shades of the display blouse behind him. With those straight, long black lashes and thick, arched brows, he could have Native American blood. The raw impact of his profile startled her—masculine, harsh, tough, lines across his forehead and around his mouth, a strong jawline that led into a muscled throat.

Fascinated, Leona stared at the pulse in that tanned throat. She could almost feel the beat of his blood pounding within her. . . .

Much taller than her five-foot-nine, he had thick straight hair that gleamed, almost blue-black, and just about reached his collar. Leona held her breath, her senses heating. Her gaze skimmed the length of his arms, the way one large hand held a fragile necklace he'd picked up from the display case. A muscle moved in his arm as he cupped it gently, sensually, the way a woman's breast should be held. His left index finger prowled slowly around the beads, and Leona noted that he wasn't wearing a wedding ring. She shivered, her breasts peaking as he touched one bead and then another.

She could almost feel the heat of that fingertip circling and arousing her nipples. She could almost feel those powerful arm muscles sliding against her skin, damp with sexual strain . . .

Leona braced herself against the hunger that vibrated deep within her. Logically, this customer was only an ordinary man; perhaps she was still aroused from her dream last night. How else could she explain her powerful attraction toward this stranger?

Crossing her arms over breasts that seemed too sensitized, she asked, "What are you looking for, a necklace?"

His deep tone seemed distracted. "Maybe. I need suggestions."

She knew how his voice would feel against her skin, a rumble that vibrated deep within her. . . . Leona drew a deep, steadying breath and flowed into her saleswoman mode: "I see. I think I can help. A good place to start might be how much you'd like to spend. We have some very nice low-end items, then some that are quite expensive, one-of-a-kind."

Warmed by that broad, callused palm, the beads rippled almost sensuously as they moved. "Something that will make my sister happy. I want to see her smile. Just for a little while. She's having a bad time."

The softness Leona often hid from outsiders quivered and warmed; she would want to do the same for her sisters. "I see. What kinds of things does she like? Dresses? What colors? Does she have any special hobbies?"

"She likes horses. Animals like her. They settle her

down." He turned his head slightly to look at the display window. "I saw a purse in the window that had horses on it."

"I'll get it for you. I should tell you that any of Claire's Bags are very expensive. They're handmade and one-of-a-kind. The artist creates each one with a special name. She does the hand stitching herself, and she's very good."

"Janice would like that . . . something handmade. She was a graphic artist and very creative. But she's not doing design anymore."

"I have two creative sisters." Leona understood: a gift from warm human hands, not machines or factories, was more personal. "I'll get it. Claire named it 'Freedom.' It's actually a tote, and many of our customers like something with horses on them. The design suits Bluegrass Country and the horse lovers around here."

She walked to the window display and bent to lift "Freedom." The design was a simple blend of tapestry and suede. Claire had stitched a mountain scene behind a tapestry of racing horses.

Leona removed the tissue packing that filled the tote and turned back to the man. "It has a lot of pockets, perfect for women's things, and an attached key ring—women are always digging for their keys—and a cell-phone pocket. Note the—"

Light eyes, set in a rugged face, pinned her. Set in his harsh face, they weren't blue but rather the color of smoke. His stare seemed to slowly absorb everything about Leona: her hair, her white blouse and black pants outfit, her black pumps. Leona held her breath as the man's gaze slowly moved over her. The intense sexual charge was immediate and shocking, and Leona's heartbeat jumped into overdrive. This man liked what he saw, and he wanted her.

The primitive need for sex pounded at Leona, and this time, it came from him. Sheer masculine hunger wrapped around her, nothing sweet or tender in it, just the raw explosive need for bodies pounding against each other, blood racing, throbbing hot in his veins. She could almost feel him in her, the pressure building frantically.

When her breath returned, Leona braced herself to walk toward him. Men had wanted her before; she'd dated infrequently, but she'd never been really interested enough to develop intimacy. She'd missed sharing it with Joel, the pillow talks and a comfortable friendship.

Joel had understood her aversion to being held too close, her claustrophobia overwhelming her in the missionary position. She doubted that another man would understand, and she wasn't explaining.

The man's expression was quickly shielded, but she'd recognized the raw, sexual tug. It had nothing to do with intimacy and pillow talks, just bodies satisfying each other until both were drained.

A guarded woman, who knew the dangers of involvement especially with the lurking danger of an energy that wanted to destroy her family, Leona held her breath. She was on edge, the night's sensual dreams still simmering in her.

On the other hand, a little relief might chase away those dreams. Leona put on her professional smile and walked toward him. "Note the stitching. The handwork is very fine."

His silvery eyes bound her. He took the tote without looking away from her eyes. "Janice will like this. It will remind her of Montana. That's where we're from . . . Montana. We're new here—two weeks. We're just getting settled in."

Montana! This information jarred her; Claire lived in Montana and had been unexpectedly and viciously attacked by a man she'd met only once, a gentle man apparently trying to rebuild his life. *Leona could be standing in the same presence of that Borg-descendant who wanted to harm her family.*

She struggled to appear calm. "It's a beautiful state. How long did you live there?"

"Always. We were born there. We lost our parents when Janice was sixteen. I've been responsible for my sister ever since. I thought moving here would be good for her, a change of scenery. I'm hoping new surroundings will make a difference. She's—she's been diagnosed as having depression and other things. It's complicated."

Pain flickered through his eyes, his lips tightening as though each word was a wound.

"I see. I hope you like it here and that she is better. If she likes horses, this is definitely horse country." Because her father had died when the triplets were four, Leona understood how traumatic losing a parent could be. But to lose both parents was unimaginable.

Leona studied the man closely. Aisling's warnings came more frequently now, the visions very clear. The Borg and the threat to her family who appeared in Leona's dreams had black, burning eyes. . . .

This man had unusual silver eyes, and he appeared to be of Native American descent. Leona pushed away her uneasiness; even if he were physically similar to the man in her dreams, she couldn't avoid every man who possibly might have descended from Vikings or from Celts. If she was uneasy at all, it was because she found this man attractive. As a woman who had just decided that sex could ease her, she naturally responded to the hot, male-hungry way he'd looked at her.

Then, because Leona remembered that his sister was "having a bad time" she added impulsively, "Tell her it was created in Montana, just for her."

Leona's impulsive words stunned her. She was usually methodical, careful, and professional when dealing with potential customers.

"Thank you. She'd know if it wasn't true."

Leona frowned slightly. Born to a psychic family where odd statements were sometimes frequent, she asked warily, "How would she know?"

"Janice is good at things like that."

Leona tried to look away from those light eyes, a sharp contrast to his high cheekbones and blunt nose. When she finally did, it was to his mouth. She knew exactly how that hard mouth would feel on her skin, exactly how his breath would warm her. She understood how his jaw would feel against her throat, how his broad shoulders would feel beneath her fingertips.

Because she knew and feared her own reaction, Leona hurried to the counter, placing distance and a barrier between them. "Is there anything else?"

He just stood there holding that feminine tote bag in his big hard hands. The froth of blouses and dresses that surrounded him emphasized his dark complexion, that straight blue-black hair, the raw masculine stance. "Are you married?" he asked suddenly.

Heat flushed her face, and her senses danced. The direct question was unexpected and probably inappropriate, and Leona heard her own breathless answer, "No. Are you?"

"No. Never have been. I'll take the bag. I'd like to clean up before I take you to dinner—if you'll go. What time do you close?"

"His name is Owen Shaw and he's just bought a small horse farm here, and is fixing up the two-story house."

As Leona prepared for her date with Owen, she used her office's speakerphone to talk with Tempest. Her sister lived near Lake Michigan, but she and her husband, Marcus Greystone, were planning to relocate. "Apparently Owen worked with his father, who was a carpenter, so he knows what he's doing on the house renovation. His sister who lives with him fell in love with the old Stillings place. Her name is Janice and she has a private nurse-caregiver who also does housekeeping. She stays with them twenty-four/seven. His sister is on antidepressant medication, and they just moved here from Montana for a change of scenery. He bought one of Claire's handbags for her, and it wasn't cheap. Right now he's spending time getting his sister settled, but Owen is looking for other real estate to fix and then sell."

"So he 'flips' real estate. You said he was in investments? For himself, or as a business?" Tempest asked.

"He was an investment broker before his sister became really ill. Then he had to care for her and couldn't work regular hours. He said he fell into one or two real estate deals. Owen found he could take care of his sister at the same time he worked on the houses and managed their private accounts. Apparently, they've tried everything to help her, and nothing has really worked so far. I really hope this move helps them both. . . . That's about it, I guess. I know you're worried about me, but you should know that I would ask a lot of questions before going out with a stranger, Tempest."

"Yeah, right. Claire said the sexual vibrations from you caused her husband to have a very good time this afternoon. Neil says to thank you."

When Tempest stopped giggling, Leona said, "I'm so glad everyone is enjoying themselves."

"Hey. Don't get your nose out of joint. You deserve payback for teasing us. It may be a once-in-a-lifetime occurrence and so unlike our cool, in control, sophisticated sister. You haven't exactly been active. Let us enjoy the moment. What's this guy look like?"

After Leona inserted pearl studs into her earlobes, she removed the cloth shielding the full-length mirror. The cloth had served to protect her from her own reflection, her resemblance to Aisling, and the constant reminder of danger to her family. Tonight, she intended to escape everything by enjoying Owen's company. A sexual apperitif might do wonders to relieve her restlessness.

She smoothed the green summer-weight sweater she'd taken from the racks. The V neckline led into tiny buttons, the fabric light and formfitting down to her hips. "Owen is tall, dark—not handsome at all, but rather . . . seasoned-looking. He looks as if he's seen life and lived it. He's maybe—oh, midthirties."

"And you're excited. I can feel the heat-vibes up here in Michigan." A sculptor with a highly creative mind, Tempest was busy visualizing. "He must be something if you didn't run him off with your usual cold freeze or your 'bite-me' attitude. I still can't believe you actually accepted a date with a stranger."

"He's very . . . I don't know . . . very sleek and lean. I don't sense anything Celtic or Viking about him, if you're worried about the so-called psychic vampire Mother thinks is after our family. He said they changed to Shaw from the tribal name long ago."

"I believe there is a psychic vampire sucking off energy from others, making himself stronger," Tempest said. "I'd felt something like that before I bonded with Marcus. My husband has settled something inside me. I'm calmer. But too many incidents have happened to our family, and coupled with the dreams of Aisling warning us, we *know* something is hunting us and it isn't sweet. Every one of us feels as if we're in danger. If it is that Borg descendant, he's much stronger than the original Big Daddy. We just need him to come out of the woodwork and stop using others to do his bad stuff. By the way, wear your brooch, will you? I like to think you're protected and speaking of which, my gosh, Leona, use protection, will you? Are you carrying any? Every woman should."

Leona looked outside to the gathering storm clouds. Owen was to meet her at the store; they'd take a short walk to the restaurant, so there was no need for her raincoat. She smoothed the brooch on her sweater; the intertwined Celtic design seemed to suit the green shade. She usually preferred no jewelry, especially anything that would remind her of her lineage. But the brooch gave her comfort on an unsteady voyage, that of spending a few hours with a very desirable, sexual man. "Listen, younger-sister-by-three-minutes, I've had a few dates since Joel died."

"Yes, but you've never set out deliberately to score, and that's what you want to do tonight, to relieve the pressure and those dreams, isn't it?"

"I have no intention of 'scoring' tonight. I just thought it would be nice to have dinner with Owen. Especially since my handyman started on my bedroom-closet design today. I had to take all my things out of the closet and stash them all around the bedroom, covering them with plastic. Vernon did such a good job here in the shop, renovating the dressing rooms and my upstairs bathroom, that I asked him to help me with a few things at home. There will be sawdust all over. I wasn't looking forward to going home to that mess, let alone fixing something for dinner."

"Okay, so you're going to check this sexy guy out, feel around a little bit to see if you feel safe with him—and then, you'll probably nail him."

Leona sighed. Tempest had always been the most direct of the triplets. "Do you have to always be so frank, Tempest Best?"

"Yeah, Leona Fiona." With gloves protecting her

psychic hands, Tempest had searched for and found the brooch. In the hunt, she'd also found love, one Marcus Greystone, a tough and powerful businessman.

Leona wasn't looking for love; she didn't want a second chance at being mortally wounded, of having half of her soul torn away. Tonight, her needs were simple: to feel like a desirable woman in the arms of a very potent male. She dug into her large tote, one handcrafted by Claire and simply called "Leona's Big Black Carry-All." After zipping open her makeup bag, she freshened her face carefully, adding just a touch of raisin eyeliner to emphasize her green eyes.

"You're all in a tizzy." Tempest said, picking up on her anticipation. "My sister, primping for a date. I think this is so funny. You, the cool, structured, guarded one, accepting a date from a guy you've never met before—"

Tiny quivering polka dots seemed to flow from Tempest, and kept Leona from connecting with her sister's thoughts.

"Ah-ah-ah, you're prowling where you shouldn't," Tempest admonished her. "Don't worry, it's okay, nothing to worry about."

Obviously both of her sisters were absolutely bubbling with news and keeping it to themselves. That irritated Leona a little, but then both had recently married and Leona had been prudent about their marital intimacy. "You could give me a hint."

"It's just . . . different. And kind of funny. You'll find out soon enough. Tell me more about this cowboy."

Leona inhaled slowly. For now, she'd allow both of her sisters to keep their little secrets to themselves. "It's a dinner date, nothing else."

Annoyed, she brushed her hair, a smooth cut turned under at her shoulders. Claire's gentle understanding earlier contrasted with the mental smirk Leona was feeling from Tempest. "I've had dinner dates before, Tempest Best."

"You *know* this one matters, and you're all primed and trembling. You're wearing lacy briefs beneath your black slacks, aren't you?"

When Leona had freshened up in the shop's tiny bathroom, she had changed her undergarments, which, of course, Tempest's psychic antenna had realized. "Thongs are so declassé, little sister," Leona teased back. "You should upgrade."

"Marcus really likes my thongs," Tempest purred. Then her tone changed as she warned, "Be careful, Leona Fiona. If you feel any energy about this guy, anything potentially dangerous at all, get the hell out of there. The Borg descendant could be the same psychic vampire who tried to kill Claire and me, by way of the poor fools he sucks into his power. We felt him. We knew he was around. And we already know what he wants—the brooch and the power that goes with it. But he'll have to kill us all to get that power. All he needs is one weak link to take us all down. With Neil and Marcus making Claire and me stronger, he's going to go after you. You're still mourning Joel, and that makes you very vulnerable to this creep's energy. Apparently, psychic vampires feed on the weak and vulnerable, ingest their energies and become stronger. They're like the real bloodsuckers, only these guys deal with minds."

"Tempest, I understand perfectly—I could be the next one on his list. But I refuse to live my life in fear. I'm living away from major bodies of water that make us vulnerable to other psychic energy. I'm safe here in Kentucky."

For her next uncertain heartbeats, Leona tried to make herself believe just that.

Three

____

OWEN HELD HIS BREATH AS LIGHTNING LIT UP THE STORMY clouds. Seconds later thunder rolled across the pastures of his farm. The dark green shade of the lush bluegrass fields reminded him of the woman he'd met today, her red hair sleek and gleaming around her face, her body lean and moving gracefully toward him.

Leona Chablis was a woman who liked to touch, to feel, a very sensual woman. Her slender pale hands had seemed to float as she had wrapped the tote bag in tissue, then placed it in a box.

From the first moment he'd really looked at her, Owen had wanted Leona's seemingly very capable hands on him.

If a woman could be compared to a sleek, long-legged, racing thoroughbred, Leona would be that woman. Add an exciting touch of a strong, untamed wind in a wild storm, and that described her even better. Like a stallion scenting a mare, Owen had been turned on by her unique fragrance. The comparison was crude, perhaps, considering all the class that Leona exuded. But there were sexual undercurrents in Leona that Owen instinctively knew were red-hot, and he intended to tap into them.

In another hour, Owen intended to hold those hands, to feel her warmth against him. He'd inhale her exotic scent; it had somehow reminded him of Montana's sweetgrass, of the smoke and sage his ancestors inhaled when cleansing themselves.

But it had been ancestral influences that had driven his sister to the brink of insanity. She'd been too receptive to the disasters in her life, too open and the wounds went deeper each time.

Owen was the only one who truly understood the dangerous bog of real and unreal in which Janice lived. He was of that same blood, descended from a unique strain of powerful Blackfoot shamans, whose gifts ran more to intuitive senses and to visions than to healing. Though the Shaws had lived modern lives they could not escape their heritage.

When he was a boy, the whispers of the ancient ones and the haunting dreams had terrified Owen; the elders had said he could walk into the past, or into the future. Owen had wanted nothing of those visions, and neither had their strict father.

He'd learned tonight that Janice was still in danger.

As Owen's pickup had pulled into the farm earlier, Janice's live-in nurse and caretaker had come running toward him.

"I'm so glad you're home," Robyn White had cried, as the rain began to pelt her stout, middle-aged frame. She held up her fists and Janice's two long, black braids dangled from them.

Robyn had seemed terrified as she explained. "Janice cut her hair. I don't know where she got the scissors or that bottle of alcohol—it must have been stashed somewhere here before you moved in. Meds and alcohol are a bad mix. She ran away again, and I couldn't stop her. She's gone to that pond again, and we have tornado warnings tonight. Owen, you've got to get her."

Fear for his sister had tightened his gut painfully. "Did she—?"

"I don't think she hurt herself. I don't think she had time."

As he got out out of the truck and began to run, the wind and rain plastered his shirt to him. Owen ignored the weather as he frantically searched for his sister. He saw that Willow, Janice's Appaloosa mare was still safe, her white-mottled rump showing clearly against the barn's black paint. Moon Shadow, a big Percheron, stood at the board fence, staring down at the pond in the hollow. The horses had come from Montana with them and were as necessary as air to Janice. They reminded her of another time, when she was safe and happy and loved on the Shaw's small farm. When their parents had both died in a car wreck, Janice was sixteen and Owen twenty-seven, just getting a start in business. As her guardian, Owen had to sell off everything but a few acres of their parents' farm to meet bills.

"She always goes to the pond," he reminded himself as he ran to the board fence and scanned the area near the basketball-court-sized pond. In the hollow beside the pond, he saw her. A low layer of mist blurred her white-clad body, the hills shadowy in the distance. He patted Moon Shadow, and murmured, "She'll be okay, boy."

When Owen opened the gate and clicked his tongue, the heavily built Percheron followed him. Instantly, Willow swung in behind them. As Owen walked toward his sister, he prayed that the horses' presence would settle Janice's stretched nerves.

The sheets of rain were cold, fierce, and gray, punctuated by lightning. Thunder rolled as Owen came to stand near his sister. He couldn't touch or hold her, because in this mood, her body battling the combination of medicine and alcohol, Janice would likely fight him. *He had to remain calm and get her out of the storm.*

Janice's white blouse and jeans clung to her as she held her head and rocked her thin body. The smell of liquor bit into the fresh scent of the rain as she spoke. "The voices, Owen. Make them stop. I came here, like they said. They said they would stop, but they didn't."

He'd been unprepared for the shock of seeing Janice without her beautiful, long, black hair; the wet, chopped strands plastered to her stark, pale face. Janice looked like the child she still was, mentally. At twenty-seven, Janice had already lived a hectic, unsteady life. Periodically, she'd escaped Owen's watchful eye and had tried to find relief in a constant flow of men and in alcohol. The move to Kentucky had been a desperate one, to pluck her from her Native American background, and the dangerous fate her spiritual ancestry brought her.

He urged the Percheron near Janice, and when the big horse nuzzled her, Owen said, "Moon Shadow needs you. So does Willow. We need to put them in the barn and dry them. Can you help me?"

Owen had to get her away from that pond and into shelter. One wrong touch from him, and Janice could bolt—she had before. . . .

Janice stared at the pond, the layer of mist over it. "The spirit needs me to help him. People died here. He's mourning them."

The spirit voices. They'd begun during Janice's obsession with her computer, when she'd spent hours in front of the monitor working on her graphic designs. Finally, Owen had removed any electronic communication from Janice's life, and the voices had stopped—for a time. They'd begun again almost immediately after the move from Montana. "Janice, it is only the wind and the storm. There aren't any voices."

The old ones had spoken of spirit guides. Sometimes, Owen almost believed she did hear voices. Was it possible that Janice could actually communicate with the dead?

She could be having a flashback, or a reaction to mixing her medicine with alcohol. Her black eyes seemed flat, her voice a monotone. "I heard them in my sleep. When I awoke, they were still there, telling me what I must do . . . help the spirit mourn the people."

"Do you hear them now?"

She tilted her head. Rain pelted her face as she seemed to listen carefully. "No. But sometimes I still do. Except not now."

Owen nudged Moon Shadow between Janice and the pond, blocking her view. Suddenly, she straightened and gasped; Janice wrapped her fingers in the Percheron's mane as if it were an anchor. Then she held on to him with both arms, pressing her head against his throat. "Moon Shadow, you won't die, will you?"

"The horses are fine. They love you, Janice. They need you." *Come back to me, sister. Come back. Let this new life heal you. . . .*

Death always seemed so close to Janice. She had already tried walking into a lake to be with their deceased parents. The pond wasn't as deep as that lake, but the storm was dangerous, lightning striking too near. Owen moved away a little and clicked his tongue. Moon Shadow nickered and started slowly following, with Janice at his side. Owen took her hand, just as he had that day when their parents had died.

After years of struggling for a degree and working at "starter" jobs, he had finally been set to launch into corporate business. But his sixteen-year-old sister had become almost his child, needing him desperately. With both parents gone, Janice began sinking into depression. At the same time she began showing signs of reading the earth's seasons and animals. Instinctively, Janice knew she had to fight. She often chose the wrong weapons—alcohol and affairs. To be loved and accepted, she gave everything to a succession of men, weakening herself even more. With each affair and rejection, she sank deeper.

Traditional treatment for depression, visits with psychologists and even brief stays at "retreats," hadn't been entirely successful. Janice's medication had helped somewhat. In the end, Owen had found that Janice responded to the simplest things, a quiet life and animals. Even now, in the slashing rain, as she walked beside Moon Shadow, she seemed more at ease.

In the barn, she helped Owen towel down the horses, but she was too quiet. When he swept her hair back from her face, the heavy mass stood out in ragged peaks. He was careful to smooth it again, to arrange the strands on her forehead, as Leona's bangs had been styled. Janice stood before him, obedient as always, accepting his gentle touch.

"I brought you a present," Owen said. "You'll like it."

Janice loved presents. But this time, she didn't respond; her head turned toward that pond as if it still drew her to it.

"I'm hungry," Owen stated, to distract her. Even now, Janice frowned and tilted her head, as if hearing something he could not. "What's for supper?"

When Janice stared at him, her black eyes seemed hollow as if she were still in a trance. "People die around me. Our parents, Uncle Dan, our cousin Merry, and Sarah Jones. Do you think that I bring death to them?"

Sarah Jones had been an elderly housekeeper living with them in Montana. With endless patience and love and caring, Sarah had given Janice a measure of stability while Owen was still working outside the home at the investment company. But when Sarah had passed, Janice had sunken into a worrisome quiet no doctor could penetrate. Owen had fought the fear that he was losing Janice. Their move to Kentucky had been her idea, and he'd been desperate to do anything to help her. "You bring life, Janice. Remember how you helped with the calving and the foals?"

"But my baby was stillborn. Because of how I am— bad. The voices said I'm bad."

An innocent at seventeen, Janice had an affair and she'd miscarried, which had resulted in more trauma to her delicate senses.

"You are not bad. How could I love you if you were bad? You're good, Janice. You'll have other babies . . . when the time and the man are right."

"You're doing all this for me, and you've never had your own life, Owen. That isn't right. You should have your own family now, not be burdened with me," she stated in one of those startlingly lucid moments that seemed to escape the darkness cloaking her.

"I haven't met the woman I want."

Her black eyes seemed to see inside him. "I think you have."

At times, Janice frightened Owen. They carried the same shaman blood, the connection real and often carrying too much truth. Normally males with gray eyes had unusual visions, but Janice was the exception. She'd proven that ancient shaman strain existed in her, a woman with black eyes.

"I would know if I met the right woman, wouldn't I?" Owen asked gently.

"You deny what you cannot see. But you know."

He smiled and ran a playful hand over her ragged hair. "I know you've cut your hair."

"Am I in trouble?" she asked with that childlike innocence.

Owen tilted her chin, his fingers in the ragged hair framing her face. He mourned her long black hair, the way it rippled with a life of its own, like sun on a black-bird's wings; Janice's hair had been like their mother's. "I think it's going to look good on you. It just needs a little trimming. Women change their looks all the time. That's all you did. We'll get some of those magazines about hairstyles. It will be a game, choosing one. I'll help you."

He'd have to warn the beautician about Janice. Knives and scissors had to be kept locked. Owen continued talking quietly as he urged his sister into the house. She submitted easily to her nurse's care, and after dinner, Janice seemed exhausted. Robyn helped her with her nighttime routine, and Janice settled into bed with art and graphic magazines.

In the meantime, Owen quickly changed his damp clothing. He would have to wait to retrieve his laptop from his locked pickup. Experience had taught him that Janice couldn't be anywhere near computers, even those locked with passwords. Especially during nights like this one.

Her fascination with a computer had been too intense. At first, she'd been excited and lively about her new computer setup, and Owen was relieved that she was investing her creative talent in learning and creating graphics. He'd begun to hope for a normal life for them both. Then Janice slowly changed, transferring her energy from learning the programs, into hours of creating primitive designs of whirling circles and bold slashes.

To keep Janice safe from herself had become almost a full-time job. To place his sister permanently in a caretaking facility wasn't an option for Owen; caretakers wouldn't understand her as well as he did. But then, how did one explain what wasn't real, what ran only in the blood from the ancient ones?

At eight-thirty in the evening, Robyn had settled into

her room to watch television. She'd been unnerved by Janice's suicide attempt, the chopping of her hair. "I don't know how she got anything to drink. I hope you won't fire me over this. I'm really trying."

"I know. This isn't your fault, and I appreciate your help. Now that's she's settled, I'll just go talk with her for a minute." Owen understood Robyn's desperation. A middle-aged woman with leg problems, she was unable to work a full nursing shift and had few other skills. Her tolerance for young children was low, and she needed periodic rest when possible. She also needed the income. Her savings had been depleted when she'd been scammed in an investment scheme. A widow, she enjoyed cooking and housekeeping, and had been exactly what the Shaws had needed. And more importantly, Janice had seemed to connect with Robyn immediately.

Alone with Janice, Owen gave her the Timeless Vintage box with the "Freedom" tote inside. At first, she was delighted; but once the tote was in her hands, she began to tremble. She clutched it to her chest. "Where did you get this?"

"A shop in town. Do you like it?"

"It has the feel of a spirit touch, a woman. Two women . . . no, three spirit women, a third close to them. All good spirits. . . . I like it. Thank you."

After Janice had snuggled down in bed, still clutching the tote to her, her statement haunted Owen. Janice had simply held a bag and knew that three women were involved. *Leona had said she had two creative sisters. . . .*

And all of that probably meant nothing. With a resigned sigh, Owen took out the business card from Timeless Vintage and prepared to make his excuses. He left a message on the shop's machine, then settled into the living room to watch the violent storm light up the windows. It shook the old two-story house and rattled windows that needed replacing.

The lights flickered, and Owen thought of all the wiring that also needed replacement. The small farm was all he could afford; the move to Kentucky had been a financial gamble. He'd have to work hard and fast, but Owen had just enough of a bankroll to keep them housed and fed for now. And Janice safe.

He opened a book and retrieved a scrap of printer paper he'd found last fall, after Janice's computer had been suspiciously wiped clean. "Go to the lake. I'm waiting for you," it read. And then Janice had tried to drown herself. Owen tensed as he remembered that night and how she'd fought his rescue.

"He's waiting for me," she'd said then. With medication and a change of scenery, and no computer time she'd improved slightly . . . until tonight. She'd been drawn to the pond, ready to walk into it. And she'd spoken of "spirit voices," just as she had when she'd become obsessed with her computer.

"Spirit voices?" Owen crushed the note in his fist. "More likely someone is having a really good laugh. Probably the same joker who sent that note."

Furious with whoever was playing with Janice's mind, Owen had once demanded she tell him who it was.

After that, whenever Janice spoke of the voices in her mind, the answer was always the same, *"He."*

Since last fall, Owen had been hunting for *He.* And when he found whoever was playing with Janice, he would end his sister's tormentor, one way or another. Even if it meant entering the spirit world himself.

Owen rubbed his jaw. The thought was reckless and traced back to his early childhood. He was a man now, coping with an ill sister. Their move to Kentucky should have helped, but now it was starting all over again.

Lightning lit up the night, followed by rolling thunder. *Three spirit women,* Janice had said. Owen turned her words over in his mind. "Three spirit women" could mean anything: spirits from the dead, or in the living; it could mean something unusual in the psyche.

Owen had sensed something unusual about Leona the moment he'd walked into Timeless. But then his body's hunger had taken over, and he had thought only of her as a woman. What was it about Leona that was unusual, other than the sensuality she expressed in the way she looked and moved, that uniquely arousing scent?

The red-haired woman interested Owen on two levels: a definite physical attraction, and one invisible, caught by Janice's unsteady senses.

Prone to be restless in storms, Janice was certain to awake tonight. With a sigh, Owen settled into working on his investments, and braced himself for the terrified scream that was certain to come.

His desire for Leona Chablis would have to wait.

"Serves me right. I've been stood up. Eight-thirty is a long way from 'pick you up at six-thirty,'" Leona muttered as she glanced at the clock in her office. Worse, Owen's message offered no excuse.

At nine-thirty, the storm abruptly stopped, allowing Leona to finally leave Timeless. She'd stayed to finish the orders she'd begun while the storm had raged earlier. The weather station had canceled a tornado warning when the storm had swept unexpectedly out of the region. Still, she'd decided to wait rather than battle the fierce wind and likely hail, or risk damage to her brand new car, which was safely tucked beneath an overhang in the back of the shop.

Nettled that she could have been home and settled by now—if she hadn't waited for Owen Shaw—Leona hitched her tote up on her shoulder and stepped out onto the back porch of Timeless. With only the door's overhead light cutting into the night, the back alley's shadows almost concealed her white Lincoln. The storm and wind had left raindrops glittering on her car and puddles on the alley's old cobblestones.

With a sigh that said she was tired and disgusted, and doomed for a frozen dinner from her freezer, Leona turned to punch in the store's security code.

When she turned back, a man stood beside her car, his face shadowed. Fear tightened Leona's throat. This could be the psychic vampire or Borg-descendant who wanted to kill her. It was only logical that she would be next, now that he had failed with her sisters.

Borg's icy curse circled Leona as she glanced around the darkened alley. Had her time come to be attacked? Was she really the weakest link in the triplets now?

The rest of the shopkeepers' cars were gone. Leona was alone, but for the stray cat that crept across the overstuffed Dumpster. She reached inside her tote and found her cell phone. Her finger poised over the 911 button as she asked the man, "Who are you?"

As he moved into the pool of light spilling from her back porch light, Owen's harsh features appeared. "You weren't answering your phone. I left another message, so I wouldn't frighten you when I arrived. When I saw a car back here, I hoped you might still be here."

Leona gripped the handrail and didn't move. Panic leaped, her pulse pounding hard and fast. His long-sleeve black sweater and jeans had blended too well into the shadows. Her senses had definitely kicked up when he'd entered the shop earlier today, which meant he *could* be psychic—it would take a psychic to rattle her defenses. *This man could be the one stalking her family.* "You would have had to walk down the side alley to do that."

"Yes. I parked out front."

He was a hunter then, set on finding her. Her senses rippled uneasily with potential danger. "I have my finger on the 911 button on my cell phone," she warned.

"Oh? Are they bringing our dinner?"

That light, teasing comment set her off. Few people had seen Leona's dark side; she preferred to keep cool, impervious, and calm. But being stood up had caused her temper to simmer.

"After my date didn't show, I gave up having dinner." Leona moved down the steps, determined to finish her bad idea, that of a date with a man she didn't really know. After a long day, and a disappointment because she'd been excited about the dinner date, she just wanted to get home. "Look, I'm tired and I'm going home. You're not invited."

"Too bad. We could still have dinner."

"I have nothing more to say to you." Leona walked to her car. She unlocked it, then decided that probably wasn't the smartest thing to do . . . not with a man she barely knew standing nearby.

Owen moved aside, but not before she saw his face. He looked as if he'd been through hell, lines cut deep into his forehead and beside his lips. He seemed as if he'd aged in the hours since she'd met him.

"I'm not good at this," he began. "I'm sorry I'm late. My sister, Janice, had a problem. I had to stay with her until she settled down. She was better when the storm quieted. Her caretaker is looking after her now."

Leona withdrew her key and opened the door, preparing to get in. "You could have said so in your message. I have a family. I understand emergencies and priorities."

"I hurried to you. I came as soon as I could."

I hurried to you, words a lover would use. *Perfect words, ones Leona had wanted to hear, the ache unknown until just now.*

She tossed her tote into the car and turned to look up at Owen. Uncertain now if she had been too quick to judge him, she said, "I don't usually accept dates from men I don't know."

"And I don't usually ask women I don't know." Owen braced both hands on the car behind her, framing her body with his. "I guess that makes us even."

"You're standing too close."

He eased back slightly. "Better?"

She hadn't been prepared for the male onslaught on her senses or that slight wave of claustrophobia. On another level, something feminine and buried deep beneath Leona's businesswoman facade quivered. She liked that bit of masculine posturing, like how Owen had moved in to make his point: that he found her desirable. She hadn't been *desirable* for a very long time. But then, maybe she hadn't been receptive to men taking the initiative in the flirtation phase. "I guess so. I'm still mad, of course."

"You have that right." Owen nodded and leaned down to nuzzle her cheek with his. The rain-scented air seemed to heat, to pulse with his scent and his need. He looked down her body and slid a long leg closer to hers. His voice was deep, husky and intimate, the sound coaxing that little feminine quiver into the bloom of sensuality. "Still want that dinner?"

Leona hadn't had *intimate* for a very long time, and she wanted more. His deep, rumbling tone caused her to imagine how he'd sound lying next to her and talking—after they were both sated and resting. "I'd better tell you up front that I'm not a fried chicken and collard greens sort of girl. I like the better things of life."

"Pizza, then."

Leona recognized the easy tease and smiled briefly. "You'll have to do better than that."

Owen's lips brushed her cheek, his face warm against

hers, and her need to be held as a desirable woman trembled through her. "The name is Owen. Say it, Leona."

On his lips, her name sounded like a song, an ache that needed filling. In that heartbeat, Leona remembered the lovers' game, the taunting, the playful seduction. She gave herself to it, her senses racing and excited. "Maybe after dinner."

Desire flared in his eyes, and his lips were hard and warm as they brushed hers.

Leona parted her lips just a bit, allowing the tip of his tongue to slip inside. That contact surprised her, and the kiss ignited. Hunger raced through her for the touch of a man's skin, the scents, the hard muscles moving beneath her hands.

Owen pressed her back against her car, his long leg between hers. The heat of his face against her throat caused warmth to ripple through her. The cool dampness of the car created an erotic contrast to his body heat, and Leona opened for him. She let him kiss her lightly at first, then hungrily, as if he needed to feed upon her.

Instinctively, she knew that Owen needed her. He needed a woman's comfort, a woman's completion to escape the darkness driving him now. He'd come to the right woman. Because tonight, Leona needed a man's arms to ease the restless tension within her. She needed one night without the nightmares and the loneliness. . . .

She held his hard-boned face between her hands and eased Owen away for a moment. He smiled then, a man who knew he almost had what he wanted by Leona's response to him. "I knew you'd be like this. Cool as a mountain meadow on the outside and fire and storm beneath."

Leona needed her hands on his skin, to feel the blood and heat coursing through him. She needed more than the dreams of a faceless lover. In contrast to her body's needs, her mind cautioned that she should walk away from Owen and the night with him and what it could be.

His finger strolled down Leona's cheek to the V in her sweater and hooked in to tug lightly. "I haven't had dinner with a woman—one that interests me—for a long time. I should have left a better message. Just now I came at you too fast. I'm sorry."

Owen's raw, primitive hunger had been shielded for a moment, and Leona wanted it back. She didn't want a civilized dinner, small talk, then another long night with her nightmares. Tonight, with Owen, she could exorcise her hunger and her nightmares briefly, at least for a few hours.

Obviously tied up with his sister's care, he wouldn't want an involvement; Leona could dance away free afterward. She debated that enticing tidbit while she ached for his hand to cup her breast, just as it had those beads in her shop today.

Leona placed her hands on Owen's chest, gently pushing him away until she stood free. Owen stepped back, his head tilted down as he waited for her next move. That was a good test, and he'd passed by allowing her boundaries. He'd moved easily to her touch and had stopped when she wanted.

She slid inside her car, closed the door, and started the engine. Owen crossed his arms as if he were settling in to deal with a difficult woman. She planned to meet his expectations. Leona rolled down her window, and said, "I'm going home. Coming?"

Not smart at all, Leona thought a few moments later as she drove over Lexington's wet streets. They were designed to circle the city in the shape of a wagon wheel, the spokes of the streets leading out of the city.

She took New Circle Road, the inner main thorough-fare, then swung south on a side street to enter Man O' War Boulevard. Owen's big farm pickup followed her through another side street. Raindrops beaded her windshield, glittering under the streetlights as they passed through a residential area and then arrived at her own cul-de-sac. The pickup's headlights swung into her driveway after she'd parked in her garage.

Leona entered her home and circled to the front door, where she found Owen waiting, a grocery sack in hand. Smoky eyes pinned Leona, as if nothing meant any-thing to him but this time with her. His expression was purely male, like that of a man who knew he could hold his own in a highly sexual battle to a final, exhausting pleasure-filled climax. He looked like a man who knew exactly how to please a woman and tonight, Leona didn't intend to hold back; she intended to take what she wanted, skin on skin.

She forced herself to breathe, and when her voice fi-nally came, it sounded like an invitation to her bed. "Come in."

Owen entered slowly, glanced at the sleek contempo-rary living room, and nodded. He glanced at the scarf Leona had hung over the hallway mirror, and said, "Janice liked the purse."

"I thought she would. And it's a bag, a handbag . . . actually it's a tote," Leona automatically corrected as she closed the door. She quickly drew the scarf away from the mirror; Owen had been too quick to notice what might be called a quirk. But this morning, riding on the edge of her nightmares and the sensual dream, Leona had wanted to block her resemblance to Aisling.

Slightly uneasy now, Leona hurried to get on with her plan. She'd come this far; she couldn't back out now. She needed everything Owen Shaw had to offer and more. "I'll make sandwiches. Make yourself comfortable."

Owen lifted the sack. "I brought dinner. I'll cook it."

"So we weren't going out, after all?"

His slow smile seemed a little sheepish. "I hurried, but had to gas up. While there, I picked up a few groceries for the house. We might as well use them. You look like you could use a real meal."

"Are you saying that I do not look well?" Leona asked tightly. Her nerves were stretched after a sleepless night. And standing too near her was a man she'd brought home for the night, a man she'd just met. Her reactions to Owen were very atypical for her, a cautious woman.

"You look tired."

"Yes, well, I usually eat a lot earlier—"

His hand was on her hair, toying with the strands as he watched. "Silk . . . dark red, but layered with fire."

Owen's soft statement sounded like a caress and held her spellbound. While Leona tried to remember what she had been saying, he searched her eyes for a long moment, then leaned down to brush his lips across hers. She braced herself for the jolt of heat ricocheting down her body. But she didn't touch Owen; she feared she would rip that sweater from him if she did. She knew instantly what his sleek, damp hair would feel like as it feathered sensually against her skin when Owen moved down her body . . .

He'd caught her reaction, those gray eyes narrowing instantly as his body seemed to tense and heat near hers. Trailing a fingertip down her cheek to the brooch resting on her chest, he said. "The design is Celtic. So you're Irish?"

"It's just a little something I picked up." *Keep it impersonal.* . . . Leona didn't want to share too much of

her life, just her body. The heat of him, along with the
scent of male soap and aftershave, mixed with scents of
the storm, had her hungry and anxious for more. She
placed her hand along his cheek, learning the shape and
texture, sensing the underlying male hunger. She let the
latter seep into her blood, warming it even more.

Owen reacted as if to an impact; he inhaled abruptly
as his hands slid lightly over her breasts and down to
grip her waist. Sensual tension throbbed and stretched
taut as they studied each other, each aware of what
could or could not happen in the next heartbeat. Then
he nodded, and eased away, as if pacing himself. "I'll
get dinner started. I guess the kitchen is over there?"

As he walked toward the doorway leading to the
kitchen, Leona tried to find her voice. She'd always kept
her home very private. Now a man she barely knew was
preparing a late dinner and would probably share her
bed—where she'd made love to her husband.

Correction: That bed was covered with her clothing
and plastic, the result of the great closet remodeling.

Still, Leona struggled to place herself into a reality
that didn't seem logical for her, a cautious, calm,
thoughtful woman. Here she was, in the small subdivi-
sion home, one she'd bought with her husband and
where they'd planned to start their family. Now the
beautiful fenced backyard had no children's swings,
and she had just brought another man home to spend
the night with her in the guest bedroom.

In the kitchen, Owen placed the chicken breasts in
the refrigerator. Then he scrubbed and wrapped the
baking potatoes, washed the salad lettuce and placed it
aside to drain. But his mind was on Leona.

He smiled briefly as he searched for a paring knife,
sliding it from the countertop's wooden holder. He
pushed the blade back into its slot and thought of how
Leona's sleek, graceful body would sheath him.

Leona. Owen decided that she'd been named well. The translation of Leona was lioness and that suited her, her heat and hunger at odds with her seemingly cool poise. And as the sleek lioness, she was definitely hunting tonight. . . .

Owen frowned slightly as he remembered how she had stood at the shop's back door, challenging, wary, and fiercely determined to tell him off. He wondered how many men had seen that side of Leona. Her prickly attitude might have cooled another man's interest but it had only peaked his. Heat and passion ran like a stream through that slender curved body, beneath that pale skin; Owen could feel it brewing like a summer storm.

Her home's open floor plan allowed his view of the living room. The decor was also a contrast to Leona's outward appearance. On one hand it was almost too neat, too orderly. Yet the pecan-shaded wood flooring was covered by expensive area rugs, their intricate patterns a blend of whimsical vines and leaves, almost as if the rooms had a magical forest floor. Did Leona enjoy walking over these rugs in her bare feet, alone in her own private forest at the midnight hour?

A standing lamp shed a pool of light onto a tabletop's small whimsical statue. Gleaming metal captured three women, their hands joined, their backs to each other. Two of the figurines were taller and lean, the third, shorter and more curved. The women seemed almost alive, as if they were dancing in a round circle, their hair in motion. *Three women* . . . the work had reminded Owen of what his sister had said.

Leona's obviously handcrafted brooch seemed to be an unusual choice for a seemingly cool businesswoman. The Celtic weave around the wolf's head seemed very eclectic. Her home reflected none of those tastes—but for the statue and the whimsical carpets.

The long, angular, contemporary cream sofa took most of the space, a few books and odds and ends in a ceiling-to-floor bookshelf, a modern computer setup and printer in one corner. Yet another contrast was the obviously feminine muted gray-green comfortable chair with a reading lamp and basket stuffed with magazines nearby. A yoga mat lay spread in front of the entertainment center.

That mat had started visions of Leona lying upon it, her slim pale body moving rhythmically. Owen's body tightened, and he sucked in his breath, controlling his need. She appeared to be a woman who would call her own time, and he wasn't pushing.

The kitchen seemed unused, the appliances ultra-modern. Owen glanced out at the backyard to find a reclining lounger and a wooden privacy fence. A neighbor's lights lit a small area of her yard, revealing a bed of flowers and several flowering pots of all sizes. The scene was typical Lexington style, where greenhouses stood on practically every street corner and gardening seemed to be an active community interest. As he'd followed Leona to her cul-de-sac, Owen had noted the small, neatly kept yards bordered by chrysanthemums. The older homes seemed ordinary, but each held its own design and unique flavor. Leona had chosen a very comfortable family-type neighborhood.

That also was a contrast to Owen's expectations of her; he'd pictured Leona Chablis in an upscale condo or apartment building.

The bricks stacked near her patio, the shovel leaning against them, could be for patio work. Owen noted the utility room just off the kitchen. From the look of a woman's gardening gloves tossed carelessly on the washer near the back door, Owen guessed Leona might be doing the brickwork herself. The task was unusual for a businesswoman with well-kept hands . . . ones Owen intended to have on his body very soon.

From the moment he'd entered her home, Owen's senses had begun to tingle uneasily. Maybe Janice's "spirit woman" label had caused it, or maybe it was his anticipation of making love to Leona, to see if she was really as passionate as he had sensed earlier.

Owen also recognized another sensation. His instincts told him that someone else with intuitive ability was nearby. While he did not play to that side of his inheritance, it leaped and quivered through him at times. And he'd had enough experiences to know its truth. If Leona was everything he suspected, she could be the key to everything he had to have. . . .

That thought jolted him. Owen suddenly realized he'd been gripping the salad tomatoes a little too hard, the juice dribbling over his hand, red as blood.

Blood. If he ever caught the son of a bitch who'd gotten into Janice's mind, he'd kill him.

And Leona, a suspected "spirit woman," just might help him find the bastard.

Leona checked her bedroom to find that Vernon O'Malley had started working on her closet as she'd asked. New shelving wood had been stacked against the wall, and plastic sheeting covered her furniture. Her design for the organized closet lay spread over the plastic covering on her bed.

"I'll be glad when this is finished," she murmured, and walked into the guest bedroom to kick off her shoes. This was where she planned to sleep for the next few nights. She studied the bed, and an image of Owen's long, tanned body sprawled upon it hit her. The image carried enough force to drive her back against the wall. This time, she was certain her precognitive ability would be correct, not smoke and mirrors. Breathless, her hand to her chest, Leona closed her eyes and shook her head. "Thank you, Aisling, for that shocking tidbit, but just maybe that won't happen."

The unexpected vision had riveted her, rippling down her body, warming it sensually. Leona had known desirable men, but her reaction had never been as shocking. Tempest and Claire were right: she was becoming stronger, and the insight into making love with Owen had shaken her.

Leona pressed her hands to her temples. Reality pounded into her: She was about to make love with a man she'd just met and had brought home—to the home Joel and she had shared for two years, hoping for children to fill that backyard.

She listened to the sound of kitchen drawers opening, the electronic beep of a stove being set, the rattle of paper, and the sound of pots and pans. Apparently Owen was busy with dinner, in her home, in her kitchen, one she had rarely used since Joel's death. *Joel? What am I doing? Am I betraying your memory?*

Uncertain now about taking another man into her body, Leona forced herself to walk toward the kitchen. She leaned against the doorway, and for a moment, savored the sight of the tall, lean man apparently comfortable with cooking tasks.

When Owen glanced at her, those gray eyes held enough heat to startle her, spreading warmth through her body. She could almost feel herself enclosed in those sleek, steely muscles, the way he would move within her arms.

In an effort to appear casual and unaffected, she walked to open her refrigerator and bent to study the contents. But her mind was on that image—Owen without his clothing . . . on her guest-room bed. . . .

The tingle running up her nape said that Claire was

calling and Leona understood: Her youngest sister was worried for her. Claire would instantly sense the high sexuality between Leona and Owen. Leona closed her eyes and tried to focus away from her sensuality, from that image of Owen's powerful body locked with hers. After a heartbeat of trying to block her sister, Leona picked up the wall telephone. "Hi, Claire. There's nothing to worry about."

She'd forgotten to let the telephone ring! Leona had answered automatically, an instinctual response to her connection to her sister. Owen's quick glance and puzzled frown said he'd noticed the missing performance she always gave when others were around. Without words, Leona knew instantly why Claire had called. Lowering her voice, she said, "I'm very safe. He's not getting me. Please don't worry."

When Owen crossed his arms, leaned back against the counter, and stared at her, she knew he sensed something amiss.

"He's there, though, isn't he? A man? The man you told Tempest about? Ohmigosh, Neil," Claire called to her husband. "Leona brought home a man. It's a first for her—he's cooking dinner now, in her kitchen."

Leona sighed loud enough to let Claire know the familiar tease wasn't welcome just now. Neil's low rumble sounded, then Claire said, "Neil said that you should have introduced him to us and gotten permission to date first."

"Like that's going to happen." Her new brother-in-law loved to tease Leona, and frankly, she enjoyed the repartee—but not now, not when she was primed and hot and yearning to take what she wanted.

"I knew something was up with you tonight—I just felt it." Claire's soft, humorous tone was exactly what Leona did not need to hear now. "First sex doesn't always go right, Leona Fiona."

"I know that, Claire. But thanks for the advice, anyway."

"You're anxious to get rid of me—and I know why. Use protection. Gloves are so important." Claire's laughter said she'd enjoyed teasing her older-by-six-minutes sister, who was usually unflappable. Claire's bond with Neil had changed her; she had emerged from her quiet protective cocoon into a woman who enjoyed life. But her little teasing remarks were still surprising.

When Leona finished the call, she explained, "My sister always calls at the same time."

Owen's gray eyes pinned her. "Why would 'Claire' worry? Are you in danger?"

"Of course not." Owen was too quick, picking up details like a hunter on a trail. Doubt moved through her once more that Owen could be the man who had been stalking her family.

She had to appear calm. While Owen returned to slicing tomatoes, Leona retrieved a bottle of wine. Her hand almost shook as she lifted it to him. "Would you like a glass?"

"I don't drink."

She lifted one of the elegant wineglasses from an overhead rack. "I do, and it's been a long day."

"You're uncomfortable." Those cool silvery eyes stared at her as he walked toward her. "I won't hurt you." He took the glass and the bottle from her and placed them aside. "You won't need that tonight."

The air around them stilled, and Leona shivered. Was it possible that he knew she drank wine in an attempt to settle her restless senses, to still her nightmares?

"Do you have trouble sleeping?" he asked, as if plucking the thought from her mind. The light stroke of Owen's hand on her hair gentled her, much the same as he would ease a nervous horse.

She should be capable of handling her restless senses,

of coping with a man in her home. Yet her body shivered at his touch, uneasiness rippling through her. She searched his eyes and found only sensual heat. Opening her senses, she let them pour around Owen, briefly capturing his energy and rummaging through the stark masculine edges. She found only desire, not harm. Could she really trust herself to him? Just for the night?

"I have dreams . . . nightmares. A glass of wine sometimes settles me." Leona's husky voice trembled between them. She was always careful not to drink too much. Her grandmother had tried drink to hide from her visions; they came anyway and had destroyed Stella Mornay's mind.

Leona looked at her window, to the backyard she'd shared with her husband. Why was she giving so much of herself to Owen's keeping, sharing her life and instinctively trusting him?

Owen's thumb stroked her temple and drew her attention back to him. "I know you're unsettled, Leona. That's why I'm here, isn't it? To give you some relief? To fill the midnight hours? Your dreams haunt you during the day, don't they? Never fully letting go?"

He understood too much, those silvery eyes intent and relentless upon her. Resenting the intrusion into her obvious needs, Leona stood back and crossed her arms. "That's enough about me."

"I understand. You're afraid of letting pieces of yourself go into someone else's keeping. I think—just for tonight—that we both want the same thing. That's all this is, Leona. It's about tonight. You and me." Owen looped out his arm, circled her body, and drew her steadily close to him. He smiled slightly as her body softened against his. "Okay. Did you miss me?"

"Have you been gone?" she countered, trying to cool her senses as she kept her arms crossed between them.

He answered that question with another. "Scared? You weren't nervous before, at the shop. What changed?"

Male to her female . . . hard, strong . . . Fear raced through her. She'd stepped out of her meticulous life, and here she was, facing a man who could be everything she wanted for a few hours—or not. Did she really want to give her body to him? When the last man had been her husband?

Instinctively, Leona knew that if she did not take this one leap, she never would. Instinctively, she decided the leap might be worth the attempt. "You realize that it's ten-thirty now and late for a full dinner. The thought is nice, but not practical with a full workday ahead tomorrow. When do you think dinner will be done?"

"About a half hour, maybe forty-five minutes. I set the oven timer for the baked potatoes. The chicken can be grilled when you're ready. . . . Are you ready?" Owen's hands smoothed her hips, then cruised up beneath her arms, his thumbs just beneath her breasts. He stared at her breasts and breathed hard as they tightened in anticipation. She had to touch Owen, to feel that solid muscle and sinew and bone. Tonight, she wouldn't be sated by a dream lover, but by flesh and blood and heat.

Her hands found Owen's shoulders, testing the power there, her fingers digging in slightly. He wasn't going anywhere, at least, not just yet.

"Ready for what?" she asked as she moved against him.

Leona hadn't expected Owen to carry her to the bedroom, his lips hot and hungry against hers. At first, she'd been startled as he'd lifted her, the gesture unexpected. Owen was making his needs clear; he wanted her and quickly. Tonight, a slower seduction wasn't on his agenda. *Perfect.*

As he stood holding her aloft at her bedroom doorway, the shaft of hallway light fell upon a pair of large paint-spotted coveralls. They hung from the boards stacked against the closet, a jumble of tools nearby. Leona answered Owen's questioning look with, "My handyman's things."

Owen scanned the picture on the wall, the framed portrait of Joel. "Your husband?"

"I told you I wasn't married."

"He's who you really want. But you have me instead now, don't you?" he asked roughly as he carried her to the guest room.

"Does it matter?"

"Yes, it does." His tone was bitter as if an old wound had just torn open. Owen dumped her on the bed as if he couldn't unload her fast enough. He stood with his legs braced apart as he rammed his hand through his hair. "I want you, but—"

Leona reacted instantly, her emotions in turmoil, her uncertainty warring with her sensual needs. On her feet now, she was shaken and furious about the sudden change from desire to dismissal. Tears burned her eyes, her body shaking. "Maybe we'd just better call it a night then, bud."

Owen stared at her, his face shadowed. "I'd just be back, or you'll come after me . . . and we both know it," he stated rawly as he took a step toward Leona. "Is it yes, or no?"

Unprepared for the bold, masculine demand, Leona took a step backward. "I—"

"You miss him. You dream of him, and I'm not taking his place."

"I know. I—You couldn't take his place. Joel was very—"

"Civilized?" Owen supplied, as his fingers slowly unfastened her sweater's top button. "Why are you so nervous of me?"

"You're the first man I've brought home." The words seemed to leap out of her mouth, shocking in their clarity. He paused, that sharp gaze stripped her face, searching for a lie. "It's true. Take it or leave it," she whispered.

Owen was too close, his heat spreading into her body. He smiled and nodded. "Thank you. I will . . . take it."

A second button came undone in his hands, and he eased back her sweater to look down at her breasts. "Lace," he murmured in approval. "You're just what I expected, all cool and prim and efficient on the outside, but inside—"

When his hand cupped her breast, Leona closed her eyes. She gave herself to the warmth and the strength and the gentleness of the caress. She gave herself to the sensuous slow touch of Owen's hands flowing along her body as he carefully undressed and caressed each part of her. The rough calluses of his hands only served to heighten her need. She opened herself to the textures and heat and scents of Owen. She let them flow within her, let them warm her.

In the end, Leona hurried to remove his clothes, to feel that hot, smooth skin against hers, the roughness and power of his legs against hers. She longed to give herself to pleasure. "There's just one thing," she whispered against that strong throat once they were naked and side by side on the bed. "I hope you don't mind."

He smiled against her lips. "Name it."

"I'm claustrophobic—fearful of tight places. I don't like to be held down."

"I don't see that as a problem," he said. With that, Owen took her mouth in a kiss that heated every inch of her body.

Four

———

ELECTRODES REACHED OUT FOR LEONA. BRIGHT LIGHTS burned her eyes, the table cold and hard beneath her. Hands covered with rubber gloves touched her, a needle pricked her arm, and unfamiliar faces peered down at her.

Leona couldn't move, her hands and ankles held tightly. She should have told her sisters to run and hide. She should have protected them. Last night, she'd dreamed the bad people were coming to take her and her sisters away. She hadn't told anyone because she didn't want to believe this horror actually existed. . . .

But it did. She fought the strap across her chest, bucking against its confinement. Her ten-year-old body was too weak against the bonds that held her. What was happening to her sisters? Where were they? Tempest would fight, but oh, Claire—sweet Claire, who felt too much, the emotions and physical pain of others. . . . If she were going through this, too, she'd be torn apart. Why? Why?

The researchers' questions traveled like a river through her senses, and her fear turned to anger and she yelled. It was a language she didn't know, but it ripped from her like a burning curse, echoing around a room filled with machines, the needles on the gauges leaping wildly.

Leona's senses prickled, picking up bits of her sisters' terror. Fearing for them, she struggled harder. "Where are my sisters?"

"Triplets, born three minutes apart." A face floated nearer and peered down at her. "Their extra senses are connected . . ."

The steady hum of voices paused, and continued, "Tell me about your dreams. Are they only at night? During the day? Do events actually happen as you've seen them in your dreams? What are the details? Are the dreams in color, or not?"

Leona struggled against her bonds. She had to get free to find Claire and Tempest. She'd seen everything in a dream: She'd seen the police and the white-coats coming. She should have told her sisters to hide.

Where was their mother? Off helping the police find some boy? She should have been home—

The voices continued to question her. "Do you feel what your sisters think? Is it exact words or images? Do you practice with your mother? Is she connected with witches?"

She had always protected her younger sisters, and now she couldn't. Where was their mother? Why wasn't she here?

Leona suddenly awoke to the echo of her own cry. "I'll never forgive you for leaving us! I don't want to be like you!"

Caught on the edge between the nightmare and reality, she fought to climb out of the nightmare. Tearing the sheet wrapped around her body, she saw the man lying next to her.

"That was some dream," Owen said slowly.

Her heart racing wildly, she stared at his hard features, that dark skin and light eyes in the shadows. She lay very still as his finger wiped away the tear sliding down her cheek. "Want to tell me about it?" he asked.

She closed her eyes, and a remnant of the nightmare floated by, just a terrifying wisp of Greer Aisling descending upon the Blair Institute of Parapsychology and tearing her daughters away.

Leona shivered slightly, because she'd never forget her mother's fierce rage. Cold as a blade of ice and armed with legalities she would enforce, the world-famous psychic had collected her daughters. But Leona had never forgiven herself for what happened—or her mother.

She turned to Owen, noting his gleaming broad shoulder, the strength in his arms, and moved closer to him. Against her bare breasts, his chest pulsed with life, his heat drawing her back into reality. Leona needed to lose herself in him, to keep away the nightmares and the dreams that came true more frequently now. She needed Owen to make her believe that she was just like any other woman.

"We have other things to do besides talk, don't we?" Leona asked as she moved over him to take what she wanted.

I'll never forgive you for leaving us. I don't want to be like you. . . . Leona's troubled words circled Owen as he sat up in bed. He studied the sleeping woman on the bed, her long, pale legs tangled in the sheets.

By the moonlight outside, Owen gauged the time to be shortly after midnight. He rolled his shoulders, and noted the light sting of her scratches on his back. He rubbed the slightly tender place where she'd bitten his throat. But then, as she'd ridden him, Owen had done some nipping of his own. *Leona tasted like honey and felt like fire.* . . .

She was even more than he'd anticipated—sensual, hungry, almost primitive at the end, an equal partner who shed everything to meet him. Instinctively, Owen had known she came from warriors who took what they wanted, this, his warrior-woman, who preferred to ride rather than be dominated. The position didn't matter; the woman did.

He stroked that silky hair back from Leona's cheek, still flushed from their second lovemaking. They'd come together on a primitive level Owen sensed only came once in a lifetime, a perfect mating.

He couldn't wait to see those eyes again—dark, mystical, loaded with secrets. Caressing her smooth thigh, he enjoyed the flowing beauty beneath his light touch. Then his fingers tightened possessively, as he'd remembered how her feminine muscles had held his body. The contrast of male and female, of dark skin lying on fair started his blood heating again.

That wouldn't do. He couldn't ask that of her so soon after this lovemaking. At first, she had been too tight to accept him. But she didn't wait, pushing him, her hunger fueling his.

Owen sensed a very unique bond had formed between them. Maybe it was true then, what Janice had said, that he'd found a special woman. *A spirit woman?*

He stood to pull on his jeans and noted the framed picture on the bedside table. Janice had said three spirit women. The three women in the photograph looked as if they were the same age, their features remarkably alike. The figurine in the living room also had three women. . . . *Three spirit women.*

Leona had murmured restlessly in her sleep. Though Owen couldn't pinpoint some of the words, he'd known they weren't English. Who had left the sisters alone and unprotected? What had she dreamed? And who didn't Leona want to be like? Who wouldn't she forgive?

"Spirit women" could be translated as anything, but Leona definitely wasn't a ghost. Janice's term meant something else, and Owen intended to find out what. His sister's readings could be exact, but sometimes these were muddled.

He showered quickly and smiled as he noted the feminine scents in the bathroom and the absence of a male presence. In the kitchen, he set the table, started the chicken on the cooktop's grill, and went to awaken Leona. He couldn't wait to see her open those dark green eyes, to see her recognize him as her lover. But there were deeper layers, too, a fascination Owen sensed was only beginning.

When he reentered the bedroom her scent and that of their lovemaking almost set him off again. She'd ache tomorrow, wearing his mark, just as she'd marked him. Maybe Leona would dream a little of him, too. Owen smiled at that thought, mocking himself for the romantic whimsy. The Shaws were notorious for not revealing their emotions, but this woman made him feel different inside, like he was caught up in a storm that heated and devoured. He sucked in his breath as he looked down that long, pale body, tangled in sheets. "Dinner is ready. Wake up."

As she turned toward Owen, her hair seemed to glow around her pale face, dark red strands sliding on the white pillowcase. Clouded with sleep, Leona's eyes were unfocused. In a heartbeat, her gaze sharpened. Owen waited for her reaction, this woman of mystery, Janice's "spirit woman."

Leona quickly drew the sheet around her. She moved off the bed and into the bathroom, closing the door behind her.

He shrugged lightly, pushing back his impulse to follow her. Leona obviously needed privacy right now. But there would be other times when he would follow, and nothing would keep him away from her. *Nothing could keep him from her, not anymore.* The starkly primitive sense that Leona was now his startled Owen. He'd never felt like that before, as if a woman were his to possess and be possessed by.

He wasn't surprised when Leona came into the kitchen fully dressed in a T-shirt and jeans. The scent of her shower clung to her. She reminded Owen of a skittish, unridden mare as she sat, keeping her distance from him. Obviously uncomfortable and tense with this situation, she carefully avoided looking at him as she picked at her food.

He wondered how many people had seen the efficient businesswoman like this: uncertain, wary, and without her shields.

Owen understood why she glanced warily at his bare chest, why her cheeks flushed. She was shy of him now, obviously aware that she'd given something precious to him.

It was clear to him that Leona feared her emotions; she feared what Owen could mean to her. He also understood her very proper, "Thank you. The dinner was wonderful, but it's very late. Don't worry about the dishes. I'll clean up."

He decided not to mention her nightmare; Leona was already uneasy. As he reached for her hand, its soft, fragile shape within his dark callused one reminded him how her hand had curled around him earlier. . . . He watched as his fingers intertwined with hers, a sensual blend of male and female. He knew he had to ask his next question, to see her reaction, despite the tension simmering between them. "I need to know what kind of women touched my sister's bag."

"Why? What do you mean?" Her damp hair shimmered in the room's dim light as she trembled, her eyes wide, those lips parted in surprise. With a hunter's instincts, Owen knew he had hit a secret Leona hid well.

"My sister is sensitive to certain unusual things. Janice says a 'spirit woman' held the bag. Actually she mentioned 'three spirit women.' I'd like to know exactly who held it."

Leona's green eyes darkened as she withdrew her hand. But not before he sensed her fear. "It's late, Owen."

"Are they your sisters? You have two right? I saw the picture. You all seem about the same age."

Leona stood suddenly and began clearing away the table. "I can't stand to come home to dirty dishes after a long day at work. I'll do these now."

Owen recognized the excuse for what it was—an attempt to stop his questions. He would ask again, but not now. "I'll help."

"No need to. I'm sure you have an early morning, too."

Her crisp tone wasn't exactly an invitation for a return to her bed. "Am I leaving?"

"Yes. I would appreciate that very much."

Protective, defensive, wary, Leona turned to face him. Owen understood: He'd gotten too close to a secret Leona held dear. She'd had a definite reaction to Janice's phrase, "spirit women." Owen had to know more. And he would. Soon.

After he dressed, a cool, composed Leona saw him to the door and shut it firmly in his face. Outside her home, with the moon high and full above him, Owen rubbed his chest where an ache had lodged to hold her, to be warmed by her fire.

Once he was in his pickup, Owen scanned the cul-de-sac, quiet in the midnight hours. His body still restless, he felt like hunting. He had only a few hours while Janice slept, and Owen knew that he had to make use of his time.

A half hour later, Owen sat at a table inside Perks, an Internet cafe, tapping on his laptop's keys to research Leona Chablis.

It wasn't long before newspaper records revealed the death of her husband, Joel, five years ago. Joel Chablis had been a medical supply salesman attending a conference in Colorado when he'd been killed by a snow avalanche. A hunt through previous articles revealed their marriage announcement: one Joel Chablis married to a Leona Bartel, seven years ago. And a search on Bartel led to the world-famous psychic Greer Aisling, mother of "gifted triplets."

Owen held his breath as he read the newspaper account. Leona Bartel had two sisters. The triplets had been born three minutes apart. No wonder she'd answered the telephone before it had rung—a psychically linked triplet might sense the other's call. Clearly Leona, born of a psychic mother, had an inherited gift. The person who called was Claire, as in Claire's Bags. *Janice had sensed that her bag from Leona's store held a spirit woman's touch.*

The connection was too strong. Owen sat back and stared at the screen. "Janice's three spirit women. Not spirits, but flesh and blood—and connected by birth."

If Leona were strong enough, she might be able to do what he could not—untangle the grip someone had wrapped around his intuitive and vulnerable sister. Leona could be the answer for Janice when traditional means had failed. . . .

Owen's senses prickled uneasily, and he glanced at the street outside Perks. The streetlights gleamed on the same late-model dark SUV that had circled the cafe twice before.

He settled back to drink his glass of milk and waited

for the return of the SUV. When it circled again, Owen knew someone else was hunting that night.

"I'm very safe . . . he's not getting me," Leona had said. But she'd obviously been uneasy with the lie.

Who hunted her? And who couldn't she forgive?

"She's finally taken a lover, has she?"

Rolf Erling's powerful hands gripped the SUV's steering wheel as he circled the block. Owen Shaw sat inside the Internet cafe, staring out into the night with a hunter's watchful eyes.

Rage boiled within Rolf. He should have had Leona first—not Owen Shaw.

While in disguise, Rolf had entered Leona's shop. That July day, he'd let her feel his extrasensory presence, that of a powerful psychic. He'd wanted her to *feel* him near, to unsettle her senses. Once unsettled, pushed and crowded, extrasensory perceptions tilted, sometimes out of control. It was always a matter of seduction to unravel another psychic, even one with limited reception, like Leona.

Disguised as a blue-eyed, Nordic-looking blond, Rolf had enjoyed holding the purse Claire had created, setting up a psychic link with Leona. He'd played her well, letting her know his energy. On some level, she'd recognize him as another of the gifted.

Rolf had known he'd have to have her body before killing her, or taking her mind. He toyed with the thought—Leona lying beneath him, obedient to his commands.

She was the most like Greer Aisling, the woman who had publicly bested and shamed him in front of his peers ten years ago. However, he'd been able to block Greer's attempt to discover his real identity as a descendant of Borg, the warrior-psychic who had challenged Thorgood for the Celtic seer, Aisling. Borg's shame and anger had been so great, Rolf had taken another name, Erling.

This time, Borg's best and last descendant would have everything that Thorgood had taken, the ancient Celtic power tied to the wolf's-head brooch.

In Rolf's dreams, he was Borg. He absorbed Borg's jealous fury as Thorgood claimed that Celtic witch for his wife.

"It's time for my revenge and that of my family's. I was just learning when I 'played' with Leona's sisters, and I made mistakes. But I am going to make my ancestor's curse come true."

As Rolf drove off into the night, he stared into his rearview mirror, into the mesmerizing eyes he'd inherited from his ancestor. *He could steal anyone's identity. He was the perfect predator.*

Moments later, he pulled into the driveway of a plantation-style home. His arrangements to assume Alex Cheslav's identity, and then dispose of him, had been meticulous.

Rolf's inherited psychic ability, the years he'd spent honing it, and his years studying theater had given him much. Electronics, connections through computers and the information freely circulating the Internet gave him the rest. Identity theft and impersonation had become easy when added to his psychic powers. He had become very methodical, enough to patiently study and befriend a potential kill. Once he was satisfied that all the little identity gaps were closed, naturally the target would have to die. His slide into his prey's identity was nearly always seamless.

This new identity had been very easy to achieve. The prey, Alex Cheslav, had been emotionally vulnerable, a perfect target. Alex had been tall enough to match Rolf's requirements, in case someone actually questioned his physical identity.

Rolf liked to think of his victims as "prey." This made the "game" so much more fun. Alex's mind had been so easy to seduce and possess. This last identity's mind had been perhaps easier than the others, the ones Rolf had sent after Claire and Tempest.

Now the real Alex was dead, enabling Rolf to assume his identity *and* his home. As Rolf descended into his special workshop, a basement room filled with audio and visual equipment, mirrors, and a worktable for his disguises, he thought of his deceased prey.

Alex Cheslav had lived with his mother until she'd died, then the seventy-year-old man had seemed without an anchor. Retirement had further isolated him. Upon a chance meeting with Alex in Utah, Rolf had immediately sensed that vulnerability. After a few discussions with Alex about his antique collections, Rolf had become a "dear friend" and had easily convinced Alex to relocate to Lexington, a town filled with beautiful plantation-style homes and a ready antique market in the surrounding towns.

After Alex had sold everything and made financial and living arrangements to settle into "Lex," Rolf no longer needed Alex. Like the others, Alex was disposable. A cruel master, Rolf had decided to end Alex's worthless life with his own hands.

A little skillful padding, a few minor adjustments—like killing a man—and the new identity transfer was complete: Rolf Erling had simply become Alex Cheslav.

Disguised as Alex, a lonely widower, Rolf had intimate access to Leona's life. He'd studied her in person and with surveillance electronics. His years of shielding his gifts from other extrasensories, of blocking them from his energy, had paid off; Leona hadn't recognized his real identity, even in close proximity. A lesser talent and one with the minor healing and nurturing urges of an empath, Leona saw what she wanted to see: a lonely widower, helpless in his new life, without a woman to care for him. If she had looked past what her emotions had told her, Leona might have seen the almost invisible clues to Rolf's Alex-disguise. Just in case, he'd been very careful about keeping to the shadows when near her.

Now Rolf understood Leona's weaknesses as well as her habits. Disguised as a workman, he'd been in her home. But he wouldn't make the mistake of moving on Leona too soon. Perhaps that was his mistake with her sisters. And now their protective husbands hovered too close.

Rolf hadn't gone to bed since he awoke last night. In his routine midnight survey of Leona's home, he was furious to find Owen Shaw's pickup parked in her driveway.

"She should have known I was coming. That I was the one to have her. Leona sensed me that day I came into the shop, I know she did. She caught the pulses I sent to her. I saw her reaction," he said to his mirror's image. "Understand me well, Leona. I'm coming for you."

He preened just that bit, twining a black braid around his finger. He found his undisguised reflection beautiful: sharply defined features, black, compelling eyes, and flowing black hair. It was the image he had imprinted upon each of the Aisling women. He wanted them to dream of him, to fear him. Because fear always served him well.

He focused on the mirror, on the image he wanted Leona eventually to see in the flesh. "Yes, I am the one powerful enough to make the curse come true. I will have the brooch and the power. Dream of me, Leona."

Leona awoke to the sound of her own terrified screams. The image of the Viking chieftain walking toward her slowly faded.

This time, Owen's image had replaced the blur of the chieftain's face, the features rugged and dark and savage. A strand of his straight black hair crossed his brows, his eyes ice-cold beneath them.

The dream shredded with the echo of her own cry, "Don't leave me here alone!"

Don't leave me here alone. She'd cried the same at Joel's funeral. But memories of her husband's tender lovemaking contrasted with Owen's stark possession; her sated body bore the aches created by the imprint of his powerful one. Her muscles had stretched to the limit to hold him, to fight him in that ancient man-woman war of pleasure.

He'd wanted to know who had held his sister's bag. . . . His sister spoke of spirit women in the specific number three, as in the Aisling-Bartel triplets.

Leona tried to slow her racing senses. She tried to reassure herself that the first lovemaking she'd had in five years hadn't backfired. That she hadn't been branded in a way she couldn't forget.

Her body at war with her heart and mind, Leona's attempt to focus and calm failed. In one lithe movement, she rose to face the dawn; dim light filtered through the plantation blinds on the guest-bedroom window.

Owen had picked her up and carried her as if nothing could stop him. But she'd known one word from her could have ended the night, if not the hunger.

Out there on that dark, hot plane of passion, she'd sensed her own savage energy-thread reach out to hunt Owen's energy and suddenly connect.

She'd connected with Owen on a level she hadn't known existed in herself—something long, dark, and forgotten in her mystical DNA. Something very fierce and primitive had slipped from her keeping. She hadn't realized she was a hunter, a predator, seeking to capture Owen's unique blend of raw male energy.

Leona rubbed her chilled body. But then, her bloodline wasn't Aisling's alone, was it? Part of her heritage came from a race that needed adventure, that needed a challenge, a battle, to remain satisfied. "Owen is definitely a battle."

She trembled as flashes of their lovemaking slid through her mind. She'd surprised herself with the need to capture him. They'd made love, but never the basic missionary position. Owen had been very careful to stop from moving over her, and to ease into another position.

In the stormy darkness of her instincts, Leona knew her fear of being crushed would rise into terror; it was an emotion she kept close. But in the hot, hungry whirlwind, she'd moved over Owen.

Owen's big hands had roamed over her body, cupping her breasts, his face rough against her skin, his breath hot and uneven. . . . *Perfect, a little savage, just right, no easy capture.* . . . Did Owen always take a woman so hungrily? Or had he reacted to Leona's unique primitive hunger?

Leona's every instinct warned that Owen was dangerous, that her hunger for him could pierce her own protective shields.

Automatically reaching for the telephone before it rang, she picked up the receiver. "Hi, Tempest. No, I don't want to talk about last night."

The sound of wind and waves in the background told Leona that her sister stood outside her home's deck overlooking Lake Michigan. "I couldn't sleep," Tempest said. "The fact that this guy comes from Montana, where Claire lives, has got me unnerved. You have to be careful, Leona."

"I am very careful. That's why I've decided not to see him again. At least not in a—"

"Bed?" Tempest supplied in a humorous tone. "I can feel it run through you, that liquid soft sense of being a woman, and very . . . feline. You've found something you want—or your body wants—and you're going to go after it or rather, him. I don't think I tapped into anything personal. I know *you* wouldn't," she teased.

Leona wasn't in the mood for teasing. She'd crossed a very important line. She'd made love with a man she'd known for only a few hours, and their lovemaking hadn't been ordinary. She'd given Owen something of herself, and she'd taken as well. "I don't intend to come that close to him again. His sister said something about 'spirit women,' and she said 'three spirit women.' She just could be an extrasensory, too."

That light, teasing energy flowing from Tempest stilled. "Then he might have it."

"Because his sister is intuitive, or has some ability, doesn't mean Owen is. It can skip generations or siblings. I didn't feel anything like that from him."

"No, you were too busy *feeling*. Sixth senses can be overridden by body responses, you know that. And you were all primed when he walked into Timeless. Admit it. Seduction is also a form of beguilement and gives power to the one who takes it. To seduce and challenge can be an addiction. The fact that you are unusually cautious and that you nailed this guy on the first night after you met him, tells me something is just not usual. And you're afraid of him, aren't you? Of what he could mean to you?"

Was it true? That her body's need of Owen had blocked her usual psychic awareness of another extrasensory? His sister definitely had ability, but did

Owen? Was her connection to Owen only physical? Or was it more?

Before Leona could deny Tempest's suggestions, a male grumble sounded in the background. Marcus Greystone, her protective husband, was checking on his wife. A sensual warmth drifted lightly around Leona, and she knew that Marcus was caressing his wife. His low whisper caused Leona to smile. Marcus's hunger for his wife wasn't always shielded. "It's damn early, Tempest. Come back to bed, honey."

"Um . . . not now Marcus, I'm on the line with Leona."

"Good *early* morning, sister-in-law," Marcus stated loudly for Leona to hear. She understood the teasing tone; Marcus had plans for his wife that did not include Leona. There was a murmur as Tempest muffled the telephone, but Leona sensed an intense discussion.

She was right. Marcus took the phone, his tone changed to that of the no-nonsense businessman who ran the complex Greystone Investments. "I think I should come and check this Owen Shaw guy out," he stated firmly. "It's not like you to forget a dangerous situation, not only to you, but to your family, Leona. If he's from Montana, this guy could be after you. With the recent attack on Claire, in Montana, it's too much of a coincidence."

While Leona appreciated her brother-in-law's concern, she wasn't ready for a takeover. As a top CEO used to running a business, Marcus sometimes wanted to handle the triplets' lives, too. A financial empire builder, Marcus hadn't had a real family, and now he considered every Aisling-Bartel, including Greer, to be under his personal protection. He meant well, but sometimes had to be gently put in his place. This was usually something Leona enjoyed immensely, but not at the moment. "Thank you for the lecture, Marcus, but I've already decided not to see him again."

They'd clashed before and she knew that Marcus wasn't paying attention to her hands-off signal. "You do that. Keep me posted. It's a day's drive down there from here, but I can fly our plane in faster. Let me know if you need me."

Leona was still adjusting to her two brothers-in-law, both ready to assume protection of her. Both were of Viking ancestry and definitely macho. "Thanks. But I can handle it. I'm safe."

"Sure. That's what they all say. That's what Tempest said before she was attacked, before we bonded. See? I'm getting used to this psychic stuff. Bonding with Neil and me has made Claire and Tempest psychically stronger, but you're not there yet, kiddo. I know—you're an adult, a capable, independent woman with one big fat attitude, yada yada. In short, you want me to butt out. But you're alone, and I'm here for you—if you need me. Good talking with you, but my wife and I are going back to bed now."

"You didn't marry *me*, Marcus. You're not taking me over," Leona warned softly.

"Get used to it," he replied in a teasing tone. "I'm family now. I hold the rank of a certified Aisling Protector. More than likely my ancestor was one of your ancestor's men and pledged to protect the bloodline. According to the family's dreams, all the men in Thorgood's Vikings had gray eyes—except Borg. Neil has gray eyes . . . I have them. The equation isn't exact science, but neither are the dreams you women have. This means I have rights. You may have to move over and let big brother handle things, Leona Fiona."

"That will be the day."

After Tempest's giggling good-bye, Leona stood with her arms crossed, her breasts sensitized, and her body aching for more of Owen. But her family had a good point: Owen was from Montana, he could be dangerous, and she was evidently very susceptible. It was better not to see him again, before she became any more entangled. On the other hand, maybe it was just a one-night stand for him, and she wouldn't have to face that problem. Some men just needed to "score," then they were finished. If that was the case with Owen, she had nothing to worry about.

With that thought, Leona braced herself for the long workday ahead. She repeated her affirmation: She had nothing to worry about.

Except her own need of him.

When Leona parked in the alley behind her shop later that morning, Owen was sitting on her back porch, drinking from a Styrofoam cup.

Bracing herself, she got out of her car. Hitching her tote up on her shoulder, she walked toward him. Though she tried to appear unaffected, her senses had spiked, taking in everything about Owen: He'd shaved and changed clothes. His suit jacket hung on the handrail. It went well with his blue pin-striped shirt, open at the collar and fitting tightly to his broad shoulders. The tie draped around his neck was maroon and navy, colors that accentuated his dark coloring. When he stood, she noticed his neatly tailored slacks ended in polished dress shoes. Obviously expensive, his suit wasn't off the rack. In contrast to yesterday's Western family man, Owen looked sleek, hard, and set to do business.

His eyes hadn't left her, quickly taking in her violet blouse and dark purple slacks, her serviceable black pumps. His gaze skimmed the brooch on her blouse, then he crushed the cup in his hands, tossing it into the Dumpster with a look of distaste.

"Chai—not very good," he explained. He picked up a sleek metal laptop case and came down the steps to meet her. "How are you?"

He studied her face and she was certain he must be seeing the well-sated, smirking sexy woman her mirror had revealed. The morning's Cheshire-cat look had seemed foreign to Leona's usual businesswoman facade. After a second glance, she had attempted to cover the shadows beneath her eyes with extra concealer. It wasn't easy, not with a scarf over her mirror. She didn't want her resemblance to Aisling to appear, not after her night with Owen. "I'm just peachy. You?"

"Let's just say it's been a long night."

Leona understood that remark to mean she'd worn him out. She didn't appreciate the reference because it was probably true. That slight red mark on his throat was from her teeth, an uncomfortable reminder that in Owen's arms, she'd shed control. Uneasy with her emotions and the potential danger to her family, she moved past Owen and up the steps. Once she was safely on the back porch, she turned to look down at him. "I don't want to see you again."

"We have to talk."

Leona wasn't in the mood for a replay. Even now, as they stood close, she didn't exactly trust herself. Her instincts told her to leap upon him, take that hard mouth, slide her hand into the open shirt collar to stroke that powerful chest and lower. From there, if Owen reacted as he had last night, they would need to find somewhere private—and quickly.

But Owen had wanted to know too much about her family, and she would protect them with her life. "Last night is over."

The morning sunlight shone in his hair in blue-black shades, that one strand crossing his forehead. His expression hardened, the lines around his mouth deepening, as he glanced at her brooch. "You wore that yesterday. Any special significance?"

Only that it was a replica of the real Viking brooch,

a very important physical connection to her family. "It just happened to be lying there when I got dressed."

Owen's silver eyes narrowed as if he didn't believe her answer. He checked his wristwatch and inhaled impatiently. "I've got a business meeting in half an hour, and we need to talk more."

"I see. Business should *always* come first." How could she possibly want more of him? But she did, and that he had other "business" irritated, an illogical, emotional, and unsettling contrast to how she *should* be feeling.

"You like to make things difficult, don't you?" A muscle moved in Owen's cheek, and his lips tightened. His impatience showed clearly as he explained, "I'm doing a lot of things these days, including meeting key people and getting acquainted in business circles. I'm renovating the farm, and that takes time. But I need to set up contacts and networking, too. There's a breakfast this morning for the local businessmen's association, and I want to sit in. I really don't know how I'm going to handle everything just now. A lot depends on Janice. She might do well if we got into thoroughbreds here. We could handle a few at the farm. Racing could come later, I don't know. Everything is on hold until I see how she does."

"I fully understand your concern for your sister. But you're not obligated to me. I don't need explanations." *Did Owen feel as though he had bonded with her? Or was Leona alone in the sense that their energy had mated, just as their bodies had joined?*

His eyes searched hers. "I just want you to know where I stand."

Owen's tone carried bitterness as he glanced at another shop owner, unlocking a back door to the shop near Leona's. He straightened his shoulders and lifted his chin, his stance reflecting his pride. Those straight black lashes shadowed his eyes, the planes of his face harsh, skin gleaming against his high cheekbones. "We grew up dirt-poor. I learned the hard way that appearances, associations, and money count. And I've got to provide for my sister's care. Private nurses and caretakers are expensive."

Those gray eyes shifted back to her. "My sister wants to meet you. Janice believes you are her special 'spirit woman.' I think you can help her. Will you?"

Leona held her breath. An invitation to meet family wasn't the clean break she'd wanted. "What makes you think that I can help her?"

"Does the name Greer Aisling and the Bartel triplets mean anything to you?" Owen asked, coming up the steps once more and handing her a folded paper. The computer printout was a twenty-two-year-old event that Leona knew well—the photo of her mother and the triplets took her back to that horrible time. The headline screamed at her: WORLD-FAMOUS PSYCHIC SUES ESP CLINIC AND OTHERS.

Leona trembled as she scanned the too-familiar story, but the words had already been burned into her memory:

Greer Aisling, a world-famous psychic, residing in an undisclosed location on the northwest Pacific coast has filed kidnapping and other charges against the Blair Institute for Parapsychology. Aisling, a widow, had been called into work with a Canadian police force to find a missing boy. Her triplets, aged ten years old, had been left in the Aisling estate under the care of their long-term guardian and housekeeper.

Reportedly, Ms. Aisling had refused the institute's efforts to test the home-schooled children.

On the suspected charge of abuse and without the mother's knowledge and consent, the triplets had been extracted from their home. They were placed in the care of the Blair Institute Child Studies Program for testing.

The children are back now in the care of their mother who has already filed several lawsuits and promises more. Observers note that the triplets seem to be well cared for and strangely gifted.

The article said nothing about the electrodes, the probing examinations, the responses to tests, *the way the triplets were isolated from each other and strapped down . . .*

"That's interesting," Leona managed, as images of her and her sisters' trauma flipped through her mind, each one horrible—each one reminding her that she had been unable to save her sisters.

"Terrible thing to happen to a child," Owen said softly.

"Yes, I suppose." Grateful that her voice revealed none of the terror she'd momentarily relived, Leona shrugged.

If he only knew how terrible. Leona's hand trembled as she quickly handed the printout back to Owen. If she could, she'd get rid of the past as easily. Her family had been well researched. Anyone wanting to harm them could find information easily. *Why was Owen so interested in her family, and in her?*

On the defensive immediately, ready to protect her family and herself, Leona fought for a bland expression. She had to hide the stark emotions chilling her now.

Owen's sister had spoken of three spirit women, and he'd linked that to the Aisling-Bartel triplets—and researched their lives. *Why?*

She'd just taken a lover who might be dangerous to her family, and to herself. She'd let her guard down for one night with Owen.

Her senses prickled as if she'd been probed, someone noting her every expression, picking at the slightest nuances in her body language, her tone. *If Owen were an extrasensory, he was standing too close, within her field of energies.*

She could be standing inches away from a man who wanted to kill her. If he succeeded, he'd weaken her family's bonds and harm them. Leona took a deep breath and braced herself.

She'd kill to protect her family. That harsh thought surprised her. Leona hadn't realized how deeply and how far she would go to protect her sisters. She would do what she must. Trying to focus on her inner calm, she attempted to build those shields she'd used for a lifetime. Her voice seemed a little husky but definitely not panicked. "You've been busy. Did you know about my family before?"

"I didn't, before last night." Owen studied her face. "Your eyes were dark green last night, with just touches of earth, and now they seem gold. You're ready to fight, aren't you? The lioness protecting her clan? Don't worry. I'm not going to hurt you, but I need you. Janice picked up traces of you and your sisters on that bag. That's why I need to talk with you. You just might be able to help my sister."

"Don't count on it. And don't believe everything you read."

"She'll know if she meets you."

"What about you? What do you know, other than what you've read?" *What did Owen sense now? Was he a psychic bloodhound, picking up traces of her psyche, and storing them away? Was he connected to the man who came into her shop in July?*

In their fiery storm of lovemaking, had she given Owen information that could harm her family?

Owen's expression remained impassive and grim. The morning shadows emphasized the hard planes of his face, those light, watchful, hunter's eyes. "Janice is right sometimes, that's all. Sometimes she's not. She can be off just slightly, or completely wrong. I've learned to be prepared for anything. This time, if she's right, then she's picked through the people who have touched that bag and isolated your connection to your sisters. The designer of Claire's Bags, and one other, and you. You spoke to Claire last night. I'm guessing that the third spirit woman is your sister, Tempest."

Owen's determined expression chilled her. He was already too deep into the Aisling-Bartel lives and far too dangerous. Then, as if to drive home that point, Owen stated coolly, "Tempest Bartel-Storm . . . recently married to Marcus Greystone. I researched her name online, and she's posted several notices to antiquities dealers and collectors. She's been hunting a ninth-century artifact for about the past year and a half, a Viking brooch. Every one of the recent photos of your family shows you and your sisters and your mother wearing this same pin. Your mother is wearing matching jewelry in her television interviews. It's in her PR photo in the back of her books. It means something to your family, doesn't it?"

He glanced meaningfully at Leona's brooch. "Except for the wolf's head, the design woven around it is Celtic. Since all of you have red hair and green eyes and that pale skin, I'd say you're of that descent, and yet your home is stripped of anything that might resemble that link. In your sleep, you said, 'I don't want to be like you, and I'll never forgive you.' You're holding a pretty deep grudge. Who would that be, Leona? Who won't you forgive? Yourself? For what?"

"Go to hell, Owen," Leona managed coolly. But her emotions zigzagged from fear for her family, back to anger at Owen. Then at herself, for taking him to her body.

"Been there. It's not much fun." He leaned close and nuzzled her cheek. "You smell good in the morning." Then he smiled. "I'll pick you up tonight. We'll have that dinner and talk."

Leona eased away; her senses were already humming and wanting to take those hard lips, to feel the heavy beat of his heart beneath her hand. She gripped the tote's handle to keep from touching him. Her blood simmered even now, when she both feared and hated him. "I'm busy tonight."

Owen leaned down to nibble on her ear. "Cancel."

She tried to ignore the shock waves ricocheting throughout her body; but desire curled into a hot, tight knot within, requiring another match with Owen. "I can't. I'm helping a friend furnish his new house. We're choosing the fabrics for his sofa. He's borrowed the swatches for the night, so I can't cancel. And I really don't think I can help your sister."

"You're afraid." His challenge hung on the morning air between them.

"No," she lied. *Of course she was afraid. Leona was afraid that whoever stalked her family would succeed in destroying them. She was afraid of Owen, of opening, of what ran deep inside her that she couldn't turn off. She was afraid of going mad like her grandmother.* "I just don't want any more involvement with you."

"'Involvement?' As in what happened last night?" Owen's anger rose now, his face hard. A muscle moved in his jaw, and that pulse in his throat had become more prominent. "There's no way to take that back, Leona."

"I don't know what you're angry about. You got what you wanted."

"So did you. I'm a little touchy about being used. Been there, done that," Owen stated grimly.

If Leona could take her psychic DNA, shove it in a box, and bury it, she would. And she'd toss in the heat and passion released last night with Owen.

The only time Leona had opened herself to her powers was to help her sisters. Then she pushed back and closed the door on what she could be if she let her extrasensory inheritance develop. Helping Janice, who might have psychic ability, could be dangerous to her. To her entire family. If there was one thing Leona did not want to do with her life, it was to be entangled with Aisling's seer gifts. They'd destroyed Leona's grandmother and could destroy her.

Owen had been studying her expression. His expression was harsh, his eyes gun-metal cold. "You're uneasy with me. I understand that. Lovers look different in the harsh daylight, don't they? Fine in the dark, but not by daylight?"

Leona's senses prickled warningly, and intuition took words to her lips. "You've been hurt, haven't you? By a woman like me?"

His eyes flashed at her, his lips hard. "Did I say that?"

And then Leona knew what Owen had told no one. She'd snagged it from him, plucked it from the brooding darkness around him.

If she could do that, they might have already developed a very deep, intangible connection of the senses. If so, she knew the exact moment it had happened: at their lovemaking's peak, when they were both out there on that white-hot plane. Owen had taken something from her. But she'd taken as well. Lovemaking had been too perfect with him they'd been too well matched.

The knowledge that Owen had loved a woman like her and he'd been badly hurt throbbed around her.

"I'm so sorry, Owen," she whispered.

Nodding abruptly, he glanced around the back alley, as if removing himself from the tense emotional moment he didn't want to revisit. "Janice thinks you can help. She's desperate to meet you. She's been through hell, Leona. You probably understand some of it from your own experiences. Think about it. . . . Some other time, then."

Just that look, that tilt of his head challenged her. Leona's hand reached for his shirtfront, gripping it before she realized she'd moved. Tugging Owen's face down to hers, she said "You have absolutely no ties on my life or who I see, and I don't like being stalked."

"Someone was keeping very close tabs on you last night, Leona, and it wasn't me."

Leona didn't hide her fear for just that heartbeat, and Owen caught it. "Last night, on the phone with your sister you said, 'he's not getting me.' What did you mean by that? Why are you afraid?"

End the Aisling and Thorgood line. Get the brooch, get the power.

"I don't know what you mean."

This time, Owen wrapped his hand around her nape and drew her close, forehead to forehead. "Sure you do. You're having nightmares. They're bad enough to make you bring some 'entertainment' home. Me. A man you'd just met, so you could sleep without nightmares. Too bad. They came anyway. It's been a long time since your husband died, right? Well, Leona, I'm not Joel Chablis or anything close. Got it?"

With that, Owen took her lips. His kiss was hard, demanding, and searing in its possession. Her instincts told her that he was branding her for his own. To her shock, Leona wrapped her arms around his shoulders and locked her body to his. Arching, she thrust her lower body hard against him, sex to sex.

When Owen broke the kiss abruptly, then strode

away, Leona trembled and wiped her hand across her burning lips. The primitive hunger between them shocked her; she'd reacted instantly, branding her mark on Owen's lips and body just as he'd branded hers.

She pitted herself against the sensual hunger raging deep within her. Too much was at risk, her family's lives and her own. She couldn't afford to be possessed, and Owen was already too close to completing that mission.

He said he needed her to help his sister.

But did he want more? Could Owen be the key to her family's destruction?

After work, Leona didn't want to go home, to remember Owen in bed. Her appointment with Alex Cheslav offered a temporary buffer.

When she pulled into his driveway, just off a busy tree-lined street, she saw that Alex stood on the shadowy porch of his elegant two-story house. Obviously in deep thought, he studied a row of giant potted hanging ferns sitting on the porch. As always when it came to renovating his plantation-style home, Alex looked adrift. His hand ran through his shoulder-length gray hair.

According to what he'd told Leona, he was a widower, retired and, having recently moved to Lexington, eager to renovate and furnish the house. He and his wife had long planned the move, but now he was alone. Leona had first met him when he'd come into her shop, two months ago. He was looking at things that reminded him of his beloved wife. After a second visit and more conversation about his wife and the move they'd planned together, Leona and Alex had shared a dinner and become friends. She soon learned that bright sunlight affected his poor eyesight and Alex preferred to move in the shadows, his home dimly lit. Almost forty years older than Leona, Alex sometimes acted as if she were his daughter though he had no children of his own.

Leona parked her car in the driveway, behind his fuel-economy one. She collected the take-out dinner sack and exited the car, enjoying the cool damp evening air as she walked to the front porch. The stained glass window on the front door had been her selection, the lily-of-the-valley pattern a favorite of his deceased wife.

Tall, stooped, and carrying a little too much weight around his middle, Alex had the well-worn comfortable look of a retired businessman. Behind his tinted and thick eyeglasses, Alex's brown eyes seemed to light at the sight of Leona. "Ferns. Have to have 'em, all these old houses do. 'Curb appeal,' you know. How do you hang the things, and how do you water them?"

After a hard day, filled with reminders of the danger Owen represented as well as aches from the passion they'd shared, Leona was set to unwind. She'd have a nice glass of wine with Alex and deal with nothing more than the great fern-dilemma and the upholstery swatches. Over dinner, she'd gently tell him the ferns he'd chosen would have to go back, replaced by ones that could withstand the outdoor temperatures. In the meantime Leona held up a sack. "I brought dinner from that home-cooking place you like. There's a salad and plenty of the entree you can have as leftovers for your lunch tomorrow."

He took the sack, peered down inside to the meat-loaf dinner, and smiled almost boyishly. "Cynthia always used to make the best meat loaf. The restaurant comes the closest to her recipe. Thank you, Leona. I forgot to eat lunch. I was watching my retirement investments online, and see now that this place is going to cost a fortune to renovate. Cynthia would have had a hissy fit at the cost. The handyman you recommended is great though, quite reasonable. I like Vernon."

"Good. Just don't take him away from me before he's done with my closet. He just started it yesterday," Leona said with a smile. "I was lucky to get him. He's just started house-sitting for Billy Balleau, the country music star. Billy's on tour now, and Vernon is doing some minor renovation and repair while he's gone."

Alex released one of his gentle, friendly teases. "Oh, Vernon made it clear right away that you were his priority and that he had other work. It seems Vernon likes you, taking special care to see that you're pleased with his work. He's very proud of working for you. He says you have class, Leona."

"He's right. I do," she returned with the ease of their friendship. Leona surveyed the large shade trees surrounding Alex's home, the row of elegant homes and gardens lining the street. They seemed like peaceful, beautiful reminders of a slower time. "I would have loved to have a home like this, but I don't have the time to give it the attention it needs. I barely have time to manage my own. I'm trying to make a brick patio."

The task of fitting the bricks together reminded her of her plan to fit her life together. Joel and she had planned to buy one of these lovely old homes. The ache of missing Joel and their plans swept gently through her. Leona frowned. She couldn't even remember his face, yet Owen's image had come easily to her mind.

A powerful psychic could imprint images into the minds of others—and the images of their lovemaking had returned too many times today. Her body still bore his touch, no matter how she'd tried to forget. *She may have made love with the man who could be dangerous to her family!*

"I know you don't have time to spare, but I really appreciate your dropping by tonight, Leona." Alex's tinted glasses glinted in the shadows as he frowned. "Is something bothering you? You seem—I don't know—very tired? And here you are, coming to help me after a full workday."

"I took a break. Sue Ann came in to help for a couple hours at noon. Between fall orders coming in and unpacking new inventory, it got a little hectic. I went to a nice quiet library for a little while to get away from it all."

"You could have come here. It's closer than your home, isn't it?"

"I needed to catch up on some designer magazines." Leona had really spent her break researching Owen Shaw, lately of Montana. He'd said that he and his sister were born there. Leona's research quickly turned up a newspaper obituary noting the accidental vehicular death of his parents. Janice and Owen were the only surviving family. *He'd been Janice's guardian for years*. . . . Another article listed Owen as a promising new partner in an investment firm. And that was it; Leona had learned nothing new. Except now she knew more—that Janice was an extrasensory, and that could mean that Owen was also.

If he was, Owen could just be the psychic vampire tracking her family. He was already questioning the significance of her brooch. Psychics could observe and pair physical objects with their own extrasensory ability in order to learn everything about someone. *They could use a viewer's emotions to create a mask over their real identity.*

The curse on the brooch ran through Leona's mind: *End the ancient seer Aisling's line. . . . Get the brooch, get the power. . . .*

Five

———

"ONCE I DESTROY LEONA, I'LL HAVE THAT BROOCH. THEN I'LL have everything," Rolf Erling promised his undisguised reflection in his rearview mirror.

In the rear of the SUV, the handyman's tools rattled slightly as Rolf drove over the street's speed bump. He slowed immediately, careful to push his temper down. Rage had always been a problem since childhood. He couldn't afford to lose control now that he had the last Aisling-Bartel triplet in his grasp.

Leona would be the true test of his power; he would kill or break her, weakening the connections to the others and their combined psychic strength.

Rolf briefly closed his eyes and saw Greer Aisling, the woman who had publicly defeated and shamed him. When he finally came for Greer—and the brooch—she would have no defenses. How he would savor that moment. . . .

Alex Cheslav, a widower, still in love with his deceased wife, had been the perfect bait for a widow like Leona. The older man touched Leona's vulnerable, aching side, reminding her of her own husband and creating an emotional tie.

From what Rolf had observed, Leona wasn't practicing, wasn't developing her gifts. Only a fool would turn away from the power she could possess. She'd easily taken the bait—the assumed identity of Alex Cheslav. Add the fact that Alex lived in the kind of gorgeous home she'd always wanted with gardens she loved and a greenhouse in the back and her connection to the lonely man was all that much stronger. Rolf's "prey" was just within his grasp.

Softened by their friendship, Leona would also be open to other things—such as the fear Rolf loved to feed upon and that made him stronger.

As Rolf drove the powerful SUV through the softly falling rain toward Leona's home, he continued to fight his anger. He'd have to be very careful around Leona Aisling-Bartel-Chablis. He'd sensed she was potentially stronger than her sisters. Glancing at the rearview mirror, he admired his image—tall, sleek, powerful—and very, very smart. The tinted contacts changed his eye color, but he much preferred his own eyes, so black that pupil and iris were one.

Since early childhood, he'd been tutored by his father. Rolf had learned that his eyes and mind and skill could take control of the vulnerable ones, to make them do things they shouldn't, like puppets. He chuckled at that, thinking of his childhood, of the tricks he'd played while developing his extrasensory gift.

He could hide who he was now, become anyone with the help of easy identity theft. He'd learned to mask himself from other psychics—even Greer Aisling, that red-haired witch. *How he hated her, and he would have her crawl before he was done, have her begging on her knees, whining, trying to protect her daughters. . . . Didn't she know that he'd already killed her beloved husband?*

Rolf chuckled, remembering how as an eight-year-old boy, he'd captured Daniel Bartel's attention. The meeting had been arranged by Rolf's father, who had also helped him arrange Bartel's death. Rolf had simply imprinted the image of himself chasing his ball across the highway in front of Bartel's car. Of course, Daniel Bartel, husband of Greer and father of the triplets, had swerved, crashed his car, and died.

Joel Chablis had been an easy kill as well. The friendly invitation to go snowmobiling on that Colorado mountain pass had ended perfectly. Joel hadn't made it through that avalanche, of course.

And now it was Leona's turn.

When she wasn't in her home, Rolf enjoyed disguising himself as a handyman; he'd walk through it and study her. When she'd occasionally left her laptop at home, he'd used it to research her even more closely.

Her sisters' psychic-residue fluff filled Leona's comfortable home. In the third bedroom, he'd sensed Greer Aisling's energy.

Greer Aisling. Rolf's psychic hackles had risen as he'd entered that tiny third bedroom. "She will be thoroughly humiliated before I'm done with her."

A fresh wave of anger washed over Rolf; Leona had taken Shaw to her home and to her bed. The psychic residue in the larger guest bedroom had held enough sexual punch to take away Rolf's breath, to harden his body. In his anger he'd almost lost control and sought out a woman to rape and kill. He'd killed before to release the building pressure. But he couldn't allow his plans to be ruined now, not when he was so close to taking down the Aislings.

After he fulfilled the revenge of the Borg curse and completed his personal vendetta against Greer Aisling, Shaw was next on Rolf's list.

But Shaw, too, was proving useful to Rolf right now. Shaw had safely transported the perfect instrument, the perfect bait for Leona's downfall. Janice Shaw's troubled soul, her minimal gift, would surely ensnare Leona. Once tangled with Janice, Leona's energies would become strained and vulnerable. She would become the perfect prey.

Then, for having Leona, Owen Shaw would die slowly, painfully.

"Leona . . . "

The eerie whisper of her name reached her above the sound of the raindrops and the rustle of the tree leaves. It was nine o'clock at night and she had just turned into her driveway, stopping her car to avoid hitting a small branch in her way. As she stood beside her car, ready to pick up the branch, she heard her name again. Frozen by terror, Leona scanned the darkness.

Her neighbors on her cul-de-sac had settled in for the night. Leona heard her next door neighbor calling her dog.

Streetlights pooled gently through a mist that foretold heavier rain. In the distance, a figure stood, barely visible.

"Hello?" she called. Fear rippled up her nape and chilled her body. Her senses quivered, and something inside her shrunk back, hiding as a child would from danger stronger than she. "Were you calling me? Who are you?"

"Leona . . . " The shadow faded back into the night, leaving only the mist surrounding her, damp on her face.

Leona frantically searched for inner calm, her protection against the fierce emotions she knew she held deep inside. In a traumatic situation, her feelings were too powerful, and she didn't like to release them. *Now all she felt was fear.*

Shaken, Leona hurried to get back into her car. She drove over the small branch, entered her garage, and quickly shut its heavy door. Inside her house moments later, she was still trembling. She hurried to check the locks on her back and front doors. Shivering, she hugged herself. What was that Owen had said that morning? *Someone was keeping very close tabs on you last night, Leona, and it wasn't me.* What did he mean? Who was it outside just now?

Earlier in the year, her sisters had heard their names called in the same eerie way. Then Leona had visited Tempest by Lake Michigan, in a town with a name that would chill any psychic—Port Salem. The lake's fog had caught her on the porch; it chilled her and took away her breath. Leona hadn't been able to move. Had that fog, as an extension of the lake, taken her energy, like a bloodhound tracing her here to Lexington?

The dampness had felt the same, almost with a pulse and a heartbeat. At the time, Leona had pushed away the unwelcome realization that she and her sisters could be reached by the fog and mist growing out of large natural bodies of water. *Someone, or something, could connect to them using the mist. Who was it tonight, the shadow in the mist?*

In her small foyer mirror, Leona caught a glimpse of her pale face and frightened green eyes. The image reminded Leona of her seer DNA and the curse that could become reality. She spoke to her ancestor who she felt hovered closely now. "Aisling, go away. Please leave me alone."

Frowning, she tossed her favorite flowing turquoise-and-teal scarf over the mirror. Her image remained behind the sheer cloth. "I want no part of you tonight, Aisling. Or any other night."

You're not to blame for your husband's death. Don't blame yourself, that familiar inner voice murmured.

"I could have stopped Joel from taking that trip to

Colorado. I could have done something. Instead, I didn't want to believe."

Believe . . .

"No, I won't. At least not for tonight. I'm bone-tired, and you'll have to wait."

Firmly resolved to push any extrasensory perception plaguing her away for the night, Leona kicked off her shoes. She walked to her desk, tossed her tote onto the chair, and stretched her shoulders. After a long day and a relaxing dinner with Alex, she was determined not to let last night's lovemaking, or Owen's disturbing research of her, ruin a good night's sleep.

She stood very still, suddenly chilled with an eerie sense that she wasn't the only person in the room. *That's ridiculous. No one is watching me*, she told herself.

The mist outside had become a pounding rain, another thunderstorm in the forecast. It reminded Leona of the sexual storm last night. She'd given herself so easily to a man who was entirely too dangerous to her calm, structured life. And perhaps to her family.

Lack of sleep made her too vulnerable to dreams prowling in her mind. The nightmare of the man with long, rippling black hair, the twin braids swinging like snakes around that sharp face, those penetrating black eyes would come too readily now.

With a sigh, Leona quickly reminded herself that it wasn't only the night dreams. Her visions came in the daytime, too, in the flash of a mirror, or images sliding by her shop's window.

Even now, Owen was probably prowling through her life. There were things no reporter had discovered, the intricate web of mystic DNA, enhanced by the trauma the triplets had suffered in the Blair Institute of Parapsychology.

That sailboat accident had changed the triplets, too,

linking them with large bodies of water, making them more vulnerable to any powerful psychic who wished to use that universal portal. Owen couldn't know that at age three, she and her sisters had been terrified in the ocean. He couldn't know that before their parents rescued them, they had linked somehow in that universal, psychic portal. He couldn't truly know what the wolf's-head brooch meant to the Aislings.

Leona remembered holding the original brooch; its image burned in her mind. She rubbed her hands together, as if she could erase the curse. But she knew the dream of the man with the black, mesmerizing eyes, the Borg-descendant, would still come. *End the line, get the brooch, get the power. . . .*

Leona rubbed her temples, a headache brewing there. She couldn't afford the so-called "gift" that had caused her grandmother to kill herself. "I am *not* the strongest, and I don't want to be."

Removing her brooch, she walked to the kitchen and retrieved her bottle of wine from the refrigerator. She'd already had two glasses at Alex's, but she still wasn't relaxed. *Stella Mornay, her grandmother, had wanted to relax, too. . . .*

"Just a little more to top off the night, Grams. No more than that," Leona murmured firmly as she poured a glass and walked back to her living room.

If she walked down the hallway, she'd remember how Owen had carried her as if nothing could stop him, but her. Maybe she should have.

She settled into her favorite chair, sipping her wine and drawing the soft, comforting weight of the afghan over her shoulders. The streetlights caught the rain as it beaded her windows. The drops streamed down the glass like little snakes waiting to strike.

Settling down to brood, Leona worried that her night with Owen was causing too much to happen, too quickly.

Just a while ago, someone had stood in the mist and called to her. . . . Had she brought danger closer by getting involved with a man who was possibly an intuitive, too?

Leona took another sip of wine and stared at the windows, rain sparkling upon the glass. The curse upon the genuine brooch was relentless, circling her. Borg's descendant still wanted revenge upon her family, and someone had gone after her sisters.

If Aisling's psychic gifts had passed to her descendants, then it was also possible that another line also had dreams of that same brutal fight over a woman. In their visions, they might have heard the grunts of men, the clashing of swords. Since the Borg family had lost the prize of a woman to Celtic seer Aisling, the Borg family believed they had cause for revenge. The need for revenge could be strong enough to last centuries. The right descendant, one who had perfected his gifts, might be stalking Leona's family right now. . . .

"It's possible. More than possible," Leona acknowledged as she lifted her glass to toast the rain, another possible extension of a psychic portal, acknowledging the link between the fog, the rain and the large body of water and how she'd felt.

Whatever was out there had come after Claire in a similar way. She'd felt that energy and heard her name as she and Neil had camped beside the Missouri River. Then Tempest experienced the same by Lake Michigan. Leona lifted her glass to the window again, toasting whoever was out in the night, calling her name, stalking her family. "Logically, I'm next. If I am, I won't go down easily. You can't have my family, you bastard. You can slink right back to whatever bog you crawled out of, curse or not."

Her gaze fell upon Tempest's statue of the triplets; in life the triplets were linked in every way, physically and with their senses. The parapsychologists had tested Leona's link with her sisters. The tests had determined that Leona could potentially be the strongest, the fiercest when aroused, capable of wielding more extrasensory powers than the rest. The tests had presumably shown that Leona could perhaps be more powerful than Greer Aisling, their mother and a proven psychic.

"Bah-humbug. Malarkey." Still . . . In her lifetime, Leona hadn't wanted to believe that she could be aroused into fighting. She was now, enough to kill. For her family, Leona would do what she must to protect them. "If that was you out there calling my name and standing beneath that streetlight, don't test me too far, you bastard. Maybe I've been saving everything I am, just as a special gift to you. *Don't you dare hurt my family.*"

With that thought, Leona finished her glass of wine and snuggled down under her afghan to doze.

She awoke to the sound of the pounding rain, the erotic hunger of her body and to the sensual sound of her own voice, "Owen . . ."

"Owen . . ."

The aching sound of a woman in sensual need caused Rolf to tense, his senses tingling. He'd been at his worktable, perfecting his disguises, when the woman's erotic tone had caught him. In that instant, he'd known his senses had caught Leona's voice. She must have been in the twilight of her dreams, when her mind floated more easily to him, her protective shields down.

That day in her shop, disguised as the blue-eyed blond, Rolf had snagged something of Leona, just as she had caught something of him. This time it wasn't electronic sound transferring her voice, and her need, it was the extrasensory connection they had made that day.

"It wasn't supposed to happen that way. *I* wasn't supposed to pick up from her. That can only mean Leona is stronger than I had guessed. But not strong enough to detect my disguise as Alex. I am still stronger."

Rolf met his own compelling black eyes in the mirror; anger flashed back at him. "She calls to Owen, does she? Soon, it will be my name on her lips . . . begging me to take her, before I kill her. I'll enjoy it, Leona. I really will."

"Owen . . . "

Owen sat up in his tangled bedding, his body aroused, his flesh hot and damp. It was Leona's voice, the sound of a woman in ecstasy. She'd sounded that way last night, just as they both went over the edge. For a moment, he held the sound in his mind, hoarding it in that margin between sleep and consciousness. In that drowsy twilight, he sensed her hunger, remembered how she felt, sleek and soft and strong, taking what she wanted, what he wanted—

His body tensed in anticipation, his erection hard. Startled awake, just at the point of release, Owen jackknifed off the bed and rubbed the tension in his nape. He almost felt her above him, taking him and he'd almost—"Dammit, I'm not a boy anymore."

Somehow Leona had conceived a lock on his senses. It had happened when they'd made love, and it wouldn't go away easily.

The discovery of Leona's psychic family, the link that Janice had made between the Bartel women, and the need to be with Leona again hadn't made it an easy day for him. It was only eleven o'clock at night and he had an early morning interviewing a carpenter, and a full day after that.

Janice was desperate to meet Leona. From what Owen had seen of Leona this morning, defensive and braced for battle, an arranged meeting wouldn't be easy.

After a stinging cold shower, Owen threw on clothes then opened the door to his bedroom and found Janice's pale, haunted face staring up at him. "I have to meet her, Owen. *Or I'll die.*"

Her statement chilled him. Would Janice kill herself if she didn't meet Leona? Owen drew his sister into his arms and rocked her with his body. Their father hadn't given her comfort and warmth, and Owen had tried to learn new ways to replace that missing element. "You're not going to die, honey."

"Help me, Owen. I feel it," Janice whispered as she shuddered and gripped him tightly. "*I know.*"

Owen stroked her hair. It had been so long and soft and sweet swirling around her when she was a child, playing in the field. Now Janice was no longer a child but a deeply troubled woman.

Owen knew Janice's predictions sometimes came true. He prayed they wouldn't this time. He would make certain they didn't. "We'll talk with Leona. Don't worry. She's nice."

Janice looked up at him, her expression hopeful. "You know what she is, don't you? You know that she can help me, your spirit woman? You have the gray eyes of the ones who see into the future. You know this truth, don't you?"

"Maybe," he answered cautiously.

Because at the moment, Owen wasn't certain of anything. There was no way he could have heard Leona call to him. No way.

Still, he fought a cold premonition that Janice could be right about Leona.

After a sleepless night and before she left to open her shop for the morning, Leona left a note for Vernon. He wasn't to allow anyone in the house without her specific permission. Someone had been out there last night, and she wasn't taking chances. That fear and her hunger for Owen had stalked her all night.

During a brief quiet moment in her shop, Leona leaned back into the shadows of a corner and gripped her wolf's-head brooch. Without sleep, she was even more sensitive to everything. Sensitive or not, too much was stirring around her.

Owen just could be part of this psychic tangle, the curse and the Borg-descendant who wanted to make it come true. Leona felt something, other than the physical bond. Owen could be a descendant of another psychic power, ready to—

Swallowing her fear, she stepped from the shadows into the air stirred by the ceiling's plantation-style fan. She repeated the firm statement she'd made many times since Tempest had first placed the brooch in Greer's hands: "I refuse to live in fear."

As she hurried to take blouses from the fitting room back out to the display room, Leona's fingers shook as she replaced a blouse's hanger on the rack. Methodically, she straightened the other blouses around it. She had too many uneven edges in her life. *She had to regain control, and do it quickly.*

Glancing at her wristwatch she wondered where Sue Ann was. It had been a hectic hour since opening and her seamstress hadn't appeared at nine-thirty, the arranged time to prepare for Mrs. Alexander's fitting—she would be arriving any moment. Sue Ann was usually early, in time to chat a bit with Leona. If delayed, Sue Ann was always very prompt to call, and her reasons were always very important.

Leona decided to call her friend. "Are you okay?" she asked.

"I've decided to quit working for you."

Sue Ann's voice lacked her usual cheerful tone, and that shook Leona; they'd been such good friends. "I see. You've probably found something better."

"No. I haven't. Don't call me—ever. I'm not going to see you again."

Sue Ann had not only decided to stop working in Leona's shop, she had decided to end their five-year friendship. Leona didn't understand her friend's sudden change. Sue Ann had been a blessing after Joel's death; she had urged Leona to keep going on the darkest of days, encouraging Leona to go to restaurants and carefully chosen movies, inviting her into her home for dinner.

And now Sue Ann wanted out of Leona's life? Deeply concerned now, Leona asked, "Is there something wrong? Can I help?"

"I just don't want to work there anymore. Or see you again," Sue Ann stated before she hung up.

Troubled by Sue Ann's behavior, Leona decided to visit her friend after work. In the meantime, she apologized to Mrs. Alexander when she came into the shop, and called to cancel Sue Ann's other appointments. Hopefully, a conversation with Sue Ann would straighten out any problems. Working arrangements were one thing, but friendship another.

Movement beyond the shop's window caused Leona to glance outside. At first she thought that Owen and the girl beside him were another vision.

Momentarily closing her eyes, she willed the images away. But Owen and the girl were flesh and blood and they were coming to see her. Their straight black hair and burnished skin marked them as family—Janice! He'd brought her here!

Leona wanted to run, to lock the door and keep them away. As unsettled as she was now, all her psychic antenna quivering and on full alert, she might just connect with Janice—if Janice possessed any psychic gift at all. The outcome could be unpleasant for both of them.

"Okay, Leona Fiona, calm down. This is your shop and your life. You don't have to do anything you don't want to do." Still, a part of her couldn't help but mourn the girl, who appeared terrified and in need of comfort.

Owen held the shop's door for his sister. At closer range, Janice Shaw was older than she first appeared. Dressed in a plain white blouse, jeans, and moccasins, the "Freedom" tote on her shoulder and beads around her wrist, she seemed very frightened, her hair in a ragged cut. When the tiny brass bell over the door tinkled, Janice glanced up as if expecting a predator to strike.

As she gripped Owen's arm, he bent to her and murmured something that seemed to quiet her.

The girl's black eyes pinned Leona, and she braced herself to meet them. She ached for the girl's fear. If she was clairvoyant, Janice may have seen terrifying things beyond the limits of reality. One look at her, and Leona wanted to hold her, to fight for her. She walked toward them, pasted her usual businesswoman's smile on her face, and prepared herself for any extrasensory impact.

But her body had started to heat and soften, alerted to Owen's raw masculinity. "Hello, Owen."

"Hello, Leona. I hope you enjoyed last night with your friend." Owen wasted no time in letting his obvious displeasure be known, his eyes the color of frost.

She didn't need extrasensory powers to perceive his anger. "I did," she replied. She would make no excuses for her life, or her friends. She had given Owen no right to act possessive.

"I see." His gaze held hers as he gestured to the girl beside him. "This is Janice, my sister—"

As Janice walked toward Leona, their eyes locked. Leona wasn't a focused empath like Claire, but still the tentacles of Janice's fear reached out to her. Leona's senses picked up the image of a dark cloak surrounding the girl, keeping her prisoner. Instinctively, Leona knew that this woman-girl had been through hell. She sensed that pieces of Janice's psyche had been methodically peeled away, leaving her exposed.

Why would anyone want to hurt this lovely, fragile girl? But the damage had been done deliberately. The odd thought shook Leona.

"Help me, spirit woman," Janice whispered desperately, her eyes pleading with Leona.

Leona fought to stay calm; her instincts told her that it had begun, the calling she had always refused and hated, the ancient seer blood calling to hers. *She would not become what her mother and grandmother had become.* Smiling gently, despite every intuitive edge quivering inside her, she replied, "I'm not a spirit woman."

"You have powers. You are strong."

Leona wanted to scream that she'd never wanted the curse of the clairvoyants or anything to do with extrasensory perceptions. Yet visions hovered all around her, no matter how she fought them. She wanted to scream that if she "opened" fully and deliberately practiced to make her gift stronger, she'd be doomed. Everything that she didn't want to be could possess her. Her memories of her grandmother's insanity were enough to stop any inclination.

"You're mistaken. I have no powers." When Leona glanced at Owen for help, he stepped back and crossed his arms, his expression hard and unrelenting. Clearly, she was on her own to deal with Janice's plea.

Suddenly, Janice's thin hand reached out to grip Leona's forearm. Everything within Leona stilled. She tried to breathe, the breath pressed from her. The impact sent her back, her hand gripping the wolf's-head brooch as a talisman. In the heartbeats it took Leona to recover, Owen had moved in protectively, his arm around her. He used the other to take Janice's hand, freeing Leona. "Take it easy. Janice, give her a moment."

Leona stared up at Owen, unable to speak. *How could she tell Owen that his sister had been gripped by a powerful evil?*

She'd only been uneasy and restless after the man had visited her shop in July, but nothing like this.

Her body chilled, Leona was momentarily glad for Owen's warmth and strength. Then she stepped clear, needing space to think and regroup.

"I cut my braids." Janice's confession seemed childlike.

"You did?" *Keep calm, keep focused, keep your shields high.* Maybe Leona was mistaken, maybe there was nothing evil in Janice. Perhaps Leona had only picked up the shadowy bits from Owen's descriptions. Leona's unwanted extrasensory perceptions could be working overtime. And they could be wrong.

"Yes. He told me to. Owen said we have to go to a beauty shop. He tried, but he's not good at fixing women's hair."

"Owen told you to cut your braids?" Leona asked carefully. She wanted to run and hide, because she already knew the answer. Lurking in the Aislings' lives was someone who wanted them dead, or mindless, and *he'd* already sent others to do his dirty work.

"No. *He.*"

He. The others the psychic vampire had used were gentle people, or young and vulnerable. Tempest's gifted hands had traced the connection; they'd all been reached through a computer, the stronger mind taking them and using them to do his bidding. The attacks on her sisters had been performed by men whose identities had been taken over by the psychic vampire. Addicted

to computers, the victims were seduced online by someone powerful, someone who wanted that Viking
brooch—and the power that went with it. This girl had
also been touched by the same evil; Leona sensed it. . . .
"Janice, do you like computers?"

Owen inhaled abruptly and stiffened. "Why?"

"She can't be near a computer, Owen. She must *not*
use one." The urgent warning left Leona's lips before
she realized she'd spoken.

"We decided that she should stay away from them for
a while. I guess we are going to have that talk after all,
aren't we, Leona?" It wasn't an invitation; it was an
order. Owen wanted to know exactly why she'd made
that exact warning.

Janice looked from her brother to Leona and back
again. "She's your woman, isn't she, Owen?"

Owen didn't react, and Leona suspected he'd told
Janice of their one night together. "Your eyes just
turned that dark gold," he noted quietly.

Leona inhaled slowly, minding her temper. She refused to speak.

"She is a lioness, a fierce hunter," Janice added. "Tell
your sister, the designer, that I love my bag, please."

"I will. She'll be very happy you're enjoying it."

"I love horses." Janice noted the display of Claire's
Bags and suddenly reached for one. It was "Date Night,"
the bag Claire had been creating when she'd been attacked. Janice stared at the bag and clutched it in both
hands. Her whisper was uneven and fearful. "*He*
touched this, didn't he? And you know, don't you?"

"He?" Leona asked cautiously.

"*He.*" Janice rummaged in her tote and came up
with a folded piece of paper. She solemnly handed it to
Leona. Leona's fingers trembled just that bit as she un-
folded the paper. The man's sketched image caused her
to shiver.

Leona had seen him in her nightmares, his long black hair waving around his sharp face, twin braids tied by gold and leather, swinging like snakes. His thin mouth had spewed words angrily, his eyes wild and furious as he'd pointed to the chieftain's brooch, cursing it. . . .

In Leona's mind, the sketch flipped into another image, that of Stella Mornay, her grandmother, leaning close to a very young Leona, trying to warn her. . . . *He's coming. He's very near, but not quite ready. He'll kill to get what he wants. Forgive me, Leona. Protect your sisters and your mother, for I cannot. You've got to stop him, Leona. . . .*

In that fleeting instant between grandmother and child, Stella Mornay transferred the man's image to Leona's mind. Then Stella Mornay had tried to avoid her nightmares and tangled images by drinking herself into stupors—and finally committing suicide.

Leona hadn't remembered that scene with her grandmother, at least not in her conscious mind. The memory had crept upward through the layers of time, bursting vivid and frightening in one heartbeat.

Shaken, Leona managed to refold the paper and gave it back to Janice. Aware that Owen watched her intently, she attempted a normal tone. "You do lovely work, Janice. You're an artist then?"

"I used to be a graphic artist. But now Owen won't let me near a computer." The ache of an artist was there, wrapped in the terror of the forbidden.

"Have you seen that man before, Leona?" Owen asked harshly.

"No." But she had in her nightmares, and from his hard, "you're-lying" look, Owen knew the truth.

"Let's talk. Tonight," Owen stated firmly to Leona before taking his sister's hand.

Smiling at Janice, Leona selected a silk scarf with large red tropical blooms, a perfect foil for the girl's darker complexion. Janice needed a talisman, or something to make her *think* that she was protected. Perhaps the scarf would seem like that talisman. "Not tonight. Here, Janice, I'd love you to have this."

When Owen reached for his billfold, Leona shook her head. "It's a gift."

With the air of one who has deep pride and who has always paid his way, Owen hesitated. Then he nodded curtly.

Leona wrapped the scarf around Janice's head and adjusted the untied ends. But inside her mind, she had focused on reaching the darkness inside Janice, easing it. "You're going to be just fine, Janice."

With a sudden cry, Janice wrapped her arms around Leona. Holding the girl's thin body tightly, Leona didn't hide her tears as she looked at Owen.

"You're going to be fine," she repeated against Janice's cheek. Leona smoothed a hand over the tension in the girl's back, and willed away the darkness hovering around her. She repeated the comfort a third time, attempting to force every particle of evil away from Janice. Leona could almost feel the evil slither away—but not quite. Its claws had sunk too deep.

Closing her eyes, Leona was shaken by her own emotions. A forgotten scene from the past, her grandmother's warning, had just popped into her mind. And she had just discovered that she could soothe a troubled mind. How had she known what to do, to find that ragged thread in the darkness and stroke it gently?

Had Aisling done the same?

Yes. You have my gift. It's time you used it. That quiet, always-present voice inside Leona answered.

Leona eased away and held Janice's face in her hands. She wondered again how anyone could harm such a beautiful creature. "You believe me, don't you?"

"Yes, I do."

Janice's brilliant smile warmed Leona, then she glimpsed Owen's fierce scowl. "Don't lead her on if you're not going to help," he warned.

"He was hurt, a long time ago," Janice explained softly. "A woman."

"I know. I'm sorry."

"You do *not* know anything." As if the women had invaded his privacy, Owen said, "We need to go, Janice."

Leona hadn't known—exactly. Now she tucked away Janice's tidbit about Owen, noting his bristling stance. Whatever had happened between Owen and this other woman, it had left a deep scar.

"He's afraid of you," Janice whispered with an impish grin. "My big bad brother, so strong and fierce. He's afraid of nothing, just one woman with red hair and green eyes. My, my."

"Cool it." Owen nodded curtly. With a last, meaningful glance at Leona, he led Janice out of the shop.

His expression said he would return and demand answers. Leona hadn't agreed to help his sister, but Owen wouldn't give up. Not when his sister needed protection. Leona didn't blame him for that; in his position, she would do the same.

Chilled by Janice's intuitive reaction to her and the sense that evil hovered around the girl, Leona watched both of them pass by the tinted window. They seemed almost like the ghostly images that slid more frequently to her mind. She'd felt so safe, away from large bodies of water, and now she was almost as vulnerable as Janice.

Instinctively Leona knew if she didn't help Janice, the girl would die.

Leaning her head back, she watched the blades of the ceiling fan, the slight whispering of the air stirring around her, the lighter fabrics rustling as if alive. Suddenly she had to know. Hurrying over to the bag Janice had held and Tempest had held before her, and Claire first, as the designer, Leona touched the bag. After Claire's attack, Tempest had picked up the evil trace in it; it had burned her psychic hands and the experience had drained her. *Tempest was strong in her own right. She possessed the ability to trace a history of an object by holding it. If she'd been so badly affected, the evil on this bag was very, very strong. . . .*

Leona had held the bag before, but never like this, seeking its mysteries. She focused on her hands, on the sensations passing from the evening bag into her fingers. She caught ordinary textures and shapes, but nothing more. The bag remained cool and unresponsive in her hands. Careless of the arranged display, Leona dropped the bag to the others. "I will not let this happen to me. I won't. I will not be the weak link that brings death—or worse—to my family."

"Touching. My heart bleeds."

In his underground workroom, Rolf clicked off the television. The camera in Leona's shop had given him the entire scene of the Shaws and Leona, of Owen Shaw asking Leona to help Janice.

Leona had taken the bait. Rolf knew Janice would be perfect for the part. Leona will help her, of course. The Aislings are all basically healers, a contrast to that Viking strain that would rather fight. When Leona helps Janice, she'll use her energy. That will drain her protective resources, and she'll be weaker. Then, Rolf would have Leona.

Flipping back a long black braid at the side of his face, he picked up a picture of Greer Aisling. The newspaper photograph had been taken as she spoke to the World Convention of Psychic Minds ten years ago. Powerful psychics had crowded the auditorium that day, and Rolf had been primed to prove he was the best of the best. He'd challenged Greer before and lost, but he'd trained hard for that one moment. He'd thought that the headaches, the nosebleeds from practicing would be worth all the honors he would receive.

That was a mistake he wouldn't make again. Greer was very strong, and he had lost, defeated and shamed in front of his peers. For that, she would pay. "Take one triplet down, then the rest, and that would leave Greer, all alone. Dear, dear . . ."

He slapped the photograph down on a cluttered workbench. "Then Greer's mind and Thorgood's brooch is mine. I know she has it stored away somewhere. But then, I'll have her mind, and I'll know how to get it, won't I? I'll have my family's revenge, and my own."

Rolf hummed as he turned back to working on the fabricated disguises that allowed him to move about easily. He expertly fluffed the gray wig that was his Alex-disguise. Everything in good time. He was closing in on Leona. One adjustment he needed to make was to move the microphone at her house. He hadn't been able to hear what she said to the mirror last night. . . . And he needed to know everything in order to destroy the Aislings.

"She would barely open the door to talk to me," Leona stated, unsettled by her attempt to talk to Sue Ann earlier. Dinner with Alex offered a respite from the traumatic day, and they'd agreed to meet at his favorite restaurant. Their usual nook was shadowed and pleasant, and Alex had been waiting when she'd arrived.

Shaking her head, she continued, "Sue Ann looked terrified. I don't understand. She was just fine yesterday, happy, chatty, full of life. After work tonight, I drove out to her place and when she saw me, she gathered up her children and hurried inside. She wouldn't even open the door to me. Goodness, Alex. I've babysat for those children. I wouldn't harm them. I've had few friends outside my family, and Sue Ann has been so dear. She helped me so much after Joel's death. This is not like her at all."

The dim light flashed on Alex's thick lenses as he nodded. "You must get help right away. The shop would be too much for you to handle without part-time help. You'll be exhausted. We can't have that," he said firmly, even as he eyed the blackberry cobbler in front of him. "I miss home cooking. Cynthia always had dinner ready when I came home. I'd thought it would always be that way after we—I retired."

Leona looked at him, but her mind was filled with that sketch, the narrow hawkish features, that long black hair, the small braids close to his face, the gold threads tying them. Nothing could change that face, the bones thrusting at the skin, the cheeks hollowed, those cruel lips. *It was the face in her nightmares, spewing curses at Aisling and Thorgood. . . .*

She picked at her chocolate cake and pulled a small portion apart, separating it into crumbs as she dissected each thought: Exactly who was Owen Shaw? There was something very different about him, something familiar from long ago.

As if one crumb held the answer, Leona suddenly understood. Owen's face had been that of the Viking in her nightmare. In her vision, she had been Aisling, watching the chieftain stride toward her, fresh from raiding her village.

Her mother had had the same dream, that of a conquering chieftain approaching the ancient Celtic seer, Aisling. . . .

Every drop of Leona's blood, her coloring, her eyes, her visions, all traced back to Aisling. But almost hid-

den was that strand of that Viking fighting blood. . . .
She could feel it stirring inside her, needing to track
down the bastard stalking her family. To protect them,
she could kill him. Every instinct told Leona to call
him out . . .

Alex's voice brought her back to their conversation.
"Mm. Good pie," he said, patting his soft middle section. "You know what the house really needs is a room
that looks like a child's, a nursery. Cynthia always
wanted a baby and children, but it just never happened.
Leona, if there's anything I can help you with at the
shop—you seem so troubled over Sue Ann leaving—let
me know. Hey, I'm retired. I can work on this for you.
Maybe I could ask around for someone to help you."

"Thank you. You're sweet, but I'm hoping this may
be a passing thing. Sue Ann may change her mind."

"How's the closet coming? Vernon was telling me
what a great layout you had. Would you mind if he used
your design for one of my closets?"

"That's fine. Just don't steal him from me."

"Oh, I'm just happy to get whatever he can do for
me. Vernon is a real craftsman, a friendly kind of guy.
We visit sometimes. I like him."

Alex frowned when she retrieved her cell phone from
her bag and noted the number. "Did it ring? I didn't
hear it."

"I had it on 'silent vibrate.'" Leona had used the lie
for years when others were near and that tingle had
told her that family was calling. This time, it was her
mother, and Leona wasn't looking forward to the conversation. She replaced the phone in her bag without
answering.

"You can answer it, if you wish. I won't mind."

"It can wait." Leona needed privacy for the discussion her mother was certain to want.

Alex looked at his watch again and grimaced. He

rubbed his shoulder. "I must have wrenched it. I thought I'd help Vernon get an easy start by moving one of the doors he's refinishing. Damn thing slid sideways and almost fell on me. They're heavy, those old doors."

Alex's injury might not have been an accident. Sue Ann's sudden change and Alex's accident could mean that someone was circling her friends. Anyone in her life could be in danger, including the already deeply troubled Janice.

And Owen was somehow tied up in everything. Leona intended to discover just how he fit within this deadly puzzle.

As Leona settled into her home for the night, she frowned at the dirty footprints Vernon had left on her utility room's rug. Vernon had apparently gone in her backyard. He must have crossed the bare ground where she had been laying bricks.

Good craftsmen-type carpenters and handymen were hard to find, and Leona didn't mind a little dirt if the job was well-done. She checked her bedroom's unfinished closet and found the smell of cigarette smoke. One glance at the open window and Leona quickly wrote a note to gently remind Vernon of their terms. He'd seemed distracted lately, not his usual meticulous self.

Then she noticed that the large plastic sheeting she'd placed over her bedroom furniture had been shifted. *All* of the plastic sheeting had been shifted slightly as if someone had been snooping. A quick check revealed that nothing was missing, but that open window could have allowed anyone entrance.

Leona hurried outside with her flashlight and checked the screens. A small piece of tape she'd placed in an exact place hadn't been moved. No one had come in. Inside her locked home, she shivered. She was too upset, too restless, too suspicious of every small thing. She had to get control. "And Vernon hasn't done one thing today. I'm going to have a chat with him. I can't live like this."

A quick change of clothes, a glass of wine, and Leona called her mother. "You rang?"

In the background, Leona heard the familiar sounds of home, the crash of the Pacific Ocean's waves, the wind sweeping through the distorted pines, and her mother's soft, soothing voice. "Be careful, Leona."

"I know the game plan . . . take one down, weaken the link. Logically, I'm the next on this creep's list."

Greer's silence said too much; she was terrified for her daughter. "He's very, very strong, Leona."

"Apparently not strong enough to take out Claire or Tempest."

"The bond with their husbands strengthened them. Both Neil and Marcus come from ancient lines, too. I believe they are the Protectors, descended from Thorgood's men, who pledged to safeguard Aisling and her children through time."

Leona let the tentative psychic probe from her mother slide away. The connection was too strong, mother to child, child to mother. She resented everything that Greer was, that Leona could be. If she wanted. Still, today, she had focused and had helped Janice. Later, she had been strangely exhausted, but enough had happened lately to tire anyone.

"You can't take him on by yourself. You have a very strong gift, but you haven't opened or developed it. You're not certain if you really want to," Greer stated softly, as if snagging that tidbit from Leona's mind.

That was a reminder for Leona to hurry away from the scene hidden inside her—the memory she'd had of her grandmother leaning close, whispering a warning. Leona pictured Janice, connecting with her, locking on to every detail.

"I may change my mind. I met a girl today, and she's very . . . different. She'd sketched a man's face. His features were narrow, sharp cheekbones, black burning eyes, long black hair, braids beside his face. She'd captured those eyes perfectly on paper as if she had actually seen them, connected with him. I haven't felt such a close connection to him since that day when that stranger came into Timeless. He wasn't the same as the Borg descendant—he was a big, blue-eyed blond—but the sensation was there. As if he was some kind of threat—"

"It's called 'imprinting.' He may not have looked like that at all. He probably used a physical disguise of some sort, but also added physic 'heft' to it. He may have connected with your own abilities on some level, and created a distracting combination of the physical and a surface image of what he wanted you to see. Layers of psychic connections with those who are clairvoyant can be complicated and confusing. Unsuspecting, you could have been too open for just that moment it took for him to connect with your senses. He might have been able to lay an image in your mind, a mask over his real appearance. He may have been strong enough to block you from feeling anything unique about him. All he'd have to do is to focus on setting up a wall—"

"I know what I saw," Leona stated curtly. "Besides I doubt a guy like the Borg-descendant, with that wild mass of hair, could walk on Lexington's streets and not be noticed."

"No, of course not. You're absolutely right." Greer's words came too quickly, as if she wanted to soothe away Leona's fears.

A quick, fierce rush of warmth immediately surrounded Leona. Greer had just sent a protective psychic hug, her motherly instincts raised to protect her young. Then Greer's sadness washed over Leona. "I didn't know they had planned to invade our home while I was gone," she said.

Leona's statement was flat and automatic. "Because you were busy elsewhere."

When Leona didn't respond, Greer continued, "I do blame myself. But you shouldn't. There was no way you could have stopped them, Leona. You were just a child. That man who came to your shop in July was linking on to you, trying to snag your energy to hold as his own, to control you. He was probably testing your reception, seeing how strong you are, if you're developed," Greer said, bypassing Leona's resentment to move on to the problem at hand. "Every emotion, every bit of resentment and guilt you feel, even any sympathy you carry now will work against you. Those things can leave you vulnerable to someone more powerful. You've got to focus on protecting yourself. You can't let yourself weaken now, Leona Fiona."

"I know exactly what's at risk, Mother: my sisters, their husbands, and you." Glancing at the mirror she'd covered with the blue-green scarf, Leona noticed the scarf was gone. Her breath caught, then she decided that Vernon must have placed it aside; her carpenter had been making himself too comfortable in her home.

"I'll come to you, Leona. I've been working through the past. I've been trying to put the pieces together, trying to find some clue as to who might be stalking our family. I must find who he truly is in flesh and blood, not just as the fiend in our dreams. Maybe together, we can—"

"You can't protect me every minute, Mom. I'll be fine. You're stronger by the ocean, not here." Leona understood Greer's intentions, feeling her mother's urge to fly to her daughter's side.

"You want to do this, don't you? To call him out? Pay him back for terrorizing your sisters? You're a fighter, Leona, and that can work against you."

"If both our dreams coincide, and this ancient Viking guy—with psychic powers—fought the chieftain, Thorgood, and lost, then I have nothing to worry about. Borg didn't get Aisling, and his descendant isn't getting me."

So much for confidence, Leona thought much later when she awoke from another dream, the shreds of terror clinging to her. The man's face lingered in her mind: sharp features, black hair with braids, his eyes piercing. She understood his terms, if not the exact language. "Like it or not, you'll be mine, witch. You'll obey me."

Leona lay in the guest bed, not the Viking's crude bed of wood and fur from her dream, her heart pounding with fear. She'd called out for help, and still tasted Owen's name on her lips. "Owen," she whispered softly in the night, wanting his arms safely around her. "Owen, come to me."

Okay, so a little midnight-hour experimenting when no one was around couldn't hurt. Could it?

Leona held the pillow with his scent, closed her eyes, and focused on Owen. She visualized his face: those silvery eyes, those long straight black lashes, that sleek raven black hair, those hard, skillful lips . . .

The bedside telephone rang, startling her. She recognized the number on the digital readout—it was the number on Owen's business card. She could let the message machine take the call, or she could—

Leona reached for the phone. As much as she didn't want to admit the attraction, or the safety she'd felt tucked close to him, Leona needed to hear his voice.

"Are you all right?" Owen's deep tone was urgent.

She glanced at her bedside clock, which read eleven o'clock. His call came too closely after her dream. "Why are you calling?"

Owen's husky statement took away her breath. "I thought I heard you call my name."

Six

——

AT SIX-THIRTY IN THE MORNING, LEONA DROVE TOWARD THE
Shaws' farm.

Owen had called at exactly the time Leona had focused her senses on him, mind and body. As they'd agreed, he'd be waiting for her now, and she intended to get answers. How could he have known she needed him?

The early-September air was cool and damp. Sunrise crept through the tops of the trees, and shadows lurked beneath, fingering across Kentucky's famous lush bluegrass fields. Horses and a few cattle grazed within the board fences, painted black. At times, two black-board fences ran parallel to each other, only a few feet apart.

Leona passed the elegant, white-and-red horse barns. With rows of shuttered windows, they appeared more like mansions for humans. Nearer to Owen's old farm, and deeper into the rolling hills toward Tennessee, the county road was lined with rock "fences," created in another century. Airy tobacco barns painted black, stood amid fields that were used for all crops. In late July and August, rows of the broadleaf tobacco plant could be seen across the fields.

Leona noted the layers of mist hovering over the ponds,

reminding her of that man standing on her street that night whispering her name. If it was Owen, he'd pay.

She smoothed the place where her brooch was usually pinned. Today, she'd chosen to take her chances without its protection. Leona intended to feel everything at the Shaw farm, to make herself open to any psychic influence, and she didn't want any interference.

Gripping her steering wheel as her new car drove roughly over a chuckhole, she felt annoyed with herself. She'd been too deep in thought about the last few days and had missed it. Without giving cause, Sue Ann had withdrawn from a sturdy five-year friendship and had abruptly stopped working for Leona. Then there was the fact that Vernon hadn't progressed on her closet, and the plastic sheeting covering her personal things had been disturbed. Since he was supposedly the only one with entry into her home, she would have to speak to him about her privacy. Finally, there was the matter of the missing scarf; Leona hoped he could explain it. Or had she been so distracted that she'd misplaced it herself?

On edge, Leona was easily distracted from performing everyday tasks as anyone would be.

One thing was for certain: She and her family were definitely being stalked. If Vernon was found to be involved, Leona would find out exactly why and how. She would have to be very careful with him now.

Owen Shaw was another problem. Leona also resented Owen Shaw appearing in her dreams and for calling—in person—at exactly the perfect time.

Too many coincidences had happened, and she only had a few hours to research before opening her shop at ten. This morning, she had decided that whether Sue Ann changed her mind or not, it wouldn't hurt to interview applicants for her job. Leona had already sent an e-mail ad to the local radio station's Help Wanted section. She hoped the arrangement would be temporary and that Sue Ann would soon return.

Leona eased her car over the old dirt road leading up to the Shaws' home. The old white two-story home was small compared to the others in the area. Owen stood beside the board fence in a typical Western pose, one booted foot on the bottom board, his arms resting on the top one. Aware that those shielded smoky eyes were watching her closely, Leona parked and got out of the car.

Owen seemed to slowly take in everything about her from her green long-sleeve T-shirt and jeans to her running shoes and then finally her face. The impact of his gaze sent a sensual jolt deep within her body, a sturdy reminder that Owen's had taken her over that shocking primitive edge.

When Owen didn't move, Leona braced herself to walk toward him. It wasn't easy; her natural instincts told her to run to him. She wanted to take him there, to feel him around her, inside her, his scents filling her. Instead, Leona managed a crisp tone, "Okay. I'm here. Now talk."

"The sun turns your hair into flame."

His deep voice wrapped around her—intimate, husky, sexual—just as it had during their lovemaking. She could be fighting for her life and for her family's. She couldn't afford to let her defenses down with Owen. "I don't like being used, Owen. You came after me for a purpose. You want to know about my so-called gift. You're curious."

"I wasn't exactly sure at the time we met. I was thinking of other things, like how you'd feel in my arms. But wouldn't you do the same for your sisters, try to help them?"

"Maybe."

"Liar. Of course, you would. You're a fighter, Leona,

and you're protective of your family, just as I am of Janice."

He was right. Leona glanced at the house and found the windows dark. "Where is she?"

"Sleeping off medication. The night wasn't good to her. If she wakes up, Robyn will call me. Janice is very restless now . . . like you and like me. I'm glad you came. I couldn't leave her to come to you. After last night, I'm not certain Robyn could handle her in the same state. Let's walk."

Leona looked at the board fence separating them, then up at the man staring at her. With a sigh, she stepped up on the fence. When she prepared to come down on the other side, Owen tugged her in his arms, holding her aloft and tight against him. "Don't be afraid," he whispered. "I'll take care of you."

Her hands had locked on to his shoulders, fingers digging into the solid, powerful muscles. Instinctively Leona knew that she'd never been so safe. "I—I'm not afraid."

"Of course you are. So am I. I can't fail my sister. If I ever find that bastard in her sketch, I just may kill him."

"And I can't fail my family."

"The stakes are high then, and you know it."

Owen still held her against him. The fresh morning scents flowed around them, the air damp and cool and sweet. His hair was damp as if he'd just showered. As his cheek nuzzled hers, his skin was taut and scented of aftershave. His open hand on her back pressed Leona more closely against him. "Mm . . . Warm . . . soft . . . woman."

His simple statement, filled with so much longing and appreciation, shook Leona. She tried not to move, but her body had already softened to his. The sensual call caused her to ache for his lips, his taste.

Shivering slightly Leona tried desperately to regain control. Owen was no easy one-night stand—he wanted more, and what he wanted could endanger her family. "Owen, let me down." When he didn't respond, she continued, "You know about my mother. Greer Aisling is a famous psychic and she's good at it. You should call her . . ."

"Janice wants you to help her. You're all she can talk about. And I saw your reaction to her. You know the man in that sketch, don't you?"

That furious warrior with the sharp face and compelling eyes was only a man in her turbulent dreams of Aisling. He was only a mystic fragment left in her blood that she wanted to reject. The reality of his descendant was another matter. Owen could be—"Do you know him?"

"If I did, he'd be dead by now. . . . Always cautious, aren't you?" Finally, Owen let her slide slowly down his body, then took her hand. Linking his fingers with hers, he studied their hands. Owen's dark broad hand seemed to capture her feminine, slender one. When his thumb caressed her skin, Leona sensed that he was thinking about their bodies, tangled and hungry just three nights ago.

Owen suddenly looked directly into her eyes, his hand pressing hers tightly. "You know him. The question is how," he stated firmly as he began to walk into the field. "Come on."

Tall, leggy, lean, powerful, and feminine, his woman had walked out of shadows toward him. Sunrise had caught the flame in Leona's hair; it flowed around her face as she moved, her body tense and sleek like a lioness on the hunt.

Owen's first instinct had been to take Leona there on

the ground, a primitive possession. But too much of civilization had wrapped around him. And too much was at stake. Smiling to himself, Owen knew Leona's cool competent look was only a shield. He knew how demanding, hot, and primitive she could be.

At the crest of a hill overlooking the large pond, Leona abruptly stopped. Owen glanced at her face; it was too pale, and her body had braced as if waiting for a blow.

He scanned the area, alert to danger. A few trees and brush separated an old farm road at the north end of his property. The road belonged to someone else. Nothing but a weathered tobacco barn lay at the end of it. Vehicles passed at times, music sounding in a heavy beat. To the east, the forest was heavy and at the south end of the field, a dangerous cliff dropped into the Kentucky River. A rocky bluff rose on the other side.

Between those perimeters and the barn and house on the west side lay the farm pond. It nestled in a hollow and mist hovered over it.

Owen saw nothing unusual, but then he remembered Janice had had the same reaction to the pond.

The recent heavy rains had filled the pond. White farm ducks and the Canadian geese swam at one end of the silvery surface, others pecked for food along the bank. "Janice's nurse sometimes comes down here to feed the birds. We're getting quite a flock in a short time. The real-estate agent said the pond was natural . . . most are man-made."

"Is this the only natural water on the place?" Leona asked suddenly.

The ragged fear in her tone alerted Owen. He glanced around the area again and still found nothing unusual. "No, there's a stream from a natural rock bluff just beyond those trees, and it leads down to the Kentucky River just over that hill."

"I didn't know you lived so close to the river," Leona whispered unsteadily. Suddenly, she turned to him. "Okay, I've had it. Who are you, Owen Shaw? You're not all Native American, or you wouldn't have those gray eyes."

"My people were Blackfoot, though they didn't keep to the old ways. My parents told me that every so often light eyes turn up in our family, always in the males. Why, does it matter?" Her question surprised Owen; he hadn't expected his bloodline to make a difference to her. He tried to keep the sharp bitterness from his tone. Unpleasant youthful experiences had taught him that some people still held that red-white difference close.

Leona's expression suddenly softened. "I didn't mean it that way. I'm sorry. You told me something of your name, but I'd like to know more. Shaw is English, isn't it? It's important that I know your ancestry."

In another century, "Shaw" had been taken as a tribute to shaman. In his bloodline, the gray-eyed shamans weren't only medicine men, but their unusual visions linked to elements not known to their people. As a boy, Owen had fought those same troubling images, had stored them away and never wanted to open them again.

Owen wasn't ready to give up that information just yet. "My family took 'Shaw'. It's easier to pronounce. Exactly why do you need to know our ancestry? Has it anything to do with what's happened to Janice? And why did you react that way to the pond? I need to know why. Janice reacts the same way."

Leona hugged herself. She watched that pond, as if she expected a terrifying monster to walk out of it. "It could be tied to her—or not."

Owen studied the streams of mist rising from the pond. To him, the mist was only nature, the water adjusting to the temperature of the air. "Why are you affected by it? Maybe there's a common link. Janice is definitely certain that you can help her. When we were in your shop, I saw how you could calm and relieve her. She believes in you."

"She shouldn't. I'm no spirit woman. You've read about my family. I've never wanted any part of being an intuitive, a clairvoyant, an extrasensory. Senses beyond the normal five can envelop your mind and your soul, until you don't know the difference between real and unreal. My grandmother killed herself because she couldn't stop it. That so-called gift literally sucked away everything she was, her essence, replaced it with an overload of terrifying visions and left her mad. She tried to wash them away with drink, and that only made them worse."

"Maybe she couldn't control it. Your mother can. *You* could."

"Control takes study and work. I've got better things to do. And I don't want it," Leona stated fiercely.

Owen noted Leona's intense, thoughtful expression. From his own experiences and his research on psychic phenomena and genetics late last night, Owen understood Leona's reluctance too well. Just as his bloodline gave the "gray-eyes" insights, Janice had probably received her share. As a woman with black eyes, her perceptions could have come more from the Shaws' Blackfoot side. "When it's in the blood, there's little chance you can escape, Leona."

She watched the three crows perch in a tree that had been struck by lightning. The sunlight touched their feathers in blue-black shades as they angled their heads, staring down at the humans. "Boy, that's right."

Owen noted Leona's attraction to the birds; he'd read that empaths could be connected to nature, and that psychics generally were more receptive. Legends about crows varied among different peoples. The crows could be an omen of some kind, good or bad.

He knew Leona understood—perhaps in some hidden layer of her senses, she knew more than she realized. Her natural instincts had told her to hold Janice close and to ease her; he had witnessed the connection between the two women. "I believe that what is in the blood eventually turns up. It can't be refused."

"Sure it can. Everything is a matter of choices."

"Sometimes we don't have a choice." His words reminded him of his own potential. If it really were true about the males with gray eyes in his family, then he might have a choice to reach her on another level. Focusing completely on Leona, he tried to catch that intangible particle she'd given to Janice, that psychic connection.

Leona suddenly glanced at him, shivered, and moved slightly away. "Stop it. You're trying to—I don't like it."

She was definitely receptive to him, in more ways than one. He'd felt his senses quiver lightly, briefly linking with Leona's. The tiny experiment drove him on. "You said to keep Janice away from computers. What do you know about a psychic connection made through a computer? I think that's when Janice started hearing voices and trying to kill herself. She usually wore earphones and seemed to talk to herself. Maybe she was actually talking to someone else. For a time, I thought the connection to someone else may have been through sound and electronics, but now I wonder. She hasn't been on a computer for a while, but the voices started up again when we arrived here. Has that happened to your family?"

"Not directly. But I've heard of it happening. From what I know, and what you've told me, trauma could have made Janice vulnerable. Every traumatic incident can heighten an intuitive's awareness, sometimes on one level only, sometimes on all levels. My grandmother may have been overloaded at *all* levels. I don't know. . . .

Janice is creative, and that means she's receptive to certain elements . . . which is why she sensed the energies on the bags she touched. And she loves and easily connects with animals. They respond more to her, another potential psychic element. She's probably very curious—all traits that could make her a perfect candidate for someone stronger."

"What do you mean, 'stronger?' Someone like the man in that sketch? Who is he, Leona?"

"A stronger mind can influence one that has been weakened by trauma, that's all. A computer is a perfect conduit and situation for the seduction of someone susceptible, or vulnerable, or both." Glancing at the pond, she said, "Let's get out of here."

Owen didn't move; he had to know why Leona seemed so eager to be far away from the pond. Perhaps it was the same thing that disturbed Janice. "You're feeling something right now, aren't you? What is it?"

Shaking her head, Leona stared at the lush bluegrass at their feet. She rubbed her arms as if chilled, though her green T-shirt should have given enough warmth against the early-morning temperature. When Owen tilted her chin up, Leona's pale complexion accentuated those terrified green eyes. Sunlight played in her dark red hair, the tendrils catching fire. "Please, Owen," she whispered desperately.

"Sure." Owen didn't question Leona's need just then. He only knew she was terrified, and he would protect her with his life.

When they turned, they saw Janice standing on the front porch of the house. Her long, pale nightgown seemed ghostly in the shadows. Robyn came quickly to her side, speaking to her and urging her inside. Before the front door closed behind her, the nurse waved and called, "She's just fine. We're going to have a little breakfast now and get dressed."

"You've got to get her out of here, Owen," Leona stated suddenly as she gripped his hand. She hadn't intended the warning, but there it was on her lips, quivering with terror. "She's picking up every psychic residue possible from that pond and stream, and the Kentucky River. She's feeling too much, all at once."

"Are you?"

Leona glanced at the pond and shivered again. She ran her hand across her chest as if seeking the missing brooch. "I just know things instinctively, and I don't want to. But Janice is in danger here. I know that without a doubt. Now what I need to understand is why you called me last night?"

As he would gentle Janice, Owen smoothed his hands over Leona's hair. How could he tell Leona that he had focused on her last night, needing her, just before he fell asleep? She was skittish of him now, fearful of what had happened between them and what her mind pushed away. "I told you. I thought I heard you call my name."

She looked back at the pond, the mist over it topped by the rising sunlight. "I'd like to talk with Janice—privately. But first, I've changed my mind. I'm walking to the pond."

"Not without me."

They walked across the field to the steam, which bubbled out of the rocks and rushed toward the river. Leona and Owen followed it to the edge of the cliff, which dropped down into the green, swirling currents of the Kentucky River.

A rabbit zigzagged out of the brush, and a squirrel scurried up an oak tree. Attuned to the familiar sounds, Owen settled into watching the red-haired, tall, slender woman as she stood beside him at the edge of his field, overlooking the Kentucky River. The tall rocky bluff on the other side served to outline her lean, tense body. Suddenly, she leaned toward the water as if entranced.

Owen wrapped his arms securely around Leona's waist. Leona had moved too close to the cliff's dangerous edge. Janice had acted the same way, as if something was in the river, drawing her to it. "Watch your step. This bank isn't that secure, and a fall down that cliff would probably kill you."

Leona tensed, then leaned slightly back against him, her hands over his. As Owen waited for her to answer, birds chirped, flitting in and out of the shadows cast by trees. "Did you call my name just now?" she asked.

"No." Owen rested his cheek against hers. In his arms, Leona's body was taut and trembling. She had definitely sensed something that terrified her. He wanted to replace whatever frightened her with the sound of his own voice, and whispered into her ear. "No, I didn't."

Her fingers dug into his hands. "Liar. Tell me you did. Don't play games now, Owen."

"I didn't say your name. Let's move back from this edge. I wouldn't want to find you at the bottom. That would not be very pretty." Taking her hand he led her back a few feet.

Leona looked toward the house and the barn. She scanned the stream and bluff, where water ran from the layers of rocky outcroppings and fell into the river. Then she looked back at the field's pond. She seemed to be measuring the distance from one to another.

Owen waited for her to speak, and when she did, Leona's whisper quivered in the morning air. "The streams, the pond, and the river create a powerful triangle here. It's said that water is a universal medium for psychics. They can transmit thoughts and impulses, sensations and feelings to each other, or to one who is receptive. We could be standing within a whole field of energy—someone's, anyone's."

"So I've heard. You're drawn to this place, aren't you? The same as Janice?" Owen's instincts told him to pick up Leona and carry her to safety, but he didn't want to frighten her when she was so vulnerable.

Leona shrugged, but Owen noted that she gripped his hands tightly. "We were three when our sailboat overturned. My sisters and I were terrified. That incident imprinted the fear of water on all of us, I suppose. My sisters and I were linked with the water somehow. It was so frightening, bobbing on the swells. I felt crushed, water pushing at me from all sides. I've never liked that too-close feeling."

She paused and breathed deeply, as if bracing herself before continuing. "Our terror, the cries of each other, opened us up to the water's energy, so to speak. We became more receptive to psychic energy, and it's easier to access when we are near large bodies of water. We grew up on the Northwest coast. Our house overlooked the Pacific Ocean. I miss it sometimes. . . . Our nightmare at the institute heightened our senses even more. Now we can't even live near each other for any period of time without tangling our senses. But we are definitely too susceptible to other intuitives when around natural bodies of water."

Owen turned her to him; he needed to see her expressions, everything held deep in her eyes. "There's more to it than that, isn't there?"

Leona searched his face, and her body trembled. Her hands gripped his shirt. "Yes. And you feel it, too, don't you? You do, damn you."

"What makes you think that?" he asked warily.

"I know *what* you are. What you *really* are," Leona stated carefully as she pushed Owen away. Her hair fanned out around her head, the tips catching fire in the sunlight. She turned to walk back toward her car. "I've got to open the shop. I'm leaving."

Owen caught her in two strides. He jerked Leona to him and held her tight. Her eyes had turned that dark, angry gold, and she stood very still. The air seemed to bristle around her, pricking him. "What's this going to prove?" she asked tightly. "That you're bigger? Stronger?"

"Oh, hell, I don't know anything anymore. What do you think I am?"

"Someone who could be dangerous, to me and to my family. Is it fun, standing out here and calling me at night? Is it?" she demanded furiously.

"Calling you?"

"Broadcasting near the water, or through the evening mist on my street. It's possible, and you're possibly strong enough to do it, aren't you? You have as much psychic gift as your sister, don't you? I feel it in you. Are you certain that you didn't whisper my name just now? As I stood by the river?"

Was Leona hearing voices, the same as Janice? Near that pond? Owen had to know if she had. "No, I didn't say your name. Why?"

Leona closed her eyes and shook her head as if clearing it. "Let me go, Owen. I have to get to work."

But she didn't move. Owen let his heart open to flow into the beat of hers. He had never tried to connect with another person, not this way. With layers of blood and flesh and sinew between, he caught the softer, feminine heartbeat and let it wrap soothingly around his, yin and yang.

"Tell me what I need to know to save my sister," he whispered against Leona's ear, even as his body hardened against hers. His hands slid to her waist and followed the shape of her body upward, until they pressed against the outer curve of her breasts. Sweeping his thumb over one fragile peak, he pressed lightly to test her response to his touch. "Tell me."

Leona's head rested on Owen's shoulder. As her face turned slowly to his, a silky red strand brushed his lips and clung to his jaw before sliding away. Her scents reminded him again of Montana's fresh winds blowing over the fields of sweetgrass. But there was nothing cool about the sensations burning them, the hunger of skin against skin.

"Owen," she whispered unevenly and lifted her lips against his. "Not here. Not so close to the water."

"Why?" Sensual fever ruled him now. His ache to make love to Leona pulsed in hot waves throughout his body. Holding her tightly, his hand over her breast, he caressed the sweet shape of it. More than that, he needed to possess her, to claim her, to burn in her fire.

"I—" Apparently torn between desire and caution, Leona shook her head. Her hair webbed momentarily across his jaw, the silk and the scent ensnaring him. "Take me away from here," she whispered desperately.

Standing in the triangle of water, Owen felt nothing but the woman in his arms and his need to protect her. He glanced around, scanning the area, finding nothing harmful. But then, they weren't dealing with physical reality, were they?

Attuned to nature's sounds, Owen heard his sister's footsteps on the grass, moving toward the hill overlooking the field. Robyn's heavier footsteps joined Janice's. When they both appeared at the crest of the hill, Robyn seemed to be whispering to Janice. His sister resisted the caretaker's attempts to tug her back toward the house. "Owen? Owen?" Janice called desperately.

"Leona and I are talking. Go inside with Robyn. We'll be up in a minute."

Leona gripped his hand, her voice hushed and desperate. "Don't let her come here."

"Are you ashamed of what we have?" Owen didn't move his hand from Leona's body.

Leona seemed startled, then she frowned. "I'm not sure what we have."

"You've got some idea. And you're afraid."

Smoothing the T-shirt's long sleeves over her arms, Owen slid his hands down to hers, leaning down to whisper in her ear. "You're going to tell me everything, including who's hunting you and if he's the same guy as in Janice's sketch."

Owen had denied whispering her name. But Leona had heard the masculine whisper coming through the dappled sunlight. It had wrapped a chill around her.

She'd also felt warmer prickles from her sisters and her mother. There had been another masculine presence, too: stronger, harsher, potentially violent, yet protective. Instinctively, she recognized that energy as Owen's.

If he hadn't whispered her name, then who had called her to the river's swirling green depths and that dangerous cliff?

As they walked toward the house, Owen's deep tone was deadly serious. "I've got a good carpenter. He can help prepare this place for sale. If you think Janice is in danger here, we're moving. If that triangle is powerful enough to affect you, then Janice is probably influenced, too."

"Exactly how did you happen to pick this special place?"

"Janice, and a combination of things," Owen answered grimly. "The pond, the stream, and the river reminded her of home. She showed me a real-estate advertisement one day. The house looked like the one we grew up in, when our parents were alive. She felt safe back then. I wanted her to feel that way again. And this place was affordable."

He breathed deeply as if regretting the move to the farm. "Janice was very excited, and I was desperate to do anything that might change her course. I thought at the time that maybe she understood that she needed to get away from where we'd grown up. Maybe she needed a clean start. Here, there was a river nearby and a freshwater creek to water the horses. In Montana, she used to stare at the lakes—natural ones—for hours. She promised if we moved, she wouldn't do that here."

"Owen—"

"I already know: My sister may not be able to keep her promises."

As they approached the Shaws' home, Leona saw the signs that it was being renovated. Boards and supplies were piled on sawhorses on the front porch. "A new delivery," Owen explained. "I had to hire a carpenter to help me get this place in shape faster and allow me time to settle into business. He's going to keep his saw and store his things in the barn, when he's not working in the house. I don't want Janice anywhere near saws. He's agreed that he'll always be on his guard about any tool that might be dangerous."

Janice hurried down the front steps to meet them. Her smile at Leona was brilliant and happy. "You came! I saw your car, and I knew. I knew you'd come. . . . For Owen, and for me."

Leona ached for the girl, who looked even more vulnerable with her roughly shorn hair. Instinctively her hand went to smooth the thick blue-black mass. "Hi, Janice."

Janice stilled at that first physical connection and Leona's senses prickled and stretched, startling her. Waves of fear and hope and struggle moved into Leona's fingers and palms, the sensations weaving up her arm. Suddenly, Janice took Leona's other hand and placed it on her head. "Heal me. I know you can," Janice whispered desperately.

"I'm not a healer." Aisling, the Celtic seer, had possessed that gift. In Leona's dreams, Aisling had bent over the wounded and the ailing, giving ease. Claire, as an empath, could ease a troubled soul to some degree. Tempest had definitely eased her troubled husband, but then love might have been his medicine.

Janice's big dark eyes looked at Owen. "She's a healer. I can feel her doing it when she touches me. Make her help me, Owen."

When Leona glanced at Owen, his expression revealed nothing. His hand warmed her shoulder, then pressed lightly. "Try," he whispered. "Just try. You've already done a little in your shop, and that was only instinctive reaction. This time, think about it."

She'd already focused on Janice once. If Leona continued, and fully opened that doorway to her inherited DNA and gifts, she might never go back.

Janice's black eyes begged her. The girl's startling pain seemed like ice crystals beneath Leona's hands, jabbing at her skin.

Damn her curiosity, native to psychics. She needed to know. . . . Leona spread her fingers over Janice's head.

"Don't be afraid to let someone cut your hair. It's beautiful and only needs a little trim," she whispered gently. The soft, soothing words had seemed to cross her lips of their own accord.

At her side, Owen stiffened. "She has been both afraid and fixated on scissors. She hasn't used them, until she cut her braids. I thought it best if we steered clear of scissors altogether."

Leona understood; Owen was afraid of what his sister would do to herself. "I'll cut it for you, Janice," she said gently as she moved her hands to frame Janice's face. "You trust me, don't you?"

"I trust you," Janice repeated, as if mesmerized.

Leona wound through her senses, intuitively seeking that latch on to Janice's psyche. Amid the red patches, the zigzagging yellow alerts, the screams of pain, a sweet nugget glowed. Leona wound her way through the past images in Janice's mind to that fragile, child-like innocence.

"So here we are, aren't we?" she murmured to Janice and to herself. Leona understood that all the quivering, uncertain threads had settled into a stream, flowing between the women.

She sensed a masculine warmth, tinged with a dark hunger for savage revenge. She hurried to protect that sweet little stream of connections against it. "Don't touch me, Owen."

"We're women, brother. You're interfering," Janice explained gently, but her stare remained locked on to Leona's.

With a quick intake of breath, Owen eased back slightly and crossed his arms. He glanced at Robyn, who had come outside with a glass of water and a white paper cup of pills. Owen's voice was calm and low as he ordered, "Not now, Robyn. Go back into the house, please."

"What is happening? What's wrong with Janice?" Robyn's voice was protective and angry. The tone jarred Leona, but she tried to hold tight to the streaming connection to Janice. The stream shifted slightly, uneasily, ready to escape Leona.

Owen moved quickly toward Robyn, his voice a low murmur as he eased her inside the house.

Leona sensed an angry prickling; the connection to Janice began to weaken and slide away from her. She reached for it, gripped tight and fought to keep her voice even and soothing. "I don't think you should go to the pond again, Janice. Or to the stream or river. You won't, will you?"

Leona thought she heard a furious scream as anger prickled and burned her hands. Still, she kept them firmly on Janice's face. The sketched image and the one from her dreams sprang into her mind. The man's expression was murderous, his eyes fiery, and his mouth spewing silent curses. His thin black braids snaked around his face as if alive.

The images blended, swerved away from each other, and the wolf's-head brooch glowed and floated to the surface.

"You come from an ancient people, ones who see the future, don't you?" Janice asked.

"My line is very old. So is yours." A silver thread spun around the brooch, then wove together in a single strand. Then the threads started to break away, tiny masculine sparks weakening it. Leona glanced at Owen and found him leaning close, too intent and grim. She understood that he was trying to latch on to that thread, to seek information. The dark shadows hovering around the thread seemed like snakes, poised to strike; the interference could be deadly to Janice's fragile psyche.

Leona held her breath, startled by the knowledge that had just leaped at her. *How did she know that?*

Whatever was joining her to Janice, Leona couldn't afford interference. "Owen, go get my bag from the car, will you?"

When he hurried away, she smiled at Janice and took her hands. Leona kept the link strong, but her mind questioned the past moments. *How did she know what to do? Why did she know everything, all at once? Was this what had happened to her grandmother, the cause for her overload and destruction?*

Leona sensed an energy swerve and immediately refocused on Janice. She kept that critical psychic link, imprinting herself over the evil that had bound the girl.

"You're mine now. The man in your drawing can't have you. He's angry, but I'm going to give you something of mine, for protection. When you wear it, you are to know that you are strong and safe. Know that me and mine are with you always."

"You wanted my brother away, so we can speak."

"Men." With a smile, Leona dismissed the male ability to understand women. In the layers of her mind and body, Owen's energy had attached too strongly. He had interfered with her clarity. Leona needed that clarity to protect Janice. Everything she did now was pure instinct; as an untrained intuitive, she was purely trusting her senses. *What if she did the wrong thing and harmed Janice even more?*

"You won't harm me. I feel as if I'm lighter, freer. Owen is your man. You feel him deep inside, where you have let no one else. He frightens you, because of what you are with him . . . what you know you can be."

Something taken, something given. Janice had picked up traces of Leona, just as Leona had foraged through Janice's senses.

In Janice, Leona had found traces of the sea and of sailing, of the angular Viking alphabet carved on stones. She had also found elements of another ancient civilization, older than the new and more dominant Viking influence. "Your brother's gray eyes say he comes from Viking ancestry. That may be what I feel around him."

"You are one with him now. Only some of the men of our family have eyes like that. It is said that these men are different somehow. It's said that we are of shaman blood, but it's said that only the light-eyed men have the sight."

Shaw for shaman, a Native American medicine man and healer. And Owen had that Viking strain running through his blood. He'd probably known all along that he was of two potentially intuitive bloodlines, a descendant with powerful gifts. . . .

Janice nodded, her eyes so black that iris seemed one with the pupil—*almost as black and mesmerizing as the man in her sketch and in Leona's nightmares.*

"Sometimes my brother knows things. He feels things I can't, but he doesn't want to talk of them. You want to give me a talisman that comes from an ancient woman, your grandmother."

Janice had caught traces of Aisling. Leona took a deep breath and admitted to herself that the forged connection had been stronger than she'd expected—in both directions. "My grandmother many times over. The brooch isn't the original, but I've worn it. It holds me and my sisters and my mother in it. You wear it. You hold it and think of me. Focus on it and me, Janice. We're going to do this. We're going to get whoever is harming you. We're going to tear you free so that he won't ever bother you again."

"But you're afraid," Janice stated solemnly, another tidbit she'd snatched from deep within Leona.

"Very. I could make a mistake that would endanger us all. The man in your sketch has hunted my family. He's caused others to harm them. Now it's time to stop him. You and I."

"And Owen."

"Owen, too." Leona glanced at Owen, who had returned to her side. If Owen had anything to do with this psychic tangle, Leona was determined to discover exactly how he was involved. Right now, Janice had to be saved.

Leona took the bag Owen had brought to her; she reached inside to find the replica of the Viking brooch. When she gave it to Janice, the girl gripped it in both hands. She closed her eyes and brought it to her chest, as if pressing everything Leona had said inside her heart. Leona placed her hand over Janice's. "Remember what I've said. And don't be afraid."

Janice nodded solemnly, then she whispered to Owen, "She gave me her protection. You must protect her now. The hunter is close. He comes from the ancient time of her family's beginnings, and of ours."

Owen's hard stare pinned Leona's. "Nothing is going to hurt either one of you. I'll be with you every step of the way."

A sudden movement caused Leona to glance at the house. A curtain had moved slightly as if they were being watched. From her expression earlier, Janice's nurse-caretaker wasn't happy. Perhaps she had the right to be suspicious of Leona.

"I have to go now, Janice. But I'll come back tonight and help you with your hair."

"Promise?"

"Promise."

Leona called Claire as soon as she left the Shaws. "I'm fine. You can call Tempest and Mom. I felt you all with me."

"We were worried."

"You felt it? It was that strong?"

Claire's soft voice had curled warmly around Leona. "Yes. I knew you were helping Owen's sister. You were moving on instinct, and you knew exactly what to do. But be careful, Leona."

"I will be."

"You know about yourself then, that you have more than the one gift? You know that you can ease and heal?"

Leona thought of how her instincts had told her to touch Janice, to calm her, of the threads weaving between them. She'd known how to dive into the stream and follow it. "Yes, I know. But I don't want to do this. I'm terrified of myself."

"You've always been strong. I've always felt it in you, and so did Mom. We all knew. Grams told me before—"

"She went off the deep end? You could have told me. Or at least let me sense it."

"Would you have believed?" Claire chided gently. "I thought Grams told you that day—just after Dad's accident. She was staying with us, and you acted petrified of her for days. We didn't know why. She wouldn't say what she had told you. We'll never know now what secrets she knew, what caused her to drink and go mad."

Her grandmother had leaned close to Leona, her green eyes brilliant with fear. Her fingers had dug into Leona's thin arms, her whisper urgent. *He's coming. . . . The one . . .*

Leona momentarily struggled with the fragmented childhood memory, but more of it escaped her. "Grams never said anything about what I could do. I've always thought of it as a curse that I wouldn't let have me."

"Yes, well," Claire stated in a crisp fierce tone, unlike her usual soft flowing one. "There is one curse that isn't getting any of us—not if I can help it."

Leona smiled to herself. Claire's Viking strain had just leaped, ready to do battle. "You're right about that. I love you. Truly, I do."

During the morning at work, Leona had replayed the scene with Janice many times. Something taken, something given, she thought, trying to understand her instinctive reactions, and her connection to Janice. Between interviews for an alterations seamstress and a part-time clerk and helping her customers, she sat in her upstairs office, fighting her claustrophobia. The new shelving reminded her of Vernon and she remembered her missing scarf. Picking up the telephone, she dialed his number.

His voice sounded drowsy. "Been feeling droopy lately, Ms. Leona, but I'll get your closets done as soon as I can. Been working overtime at Billy Balleau's and Cheslav's. I don't touch personal stuff. Haven't seen that scarf."

Could she believe him? She had to be very careful now. "Okay, just get well, Vernon. And let me know when you're working at my house from now on, will you?"

"Huh? Is something wrong?"

"No, but I just like to know when you're there. I'm expecting company in the next day or so, so no need to do any work then. Take some time to get well, then we may have to discuss moving this shelving in my office back a little. It's taking up too much space." Leona needed time to determine whether the handyman could be dangerous to her.

Strangely, Vernon didn't argue the point before the call ended.

Of course, Leona wasn't expecting anyone. Her sisters had called with a warning, prior to Greer's midmorning call. "I thought I'd just hop over to see you for a bit. Is that all right?"

"Is there a reason?" Leona had asked.

"You know there is," Greer had answered softly. "It's your life and I don't want to interfere but I'd like to see you."

Greer's maternal link, combined with her powerful extrasensories, usually set Leona on edge. However, for Janice's sake, Leona wanted her mother's help. "Could you do me a favor?"

"Of course. I'll make arrangements to come to you right away."

"I'd rather you wouldn't."

The slight trembling of her senses told Leona that she had wounded Greer by once again rejecting her mother's offer of help. Leona hadn't asked anything of her mother since the parapsychologists and doctors had swept the Aisling-Bartel triplets into a nightmare of psychic testing.

"You're going to need help, Leona." Greer's voice was as uncertain and trembling as the tingling in Leona's senses.

She wasn't as strong an empath as Claire. She didn't have the developed powers of her mother. She may have endangered Janice even more by promising protection that she might not be able to deliver.

After years of closing the door on what she was, Leona was also uncertain. "There's someone I need you to protect. Could she stay with you?"

Greer's answer was immediate and firm. "Yes. She'll be safe with me."

Just as the triplets had always been safe with their mother . . . Greer had done everything she'd known to protect them. Her mother had done the best she could. . . .

Leona's resentment began to shatter, the shards spilling at her feet.

Seven

OF COURSE HE HAD LEONA'S SCARF.

Rolf Erling brought the silky, swirling shades of teal and turquoise to his face. As he nuzzled Leona's exotic, unique scent, he smiled. "Yes, I have your scarf, my lovely."

She'd sounded upset on the telephone when she'd thought she was speaking with Vernon. The shelving that had been deliberately created to consume Leona's personal space had done its job, jump-starting Leona's claustrophobia. Then, she was already suspicious that her little safe nest had been invaded, creating another pressure on her psychic antenna.

Rolf smiled again, his plan coming together perfectly. With all her concerns, Leona didn't have enough reserve energy to block him—even if she knew how. He'd been watching her startled reaction to his mental broadcast today. He'd actually used that watery triangle, a perfect psychic portal, to connect with her senses and take her very close to that river. Just a few more extrasensory pushes, and Leona would have tried to see who was calling her from the river. She would have gone over the cliff and into the deadly currents.

"Maybe next time, sweet Leona." A skilled master at

traps and seduction, Rolf was in control of all the little pieces. Leona had definitely taken the bait. To ease Janice would draw away even more of Leona's energy. Then she was deeply troubled by the inexplicable actions of her closest friend, Sue Ann. Leona was also under pressure to find help for her shop. Then Alex, a grieving widower, had snagged bits of her sympathy. Every time Alex brought up his wife, Leona's unresolved grief for her husband quickened.

Poor Alex. He never should have tripped over that carpenter's plastic. The newest faked injury was just another stress on Leona, a little nudge to weaken the cracks in her psychic gifts. Before Janice, she'd only revealed that deeply hidden nurturing streak with Sue Ann and with Alex.

Alex's faked injury would be a physical drain on Leona, a weakness to siphon Leona's energies and make her more vulnerable. There were always pinpoints, weaknesses in all the people Rolf chose, even Leona's sisters.

By water, they'd been more susceptible, and by using fog as an extension, he'd been able to reach them easily. But Neil Olafson and Marcus Greystone had bonded with the sisters and he couldn't get to them as easily.

Rolf crushed the scarf in his fist, then twisted it with his other hand. Now only Leona was left unprotected.

Weaken one, weaken them all. Then humiliate and destroy Greer, and take the brooch that would give him everything, power and revenge.

He wrapped the scarf around his fists and drew it tight; it would make a perfect garrote. The colors suited Leona, but her choices had probably been based on her heritage, an affinity for the earth's green and the water's power. According to the information Rolf had inherited from his ancestors, Aisling descendants with their red hair and green eyes usually had that water affinity and were usually stronger by the water.

But the triplets' sailing accident had linked them with the water and each other in a different way. Water, large bodies, and now fog, weakened their psychic protections. *Rolf's father had passed down many interesting facts about the Aisling-Bartel triplets, derived from his time with Stella Mornay.*

Rolf had been infuriated when Shaw had stopped Leona from looking over that cliff. He'd been furious when their bodies moved in sensual harmony. Shaw and Leona had stood in that powerful triangle of the pond, the stream, and the Kentucky River—and Shaw had protected Leona at her weakest. After five years, Leona had finally taken a lover, and no ordinary one, either. Through contact with Janice, Rolf had caught traces of an unidentifiable ancient psychic power.

Before Leona bonded with Janice's brother, Shaw had to be removed from the equation.

Rolf could not fail, not after studying the Aislings for so many years. Not after all the practice on others and his success. Not after Greer had made such a fool of him. He turned to the mirror and spoke to his reflection. "Damn Shaw. I've gotten a strong link with Leona's energy. Without Shaw's interference, I'd have had her bouncing down that rocky cliff and into that water. It wouldn't have been a hands-on death, but it would have served. Shaw is more powerful than Janice. I've known that all along, but I needed him to transport Janice to Lexington. Now I'll have to take him out of the picture. I made the mistake of letting Leona's sisters' lovers live . . . Shaw won't."

Rolf preened just a little in the privacy of his underground workshop. He admired his undisguised lean, angular face, his compelling eyes and crooned, using the same tone he'd used to mesmerize those with weaker minds, including Janice's. Once his psychic tentacles captured a vulnerable person, he could make them do anything. "Leona . . . Leona . . . you are mine."

His fury almost rebounded, burning him, as he thought of Greer Aisling.

Greer had caused his peers to laugh at him, as if he were nothing—he, Rolf Erling, Borg's descendant, in a line as old and strong as hers.

Greer really shouldn't have done that.

"Janice?"

In his hurry to ready Janice for the next morning's flight, Owen had left his laptop case on his bed. Now his laptop was missing.

He'd tossed his key ring onto the dresser, and it was gone, too. In its place was the wolf's-head brooch Leona had given Janice. Owen grabbed it. Panic raced through him, and he called Janice again. But the house remained quiet.

Earlier, Robyn hadn't left easily. She'd alternately pleaded, then argued furiously. "Janice will be alone, without me, without her medications. You can't just take her into an environment where she doesn't know anyone, doesn't have me! *Don't you love your sister?*"

Owen had explained to Robyn that he had talked with Greer Aisling and believed that Janice would be well treated.

In the end, Robyn had grabbed his shirt and pleaded, "Don't do this to your sister. Don't do this to me. You don't know what you're doing, Owen. Take me with you."

Her desperation and fear had startled him. Owen suspected she feared losing her income and assured Robyn that she'd be kept on retainer. He wanted her to consider the time away as a little vacation.

"I don't need a vacation, you fool!" Robyn had screamed. "I need to be with Janice."

"We'll talk when I get back," he'd stated firmly. In the end, Robyn had asked to say a private good-bye. She wanted to reassure Janice that they'd see each other again. When she returned to Owen, Robyn was set to argue again. He'd been forced to leave Janice momentarily alone and usher Robyn to her small, economy car.

Her last words had burned him, "Oh, I hate you for this. *You've killed me.*"

Owen had no time to deal with Robyn's sudden, dramatic change; he'd hurried back into the house to pack. Now Janice was missing.

Fearing his sister had returned to the pond, Owen hurried out into the evening. The sunset sent a scarlet ribbon trailing across the top of the hills.

Moon Shadow stood at the fence near the barn, staring at it as he always did when Janice was inside.

"Good boy," Owen murmured as he ran toward the barn.

When he found the barn unlocked, Owen's heart raced. *How could he have been so careless as to leave his keys where Janice could find them?* As he searched the shadows, he eased around the sawhorses and standing saw that the carpenter had been using.

Janice stood in a far corner. As he walked slowly toward her, Owen didn't like the dull gleam in her hand. As he came closer, the handgun aimed at his heart. The revolver had been a gift from his father, one of the few family treasures he'd been able to keep. How could she have found the handgun? He'd carefully pried open a weathered board in the loft and laid its case inside; he'd even covered the board with a bale of hay. The barn had been locked, the carpenter instructed carefully on safety issues. "Hi, Janice," Owen said lightly, as the revolver raised and pointed at him.

Her expression was blank, just as it had been when she'd tried to drown herself.

"You won't let me talk to him."

"Who, Janice?"

"You know who. I miss him. And you kept me from talking to him." Her speech pattern was robotic, stripped of emotion, the pace almost mechanical. She'd sounded that way after her computer sessions.

"You mean someone you know through the computer? The man you drew?"

"Yes. You're evil, Owen. And you have to die. I found the cartridges. The gun is loaded."

He edged closer. He'd deliberately hidden the cartridges in a location separate from the handgun. How could she possibly have found both the revolver and the cartridges? He had to distract Janice for just one instant, then he'd have the gun. . . .

"Where's my laptop, Janice?"

"I threw it in the pond. If I can't have it, you can't either."

"That's fair," Owen soothed. As Janice's thumb drew back the hammer, the deadly clicks echoed in the shadows. "Let me have the gun, Janice."

"You hid Dad's gun from me. It's mine, too. I don't like how you keep things from me. You don't love me anymore. You had sex with Leona. Now you're hers, not mine anymore. I'm alone, and I don't want to leave here. I want to stay here, with him. But you want *her* here, not me. You're planning to put me away again. That's why we're leaving in the morning. But we're not. I'm going to stay here forever."

Owen fought his fear, trying to focus on moving closer and disarming Janice.

"Stay where you are," Janice ordered quietly.

"You forgot something." Owen held out the brooch. If Janice took it, the distraction might be enough for him to act. "Leona gave it to you this morning, remember? It's her good-luck piece, and she gave it to you."

"It's evil. I won't wear it. It's a part of her, and she's evil, too. She lied. She said she'd come back tonight, and she didn't. She broke her promise."

Owen didn't turn when the barn door creaked slightly. Light, feminine footsteps sounded, now. Bits of straw snapped and Owen's hunter senses detected she was coming straight to him. As a cool fresh scent curled around him, Owen quietly ordered, "Leona, get out of here."

Even as he spoke, Owen knew Leona wouldn't back away in fear. Her footsteps came closer, until she stood at his side. Her hand opened on his back. A steady, warm, reasurring pulse flowed from her.

"Hello, Janice," Leona murmured quietly. "I said I'd come back to cut your hair. I brought my hair-cutting shears and some new traveling clothes for you. My mother will take you shopping on the coast. They have lovely stores there, and she'll know how to help you. *She'll protect you better than I can.*"

Janice's eyes flickered toward Leona, and the revolver moved slightly, aimed at her. "You promised. I waited and you didn't come."

"One of my friends had an accident. I took dinner to him and saw that he was comfortable. I came as soon as I could. The new clothes I brought are from my shop. Didn't you like the brooch I gave you?"

Owen suddenly remembered the brooch now clenched in his fist. He'd been gripping it and had to force his fingers to open. *He had to draw Janice's aim from Leona.* He held the brooch out to Janice. "Trade you."

Trade you. It had been a game they'd often played, a bargaining game to get Janice to respond in the worst of times. Janice's eyes flickered to the brooch. "It has a wolf on it . . . a wolf is a hunter . . . like your name, Owen."

At his side, Leona inhaled suddenly, her fingers gripping his shirt. "Like Owen? What do you mean, Janice?"

"His name is Wolf . . . Owen Wolf Shaw. It comes from the old ones. He wants to forget those things the old ones told around the campfires, but he can't. Neither can I."

Within the shadows, Owen sensed Leona's pulse as if it were his own—frantic, panicked, uncertain. She moved just a few inches closer to Janice. Leona took the brooch from Owen, looking into his eyes as if seeing him as another person. Her tone was a little breathless, but soothing. "Yes, of course. I should have known by his light eyes. Wolf is a good name for a man, isn't it?"

Owen frowned slightly. *Why should Leona have known?*

When Leona moved slightly in front of him, Owen realized that she was protecting him. He reached for the waistband of her slacks and held tight. If he had to, he would push Leona aside and take that slug himself.

Since Leona had begun talking, Janice's eyes changed slightly. Her hollow look shifted more into lifelike. Still, the revolver's hammer remained cocked and dangerous. Owen had to protect Leona. "Let me have the gun, Janice. You can have the brooch. You want it, don't you? Trade you."

One wrong move, and that hammer would set a deadly slug spiraling through that barrel. . . .

"My brother is sending me away, so he can have you." Janice's monotone had wavered and slid into uncertainty.

Leona took the brooch from Owen, her eyes meeting his. *We can do this. Don't frighten her.*

When he nodded slightly, Leona looked at Janice, her voice smooth and flowing. "He's taking you to my mother's home by the ocean. She's waiting to meet you, and you'll love it there. Just for a time, and then you can come back. I grew up there."

"With your sisters . . . you're one of triplets." Janice spoke as if trying to grasp a thread she remembered from another time.

Leona smoothly supplied an anchor for Janice to grasp. "Yes. We were born three minutes apart, and I'm the oldest. There's Tempest and Claire. They both just got married this year."

"And they're both going to have babies. Not soon, but sometime. And you're terribly afraid for them." Fear suddenly leaped in Janice's eyes, and the slender hands holding the gun trembled. "Owen, I don't know what to do with this. Help me. I can't let go."

Owen moved quickly to his sister's side. Placing his hands over hers, he turned the revolver from Leona. "Let me do it, Janice."

He slowly released the cocked hammer and eased the revolver from Janice's hands.

"There now," Leona soothed as she pinned the brooch on Janice's blouse. Leona's eyes held Janice's as she touched and smoothed the girl's hair, face, and arms. Owen held his breath as Leona smiled and spoke softly of Janice's new haircut and of Janice's upcoming visit to Greer Aisling, of how it was only for a short time. "You'll have to ask my mother, but she has a very special computer. It's been . . . adjusted. She might let you use it, too. You'll feel very—calm and very strong when you're with her. She'll never leave you alone, and she'll know how to help you."

"Like you. That's how you make me feel—calm and strong. You'll take care of my horses when I'm gone, won't you?"

"I will see them every day. I promise. And I'll tell you how they are."

"And Owen, too? You'll care for him?"

Leona hesitated just that fraction of a heartbeat. "Yes, him, too. You'll do what my mother says, won't you?"

Janice nodded. "I'll see the real brooch, won't I? The one with the old writing on it? And you'll wear this one?"

Puzzled by Janice's phrase, "old writing," Owen glanced at Leona. What "old writing?" What did his sister mean? Apparently, the phrase meant something to Leona because for a moment, she looked stunned. Then she said smoothly, "I will. But I want you to wear it on your trip and think of me. My sister, Tempest, is making one for you now, so you'll be our sister."

"She is?" Janice's childlike excitement caused Owen to relax slightly.

"Tempest is an artist, like you. You'll like her. Let's go back to the house now, shall we? I can help you with your hair. I want to see what you've packed." Leona continued speaking in that same calm tone. She glanced warily at Owen, and he thought of the two-way connection. He'd said nothing to Janice about the Aisling triplets' births. He hadn't even known there was a genuine brooch. Yet Janice seemed to know everything. While Leona could obviously communicate and calm Janice, his sister was obviously picking up tidbits from Leona.

"Your mother knows the man I drew, doesn't she?"

Janice's question obviously startled Leona. She glanced at Owen again before answering curtly. "In a way—she knows him."

Every muscle in Owen's body tensed. *Greer Aisling knew that bastard? How?*

Instantly, Leona looked at Owen again, her slight frown warning him. *Not now.*

She'd understood his emotions and thoughts instantly. She'd just warned him against disturbing the link she'd made with Janice. Then Leona turned slowly to look at Janice as though willing the girl to understand. "You remember how I said that you are mine now, Janice? You're not that man's any longer. You belong to my family, like a sister."

When Janice smiled timidly, Owen let out a shuddered breath, a release of tension in the aftermath of his terror. If Greer Aisling was anything like Leona, he had no reservations about taking his sister to her.

Familiar with the revolver's wooden grip, Owen wrapped his hand around it. He expertly removed the six deadly cartridges from the cylinder. They gleamed in his hand, and he remembered how Janice had looked—one wrong move, and he could have been killed. His death would have also resulted in his sister's, one way or another.

Or Leona could have died. The thought terrified him. Ignoring his attempts to keep her out of the line of fire, she'd deliberately used her body as a shield for his. Now that was real irritating. A man liked to know his woman listened to him.

The lady wasn't afraid of much. But maybe she should be.

Shaken by Janice's latest episode, Owen was relieved to see how his sister continued responding to Leona. Janice seemed like she was back to normal. She was delighted with the short haircut that Leona gave her, which Leona described as almost like Tempest's. Now, with Janice settled in for the night, Leona sat with Owen on the front porch steps. The early September night was soft and fragrant around them, scented of the approaching fall.

"I shouldn't have left my laptop or my keys where she could get them," Owen said. "I was trying to get ahead of a stock split and some investments at the last minute.

I didn't think she'd go into my room." He looked at her. "Thank you for helping my sister."

Owen was still amazed at how gentle and normal Janice had seemed with Leona. But now it was close to eleven o'clock and after two hours of soothing Janice, Leona appeared drained.

"Owen, make certain that she doesn't take any of her usual jewelry or clothing with her. She's got to be 'clean' of any of this guy's creepy residue. On the other hand, her braids were a part of her. It's important that they are not left where anyone can get them. If you still have them, they should go with her. She'll be safe. Just keep her from any electronics on the way. If someone lights up a laptop or anything that transmits, get her to focus on that brooch. Don't leave her alone for a minute."

"It's going to be hard to watch her in the ladies' room."

His grumble sounded so male and disgusted that Leona couldn't help smiling. "You'll manage." Glancing at her watch, she said, "I have to go check on my friend yet tonight."

"Alex." Owen's tone bit into the night air, sharper than he would have liked.

"Yes. I'm worried about him. He's a retired widower and not used to taking care of himself quite yet. Today he fell and got bruised quite badly. I just want to check to see if he's better. I thought he should go to the emergency room, but he wouldn't. If you need me, call my cell phone." Leona looped her arms around her knees and rested her forehead on them.

"Oh, I need you," Owen admitted roughly. "Is it necessary that you check on him tonight?"

"I said I would. Owen, he's exactly the kind of vulnerable personality that whoever is using Janice preys upon. I'd never forgive myself if anything happened to him."

"You think you can protect him, do you?" he asked a little too sharply.

"If I have to."

Owen smoothed back Leona's hair, then slowly rubbed her shoulders and back. The tension there pounded at him. In the quiet evening air, Leona turned her face to him. "Alex has no one else to help him. I'm all he has for now. He doesn't make friends easily."

"I see."

"No, you don't. Don't be jealous, Owen. He's a friend, he's lonely, and he needs me."

Removing his hand, he clasped it in the other. The chilling scene with Janice had revealed more information about the Aislings. "Tell me about that brooch, what it means to your family. Janice said she's going to see the real one. And what is the 'old writing' she mentioned?"

Leona didn't answer. In that terrifying scene with Janice, she had also gotten new information about Owen. "You didn't tell me your name was 'Wolf.'"

"It's a middle name, and not unusual for a Native American. Why? Does it matter?"

Leona turned her face to study him. "Yes, it does. I'm going after this creep, and you're involved somehow. There's a wolf's head on that brooch, and your middle name is Wolf. There could be a connection."

"Oh, I'm involved, all right, and not only because of my sister," Owen murmured, as his hand smoothed her hair, letting the silky warmth flow around his fingers. He gently drew Leona into his arms and let her rest against him.

Leona trembled, but she held him tightly. Her face pressed against his throat as she whispered, "I'm so scared, Owen. My sisters, my family could be at risk. Janice was right. Claire and Tempest will be pregnant soon, and so vulnerable. For years, I—I've seen flashes, images of them pregnant, and with babies in their arms. Claire was pregnant, before she walked into a bank robbery. That trauma and the one at the hospital caused her to miscarry. Before that happens again, I've got to get this bastard out of our lives now. But I've got to open myself to what I am, and I've fought it all my life. My grandmother killed herself because she'd 'opened,' and had become too strong. She'd fought it all her life, then suddenly she changed. When I was four or five, she stayed with us after Dad's accident. She told me something—I'd forgotten until recently what it was, then only parts. She was already losing her mind, and it could have been the start of her madness, which lasted for years."

"Tell me about the original brooch. It's not just a piece of jewelry, is it?" Owen had to know why all the Aisling-Bartels wore replicas, why Janice had said that Greer had the original brooch. "You don't have anything Celtic in your home—or that I noticed. And yet your brooch has that definite style."

"It's a family brooch, like one my Viking ancestor wore—the chieftain who captured the seer called Aisling. His name was Thorgood. My family is descended from them, and my mother took Aisling as a professional name. In our family, clairvoyant gifts usually come to the red-haired, green-eyed females. I wanted nothing in my home to remind me of a gift I have never wanted, but I can't escape. It is a curse in itself. When I see myself in the mirror, I remind myself so much of the Aisling of my dreams that I can almost hear her whispering to me, warning me."

"Anything else?"

"The brooch has a curse. Thorgood got Aisling, Borg didn't, and so he cursed the brooch and their bloodline. He's the bad guy in this unbelievable story, or rather his descendant is."

Owen shook his head. "How do you know all this—the exact names and what happened?"

"Dreams. Flashes in mirrors, in glass, and just plain old-fashioned nightmares. We know the names very well. The man in Janice's sketch is a psychic vampire, Owen. He seduces at first, then gradually takes control and becomes stronger than his victim. Soon his victims no longer belong to themselves. They move at his command. He's very powerful. He wants that original brooch, and he's going to kill to get it. He's *already* killed," Leona corrected.

"You've seen him, too?"

"Yes. In my dreams. Now I'm questioning if my grandmother actually transferred an image of him into my mind. My mother has the same dreams, very real. Sometimes it's as if we're Aisling, experiencing what she did. Sometimes we see her in that Celt village, as she watches Thorgood come toward her. But the visions of Borg challenging Thorgood for Aisling are the same. Whatever the case, this psychic vampire is a descendant of Borg, and he wants revenge. He wants to make that curse come true . . . he wants to kill us and get that brooch. He has some mad idea that he'll have whatever so-called power it holds."

She shivered against Owen before continuing. "Once he gets control of someone—always the vulnerable—he has them do his dirty work, then commit suicide. He uses them, and he discards them like trash. His attempts on my sisters' lives resulted in several suicides or deadly accidents. In Claire's case, when she miscarried, it was a doctor and nurse and a man trying to reform. In Tempest's, it was only a boy trying to survive a rough life. All of them had connected with him, just like Janice. A computer is his usual choice. This man, whoever he is, is like a puppet-master, pulling psychic strings, using his minions."

Owen thought of his sister's suicide attempts. *He* was always the explanation, what *He* wanted her to do. "Do you really think there is a connection to my family name, 'Wolf'?"

"With your light eyes, I'd say there's a good chance."

"Explain."

"They're gray, not blue."

"So?"

"I don't know exactly how you fit into this, but you do."

"And you have some idea. I need to know anything even somewhat possible." Leona leaned back to look at him. Her hand stroked away the strand of hair at his forehead. A wave of euphoria curled around him, and Owen smiled, "It feels good, honey, but I'd appreciate you not practicing with me. I like to understand any psychic connection we may have but I'd rather have the real flesh-and-blood thing with you."

With Leona so close in his arms, Owen couldn't stop his body hardening, his need for her swelling inside him. As his hand lowered to caress her breast, Leona's eyes searched his face. Then, gripping his hair, she tugged Owen to her. Against his lips, she whispered, "We don't have much time."

"No, we sure don't." Owen had expected a soft kiss. Instead, Leona's body heated and melded to his, her fingers pressed deep into his upper thigh, her hand moving upward to cup and stroke him. When she leaned back, the hunger in her expression matched his. She licked her lips, a reminder of what that tongue had done three evenings ago.

In one movement, Owen stood and scooped Leona into his arms. He moved swiftly toward the barn, carrying her.

"You like this big, strong macho stuff, don't you, big guy?" she teased between kisses. But her hand had already slid inside Owen's shirt, caressing his chest. Her fingertip prowled his nipple and sent a jolt straight southward until he almost missed a step.

Leona's change of mood was too sudden, but at the moment, Owen wasn't refusing. "Like you said, we don't have much time. Is it always this way with you? Changing gears at the speed of light?"

"No."

Owen decided that he'd take that firm "No." He wanted Leona to react differently to him than she had with any other man, and that was good enough.

Within heartbeats of entering the dark barn, of closing the door, Owen eased inside Leona. Their clothing had been strewn upon the plastic sheeting covering the standing saw and they stood in a corner, his back braced against the wall. Shuddering, he lifted her to accept him better, then thrust deeply within her.

He stopped, holding her on that peak and withdrawing slightly. Leona dug in for the battle, set to complete it. Her nails pressed into his back; her legs wrapped around his. Instinctively, Owen knew that she'd never given another man everything; she'd never fought for her pleasure so desperately or so quickly. Other men probably hadn't seen her primitive side. Owen had, and he intended to give Leona something she wouldn't forget.

Lost in passion, her body at its throbbing peak, tightly gloving his, Leona threw back her head, her hair webbing her damp cheek. Her eyes shone bright and furious upon him. Torn away was that perfect calm, that poise and soothing cool voice. She looked as if she would fight all odds to pay him back. *Perfect,* Owen thought, before his mind went blank and his body took over.

When the pounding red haze passed, Leona stood limp against him, her body quivering. Owen pressed his face against her damp throat, taking in her scent. "What was that?" she whispered unevenly.

He nibbled on her skin, licked it lightly, and tasted her sweat. She'd matched his passion in every heartbeat. "I think you know. Now tell me what turned you on so fast. . . . For future reference."

"What? I can't be the one to make advances? That's old-fashioned, isn't it, Owen?"

"I'm not complaining. I just want to know what I'm dealing with."

Leona nuzzled her cheek against his, then against his throat and over his shoulder. She nipped her way back to his ear, and whispered, "I guess that's only fair. . . . I'm not used to releasing so much of myself to another person. I'd just told you the family secrets. I'd just come down from helping Janice. I'd had to push myself to connect and soothe her, and it's causing me to grow and change. This is new for me. Our relationship, and—and finding out what I can do, when I push, or try to open to another. A little success, and I'm flying high. I was all charged up, and you just tapped all that energy."

"Uh-huh. So it had to go somewhere? You had to use it somehow?"

"I was coming off a psychic high, exhilarated, highly charged. You did just the wrong thing."

He felt his grin all over his body. "Hmm. It felt right to me."

"You're full of yourself right now, aren't you? I don't think you're very sweet, Owen Wolf Shaw. You were also making a macho possessive point—that you have some claim on me. You do that to me again, and you'll pay."

"Promises, promises. I can't wait."

Leona bit his shoulder lightly, then rested her cheek on that same spot, nuzzling him. As Owen let all the tension in his life simply flow away, his senses filled with this one woman, her body soft and curving in his arms. As they stood naked and still joined in the shadowy cool barn, time drifted sweetly by, the aftermath of a primitive mating. He caressed her back, smoothed her breast, and waited until her trembling had stopped. Then he couldn't resist cupping her breasts, studying the shape and pale flesh within his hands. Leaning back slightly, he looked down where they joined and became one, lock and key.

"Stop that. . . . I have to go," Leona whispered desperately against his shoulder.

"I know." Owen forced himself to ease away. He helped Leona dress, then tended himself. Then he took her hand, pressed it to his lips and placed it over his heart. "Thank you."

She smiled softly and arched a brow, her cool, protective poise sliding back into place. "For this?"

"For helping Janice." Owen smoothed her hair. He let the silky strands slide between his fingers. "You'll be safe?"

She tilted her head, those earth-green eyes mocking him slightly. "I'm a big girl, Owen."

"Oh, I know that," he answered with a grin as he patted her bottom. Leona stiffened slightly and frowned. He patted her again, testing her uncertain expression.

"You're going to be difficult, aren't you?" she said as she pushed away and sauntered toward the door.

Owen drew in a deep ragged breath. As he watched those swaying hips, his body hardened once again. Raising his gaze, he saw the seductive look Leona gave him over her shoulder and grinned again because he knew exactly how he was going to pay. . . .

In his underground workshop, Rolf switched off the screen fed by the camera in the Shaws' barn.

He couldn't see Shaw and Leona in the darkness, but the motion sensor had picked up movement. A brief glimpse told him what they'd been doing. "So he carried her into the barn. She clung to him, and it only took a few moments. They must have been desperate," he said, hatred burning him.

He expected the phone to ring and when it did, he picked it up and listened to the report closely. Furious to learn of the setback in his plans, Rolf focused on the message he must imprint on the caller to ensure no further damage came to his mission. He was too close to success. A wrong word to his minion could destroy a precious connection he had spent hours developing. Pushing back his fury, he kept his voice calm and soothing, his words logical. The caller had to understand. . . .

Once he hung up the phone, Rolf released his anger in a storm of curses. He picked up a hammer from the workbench and smashed it into the mirror. One shard of the mirror reflected his image, the violence circling him, his eyes wild. He sent the hammer into it and stood back, panting, as the shards flew into the shadows. "Shaw thinks he's going to protect Janice by taking her to that witch-mother, Greer. Maybe he is—for a while, but I'll have Janice again. I needed that girl to help me with Leona. Shaw will pay for ruining my plans, and so will Leona, and Greer. I hate all of them, but Greer the most. How dare she put me down!"

Rolf glanced around his cluttered workshop, the electronics that fed him scenes from several cameras and microphones.

Everything was going perfectly. Janice had the revolver, just as she was supposed to. She had Shaw in her sights. If that interfering witch, Leona, hadn't stopped her, in another minute he would have been dead. There would be no one for Janice to turn to, but Leona. Leona would have taken Janice in immediately, and caring for her would have further exhausted Leona's energy.

Rolf braced both hands on the work counter and spoke to his reflection. "I could just shoot Leona . . . kill her somehow. But that isn't the plan. I prefer the prey to fear me and to know that I am hunting. What kind of a predator would I be if I just killed her outright? No, it's better that she didn't go off that cliff. Feeding on her fear is making my energy stronger. And this game is ever so much more pleasurable than an outright kill."

Picking up a three-foot-long sword, a replica of his ancestor's, the pommel inlaid with silver and copper, Rolf studied the deadly blade. He had seen flashes of Borg's actual sword, tossed to the very bottom of the ocean by Thorgood's men, where it could never be retrieved. In doing so, Thorgood's warriors had damned Borg's spirit to roam for an eternity.

"There's no spirit haunting me. Nothing but a thirst to take what's rightfully mine, and bring Greer down." Rolf ran his thumb over the sword's gleaming edge, then sucked the blood from the small wound. "With this sword, I'll mark Shaw for my kill. That's more sporting, to give him time to understand he will die. And then, when his fear is strong enough, I'll have the pleasure of finishing him."

Eight

VERNON CHOSE THE WRONG TIME TO STOP AT ALEX'S house. Leona was there first.

Before she opened her shop that morning, Leona had stopped by Alex's to make certain that he was comfortable. Yesterday, he'd fallen on his way to the kitchen and Leona had seen why—the carpentry clutter in the hallway had been carelessly covered with plastic sheeting. She'd almost fallen, too, her foot tangled in the sheeting.

"Come in, Vernon. I'd like to have a talk with you. I see you're feeling better."

"Never better." As always, Alex's house was shadowy, but there was no missing the scowl on Vernon's craggy face. At six-foot-six and with a powerful build, he looked around Alex's living room, then placed his large wooden toolbox on the floor. Hitching up his bib overalls, he took a cigarette out of his pocket, squinting at Leona as he lit it. He blew smoke in the air. "You're up and eager to start tossing orders around. Where's Alex?"

"He's lying down. He isn't feeling well, and because of you. Yesterday he had a bad spill."

"Is that so?" Vernon's tone challenged her.

She looked down at his boots. He'd tracked mud onto

the newly refinished hardwood floors and Alex's expensive oriental rug. "Look at that. I don't know what's gotten into you."

Behind the cigarette smoke, Vernon's eyes went flat. "You got a bee in your bonnet, lady."

"I'd like you to be more careful with your equipment. Alex tripped on that loose plastic. And at my house, your things are all over the place. You've been smoking there, and we agreed you wouldn't. You left a window open and tracked in mud."

"I had to have some fresh air, didn't I?"

He glanced up at Alex, who had come partially down the stairway. "I'll be more careful," Vernon stated quietly.

"Please do. When do you think you'll be finished with my closet?"

"Everything takes time. Balleau wants some extra work on the job I'm doing for him that I hadn't planned. I'm full up with jobs."

"Then maybe you should just take one at a time."

Vernon's anger trembled around her. Leaning down to her face, he said "Why, you little—" Stopping abruptly, he glared at her.

Leona's body chilled instantly. Vernon's temper was either new, or he'd been good at concealing it. *Was he the one stalking her family?*

"Vernon?" Alex called as he came down the stairs. "Ah. I thought I heard your voice. It's all right, Vernon, if you want to take this morning off as we discussed. Call me later."

Vernon stared at Alex for a moment, as if preparing to say something. Then he nodded and quickly left.

Leona watched him get into his battered work pickup, then she turned to Alex. A gentle man, he would be no match for Vernon in a rage. "I'm sorry I recommended him. He did a good job in the shop's display room and office. His references were good. But I don't like what's happening to him."

"Everyone has difficult times, Leona. Have patience. You're just worried about finding a new helper at the shop, and you seem stressed. Is there anything I can do to help?"

Leona turned to smile at him. "I don't suppose you know anything about ladies' wear, do you?"

"I'll take care of your sister," Greer Aisling said when she met Owen and Janice at Sea-Tac, Seattle's major airport.

Greer's earth-green eyes were amazingly like Leona's. Though gray touched the older woman's hair, which Greer wore in a smooth chignon, that dark red shade was still alive, fiery when touched by bright light. A replica brooch like her daughter's was pinned to her soft green jacket. After they'd deplaned Greer had immediately walked to Janice. Greer had hugged Janice as would a mother.

A tall, older man stood near Greer, keeping a watchful eye on their surroundings. "This is Kenneth Ragnar," Greer stated, clearly uneasy with the man. "This is Owen and Janice Shaw."

Kenneth nodded curtly, extending his left hand to Owen. "Shaw."

As they shook hands, Owen sensed that the other man was gauging him as he stepped back instantly, almost behind the women, his stance casual but his gaze alert, like that of a guard on duty. "She'll be fine. Greer knows what to do."

"I see that."

In Greer's embrace, Janice reacted immediately to the world-famous psychic. Her body relaxed, and her arms went around the older woman, as if grasping a lifeline. Greer touched and soothed Janice in almost the same manner as Leona had, and Owen instantly trusted her. But then he'd trusted Greer from the moment he'd spoken to her on the telephone last night.

"How lovely to have a daughter in my home again. I see you like Claire's work. That's a lovely tote," Greer said warmly as she eased away but continued to hold Janice's hand. "Owen says you're a graphic designer. All of my daughters are creative, too. I've prepared a perfect computer just for you. I'm sorry, but my Internet connection is out temporarily. But it has everything you'll need for your graphic work. And I think some of my daughters' clothes are going to fit you. If not, we'll alter them. You like to sew, don't you? Maybe you'd like to make your own."

"I love to sew. I'd love to make a patchwork quilt and use my own graphic designs."

Janice's excitement startled Owen. He hadn't known that Janice liked to sew; no wonder keeping scissors from her had been such a task.

"She'll be fine," Greer murmured, when he'd tensed and prepared to make a financial arrangement. Owen hadn't much to offer. The move from Montana and Janice's depression had run his savings into a dangerous margin.

Before Owen could reach for his wallet, Greer's earth-green eyes locked with his. "Money doesn't matter now. I'm glad to have Janice stay with me. We have lots to talk about. . . . I know this is difficult for you, Owen Wolf Shaw. But there are bigger things to worry about than your pride, aren't there? You've kept Janice safe for years. You've done the right thing, bringing her to me. Please don't worry."

Owen Wolf Shaw. . . . Greer had spoken his name as if it held special significance. Leona evidently had been startled by his family name when she'd first heard it. What was the connection?

Janice gripped Owen's hand. "Don't worry about me, Owen. I know what to do. Please don't let anything happen to you or to Greer's firstborn."

Firstborn had been an unusual choice of words for Janice. The women seemed to be already sharing communication on a look-and-touch level that Owen didn't understand. "Because you're a man it's harder for you to communicate that way," Janice informed him quietly, as if reading his thoughts. "Women do it better . . . or at least the Aislings do. I'm in their circle now, Owen. I'm safe. Don't feel bad, please. It's just *different* with them."

Ragnar spoke up again. "Women are different. . . . Contrary."

Greer frowned at Ragnar, but his tough, lined face seemed to ease. His steel-colored eyes held humor as he looked at Owen. Apparently, Greer didn't appreciate Ragnar's presence. However, the older man seemed to enjoy her unease. Owen liked Ragnar immediately; he knew he could trust him.

Since meeting Greer, Janice seemed stronger, brighter, more confident. Owen studied the two women, with Ragnar towering over them. There was the usual small talk and Owen noted Janice's speech pattern had changed. Instead of her earlier stilted, formal style, Janice's speech had softened to a modern flow.

His sister had changed instantly, responding to these strangers with a natural warmth that surprised Owen. As Leona had asked, Janice wore none of her own clothes. She took nothing with her, but her braids and the tote from Timeless. In the feminine blouse and jeans that Leona had given her, his sister looked nothing like the troubled girl-woman she'd been.

On his return trip hours later, Owen shifted restlessly in his airline seat. Being in the enclosed quarters of the place ignited his worries about the danger surrounding the Aisling-Bartels and his sister. When Greer's eyes had locked with his, he'd understood immediately that she was terrified for Leona. He opened a large envelope she'd given him and pulled out a photograph of a Viking brooch that matched the Aislings' replica, and Greer's handwritten note: *Your sister is safe. Take care of my daughter. I love her very much. Greer.*

Owen closed his eyes and leaned back into his seat. He rubbed his cheek where Janice had kissed him, a completely new gesture. As a child, she'd kissed him. But this time her affection wasn't impulsive or quick. Her kiss had been intended to comfort, one adult to another, and it had caught him by surprise. A show of affection hadn't been the Shaws' family trait, and for a heartbeat, Owen hadn't known how to respond. Stunned, he'd stood stiffly between the two women, then Greer's hand had touched his arm. Her eyes had said she understood.

Tears weren't something anyone in the Shaw family shed easily, especially the men, but today they had burned in Owen's eyes. Janice's brilliant smile and laughter at the airport had startled him. She'd seemed as if she'd escaped an ugly cocoon, and was now a beautiful butterfly set free. For the first time, Owen had glimpsed the vibrant woman she should have been for all these years.

Owen would kill the bastard who had taken those years away from Janice.

Remembering how Greer had known his middle name, he took from his pocket the replica brooch Janice had asked him to return to Leona, studying the wolf's head. Then he compared this replica Tempest had created to the glossy photograph of the original, noticing the Viking alphabet, what Janice had called "old writing."

As he traced the wolf's head on the replica brooch with his thumb, he wondered why it seemed familiar. Then he realized that it was probably because as a boy, he'd seen several wolves in the mountains. However, if his family name, Wolf, had anything to do with the Aislings, he intended to find out. And he intended to protect Leona.

Leona hadn't answered his question about the color of his eyes. What difference did it make to her if they were blue, brown, or gray?

As he watched the mountains of clouds outside his flight's window seat, he suddenly longed for Leona. As soon as his plane landed for the connection in Denver, he hurried to call her. He had hours until his next flight but needed to hear her voice.

"Timeless Vintage. Leona speaking." Her voice was cool, crisp, and perfect. He intended to hear a different, sensual sound in a few hours—while they were making love.

"I'll see you tonight."

"Oh? And who would this be?"

Owen settled in to enjoy the flirtation. He smiled at himself, a man who rarely wasted time on unnecessary calls. Apparently, Leona was necessary. "What are you doing?"

"Steaming down a shipment of blouses."

"Mm. Sounds like fun."

"You have no idea what I mean, do you? You probably haven't ironed or steamed anything in your lifetime, buddy."

"Oh, I think I've steamed a little in my time, just last night as a matter of fact. I'm hoping for the same thing tonight," he returned, and smiled at Leona's slight gasp. The reference to their lovemaking had obviously startled her.

Neither one of them were leisurely, relaxed, playful

people, and Owen was surprised at how much he enjoyed teasing Leona. "I'm busy, Owen," she returned huskily.

"See you tonight."

He waited until she replied curtly, "Fine."

Leona's "Fine" wasn't exactly a lover's gushing welcome. But hey, she hadn't said no. He spotted a florist shop and whistled as he walked toward it.

On his connecting flight to Lexington, Owen glanced at the bouquet on the empty seat beside him. The flowers were worth the effort to pass the security check. The calla lilies reminded him of Leona's creamy breasts, the rosebuds of—Owen took a deep breath and settled more comfortably in his seat, his body hardened.

Owen picked up the bouquet and nuzzled the blooms. He found the female flight attendant smiling softly down at him. He was almost positive that no Shaw male had ever looked gooey over a florist's bouquet. Embarrassed, Owen quickly placed the bouquet aside and picked up a magazine. As she passed again, the flight attendant patted his shoulder. "Your girlfriend will love them."

Owen stared blankly at the travel magazine in his hands. *A girlfriend*. That's what he had, a real girlfriend, for the first time in his life.

Seven hours after he'd talked to Leona, Owen hurriedly checked on Moon Shadow and Willow; he glanced at the dark house and headed for the barn. Opening the side door, he stood in the entryway, a flashlight in his hand. He had to secure that revolver where no one else could find it. Then tonight and tomorrow, he could relax with Leona.

Owen smiled at himself. He hadn't considered himself to be a relaxed sort of guy, playing house on a Sunday afternoon.

He realized he was grinning again and hurried to finish his task. He didn't want anyone else getting that revolver, not with trouble afoot. Clicking on the overhead light, he went straight to the wooden ladder leading up to the loft. He moved up the worn boards serving as rungs. Suddenly a board creaked beneath his weight and broke. He grabbed the edge of the loft above him and worked his way over the top.

Owen gauged the fall he could have taken. It was enough to have broken a few bones, or maybe his neck. The ladder was old, and he should have already replaced it.

After easing aside that concealing bale of hay, Owen lifted the rough wooden planking where he had hidden the handgun. His father's revolver wasn't there.

Who had it now? The carpenter was the only other person with a key to the barn. Owen had already cautioned him about locking the door.

Owen skimmed the shadows with his flashlight beam, searching . . . Then a fresh nick in the barn's old wood caught his eye. He went to the board, noted the splintering where nails had been, as if something had been pulled free.

He put his back to the wall, bent his knees a little to place his head level with the freshly disturbed wood, and looked around the loft.

From that angle, the place where Owen had hidden the revolver could plainly be seen.

Owen straightened suddenly. Someone was playing a very ugly game.

Since they'd moved, several people had been on the place: deliverymen, the carpenter, Vernon O'Malley, and the veterinarian. Robyn had lived with them, though she still kept an apartment in town.

Owen frowned as he remembered how desperately Robyn White had wanted to go with Janice. Robyn

had been unusually upset and persistent, almost clinging to Janice last night. Before she left, Robyn had
whispered furiously to Janice. Later, his sister had
found the revolver. Had Robyn known where he'd hidden the handgun?

Owen walked to the edge of the loft, tracing the
shadows with his flashlight beam. The standing saw
and the handyman's toolbox were in the same place.

After carefully making his way down, Owen picked
up the broken board and noted the too-even saw marks
halfway through the center. As he thought about the
trauma last night, Owen rhythmically slapped that
piece against his thigh. He'd been up in the loft just last
night, and the board had held his weight. Someone had
damaged that board while he was away.

If anything happened to Leona . . . Owen hurried
out into the moonlight, glanced at the fog layering the
pond, and knew he had to get to Leona—fast.

After a long hard day, Leona stripped off her clothes,
pulled on a T-shirt, and settled onto her living room's
yoga mat. Owen's message on her machine had said he
had a few tasks to do before coming to her house, but
he would hurry. He'd said that Janice had responded
warmly to Greer, but his tone had seemed distracted.
He was probably very tired after last night's episode,
and the early-morning and return flights in one day.

At ten o'clock at night, Leona was determined to find
her inner calm. She took the lotus position, folding her
bare legs; she rested her forearms on them and formed
circles with her fingers. With the melodic strands of her
meditation music in her sound system, Leona focused
on tension relief.

The prickle up her neck said Tempest was calling.
With a resigned sigh, Leona picked up the telephone.
Lying on her back she did leg lifts while talking to her

sister. Tempest wasted no time in getting to the point. "I've just talked to Mom. You didn't say anything about Owen Wolf Shaw having gray eyes. You deliberately skipped that part, didn't you?"

Leona sighed again and turned off her meditation music. Tempest's accusatory tone said she was just getting warmed up, and Leona would definitely need the music later. "Maybe."

"No 'maybe' about it. Owen Shaw is just like Neil and Marcus. He's a 'Protector,' the same as Claire's husband, Neil . . . and mine. Owen's very protective of his sister, and you've bonded with him. You know it, and so do we. Owen could be descended from one of Thorgood's men. . . . You know: Thorgood, the Wolf, Men of the Wolf, Aisling's protectors, sworn to protect, and all that stuff Mom and you have seen in your visions. You could have said something about this 'Wolf' business. But oh, no, you blocked me, didn't you? You're getting stronger, and you know it. That's not fair, Leona Fiona."

Leona settled into the gentle, rhythmic hum underlying Tempest's frustration. Sensations had flown between the triplets since birth, but this vibration emanating from Tempest was very new and different.

Leona caught one soft, pastel thread. She separated it from the rest and traced it down to a quivering tiny egg, already fertilized. In her mind, an image of a tiny girl, her hair blazing red in the sun, leaping from rock to rock, suddenly turned. She stared at Leona with those green Aisling eyes. *Tempest was pregnant and didn't know it yet.*

"Don't play with me, Leona Fiona," Tempest ordered unevenly. "You're feeling around inside me, aren't you? Stop it."

Leona smiled and stretched on her yoga mat. Images of red-haired tomboys, scrambling over rocks and grinning, danced around her; Tempest would be a mother in nine months. Leona would be an aunt spoiling every one of her nieces and nephews. "Tempest Best, I wouldn't do a thing like that."

"The hell you wouldn't. What are you so damn happy about? Here you are, in danger from some creep, and you sound like you're grinning. What's up?"

"Um . . . nothing. Talked to Claire recently?"

"Minutes ago. She sounded funny, like she had some sort of a happy polka-dot secret, too. They seem to bubble out of her when she's happy."

"Oh, it's probably just a little something she has going on with Neil," Leona said lightly. As an empath, Claire would have already sensed that Tempest had just become pregnant.

"We've got to get this guy. I'm coming to help. I can take off my gloves and feel around and see if—"

Leona stopped smiling and sat up. She couldn't endanger Tempest. "The hell you are. You stay exactly where you are. I've got this under control."

"Oh, no, you don't," Tempest singsonged. "And the only way that I'm staying out of this is if you admit what everyone knows now. Owen Shaw is your Protector. I have Marcus, Claire has Neil, and now you've got Owen. You've already bonded with him. We can feel it. You're all feline and sensual now, practically purring when his name is mentioned. So the sex must have been real good. You're excited now and waiting for him, aren't you? Bet you nail him on the doorstep. Don't embarrass your neighbors, will you? That seems like a nice neighborhood, kids and all."

There were limits to what a three-minute-younger sister should know. "Stay out of this, Tempest."

Leona frowned at Tempest's burst of laughter. "Got you."

"I don't want to talk about it."

Unlike Claire, who was very sensitive to personal privacy, Tempest immediately challenged her. "Oh. So you can feel around inside me, block me, and I can't point out to you that this Owen-guy is different?"

"Lay off."

"Sure. Can't wait to see him, can you? Is your little heart pitter-pattering, just waiting until you see Owen again?"

"Good night, Tempest."

Leona hung up the phone. She studied the picture of the Aisling triplets, all wearing pink T-shirts and grins and holding cakes with seven candles on them. Tempest's pregnancy put an even-more-urgent light on catching the beast stalking their family. She folded her arms around her knees and looked at the picture of her mother, snuggled to Daniel Bartel.

Leona had loved Joel just as deeply. She'd been devastated by his death. Now she was uneasy about the emotions that Owen raised in her. What if something happened to him because of the curse? Every trauma in a psychic's life rebounded and rippled and affected those around them. She should have stopped Joel from going to Colorado; she should have stopped him from taking that snowmobile trip. She should have warned her sisters about the parapsychologists' coming to take them . . .

Leona focused on her mother's glowing expression in the photograph. Greer had lost the love of her life, too. But were they linked, Daniel Bartel's death and Joel's?

Leona always been uneasy about her father's death and what had caused his deadly accident. She concentrated on those images, sliding through her memories of a father who had died when the triplets were only four. Suddenly her father's face appeared; Leona closed her eyes and pressed her hands over them, sealing his image into her mind. She'd seen shards of him tumbling through her mind, but she could never truly put the pieces together.

Tonight, they slid into one picture—a small boy, maybe eight years old, with black compelling eyes, stared back at her. The picture began to move, slowly sliding into other images. The boy was holding someone else's hand—an adult's. . . .

Unable to stop, Leona let herself circle the images as if caught in a gray, glittering whirlpool. She caught a single red thread and held it. She let it draw her deeper into the funnel. . . .

Pain tore through her heart as she saw her father. Daniel Bartel looked down at the boy, and their stares locked. Daniel frowned slightly, but he didn't look away. The next image was of that same boy, crossing that highway in front of Daniel's car, then suddenly stopping. He stood and waited for the impact that never came, because Daniel had swerved, taking his life, instead of the boy's. . . . *It wasn't Dad's fault! That boy wasn't actually there! He'd put that image into Dad's mind!*

With a gasp, Leona mentally gripped the sides of the funnel she was looking though to the past. Working her mind back to reality, she forced herself out of the vision. Shaken, she stood, bracing both hands on her desk and trying to catch her breath. *That boy's features mirrored the adult's in Janice's sketch, the same face that had come prowling through Leona's nightmares.*

Chilled, Leona wrapped her arms around herself. Did her mother know that Daniel had been deliberately imprinted with an image that would replay at a certain place on the highway, just as he was hurrying home?

Greer knew that face—she'd dreamed of it—the adult in the sketch. But did she know that the boy was instrumental in Daniel's death?

"I've got to get control . . . Stop . . . think . . . focus,"

Leona whispered. She turned up her meditation music and lay back down on her mat. Shaken by a journey she'd never taken before, her heart raced, and she tried to breathe slowly.

Stop . . . Think . . . Focus was the mantra her mother had taught the triplets, and now it sprang to Leona's mind.

How had she known to slide into the stream of Janice's mind, to follow the threads and latch on to that precious, clean warmth deep within the girl? How had she known to touch in a certain way, to soothe Janice's frayed psyche?

Was she, in fact, potentially the strongest of her family? Perhaps even a match for her mother?

Did her mother know that Daniel's death wasn't an accident?

Leona opened her eyes to Greer's and her sisters' photographs just as a shadow passed by her living-room window. "If that creep is prowling around my house, I'm going to catch him."

Easing out her back door, Leona opened the gate to her privacy fence and circled her house. Owen's truck was in her driveway and he stood on her front porch. Suddenly, he placed a box on the front porch and sprinted toward the end of the block.

At the corner, he leaped over a row of shrubs and disappeared into the night. A tall man and evidently a runner, Owen had crossed the area quickly.

Puzzled, Leona picked up the box, which contained a new laptop, the manila envelope, and mixed bouquet next to it. She nuzzled the mixed bouquet of calla lilies and miniature red roses, then sat on a wooden Cape-Cod-style lawn chair to wait. And waiting wasn't easy, not when she wanted to follow Owen. She smelled the bouquet, and whispered, "He can't just drop off something like this, then run into the bushes. I'll give Owen just one minute, then I'm going after him."

Leona suddenly realized that she would follow Owen anywhere. The thought shocked her, her heart racing. *She loved him. Not the gentle, tender kind alone, but with fierce layers of protection and need and excitement. . . . Owen was the other part of her. She'd been incomplete even in her marriage to Joel. Deep inside, she'd always known that a man like Owen would come one day, and now—*

Owen suddenly reappeared on the sidewalk, his light short-sleeve shirt catching the streetlight. He spoke briefly to the Donaldsons, a young couple who were taking their German shepherd, Max, out for a walk. Owen crouched down to pet Max and Leona held her breath; Max wasn't exactly a friendly dog. A "pound puppy," Max had been mistreated and could react unexpectedly. Apparently, Owen was the exception, because the dog moved away from his owners and sat beside Owen.

When Owen stood, Max's owners tugged on his leash, but the dog didn't move. Fred Donaldson's voice rose, the words indistinct, but the anger clear. He drew the leash taut, and Max barked, refusing to move. Owen crouched again and spoke to the dog. After a few moments, Max obediently returned to his owners, and the Donaldsons walked off into the night.

Owen stood and walked toward her home. As if alert to danger, he glanced warily at the night around him. As he came up her steps, he instantly found Leona sitting in the shadows. He reached for her, taking her to her feet. "Let's go inside."

"You're lucky Max didn't bite you. He's nipped Fred. The Donaldsons are thinking about returning him to the pound. I'll have to go around the back. Wait here."

"He just needs a little one-on-one, and a lot more space. He's confined all day in the house. He needs more running room in the backyard. In fact, he needs a lot of room to work off what happened to him." Owen's tone was grim as he took the laptop box. He looked at the crushed bouquet and grimaced. "I'll come with you."

Aware that he moved closely behind her, Leona turned to see Owen glancing out into the night again. "What's going on?"

His open hand on her back pushed gently. "You tell me. You circled the house rather than coming to the front door."

"I saw your shadow from the living-room window."

"And you couldn't wait for the doorbell? Don't you know what could happen if you don't ask who's at the door?"

Apparently, the downside of having a protector around was the darned superior male attitude that came with him. At her back patio, Leona turned to face him. "Wait a minute. I don't like being bossed around. You should have called. It's ten o'clock—"

"It's all about the attitude, isn't it? Lady, you've got one." Owen glanced at the moon, rather than at his wristwatch. His hand, riding low at her back, pushed her gently toward the door again. "It's closer to eleven. I stopped at an electronics store. I wanted a laptop to work on tomorrow just to get some things done before we relax. I thought we could each do some work—and then relax."

"That's the second time you've said relax." Leona caught an image of her naked and straddling Owen's darker body, and knew exactly the source of that image. Owen's body was already hard; her senses snagged something from his that concerned her breasts and calla lilies and rosebuds.

She studied him, and Owen looked slightly embarrassed. "Ah . . . relax, sleep in, have a late breakfast, whatever you want to do. I'm sorry I didn't have time to call before I came. Then I saw someone suspicious circling around in a black SUV when I pulled into your driveway. I thought I might be able to cut through the woods and catch him off guard, but I lost him. Let's get in the house."

"I'm inviting you in, am I?" *Of course, she was.* If someone out there in the night, the driver of that black SUV, had harmed Owen. . . . She shivered, wanting to wrap her arms around Owen and hold him tight and safe. Instead she entered the back door with Owen close behind her. In her utility room, Leona watched him lock the door and shoot the dead bolt. "Do you have any idea who that might be in the SUV?"

"If I did, I'd already have had a little discussion with him." Owen pushed his hand through his hair, glanced at the flowers, and grimaced. "Sorry about the flowers."

"They're lovely." Leona tried to smooth the poor crushed and bruised petals, the broken stems. She noted the Denver florist's label on the plastic and clutched the bouquet close to her. They were the most beautiful flowers she'd ever seen.

In the soft light of her utility room, Leona noted how tired Owen looked, lines deep around his mouth. She wanted to touch him, her need to comfort guiding her hands. But Owen had other things on his mind, placing the laptop box on her washing machine. The bouquet followed. Then he closed the utility-room door to the kitchen and agilely moved to stand on the dryer. Unscrewing the overhead light fixture, he studied it for a moment and then reattached it.

"What's going on, Owen?"

"Just checking for cameras, sound equipment. . . ." He jumped down, then scooped her into his arms. "Now for you."

As his lips fused to hers, igniting her senses, Leona's hands gripped his hair. The poise she'd planned when seeing Owen again flew away as the hunger for him enveloped her.

"I promised myself that this time would be different," he whispered roughly against her ear before gently biting it. His hands were already sliding beneath her T-shirt, stroking her body. She sighed as his hands cupped her breasts.

Leona turned her head quickly, found his lips and slid her tongue inside his mouth. She needed all of him, her body aching as she found him with her hand. He was hard and ready and—something else was in his jeans. She slid both hands into his pockets and withdrew several foil packages. When Leona looked at Owen, he seemed wary. "Had plans for these, did you?" she asked.

"Big plans."

"Mm. Everything is big about you." Leona unsnapped his jeans and eased the zipper down to hold him. "Did you miss me or not?"

Why had she asked that? Why was it so important to know that Owen needed her as much as she needed him? Why couldn't she just take what she wanted and forget the rest? *Because with Owen, "the rest" was important to her.*

"Dammit, Leona," Owen groaned as she slipped out of her pants and took him into her.

Inside her now, Owen trembled and paused, his eyes closing. "You just ruined my plans," he stated roughly.

Leona suddenly felt lighter, happier. "I did? It doesn't feel like it."

"Flowers . . . telling you how pretty you are. All that good stuff, before . . . ah, this . . ."

She cradled his face in her hands and nibbled at his lips. The exhilarating sensation of being pure female, desirable, and flirtatious couldn't be better. Add sensually playful into the mix, and she was truly enjoying this man. "Oh, that's so sweet."

Owen's nostrils flared, his expression tightened, those gray eyes slitted down at her. "Yeah, sweet. That's *not* how I'm feeling now."

"You hurried to see me, didn't you?" Leona studied Owen's expression, intrigued suddenly by this side of him she didn't know. Connected with him, she instantly understood everything: He'd hurried to her—because he'd wanted to see her, to hold her, to make love with her. It was sex and lovemaking and more. She knew now that she gave him a warmth and a home base he had not had before. Her senses tingled slightly with a happy glow of a woman whose man had come home to her—the age-old sense of a fulfillment wrapping warmly around her.

Known as a woman with "attitude" and as a self-reliant professional to some, Leona savored this moment. As she leaned her head on Owen's shoulder, her lashes fluttered against his throat. He held very still, but his fingers pressed into her bottom, easing her closer.

"I don't know what's going on with you, but I'm not complaining. Yes, I did hurry—but I had a few things . . ." He groaned and eased deeper, his body hot against hers. "Ah . . . do we have to talk about this now?"

Leona brought his face to hers and rubbed his nose with hers. He looked so distracted, so hot and hungry. But something else emanated from his energy; it was uncertain and shy, almost boyish. Leona welcomed that energy tidbit, cherishing it, a small gift too precious to ignore. She couldn't resist a flurry of tiny kisses across his hot cheeks. "You're embarrassed, Owen Wolf Shaw."

"Correction: If you don't stop playing around, I'm going to embarrass myself pretty soon," he stated grimly.

Leona smiled and moved her hands down to smooth his butt. Muscles contracted, sending a hard thrust into her. Owen watched her warily, his body trembling. "I thought we might shower together—later. Much later."

His body locked with hers, pulsing within her. The suggestion seemed at odds with their lovemaking. "That would be nice."

"I intended to clean up after the trip. But—It's okay, then, if we shower together?" he asked almost formally with just that little thrust to keep her simmering.

"How nice. You want to conserve water," Leona teased after she caught her breath. Strange, she thought distantly, even as her body moved into a rhythm to match Owen's. Strange, that he would ask if they could shower together. And somehow very nice.

"I can't play this game, if I don't know all the pieces . . . and there are a lot missing. Fill me in."

Owen leaned back against the kitchen counter. Placing Leona's brooch onto the counter beside her, he crossed his arms, his narrowed gray eyes pinning her.

It was six in the morning and they'd slept little. Sunlight from the kitchen window stroked his broad bare chest, that six-pack stomach. The sagging waistband of his jeans did little to settle Leona's simmering need of him. But she sensed Owen would wait all day for her answers. Sighing, she filled their glasses, her hand trembling on the pitcher of orange juice.

He glanced at the juice she had just spilled on the counter. "Why are you nervous around me?"

Leona took her time wiping away the spill. After making love to Owen several times during the night, she should be sated.

Uncomfortable with her own desire, and with having

a man occupy her space, her bathroom, and her life, she said, "You're very direct. I'm not used to that."

"Get used to it."

When Leona turned to Owen, prepared to tell him that he wasn't giving *her* orders, he brushed her damp hair away from her temple, his fingertip tracing her eyebrow before he crossed his arms again. "Your eyes are that gold color. You're mad."

Leona tightened the belt on her cream robe, and Owen's eyes immediately focused on her breasts. The reminder of his lips on her skin took away her breath. She lifted the drink to her lips and sipped slowly, watching him over the rim of the glass. "Stop that. You know what you're doing."

He watched her lick her lips. "So do you. Tell me about that brooch, *Firstborn*. Tell me what you dreamed last night and why you cried out, 'I'm sorry.' Sorry for what?"

Nine

"I'M SORRY FOR SO MANY THINGS." LEONA STARED AT THE large glossy photograph of the original Viking brooch that Owen had placed on her kitchen counter next to her replica.

In the filtered morning light from the windows, the fragments of her life seemed to churn around her. She traced the photograph with her fingertip. "When we were ten, I should have told my sisters that the parapsychologists were coming. The night before, I dreamed they would. I should have told Joel that I'd seen him crushed in my dreams. But I didn't want to be like—"

"Your mother, a psychic. Your grandmother, who drank and gradually went insane. I get that. But you couldn't have helped any of that, Leona."

"Maybe I could have. But I didn't. I'll regret it for the rest of my life. I'm sorry for not saving my sisters, my husband, and just maybe my father, Owen." Leona rubbed her cold hands. To avoid Owen's puzzled frown, she walked to the washer and collected the crushed bouquet. Leona ached for the bruised calla lilies, for the tiny rose petals that littered the floor.

In their hurry to make love, the bouquet had been forgotten. Now she hurried to place the wilted bouquet into an elegant crystal vase filled with water. The vase was tall and contemporary, and she traced the delicate flutes.

Her fingertip trailed across the kitchen counter to the photograph. "We're dealing with a psychic vampire, Owen . . . one who wants to destroy us. I saw—in my mind, I saw an eight-year-old boy fixating upon my father. The boy had help, implanting a scene into my father's mind that caused his accident."

Owen cursed softly. "Eight years old and that strong?"

"He had help from his father, I think."

Shaken by the facts she had just voiced, Leona moved into Owen's arms. Held safe against him, her head on his shoulder, she whispered, "I'm starting to spin out of control, and it's taking over, just like Grams."

"You won't let that happen." Owen stroked her hair and nuzzled her cheek. "Go on."

"At a certain point on the highway, Dad would have imagined he saw that boy run in front of his car. When I—saw him, the boy, he was holding someone's hand. If someone else with that same hatred and drive and ability held his hand, and joined forces with him—it's possible. If he's the Borg-descendant I think he is, he's been well tutored and has teethed on hatred. He's already proven he can direct others to do his dirty work."

Leona ignored the tears streaming down her cheeks and buried her face against Owen's throat. His pulse was strong and good against her skin; his hand smoothed her hair, calming her. She shuddered, unaccustomed to releasing her thoughts and her life to others, without that family connection. "He wants that brooch. He believes that killing our bloodline and possessing the brooch will give him everything—the world. He believes he will have Aisling's power, and she was very gifted."

"*He,* as in Janice's sketch," Owen repeated darkly. He leaned back against the counter with Leona in his arms. "Go on."

Within his arms, Leona sensed how powerful they could be together. "You terrify me."

"So what? You terrify me. What does the brooch's inscription mean?"

"The usual brag of a warrior: House of the Wolf, Thorgood the Great, whose mighty hand holds his people safe, who will kill those who defy him. His line will be long and powerful, reigning after him, for he who holds the wolf, holds the power."

Owen cursed softly, his lips against her forehead. "That doesn't sound like a curse."

"Borg's curse is like a blanket over the brooch, dark and flowing. It's so venomous that it burns. The brooch is at my mother's, and I've felt its burn with my own hands. The curse has been waiting for a very strong descendant. Apparently, with everything that is happening, there is one now. We're strong together, but if he can take one down, the rest will weaken and—"

"And that will do it," Owen finished grimly.

Leona pushed back and placed her hands over her face. She was becoming too strong, her psychic powers leaping out of control. "Sometimes, when I dream, I'm Aisling. I feel what she felt. I know how terrified she was for her people and how she offered herself instead. She *knew* that the chieftain—Thorgood—would love her and she loved him . . . she saw into their future. She also knew that Borg had psychic powers and that he was evil."

When she removed her hands from her face, Owen stared at the floor, his expression harsh. Leona pushed away from him, furious with herself for revealing so much. "You think I'm crazy, don't you?"

Owen caught her wrists. "Stop that."

Leona pulled her hands away and folded her arms

around her shaking body. "Don't you get it? I'm his last chance. This . . . descendant, this lowlife scum with a bloodline as old as ours *and* with strong psychic ability, tried first with Claire. When he couldn't get past Neil—because Neil caused Claire's energy to be stronger—this beast started in on Tempest. He was actually able to imprint his energy, to get a lock on her. When Tempest and Marcus fell in love, this jerk lost his chance with her. He's strong enough to use fog . . . mist . . . rain to connect with us. He can make us hear things, or think that we do."

"Hear things? Like Janice thinks she hears things? Someone telling her to kill herself?" Owen demanded fiercely.

Leona nodded slowly. "First, he makes a connection, like through a computer. He probably sounds very normal at first, sending out psychic hooks to find vulnerable and sensitive areas. After that, he plays his games, slowly sucking away resistance to him. Then he begins suggesting, placing his will over his victim's. Once connected, he can find ways to continue his control and awareness through his victim. It's like someone is whispering to you, calling your name."

The violence in Owen seemed to rock the room. "I swear I will kill him."

"He left enough residual energy on a bag he'd handled in Timeless to almost make Tempest faint. Claire was working on one when she was attacked. Tempest felt that one, too. It's the same evil. Janice also recognized the bag he'd touched. There were bags around, and other people had held them. But she picked up his energy. I felt his energy on her, that day in the shop."

"Bastard."

Owen's hands shot out to grip her upper arms. "And?" he demanded, as if all that information wasn't enough. "And what about you?"

"I'm starting to be all over the place, hop-skipping-zooming. I'm starting to pick up bits of threads, the sensations of other people, their emotions. One day a man came into my shop and I knew just what he was. I sensed him. But that man was blond and had blue eyes, not like the sketch. . . . Owen, he's strong enough to conceal himself by setting up some kind of psychic mask. It's apparently effective enough to block me. I guess he wanted me to know that he was circling me, to make me uneasy. Psychic ability doesn't fare well when the intuitive is uneasy. He took something from me, some small particle of my energy. I think that's why I heard him call me by the river. Since that day, my dreams have become stronger. Sometimes vision-flashes happen when I see glass or a mirror—especially when I see myself. My image is a trigger back to the original Aisling. She's been warning me—or I *think* so anyway."

Owen glanced at the hallway mirror Leona had covered with a red challis scarf. "So that's no decorator style."

"No. When I look into a mirror to put on my makeup, I've tried using a sheer cloth. It doesn't work. I still remind myself of the Aisling in my dreams." Leona held her breath, then served the last damning tidbit to him. "I think that's why my grandmother drank and why she killed herself. I think she had to escape someone of that bloodline."

Owen looked around to the living-room mirror, covered with a scarf. He glanced at the sheers at every window. "Why isn't your mother affected?"

"Simple. She's too strong. She studied and practiced. She's connected with the ocean somehow. She's stronger by it. Grams never wanted it, and she wasn't prepared when it opened and devoured her."

"I get the picture."

"The only way he can reach Mother is to make her vulnerable by taking one of us down." Leona shuddered and whispered, "Nothing can happen to my sisters."

"It won't. Why don't you fix us some breakfast?" Owen walked over to the mirror. He removed the scarf, then studied himself in it. He angled his jaw as if checking a morning shave he hadn't yet completed.

"Owen? Don't you have anything else to say—like I'm losing my mind?"

"You're not losing your mind." He sat at her desk and started pulling his new laptop out of the shipping box as if she were an ordinary woman talking about a frivolous laundry spot that wouldn't come out.

She'd just bared her deepest heart to Owen, and he seemed unconcerned. "Listen, I just told you something pretty horrifying, and you're—"

"Hungry." Owen opened his new laptop and angled the screen. He moved slowly, methodically, as if considering each move. Then he turned to Leona and leveled a cold angry stare at her. His tone rippled with violence, reminding Leona of Max's low warning growl. "On second thought, let's go for a walk, *right now*. Just put a raincoat over that robe. Just do it, Leona. No arguing for once."

Leona wasted no time. On her way to her doorway's closet, she collected the shirt Owen had discarded last night. She tossed it to him. "Let's go."

Owen didn't speak as they entered the low-lying mist, but his expression was grim. His hand remained on Leona's back as they walked down her porch steps and down the walkway. The morning air was fragrant with the scent of newly planted mums and sunlight had started to burn its way through the mist as they left her cul-de-sac. They walked along a block lined with two-story, well-tended homes, then Owen stopped.

"Where are we going?" she asked. Owen scanned the streets as if he were hunting. They began walking again. His hand stayed at her back, guiding her. "What's wrong? What are you looking for?"

"That black SUV . . . just making certain it wasn't around. Tell me exactly what you feel when you look into that mirror. Why you've hung a scarf over it."

"I just told you: I see images in glass, Owen. Sometimes in my shop's windows, my windows when they're not covered by sheers, and in mirrors. Okay, I admit it. I'm a clairvoyant, a precognitive, and probably more . . . like an empath. I see things . . . events, so it isn't just blurred premonitions. I feel things. I'm getting stronger. I'm trying not to develop, but I am whether I like it or not. Owen, as restless as I am, as upset, I could cause my sisters to be affected. Tempest is pregnant. I think it happened yesterday, and she doesn't know. I can't let anything happen to my sisters."

Owen didn't seem surprised. "Claire is pregnant, too."

Leona stared at him. "Not that I know of. Why would you think that?"

"It came to me," he stated warily.

Fascinated, Leona leaned closer. "When?"

Obviously uncertain of her reaction, Owen looked away and rolled his shoulder. "How would I know? Sometime when I was talking with your mother."

"You connected to my mother's energy?"

He seemed irritated and uncomfortable. "Don't get all snarly. I don't know what happened. It just did . . . What are you looking at?"

Leona held very still, terror racing through her. In the shadows that sunlight had not yet touched, mist swirled around their legs. It slid beneath Leona's raincoat and up her bare skin. She watched it slowly wrap around Owen, and, suddenly, Leona couldn't breathe. "Owen?"

Owen studied her face for a heartbeat, then glanced at the mist around them. He hurried her to a sunlit spot, then took her face in his hands, lifting it to the warmth of the sun. "Take it easy. I'm here, and nothing is going to happen to you."

"I can't . . . I can't breathe."

"You can. You will. Do it. Feel my hands? Connect with me, Leona. Do your thing. Get strong."

Leona closed her eyes. She focused on the hard, rough texture of Owen's hands. She followed the heated pulse she felt up through his arm. His pulse swerved, churned through a wilderness of fresh woodland scents, and came to rest on a particular strand of forgotten DNA. She glanced up to see Owen frowning. "What?"

"You come from Vikings. That's why you have those gray eyes."

"So? It's said that they came down from the Great Lakes. I suppose it's possible." As the sun warmed them, Owen glanced down the streets, first one way, then the other. As if assured that it was just an ordinary morning with someone's dog barking, and sunlight fingering through the street's shadows, he turned back to her. His tone was cautious as he asked, "Is it important?"

Viking blood, mixed with shaman, could be very strong. "Probably. Drop in the family name of 'Wolf,' add that to the brooch, and there could be a connection. I think you feel it, too. Do you? You do, don't you?"

"I wouldn't give too much weight to that family name. Feather, bird, hawk, eagle are all commonplace." Owen's dark skin gleamed tight across those high cheekbones; his straight, long black lashes gleamed almost blue-black. He seemed to be wading through his thoughts, placing facts in order. "This psychic vampire comes from an ancient bloodline—and you think *my* bloodline might be connected somehow."

"I'm thinking . . . and wondering why I'm standing out here on a chilly morning, wearing only my short robe under this raincoat."

"So we can talk privately. There's a surveillance camera attached to your living room's recessed lighting. It can get angled shots from that mirror. If you feel like you've been watched, you have been. There was a little flash at the ceiling. The reflection of the lens caught in my laptop screen. The hidden camera is motion-sensitive."

"Owen!"

"You think you're dealing with a psychic. You may be just dealing with a high-tech lunatic. Just who's been in your house? Who has access?"

"A handyman . . . Vernon O'Malley. He's also renovated the shop."

"O'Malley?" Owen's tone was too sharp. "Vernon O'Malley is your handyman?"

"Yes, is that a problem?" she asked.

"Probably not. But he's mine, too. He gets around a lot. Maybe I should have a talk with him."

"*We* should talk with him," Leona corrected and shuddered. "I don't like the idea of being spied on. I can't see him setting up electronic equipment, but he has had other workmen in my home. I feel so exposed."

"He's got a lot to answer for," Owen stated grimly.

From his dark expression, Leona knew that Owen wouldn't stop, danger or not, until he had every answer he wanted . . .

On their way to the Shaw farm, Owen collected his cup of black chai from the pickup's holder. After sipping it, he grimaced. "Sugar. They didn't ask at the drive-in coffee shop, and I didn't think to tell them. Southern sweet."

Owen glanced at Leona, who wasn't happy. "I still think we should have gone after Vernon first. Or to Timeless to see if there are cameras there," she said.

"I don't. If there are cameras at your shop, they can wait. It's probably ruined, but the longer my laptop is in the water, the less chance anything might be on it. I want to know if my laptop had anything that might be a connection to Janice. If this Borg-descendant guy can get others to obey him, we need to be very careful. We need to check everything and make certain that Vernon isn't being controlled by him. Or that he doesn't have a whole gang of friends sneaking around."

Seated between them on the bench seat, Max stared straight ahead. The German shepherd seemed to sense that he was heading for his new home, one with an understanding master and plenty of running room. The Donaldsons had been surprised, but relieved by Owen's offer to adopt Max. When Leona questioned his sudden decision, he'd explained that German shepherds were born protectors and that they could use a watchdog now.

Glancing at the sweet roll sitting untouched on Leona's lap, he asked, "Are you going to eat that? Or am I?"

Leona stared at him, her face too pale beneath that fringe of dark red hair; the morning sunlight sending fiery sparks through the strands. "How can you eat at a time like this? We've just discovered that my house is bugged. Do you realize that—that camera thingie probably saw me naked? And maybe you? And maybe both of us *together,* Owen Shaw?"

If he got his hands on whoever was terrifying Leona, Owen wasn't certain what he would do. "High-tech stuff is great, isn't it?" he asked darkly.

"Don't be funny. Returning to my house wasn't easy after our walk. Are you sure there's only the one in my living room?" Leona crossed her arms and settled in to brood.

"Pretty sure. Vernon, or whoever this guy is, put the cameras up high, so as to make certain nothing blocked his view. He didn't have to stand on anything either, so that means he's tall."

"Wait a minute. 'Cameras?' Where were the others?"

Owen finished the cinnamon roll and licked his fingers. He leaned slightly toward Leona as she brushed a crumb from his lip. He could get used to those soft pale hands touching him. "I found what might have been an ideal place for a camera in my barn. It was aimed right where I had hidden the revolver. I checked the rest of your house briefly when you took that shower. Don't worry. He wasn't interested in watching you cook or sleep or take a bath. But I didn't spot the camera in the living room until this morning."

Owen glanced at Leona's body and visually savored the curves he'd held and tasted throughout the night. "As a man, I find that really odd. I could tell you had a great body the minute I saw you. You look good in jeans and that gray sweatshirt and joggers, by the way."

"Thanks." Leona relaxed slightly and wrapped her arm around Max. "So then, you don't think he saw us this morning—or last night? What we did?"

Owen momentarily envied Max; Leona's soft breast rested against the dog. "I checked the guest room. It was clean . . . no sound equipment. He could have heard us, if that SUV has high-tech sound equipment in it. You really shouldn't have gotten up on your desk and sprayed the camera with paint. We might have been able to get fingerprints."

After their hurried walk, Leona had gone into action the moment they'd just stepped into her home. She'd moved too quickly for Owen to understand what she was doing.

"The paint matched the ceiling's. I was just touching up," Leona stated righteously.

Owen glanced at her and found those dark gold eyes staring back. Leona was real mad, the vibrations of her anger pounding at him in the pickup cab. "Sure." Then he asked, "If you sensed that the guy in the shop was a psychic, could you sense if Vernon was either this psychic vampire or one of his flunkies?"

"I—I don't know."

Owen sighed. "Okay. What aren't you telling me?"

"There's this thing called 'blocking.' It's like putting up a mental wall to prevent detection or intrusion. Sometimes there's just that little recognition tug with other people, and you just know they are intuitives. I've had customers who seemed to be a little gifted. I was able to work well around them by focusing on my sisters."

Owen stared at her, and remarked dryly, "Oh, boy. Learn something new every minute."

He turned back to the county road, glancing at the rock "fence" piled beside it, and the tobacco field leading up to an old weathered, black barn. Sunshine passed through the places between the boards and crossed into the shadows on the ground. "Strange that we have the same handyman and carpenter, isn't it? Who recommended Vernon to you?"

"Sue Ann, my friend—or former friend. Vernon helped her husband, Dean, do some remodeling." She looked at Owen "Do you think Sue Ann is involved?" she asked fiercely, her hand reaching to grip his.

Owen saw fear dancing in those earth-green eyes, and her voice was uneven. "Do you think he saw the pictures of my family? Do you think he heard anything about Tempest's or Claire's pregnancies?"

Turning his hand over and giving her a comforting squeeze, he said, "I don't know. High-tech sound equipment can be set up in a vehicle and catch quite a bit."

"Vernon is an old-fashioned workman. He can barely use his cell phone or an ATM. I can't see him managing high-tech equipment."

At this point, Owen wasn't certain of anything. "Let me get this straight: You triplets can't live by large bodies of water. But you think that the pond, the stream, and the river can create a large enough amount of natural water to act as some kind of a psychic portal?"

"A natural triangle. Very powerful." Leona nodded, speaking carefully as she watched a small herd of leggy thoroughbreds graze in the field's dew-damp grass, their coats gleaming in brownish red. "Fog and mist are water's natural extension and we were always more sensitive while in it. We were always stronger together, and Mother was—"

"She protected you." As if in agreement with Owen's statement, Max huffed twice.

"I suppose," Leona admitted reluctantly.

Owen bit into the sweet roll. "Get over it. You know she did her best."

"Maybe I *do* know it." She glanced at him "How can you eat at a time like this?"

"Easy. I'm hungry. By the way, what's the story on the guy with your mother, that watchdog?"

"Huh?" Leona's green eyes stared blankly at him, her lips parted slightly. "Who do you mean? What guy?"

"Kenneth Ragnar. He's got the look of a bodyguard. He was with Greer at the airport. Apparently, he's living with her."

Leona didn't waste a heartbeat. Reaching into her tote bag, she retrieved her cell phone. She stared at Owen as she waited. "Okay, Tempest. Marcus's father is on the coast, guarding our mother, and no one told me."

Owen smiled when he heard a bubble of laughter from Tempest.

She frowned at him. "Let me talk to Marcus. Yes, right now."

Leona explained quickly to Owen, "Kenneth Ragnar is Marcus Greystone's biological father and Tempest's father-in-law, that's who he is. And no one told me he was with my mother. He's not married, by the way."

"Maybe she's dating," Owen offered lightly, thoroughly enjoying Leona's steamy, frustrated look. "Just because you're the oldest, dear heart, doesn't mean that your mother needs your permission to date."

Leona glared at him. "Marcus? What's this about *your* father staying at *my* mother's place?"

Though Owen forced himself to watch the road, he couldn't stop his grin as a male roar of laughter erupted from Leona's cell. Clearly, Marcus wasn't upset by her tone. Leona breathed in deeply and held her breath as he spoke; Owen settled in to enjoy the fireworks.

"You mean that you *and* Neil got your pointy little heads together. . . . I know your father is tough and able. That's not the problem here. The both of you decided that *my* mother needed a protector? You think *she* needs one? You fixed her up, Marcus, and you know it. You just wait until I talk to Neil. Why wasn't I told? What? You think that—"

Leona glanced warily at Owen and lowered her voice. "Okay. Backup plans are good. I understand. Tempest already told you that Owen is sitting beside me, huh? She just felt her little way into this pickup cab and tapped into Owen sitting next to me. . . . Okay. Good-bye, and just don't keep any more stuff from me, or you'll pay, brother-in-law."

Leona's smile was almost evil as she added, "Huh? You're nauseated? Oh, that's too bad. It's probably just a little something you ate. Nothing to worry about."

She clicked her cell phone closed. "Men. Marcus is having morning sickness. Mr. CEO and running-my-life is already feeling the effect of his wife's pregnancy before either one of them know about the baby. I'll bet Tempest and Claire will be feeling full of energy and tiptop for the next nine months. Neil and Marcus won't be, the big babies."

"You're scaring me, honey."

"I've been fending off my brothers-in-law for months now. They mean well, but sometimes I feel like I'm being taken over. I'd say a little payback is due. . . . Oh, Owen, it is really a scary time." Sniffing delicately, Leona looked out the window at the overgrown brush and trees bordering the road. "At least your sister is in good hands. Kenneth Ragnar can be trusted. He won't let anything happen to her—or my mother."

Owen opened his hands on the steering wheel and gripped it again. The Aislings were very fond of the word "protector." Neil was apparently Claire's, and Marcus was Tempest's. Owen hoped that left him as Leona's protector. Owen Wolf Shaw, labeled "Protector" and permanently attached to one Leona Chablis. But then "Chablis" really belonged to another man . . . "Leona Shaw" made her all his. . . .

He blinked at the winding road ahead of him, stunned by the thought of a marriage to Leona. But, the picture the thought conjured was good. In fact, mighty appealing.

One brief, barely audible sniff caused Owen to glance at Leona. Tears rolled down her cheeks. Her bottom lip quivered, and she looked shattered. "My sisters are going to . . . to have babies."

Leona was crying. What to do . . . what to do? This wasn't just any woman, but Leona . . . His Leona.

"Oh, honey." Owen followed his instincts and quickly pulled off the road, cutting the engine. After putting Max back in the pickup's bed, he gathered Leona into his arms and held her as she cried. She seemed so fragile, and yet, she terrified him. What if he couldn't help her?

Owen struggled to find the right words to soothe her. "Babies are good things, right? Ragnar is protecting your mother and Janice. Your sisters have their husbands—"

Leona snuggled closer and sniffed. "Protectors. Neil and Marcus and Kenneth are all very protective."

Protectors. Owen struggled to find the correlation between the label and Leona's brothers-in-law and Kenneth. "You like them, don't you? What's the problem?"

"I *adore* them. They're all absolutely perfect."

" 'Adore,' " Owen repeated softly, as if feeling his way around a new territory. He smoothed Leona's back and rocked her against him. "Adore" was a very big word— that's what he did, *adore* Leona. Did Leona *adore* him? If so, how much? This relationship business was like moving through a mine field. Finally, he asked, "What's the problem then?"

Leona shivered and held him tighter. "I don't know. . . . Everything is changing. They're having babies—I'm going to be an aunt. . . . Don't say anything to them, just now. I'm not certain who knows what yet . . . They'll have girls, both of them . . . With Aisling's green eyes and red hair. Tempest's daughter is going to need constant watching. She'll be into everything, and—Oh, Owen, I'm going to be an aunt. How can I babysit when we can't live too close together and our thoughts mesh and—"

Owen watched a squirrel race up an oak tree. He tried to understand with everything else going on, the threats to her and her family, why Leona was crying about the coming babies. "I think . . . this will work out."

She lifted away to stare at him. "Do you really, Owen?"

"Uh-huh."

Of course he had no idea, but Leona was now smiling at him as if he were ten feet tall. "Thanks. I knew you'd say the right thing," she said.

With the canopy of the trees overhead, the old tobacco barn in the field, and racing thoroughbreds grazing nearby, the setting seemed just right for his next words.

"I guess that leaves you—and me, doesn't it? Just you *and* me?" he repeated for emphasis. Owen couldn't understand his woman—that's how he thought of Leona, as his girlfriend, his woman. Yet somehow, he'd just passed a test he didn't know about.

"Maybe," she answered lightly, as if they hadn't made love last night and the night before. Leona tilted his head between her hands and studied him.

Tightening his arms around her, he lifted her to his lap; he ignored her delighted grin as he dived in for a kiss to prove just what they were together.

"That was nice," Leona said as she cuddled closer to Owen, her head on his shoulder. The static silence around him caused her to look up at his face. "What's going on?"

Owen watched her closely as his open hands roamed the length of her body. "There's not much room in here. That steering wheel is only a couple of inches from your back, and I'm taking up the rest of the room."

As Leona eased her hand inside his shirt, Owen slowly, firmly gathered her against him as she drifted peacefully in the September sunshine. His silence palpitated now, those gray eyes watchful. When she lifted her head to brush her lips against his, his hand went to her bottom, rolling her even closer. "What are you doing, Owen?"

"Experimenting."

She lifted her eyebrows. "With me?"

"Uh-huh. You know, we've been doing it your way—nontraditional."

"You've been very kind not to press the issue. You can be very sweet, like just now."

"No one has ever called me 'sweet'." He looked at her. "You trust me, don't you?"

While she did, Leona couldn't admit everything at once. She'd only known Owen for six days, and he was still a mystery. "In some ways."

"When a woman trusts a man like this, it's instinct, isn't it? Or have you sensed something I don't know about?"

"Yes, in some ways, I trust you completely. What's this all about?"

Owen eased her back into the passenger seat. In a playful gesture he might have done to his sister, he reached over and wagged Leona's head back and forth. "Just something I've been considering."

"Did I pass?"

"I haven't tested it yet."

"Tell me," she demanded.

"You'll have to get it out of me—later."

Leona stared at him. "You like to make me wait, don't you?"

"Yep. Sometimes."

After Owen parked the pickup at the end of his graveled driveway, he got out and stood with his hands on his hips, scanning the rolling green hills, the fields surrounding the farm. When Leona came to stand beside him, he crouched to run his hand over the gravel on the driveway, picking up a long thin stick, broken in two places. "Someone's been here."

"Are you sure it's not deer? I saw them out in the field the other night."

Max started sniffing the ground and, with a bark, raced off in the direction of the pond.

Owen didn't answer, but indicated the gravel on the other side of the rough driveway. "That gravel has been turned, too. . . . The width runs across in a solid pattern that suits a tire, not a deer track. The gravel is pressed down, so the vehicle was heavy—like an SUV. He's probably been in the house. Stay here. I'll be right back."

He stood suddenly and began to stride toward the pond.

"I am not staying here," Leona muttered, and took off at a run after Owen. She grabbed the back of his belt and hung on.

Owen slowed slightly. "This isn't a good place for you."

"Or for you either. How do you expect to get that laptop without diving equipment?"

"The old-fashioned way. Diving buck-naked."

When Leona and Owen came to the knoll overlooking the pond, they stopped. Max was sitting and staring at the water.

Mist seemed to spiral upward, the pond warmer than the morning's chill. The usual ducks and geese were at one end.

But in the center of the pond, a body floated, facedown.

Ten

——

"ROBYN WHITE'S DEATH APPEARS TO BE AN ACCIDENTAL drowning—unofficially." The deputy coroner stood up from the Shaws' kitchen table.

Ray Fielding delivered his sentences in the chopped manner of an old television detective. Slightly balding and carrying too much weight around his midsection, Fielding stood ramrod straight, like a man with a military background.

He reached for the coffee Leona had made and took a last sip. "Thanks. Looks like Ms. White came down here to feed the geese. Somehow she got in the water and got tangled up in that old fishing line. We'll have to run tests, of course, but I'd say it happened sometime early this morning. Just for the record, you say you came out to check the horses last night, and she wasn't here?"

"Everything seemed okay. I didn't walk down to the pond . . . I just checked on the horses and left." Owen omitted his suspicions about the camera placed in his barn. He didn't want to bring up his father's missing revolver. He was certain who had it—the same man who had messed with Janice's mind in Montana and here in Kentucky. If he was the same man as Leona suspected, Owen wanted to personally settle that debt.

Leona took Owen's hand. "Owen stayed the night with me. I'll sign whatever legal statement you need."

She'd already moved in to protect Owen earlier, when he'd hesitated about stating his whereabouts last night. He suspected that Leona would have backed him up, no matter what he'd told the deputy coroner. It was a good feeling to have his woman behind him.

Owen glanced at the ambulance just pulling out of his driveway, lights flashing and siren blaring. He curled his hand around the cup of hot tea Leona had made for him, and absorbed the warmth. The sight of Robyn, tangled in that fishing line, lying facedown in the pond with a scarf floating out beside her, had chilled him more deeply than the cold water.

"Robyn liked to—*used* to like to feed those geese at sunrise. We've only been here over two weeks. We've been pretty well tied up with getting settled in and fixing up the house. I didn't know any line was in the pond, or I would have taken it out."

"Your horses watered down there. The mud was beat-up pretty bad. Did Ms. White ever feed them special treats?"

"Sometimes."

"Mm. When horses want something, they can nudge pretty hard. That big Percheron tried to nudge me before you put the horses in the barn. He might have gotten her in the water, but the line did the rest. She was so tangled in it that she couldn't move. You say that Ms. White had her own car, but it isn't here. We'll need to know who dropped her off and talk with them. We'll check around the apartment she kept in town . . . see if anyone can help us out. If you hear of anything that might help us give me a call. Here's my card."

The deputy coroner jotted a note and snapped his case closed. He looked at Leona who stood with Owen, her hand on his shoulder. "Too bad you decided to stay in town, Shaw. You might have saved her. We'll know more later and will be in touch. Better do something about that chill. You're shivering. You're lucky you didn't get tangled up in that line when you were hauling her in."

Fielding shook Owen's hand. "I have all the information I need for now." He turned to Leona. "Ms. Chablis, my wife loves your shop, but my credit card doesn't," he stated with a grin.

Leona shook his hand. "Tell Sylvia that I've got a sale coming up soon, and there are a lot of things in her size."

His grin widened. "Maybe I'll just skip that part. Ms. Chablis. . . . Shaw, I'll be in touch. Looks like you're doing lots of work here. My wife's folks used to talk about this place. The old Stillings woman, who owned it, was quite a character. She said she was related to Daniel Boone and that he fought some big hand-to-hand Indian fracas down there by the pond. Every time she told the story, the number of dead Indians increased."

"That happens." Owen's dark tone indicated he'd heard other magnified accounts.

Leona and Owen walked out to stand on the front porch with the coroner. Fielding glanced around Owen's property. "Shaw, there's been some car theft around this area. Usually high-priced stuff. I don't think you'll have to worry about your farm pickup, though. Or about break-ins like some of the wealthy homes hereabouts. But this place sat empty for a few years, and the real-estate agents said it had been used for parties. The mess made the agents mad as hell. . . . But just keep on the lookout for anything unusual, okay?"

"Sure."

Leona and Owen watched Fielding drive away.

"Do you think there's anything to that story about the pond and the spirits that Janice heard?" Owen asked quietly.

"Maybe. There are mediums for the dead. She could be one. But I doubt it."

"So do I."

Owen noted Leona's icy hand in his and the way her body trembled as she leaned against him. He put his arm around her; the sight would have been enough to make any woman faint, but Leona had been very calm, if strained.

The static silence from her now ricocheted around him. He glanced around the property and found no apparent danger. "Okay, what's going on?"

Her fingers dug into his hand. "Just get me inside."

Once inside the door, Leona turned to Owen. She held him tight, and her body quaked in his arms. Against his throat, she whispered unevenly, "Just hold me."

"Leona, we couldn't have saved Robyn. She was already dead when I pulled her out."

"When Robyn couldn't manage Janice anymore, manipulate her, he was done with her. From the way you said she acted before Janice left, Robyn was desperate. She knew if she failed, she had to kill herself. Isn't that what she said? 'You've killed me?' She was probably spying and telling him everything. That was my scarf around her throat. I'd put it over the mirror at my house, and it was missing. It's a signal to me. He's coming after me. If he gets to me, one way or the other, my whole family is at risk. . . ."

"Nothing is going to happen to you or your family." Owen held Leona tighter and buried his face in her hair.

It was a promise he'd keep, even if it meant his life.

"You are not going out there without me, Owen."

Early-afternoon sunlight danced on the pond, the

depths murky as Leona gripped Owen's arm. He was determined to retrieve his old laptop, to see if Janice had really thrown it into the water. Leona was just as determined not to let Owen be harmed. "You don't know what's in that pond—more line or old farm equipment, or—"

"I told you to stay in the house. How is this going to work if I can't trust you to do what I say?" Owen hefted the rake he intended to use and jammed the handle into the mud.

"Oh, I'm not leaving you alone out here."

"Then I'd better hurry." He scanned Leona's tense expression. "Are you okay? Feel anything out here?"

"No, but—"

Owen kicked off his worn, comfortable moccasins; he stripped off his shirt and tossed it to her. His jeans lay crumpled at her feet. In the next instant he was holding that rake and wading into the water.

He didn't seem to hear her threat, "If you aren't out of there by the time I count to twenty, I'm coming in."

When Owen's head slowly submerged and bubbles broke the surface, Leona held her breath. Chilled despite the warm September day, Leona wrapped her arms around herself. She scanned the woods, the stream running just beyond that barrier, then looked toward the river. The pond added the third side to the potentially deadly triangle. Just what had happened to Robyn? Could it happen to Owen?

"If ever I wanted to be a medium for the dead, it would be now."

The trees seemed to rustle with a light breeze. Everything inside Leona stilled and waited. Just maybe she could—"Robyn?" She called. "What happened? Who is he? *Where* is he?"

At her side, Max started to bark excitedly. "Be quiet, Max."

Leona settled inside herself and waited for what would come. Then she heard an eerie whisper. "*Leona . . .*"

The masculine whisper circled her. "*Leona, come to me. . . .*"

She watched the ripples in the pond and waited for Owen to surface. How long had it been? A few minutes? Or just a few heartbeats? If only she'd had a chance to talk with Robyn privately. "I'm not coming to you, now or ever," she challenged the voice. "This is where you held her, isn't it? Right in this triangle of water, where you're the strongest. Did you ever think that I might also be stronger in this triangle, strong enough to take you down, you bastard?"

Max started barking again, this time because Owen had suddenly surfaced. As he tossed his head, sunlight sparkled on the water as it spun away from him. Holding the laptop in one hand, he tossed the rake on to the shore with the other. "Got it."

Then he spotted Leona. "What are you doing? Get out of the water!"

Leona looked down at her joggers beneath the murky surface, the mud swirling around her calves, her jeans wet. Without knowing it, she had moved into the pond. The mud seemed to be pulling at her, sucking her deeper into the water.

Unable to move, Leona felt the band of Owen's arm cross her chest. As if outside her own body, she felt him lift and carry her to the lush bluegrass of the field. Once her feet touched the earth, Owen quickly scooped up his clothes. With them over his shoulder and the laptop and moccasins in one hand, he took Leona's hand with his other and began hurrying toward the house. At the front porch, he dropped his clothes, putting the laptop beside them, then standing to grip Leona's upper arms. He shook her gently. "Leona, come out of it."

The icy chill seemed to crack around her, the shards flying off into the brilliant sunlight and leaving her free. "I'm fine."

Tugging her close, he scanned the hillside. "This place isn't good for you."

Leona eased away, leaning over to scoop up Owen's clothing, holding it to her chest. She didn't want to leave any part of him unprotected now. "I felt him. Just here, just now."

"There's no one around, Leona."

"I heard him say my name."

"Janice, before she tried to kill herself, said something like that—that he'd whispered her name." Owen retrieved the laptop, his powerful hands gripping it tightly, his knuckles going bone white beneath the skin, as if he wanted to crush the throat of anyone who tried to harm his sister.

"Triggers. I think that's how he gets them to do something, when he's not in actual contact. As a boy, he set up an image in my father's mind. I'm just guessing but he could do the same with words and associations. He probably sets up a trigger word or phrase, something designed to create a specific action, like hypnotists might do. Anyone using that word could have set the affected person into doing what he wanted. In Montana, he may have primed Janice to walk into the water—just as she tried to do here—when she heard that specific word or phrase. I think that's how he got the others to commit suicide."

Leona glanced at the wet laptop in Owen's hands. "Owen, Janice may have been set up to kill you when she pulled that gun on you in the barn. Was Robyn alone with Janice at any time before that?"

Owen nodded. "I had a lot to do, the night before the flight. Robyn didn't make it easy—she argued every bit of the way, even wanted to come with us. Then she wanted to say a private good-bye to Janice. So yes, I did leave her alone with Janice."

"Okay, then. That's why your sister acted as she were on automatic pilot. Janice actually was. We already know he likes games." Leona's expression hardened. "Seduction can work two ways, though. Sometimes the prey can turn into the predator."

"I don't like the sound of that." Owen frowned at her. "Don't tell me that you think you're going to take this guy on, Leona."

"Someone has to get him out in the open. He wants me. I want him. From now on, it's just which one of us is stronger. I think I can be. *Something taken, something given*. He's afraid. I felt it just now, a bit of fear that wasn't mine. Maybe now he knows that I saw him as a boy, and I know what he did. Owen, I think that he *knows* that I know about him, that he's a Borg-descendant. *That I know he killed my father*."

Owen shook his head and stared out at the bluegrass fields. The horses grazed peacefully, and the geese and ducks floated on that pond. The scene was at odds with the violence within him. *Janice could have been primed to kill him and probably herself.* "That's a lot of knowing. Are you sure you're not just jumping to conclusions or are you really sensing something?"

"A lot of it is guesswork. Sometimes it pays off. But I did get fear from his energy just now. I must have taken some of his energy at my shop that day. I didn't know I had. Sometimes energy can be captured in little pockets, forgotten, then released at odd times. But I know more about him now. He's not going to like someone else uncovering his dirty secrets."

The hair on Owen's nape lifted. The line of thought Leona was following now could get her killed; *she* was scaring him. "No, he's not going to like you playing in his sandbox. I don't like any of this. It's dangerous for you. Just as dangerous as it was for Janice. No wonder there wasn't any surveillance equipment in my house. He didn't need it. He probably had Robyn doing his dirty work for him. She was probably working on Janice the whole time." As Owen thought back to the hours he'd left Janice with Robyn, he was horrified. "*Every time I left them alone, she could have been working on Janice.*"

"Owen, don't be so hard on yourself. I need you to think clearly. Exactly how did you hire Robyn?"

"We needed a nurse and a light housekeeper for the odd hours when I couldn't be home, someone with flexible hours. When we were still in Montana, I placed an ad in the newspapers here. It was—it was at Janice's suggestion. I thought it was a good idea. We'd had a mix of different people helping us through the years, mostly family, or people we'd known or who had been recommended through someone we knew. We didn't know anyone here. Robyn answered the ad . . . I interviewed her over the phone. She seemed perfect, and qualified. Robyn said she had to e-mail her family frequently—some family illness was going on. She promised to keep her laptop from Janice, to keep it locked in her car. To my knowledge, Robyn always did. Now I question that."

He placed the laptop on the porch as if he couldn't bear to touch it. With his hands on his hips, Owen stared back at the pond.

Leona quickly gripped his arm. Owen had already shown signs of extrasensory perception, and he had the bloodline to do many illogical things. If he was feeling drawn to that pond, too, Leona would fight him every step. "Owen? Owen, do you feel anything about that pond? Are you—?"

"Hell, no. But I know I'd like to drown that bastard in that water."

Relieved, Leona handed Owen's clothes to him. "We could call the police and tell them about the camera at my house. Maybe they could get fingerprints or track down the buyer of that equipment."

"The camera you spray-painted?" Owen slid on his jeans and moccasins, then shrugged on his shirt. Leona stood close and buttoned it for him. Smoothing the fabric over his chest, she felt the solid beat of his heart and relaxed slightly. There was no question in her mind that if Owen had not emerged from that pond, she would have gone in after him. "What do you think, Owen? Should we call the police?"

"That might be the right and logical thing to do. We could tell them about Vernon having access to our lives and about Sue Ann. We *could* do a lot of things. But we don't know how far this ripples out, do we? And we're not dealing with someone who is normal, are we?"

"You mean, an investigation could lead to another probing of my family? That I'll be accused of not being normal and told that my hazy dreams are the visions of someone going insane, like my grandmother?"

Owen framed her face with his hands and looked down into her eyes. "If you're going insane, then I am, too. I believe everything you've told me. But police investigations deal with reality. We're not in the real-zone now."

"We should go talk to Vernon. He's a link in all of this somehow. And Owen? Do you think it's possible that Vernon *is*—"

"Let's just hold off until we have more information. This bastard gets scared, and he could go underground. You said it was a big blond in your shop, someone worldly-looking. Vernon is definitely pure country-bred. I checked him out. He grew up here."

Leona smoothed the shirt over his chest again and adjusted the collar. She loved touching Owen, enjoying the feel of his heartbeat running strong and even and safe beneath her hands. Standing on tiptoe, she whispered against his lips, "I think we should find a way to get this creep out in the open, don't you?"

Owen watched Leona's expression as she leaned back again and smoothed his hair. While he loved the attention, his senses were humming uneasily. At the moment, he didn't quite trust Leona to keep herself out of harm's way.

"You really want to set yourself up as bait, don't you? No way."

"Um, Owen?"

He was suspicious of Leona's wide-eyed innocent look. "Huh?"

Leona glanced around the farm. "Unless someone drove her out here, her car would still be around, wouldn't it? Do you think there would be anything in it?"

"I'd like to know where her laptop is, and anything else she might have had at my house. I checked her room right away—before the coroner came—and it was cleaned out . . . too empty. There was always a clutter of cassette tapes the few times I talked to her from her room's doorway. I'd like to know what was on them, too." Owen bent his head to give Leona a quick kiss. "I know just where she might have parked. Stay here."

"Oh, no. You're not leaving me out of this one."

Owen and Leona walked to the opposite side of the pond from the house. An expert tracker with Max at his heels, Owen followed the trail of bent blades of bluegrass away from the pond. Behind a stand of brush, Robyn's new, compact white sedan sat facing the pond, mud-splattered, the tires stuck deeply in the moist earth with the driver's door open. The keys were still in the ignition.

"She must have hurried." Owen gauged the distance

to the pond. "She must have come in from that old farm road. She used to complain about the loud music coming from the kids' cars, as they drove by. Seems like she drove straight for that pond, but got stuck. If she'd tried it the other way, she would have had to drive through the board fences. That farm road was the easiest route."

Leona glanced around at the deadly triangle of the stream, pond, and river. "I can still feel him . . . or his psychic residue. I think he came to check on her—to see if she'd managed to kill herself. He might have been afraid that she'd live and expose him," she whispered unsteadily, her senses jumping.

Max faced the river. He growled, his hackles raised, all four legs braced defensively.

"If he's out there watching us, he probably came to gut the car. He'd want to clean out anything linking Robyn to him."

Leona looked at the stream of mist that seemed to float from the pond toward her. "Owen, hurry."

"Bastard," Owen muttered as he slid into the car. He turned on the ignition, and the car sputtered to life. "The engine was working. There's an opened box of crackers and duck food in here."

Killing the engine, Owen took the key and opened the trunk. With Leona close at his side, he rummaged through it. "Nothing here."

When he returned to the driver's seat, Owen took the tape from the sound system. He grabbed a shoe box of tapes and medications from the passenger seat, then handed them to Leona. "Take care of these."

"*Leona . . .*" The whisper circled her eerily. Leona's senses stilled as it continued softly, "*You know me, don't you? You know what I can do? You know that you are mine, and that you'll do what I say, don't you?*"

She scanned the brush and the trees, found no one

near. She tried to breathe, her lungs crushed inside her chest. The chilling mist had reached her; it began to rise up her body, and she managed to whisper, "Owen?"

Max growled and clamped his teeth onto Owen's jeans. The dog began to back up, trying to draw Owen from the car.

"Dammit. Stop it, Max. Leona, get him off me." Owen bent to reach for something on the passenger's floorboard. "Here's her laptop."

Leona wanted to cry out to warn him, but she couldn't. Then suddenly, Owen turned to her.

The mist began to trail into the car, curling around Owen's body. Terror clogged Leona's throat. She wanted to move, to scream for Owen, but she couldn't. She wanted to tell him that nothing could happen to him, that he was the other part of her soul and her heartbeat. She wanted to tell him she loved him. But the words lay trapped in her throat.

Owen suddenly sat up and turned to her. His expression was puzzled. "Leona? You just screamed? Why?"

Unable to speak, she looked down at the mist curling around her body. It seemed to be exploring her, sliding along her body almost sensually. Owen glanced at her, then at the mist filling the car, lying damp upon his skin. Cursing softly, he got out of the car and, gripping Leona's upper arm, hurried toward the house, almost dragging her with him. "I've got Robyn's laptop, her cassette player, and the tapes. Let's get the hell out of here."

When they reached the front porch, Leona pulled away to catch her breath. Her heart pounded from fear and from keeping up with Owen's fast pace. She turned to see if she had passed from one dimension to another, from the unreal to the real.

When she surveyed the farm, the day was bright and scented of the coming fall. In midafternoon, the horses grazed peacefully in the September sunshine, the blue-grass lush in the fields.

"Are you all right?" Owen asked as he held the house's front door for Leona.

Her mind on how Owen had *thought* she'd called to him, Leona watched Max walk into the house. She carefully replayed the scene by the pond. She was certain she'd said nothing; she'd been too terrified. Max's tail brushed Leona's leg and startled her. "I didn't scream, Owen. I couldn't move or speak."

"I heard you. You were terrified. You called out to me. You told me that—"

"No, I definitely couldn't say anything, but I was terrified—it knows you, Owen. It's gotten to know how you feel, who you are—through me. Psychic energy is transferable, like lint catching on those nearby, it can capture anyone emotionally attached."

Easing Leona inside the house, Owen firmly closed the door. He placed the laptops and the shoe box on the kitchen table. "Let's get back to the part where you didn't scream. Maybe you just didn't *think* you did."

"I would know, wouldn't I?" In the aftermath of her fear, Leona shivered and wrapped her arms around herself. She went to the kitchen window that overlooked the pond. The surface wasn't murky now, but golden in the sunlight; geese and ducks floated peacefully on top. "Do you think this is all in my mind?"

Owen's look narrowed as he studied her; the way his head tilted with a challenge, set her off. "You do, don't you?"

"Of course, it's in your mind—and your senses. You're a psychic, aren't you?" He rubbed the bridge of his nose. "Okay, I know something was going on out there. I know it because of how you react. . . . Your eyes just turned that gold shade. You're getting mad now, aren't you?"

He leaned back against the counter and watched as Leona ran water into the teakettle. She placed it on the stove, her movements jerky. Leona was obviously furious. Tearing open the cabinet, she grabbed two cups and placed them on the counter. "Yes, dammit, I'm mad . . . at myself. I got scared, and I let him have a little bit more of me, of my energy, and that's why I'm mad. Because I didn't focus. You were in that car. The mist was wrapping around you, and I lost it. Stop staring at me like that, as if you don't know what to think."

Owen shrugged and moved to the table. He stood as he sorted through the shoe box of tapes and medications. "I was just thinking of something else."

"Like?" This time Leona challenged him, her hands on her hips.

He studied the cassette tape in his hand. "I never heard music come out of Robyn's room. But then, she had earphones. . . ."

Owen thumbed through the tapes. Most were older, commercial and concerned self-improvement, balancing life, and building confidence. He glanced up at her. "I'd really like a good cup of loose tea. This bag stuff tastes awful. My laptop is shot, by the way."

The teakettle hissed, but Leona didn't care. She threw up her hands. "How can you think of tea at a time like this? There was a body in that pond this morning. All the information on your laptop is probably ruined, a gun is missing, and—"

"Take it easy. Nothing is ever gone. I'll download information from my investment accounts, and the rest is backed up online. It just takes time to reconstruct. I thought you were supposed to be calm and cool."

"Oh, I am. . . . Usually. You just smiled. . . . Why? There's no reason to smile now. We're in a bad, desperate, deadly situation here, Owen, and so are our families."

"Uh-huh. That's what it seems like. So you were

worried about me, huh? When I was in the car? What were you thinking? I mean, other than you were scared."

"I was just terrified, obviously. I heard him whisper my name. Rather, maybe he's just placed the idea in my mind—that I'd heard him whisper."

Owen looked at his fingers as they circled the cup's rim. He seemed to be deep in thought. "Uh-huh. Nothing else? You weren't thinking about anything else?"

Leona glanced at the muddy spots on her jeans, rubbing them as if she could erase what had happened. "I—I may have been thinking that Max could somehow sense what I could, an unseen danger. Maybe I was wondering how that all connects, the animal and the psychic. Is it important? What I was thinking?"

"Probably not. That's a good note on Max, though. We might be able to use him to track this maniac down."

Owen inserted a tape into the small cassette player. Immediately that low-pitched, soothing male voice Leona had heard at the pond began. The tone almost crooned, a mesmerizing softness. "You're mine now, aren't you, Janice? No one else but me is important to you. We've talked many times about how you ache for your parents, for your baby that never drew breath? You've told me all about how a man led you on. *I* would never hurt you. You can trust me, Janice. You are a part of me now. I can help you. Trust me. Everything will be fine, if you trust me."

Owen clicked off the tape. "Bastard. Robyn must have played these to Janice. She's lucky I didn't catch her."

He sat down at the table and started up Robyn's laptop. As he started searching its contents, Leona came to stand beside him. "Anything?"

"It's strange that there is absolutely no e-mail on this

machine. Robyn said she used it for contacting her family." Owen nodded toward the screen, filled with swirling blue-and-green designs. He moved through several screens of designs, some gentle and some violent, the colors harsh. Stick people seemed to float around the designs. "That's Janice's work, but different. She used to draw horses and real people. She was good at layouts. Then she started on these primitive designs—they looked like something off a cave wall, hunters, men and women, fertility . . . Sometimes she'd work all night on them. She couldn't rest until she finished them."

Leona had caught something of those drawings when she'd calmed Janice—*something given, something taken. . . .*

Owen reached down to pat Max, who had come to sit at his side. "She was caught in a living nightmare."

"He likes that—games, playing with people. Owen, these are very hypnotic. The swirls . . . they're almost like a path to the center. Look at that one. The swirl leads the stick figure down to—"

Owen leaned closer to the image. He traced the blue-green spiral down to a dark spot, then slammed his hand down on the table. "If that's not a path into the water, I don't know what is. I hope he enjoyed himself when she tried to drown herself. He should have had a real good laugh. The bastard has put her through hell." He frowned. "But why Janice? She has nothing to do with the curse on your family."

Suddenly he stopped and stared at Leona as if placing the pieces of a puzzle together. "Maybe he was preparing the bait—my sister. Just maybe he set this whole thing up. He's evidently scouted this place. If he's researched your family so closely, he might know about your being more susceptible near natural bodies of water—about the triangle where you'd be weak. Maybe you were the target. All this—the move here—could have been designed to get you. My sister was only a toy, bait to get to you somehow," he added bitterly.

Leona shivered; her mind had already been running along the same track. "I might not have saved her. And I might not have saved myself."

Owen got up abruptly and left the room. He returned with a thick dictionary of prescription drugs and his sister's half-empty pill bottles and those made out to Robyn. "Good thing we didn't pack Janice's pills—you said to leave everything here. At the time, I felt bad having to ask your mother to fill her prescriptions again on top of everything else, but now I'm glad I have these. He poured the tablets onto a sheet of paper and methodically compared them to the drug information in the book. "Just like I thought. These pills aren't the antidepressants Janice was prescribed. Most of these can cause anxiety if used wrong. Janice exhibited signs of that, just after Robyn moved in. She was probably giving them to my sister instead of her regular medicine." He shook his head in disbelief. "And I left her in Robyn's care."

"While Janice is staying with my mother, she may not need any prescriptions. Owen, you can't feel guilty about this."

He was already on his feet, stalking back and forth across the kitchen. "I'm all Janice has, and I didn't protect her."

Leona remembered how she couldn't protect her sisters in the Blair Institute for Parapsychology. "You can't blame yourself."

"You just blamed yourself again, didn't you?" he asked sharply.

Shaken that he had just captured her fleeting thought, Leona shook her head. "How did you know that?"

Owen rubbed his forehead. "I don't know. Maybe I just remember what you'd said earlier, about not protecting your sisters. I'm all worked up right now. I really think I could kill this guy pretty easily."

"Why don't you call the coroner instead and tell him about Robyn's car?"

"That makes sense. I think we'll replace her laptop there but keep the tapes and the drugs to ourselves for now." Owen drew her close as if needing to hold her. "Better call your sisters and mother now. They're probably worried."

Leona snuggled close, holding him tightly in her arms. It was a good feeling to be needed, a comfort to a strong man. "They are. I felt that, too, out there."

She looked up at him. "How did you know they are probably worried—just now?"

"It just came to me." Owen bent down to kiss her softly. His hands opened and smoothed her back, then moved down to caress her bottom. His touch wasn't sensual, just pleasant and affectionate. "Are you *sure* you can't remember what you were thinking beside the car . . . honey?"

Honey. Owen wasn't the kind of man to give endearments. He'd seemed to have chosen that one carefully. Alarms jingled all over Leona's body, and the hair on her nape lifted. "Just what I told you."

Owen's strange behavoir, his questions about what Leona had been thinking, seemed very unusual. They seemed out of place with such danger surrounding them.

But then, playing in a psychic field where anything could happen didn't leave much room for normal behavior.

"You're pouting, aren't you? What makes you think that I would close my shop—or let someone else run it—and leave Lexington, everything I have and built, because of this . . . monster? Of course, I won't, Owen."

In contrast to the traumatic day, cooking in the big farm kitchen that evening seemed almost too ordinary. She was hoping that her spaghetti and apple pie would take the edge off Owen's brooding silence. She could brood as well as anyone, but Owen's mood was stonier, darker, more savage. When he did speak, it was only to make his point that for her protection she should leave town. "I just need you somewhere safe until I can catch this creep."

She hadn't dealt with a man's dark moods, even in her marriage. Though Owen was worth the effort, he was definitely not as easygoing as Joel—especially when set to win an argument. Cooking the meal had given Leona space and time to think.

Calls to her family also took time. Clearly Tempest and Claire were worried, their husbands ready to swoop down and protect Leona. Greer was deeply concerned, but there were odd layers to Leona's mother now, as if she were blocking an intrusion into a very personal irritation—and uncertainty.

On the phone with her earlier, Leona had decided to ask the foremost question on her mind: "How's life with a man like Kenneth Ragnar around the house?"

The spiking in Leona's senses told her that Greer was surprised. Within one heartbeat, her mother regrouped and murmured smoothly, "That's a very nice probe, dear. You are definitely getting stronger. Don't forget to focus."

"Kenneth is one of them, isn't he? A Protector like Tempest's and Claire's husbands? Standing guard over their women, defending them?" Leona had teased. The thought that her mother could be irritated and uncertain, like any normal woman, was amusing. She hadn't thought of her mother as anything other than cool and collected, filled with logic and capability.

Greer was definitely in a snit. It was the first time in

Leona's memory, and it was over a man. "He is Marcus's father. They both come from Viking heritage, that's all. He's exhibiting signs of—never mind. It's just irritating."

Leona held very still, then set words to the warm flush and feminine fear she'd just received from Greer. "That's all? He's in pursuit, isn't he, Mom? And you're running, but—"

The sound of her mother's abruptly inhaled breath and the little spiking prickles of temper caused Leona to smile. "Gotcha, didn't I?"

"You could be very good, Leona. But in this case, please mind your own business. Kenneth seems to have taken over my home. He is a good influence on Janice, however. But he is always there—"

"Protecting?"

Greer sighed wearily. "Yes. Just give them all a shield and a sword, and they're ready. Marcus thought it would be a good idea. He likes to run things, as you well know. Everyone, including you, seem to be enjoying Kenneth's improvised stay at my house. Neil is in full support of Marcus's silly idea. He's usually so easygoing, but I couldn't sway him to intervene for me. Neil just went into that male lockdown stance. Overly protective sons-in-law are not easy things to accept."

"Maybe not *overly protective*. This beast means business."

When the call had ended, Leona's thoughts settled into circling the "beast." As a boy, Vernon or perhaps someone else, the big blond with the blue eyes, had likely caused her father to be killed and others, too, including Robyn. "Accidental death, my foot."

Meanwhile, Owen had been very careful to take Max around every foot of the house and acreage. He'd returned to settle down at the country-kitchen table. For a time, he was silent and impassive, and obviously deep in thought.

Then he'd begun to state his case that Leona should leave. His reasoning came in short bursts, an odd combination of harsh reality, practicality, and comfort. "Leona, this place is dangerous for you—the pond, water, river-triangle thing. The safest thing would be for you to visit your mother . . . until this guy is caught. And he will be. Nothing is going to happen to you or your family—or my sister."

"You don't have a chance without me, Owen. I'm what he wants. I'm the perfect bait. And this product, me—I, am *not* returnable. You are not shipping me off to my mother's. I'm not going anywhere," Leona stated. She wasn't leaving Owen to face any danger alone, especially since he'd told her about the missing handgun. "Not a consideration. Don't even think about it."

Owen scowled at her. "You are one damn stubborn woman."

Leona understood that Owen was upset on two levels. One, because she intended to face the monster who had stalked her family.

Number two was as yet uncertain, but seemed more personal.

One thing was certain. Owen's hungry appetite at dinner pleased her. Was she getting to be old-fashioned, domesticated, wanting to feed her man and take away his worries sort of woman?

"Good," he said, finishing his apple pie. "Thanks."

"You're welcome." She began clearing the table, and he stood to help her. She sensed that he had something else he needed to say. As if sensing the human tension, too, Max watched them from the corner where he lay on a rug.

Leona's hands were in the soapy dishwater when Owen suddenly said, "I loved a woman once."

Number two had just popped up in a big flashing danger sign. Leona finished washing the dish, rinsed it under running water, and handed it to him. As if dealing with his thoughts, Owen slowly, methodically dried the dish. Unaccustomed to handling intimate emotions, Owen seemed to need to come the whole distance to her.

He slowly dried another dish, and Leona's heart beat heavily. If Owen still loved the other woman, she could understand. At the same time, a sweet pain circled her.

That ache lightened miraculously when he said, "I loved her, but it's different with you. That's why nothing can happen to you."

Owen's expression darkened as he suddenly faced Leona. "He's getting closer Leona. He's been parking in the woods on the other side of that pond. He drove in from that old farm road. He hasn't been in the house, or Max would have picked up his scent. By his tracks, I figure he's over six feet by a few inches, maybe around two hundred pounds. And he's probably got my father's revolver. He's done some clearing to make way for a heavy vehicle. Judging by the size of the rocks, and wood he's moved, he's strong. From the prints, he carried the rocks and that means he likes to keep in shape and do things himself—like killing."

"But Owen, I didn't see his tracks or any tire tracks other than Robyn's."

Owen shook his head. "They were there. We were exposed . . . I saw no point in telling you. I followed his tracks, where he stopped. He was watching us and moved to get better views. He's a predator, an expert hunter, someone who enjoys stalking, and hiding and watching."

Leona wrapped her arms around her chilled body. "And I *felt* him."

"I don't think he's walking around in the open looking like the man in Janice's sketch. Chances are, he's in disguise. He could have been that man who came into your shop, the one you sensed was psychic. He knows how to change his appearance—maybe he's someone with a stage background. If this guy is Vernon, he's doing a damn fine job of disguising himself. We have to play this out very carefully." Owen's hands gripped her shoulders and pivoted her to him. "And you honestly think you can match this guy?"

"I didn't say I *wanted* to match him. But I want to catch him. I *have* to."

"Acting as bait is the dumbest thing I ever heard," Owen stated flatly.

"I thought we'd decided that he'd arranged this whole thing, setting up Janice to connect with me. She was the bait, then, Owen. I want to be the bait now. All I want is a chance at him."

"You're not getting it."

"Owen, don't tell me what I'm *not* going to do."

"Okay, I'll tell you what you *are* going to do. Pack up your things, close your shop, and wait this out with your mother."

Before she could react, Leona glimpsed Owen's determined expression. A heartbeat later, he pulled Leona into his arms, his lips hard and demanding upon hers.

Caught on the edge of her emotions, Leona didn't hesitate. She reacted immediately and threw herself into their hunger.

Rolf smiled into the darkness. "Leona got the message. She's afraid—I saw how she acted when Shaw was inside Robyn's car. Fear is good. I can feed on that. That damn dog. I had to use binoculars to keep out of his scent, and that put me too far away. But I'll get them both, Borg."

Far away from the farm, Rolf stood on another hill. Moonlight spread over the Shaw farm, and he focused his binoculars on Shaw's house. Near the farmhouse, the tall pole light revealed everything perfectly. The lights had just gone out, and fury rose in him. "The prey is staying the night. Isn't that sweet?"

He tapped his fingers on the steering wheel, rage building inside him. "I should kill them both now and put an end to it. I could make it look like—Now that's interesting," Rolf stated as he picked up his binoculars again.

Shaw's pickup had just raced out of the driveway.

Rolf swung the binoculars back to the farmhouse. Shaw stood on the lit front porch, his hands on his hips, his chest bare. "My, my. Trouble in paradise. Don't you just love it, Borg?"

Climbing back into his SUV, he eased it down the hill and onto the highway. If Leona returned to her home, he had work to do. Without Shaw around, she'd be more receptive, more fearful, and Rolf really liked his prey's fear.

He decided to give Leona time to settle into her home, then he would begin. . . .

Two hours later, Rolf cursed furiously as he drove away from Leona's home. "She brought that damn animal home with her. From the way he hit her windows, he could have ripped out my throat. I couldn't get close enough to play. I'm going to take care of that damn dog."

Okay, maybe that wasn't the best way to handle Leona. Owen admitted to himself the next morning as his hired cab pulled up to Leona's house. His truck sat in her driveway.

Max came running out to meet him. Then Leona's front door closed firmly. After last night's fiery, hurried lovemaking session at the farm, Leona had scrambled from his bed, dragging her clothes up in front of her.

Flushed and angry, her eyes had flashed at him. "Well, that didn't settle anything, did it? I want to go home. Now. Either take me, or I'm calling a cab."

At the time, Owen had thought her passionate response to him had settled quite a bit. "You're not leaving here until I have your promise that you'll leave Lexington."

By the time he'd finished speaking, Leona had dragged on her clothing—somewhat. Apparently, a really mad woman didn't need her underwear to move quickly. Then she had grabbed his truck keys on her way out of the bedroom. Before Owen could get on his jeans, Max had barked and the front door slammed. He had gone outside just in time to see his pickup's tires spinning up gravel. More gravel flew as the pickup raced down the winding driveway to the county road. In the lit pickup cab, Max had been beside Leona, and Owen had been alone.

He'd sat down to eat a large slice of apple pie and brood.

As he waded through the apples and cinnamon, he had compared the flaky crust with the different layers of Leona Chablis. The woman could cook.

This morning, as he stood looking at Leona's closed front door, Owen thought of other things she did well. Maybe he'd made a mistake by laying down the law as he'd heard his father do. But then, Owen's handling of emotional women, those he wanted to keep in his bed, had been minimal.

He began to walk up to the front door; when it opened, he hesitated and waited for Leona to appear. Instead, his pickup keys landed on the walkway bricks in front of him. A feminine hand placed his new laptop in front of the door. Then it closed again.

Owen had braced himself to apologize, to back up and rephrase his "dumbest thing" he'd ever heard. But

Leona's plan to use herself as bait didn't make any sense. "I'm right, aren't I, Max?" he asked the dog.

Max turned and walked back to the pickup, then sat and wagged his tail.

Owen took the hint. Maybe right now wasn't the best time to try to talk sense to his woman.

Besides, he had other things to do.

Eleven

"OWEN PROVIDED SOME HELPFUL INFORMATION, MOM. Unfortunately, that description could match any handyman's," Leona stated in her call to Greer.

On Monday morning, she prepared for her role as "bait." Since she had no idea where to hunt the monster stalking her family, she'd decided to open her shop and wait. If there were hidden cameras, she wanted the Borg-descendant to know that she wasn't afraid and would continue her life as usual.

Still, she took some precautions. At the first tingle signaling her mother's call, she'd turned up the radio, hoping the sound would override any high-tech sound equipment Owen hadn't found and removed.

"We think it's someone with theatrical or stage background . . . someone who knows high-tech stuff, who knows how to disguise himself, like a good special-effects man in Hollywood. They can do fantastic work, and you can't even recognize the movie stars. If that's true, then the big blue-eyed blond in my shop could be the same man as the one in the sketch. With more padding around his face and some makeup, those eyes wouldn't have stood out as much as in the sketch."

"Or in your dreams?" Greer questioned softly.

Leona caught the sounds of the ocean waves and the wind in the background. She ached for the safety of her family home. *Safe. Tempest and Claire had to be kept safe.*

Leona shivered as she thought about Greer's dreams and her own. *She'd made love with someone in her dreams, before Owen. If that monster had actually entered her body*... Leona forced herself back into the call with her mother.

Cradling her telephone between her shoulder and her neck, she dressed in her guest bedroom. The bed's sheets and coverlet looked as if they'd been kicked and pulled; the pillows were still rumpled where she'd held them against her. Last night, Max reluctantly leaped up on the bed at her coaxing. Lying along Leona's back, the dog had been a warm, heavy comfort, though a poor substitute for the man she really needed to hold her.

She bent to nuzzle the bouquet Owen had given her, the poor blooms crushed and wilted. The calla lilies were more brown than creamy. Rose petals had fallen away. She scooped a few of them up carefully in her hand and slid them into her slacks pocket.

The earlier image of Owen standing on her driveway caused Leona to ache. He'd looked down at the pickup keys as if uncertain of his next move. It was clear he hadn't slept much. Shadows ran beneath his eyes, the lines deeper on his face. Leona wished she could drop her pride and call him, but her emotions concerning Owen were still unsteady.

Last night, she'd entered her house with enough anger at herself and at Owen to rattle any extra energy tidbits lying around. Losing control wasn't something she liked to do. At his house, she'd devoured him, running across the finish line with him, when she would have preferred to enjoy the journey. They'd reacted to the aftermath of danger, clinging to one another as a reassurance that the other was safe and alive. Still, she resented her raw, sexual, demanding side, triggered by Owen's hunger.

With no basic foreplay or afterplay, Leona's body still hummed restlessly. But the last thing she needed was a male dominating her life, demanding that she leave her home.

"How's Janice doing?" she asked her mother now.

"She's worried about Owen, and you. Try not to be angry with him, Leona. Owen just wanted to reassure himself that you were alive, and you wanted the same. Words don't always suit."

Leona held her breath. She worked furiously to build a mental wall. She had to prevent her mother from entering her thoughts about making love so primitively with Owen. *It had been a celebration that they were both alive and in each other's arms . . . but Owen had also wanted her to obey him*. "I'd rather we didn't talk about this."

Greer spoke urgently, "You're getting stronger, and you're angry, sending sparks all over the place. That makes you vulnerable. Control it, before it controls you. . . . Focus, Leona. You did that last night when you came into the house. You focused on your senses, on how you felt. Trust yourself, Leona."

Focus, Leona . . . trust me, her mother had said as she'd fought to haul Claire and Leona back to the capsized sailboat. *You're strong. . . . I know you can do this. Do it for Tempest and for Claire, make yourself strong . . . focus, dear. Don't let Claire feel your fear. We'll do this together, get Claire and Tempest, all of us back to the boat.*

Despite the towering swells around them, Greer's compelling eyes had locked with three-year-old Leona's. But had her mother actually spoken? "Did you . . . did you actually talk to me when the boat capsized?

Did you think that something was out there in the water? Something using that psychic portal to harm us?"

Greer's silence said that she'd protected her daughters from any other psychic influence in those dangerous moments. She'd locked on to her daughters' gifts and cast a protective psychic net over them; she'd willed them to concentrate on her, on living. "I just knew that nothing could happen to my daughters."

All these years, Leona had never forgiven Greer for leaving the triplets alone while she'd made a necessary living. "I . . . thank you," Leona stated simply.

"You're upset now, but you can do this, Leona. Owen will understand. He's just terribly worried for you."

You can do this, Leona. How many times had her mother said the same when Leona had been a fiercely resentful, angry child, detesting the gift that had made her different?

Leona frowned at the wrinkles in her practical blue blouse and black slacks. "It's this house. Everything is all in turmoil. I had to dig through my clothes this morning, just to get something to wear. All my things are under that plastic in my bedroom."

"Ah. The handyman, Vernon. He's on your to-do list."

"Yes. He matches Owen's description. And so far as I know, he's the only one—other than Owen—who has been in my house. I take that back—Vernon had another man come in to help him with a stopped drain. . . . To think that guy actually could have seen me doing yoga exercises—disgusting. Do you know that was my scarf wrapped around Robyn's neck?"

"You're developing very quickly. . . ." Greer's voice changed suddenly, fear threading through it. "Do you feel anything unusual about Vernon?"

"When I hired him, I felt nothing at all about his psychic energy. He seemed like just a simple man, trying to make a living with odd jobs. . . . That was this spring, when Sue Ann—"

When Sue Ann had recommended Vernon. And now, Sue Ann had distanced herself from her.

"I have to go," Leona said before her mother could tap into her fears for Sue Ann. She suspected it was already too late.

"It was nice to hear your voice, dear," Greer stated softly. "And you're right about Robyn's involvement. As Janice's memory of this empties, she's having flashbacks. Robyn was definitely a link. She wanted Janice to listen to tapes, always when Owen wasn't around. Robyn let her use a computer then, too, and that's how that monster communicated with Janice. He's used a combination of subliminal suggestions, hypnotism, brainwashing by sleep deprivation, and his gift. He's played on her every vulnerability. He'd instilled key words and phrases in her that triggered her to react in certain ways. We're working with that now, deprogramming her. Janice is horrified at what she did now, but she's healing. She may not even need those prescriptions at this rate."

"You're probably working with Janice the same as you did with us—after we were taken." Tears burned Leona's eyes; it was time to forgive.

Greer's next words captured Leona's thoughts. "I know, Leona. I've always known that you love me. Just do what you have to."

"I will." After the call finished. Leona stood very still and closed her eyes. The sense of being watched was gone, replaced by the need to see Owen.

But not just yet, not until she was calmer.

He'd loved a woman. Did he still love her? Had he made love to her as passionately?

The dream Leona had in her restless night without Owen was almost a replay of their passion. But in her dream, she'd been Aisling, defying Thorgood's wishes. Aisling had gone out to seek Borg, to make him remove the curse from the brooch. In pursuit, Thorgood had reclaimed her, bearing her back to their bed. His lovemaking had been to prove his point, that he was bigger, stronger, and in command of her life and actions. In a rare loss of her control, Aisling's temper had ignited, challenging him. Thorgood had been stunned, because she was usually so calm and sensible. His demand that she leave her safety to him mirrored Owen's. In the aftermath of their passion, Aisling had banned him from their bed. Sulking, Thorgood had spent a cold, brooding night outside their room. But Aisling had missed him, too; she'd spent a long night hugging the fur pelt where his body had been.

"Just great, Aisling. Thanks for that tidbit. Men give orders and think we should obey. So the point is: Men will be men, right? High lords over us helpless little females?"

In Leona's mirror, her reflection seemed to smile. *We'll have to teach them manners, won't we? They're really worth it. They mean well and only want to protect us. It is their nature. But it is up to us to teach them. Do you agree?*

"Absolutely." Still nettled by Owen's orders to leave Lexington, Leona walked into the kitchen. She poured a glass of orange juice, and settled in to appreciate Tempest's latest gift. The small package had been in her mailbox on Saturday. Leona had been too angry with herself and with Owen to appreciate it fully. Now she opened the box and lifted the silver bracelet with the detachable, retangular runes. "Perfect. I'll call Tempest later to thank her."

In the next heartbeat, Leona rummaged through her kitchen shelves until she came to another box. She opened it and prowled through the Celtic-styled jewelry.

In her lifetime, she'd tried to avoid anything to do with her ancient heritage. "If I'm baiting this creep, I'd better dress the part."

While she loved Tempest's jewelry and appreciated her sister's artistry, Leona had worn little of any kind. Now she chose a wide silver cuff bracelet and a ring with swirling Celtic designs. She studied the jewelry on her wrist and fingers, then added the rune bracelet. This time, she didn't care if that high-tech equipment was picking up sound. "Okay, Mr. Vampire. This is what I am. Come and get me."

The tingle on her neck told her that Tempest was calling again. Leona quickly clicked on her kitchen television set before picking up the telephone. In a hushed tone, she said, "Someone could be listening. Owen thinks this creep uses high-tech sound equipment, so you're going to have to listen to the weather report while we're talking. Thank you for the lovely bracelet. If I were Aisling, I'm sure I would be detaching the runes and using them now. I've never wanted to do that, but—"

She had focused on each individual rune—upright, the character could be interpreted with one meaning. In reverse, the meaning changed. Viking seers had used the runes often, but Aisling had only relied on her gifts.

Leona's methodical mental separation of the runes, their design and interpretations, prevented Tempest from entering her emotions. Then Tempest suddenly exploded with her news. "I'm preggers! Picked it up from Claire last night. She's so easy to read. Marcus is—my gosh, you'd think he was the only guy with sperm. He's actually swaggering. He can't wait to tell everyone, but we're waiting for the usual timing. He's so traditional, you know. Imagine that, me—pregnant."

"I'm so glad for you." Leona smiled, and a crop of little red-haired, green-eyed girls running wildly about

Tempest and Marcus floated across her mind. She decided not to tell Tempest that Claire was also expecting. Polka dots could be so confusing, and they could have blended. Once off her excitement cloud, Tempest would probably realize on her own that some of the polka dots weren't hers.

"Yeah . . . kids . . . me and Marcus," Tempest murmured dreamily. "Scary, huh?"

"If they're like you, yes. Ah . . . Tempest? You've always blamed Dad's accident on yourself, the time you broke your arm and he was rushing home to see you?"

A jagged scarlet streak of pain cut through Tempest's happy glow. "My fault. I shouldn't have been—"

"Listen to me. Focus on me, Tempest Best," Leona ordered. With a new baby on the way, it was time to erase Tempest's guilt.

Tempest's silence and the energy coming from her said she had focused, the link strong. "You're getting very strong," she said breathlessly. "I'm reading you loud and clear."

"Open for me. Let me in."

"I'll try."

Leona waited until the plane between her and her sister started rippling. It slowly smoothed into a light, soothing blue-gray palette. Then she began a pinpoint of light, seizing on to it and waiting as it grew larger. She gently probed for the perfect spot, then pulsed slowly through it, opening the path to Tempest. If she was successful, Tempest would never again feel guilty about their father's "accidental" death. Leona slowly visualized that eight-year-old boy looking at Daniel Bartel, imprinting him with the image of that nonexistent boy running across in front of his car. . . .

The vision squeezed closed suddenly. Tempest's anger exploded as she yelled, "He did that? That monster? I'll kill him!"

"Not if I get to him first. He had help though. At that age, I don't think he could have done it himself. Someone, probably his father, stood beside him that day and joined with him. It was no accident that he came to stand beside Dad that day. Someone had to get that boy in that exact place. Someone studied Dad's routine and arranged the meeting."

"It wasn't my fault," Tempest repeated as if she were slowly erasing her years-long guilt.

Leona held her breath and tried to dim the violence within her, but it was too late. Tempest had snagged it. "You're playing with those runes and thinking about how you're going to call him out, aren't you? My gosh, you're standing there, wearing every bit of Celtic designs and all decked out to notify this guy—"

Leona frowned; *something given, something taken.* Tempest had grabbed her emotions. She moved in to distract her sister. "You create lovely jewelry. You're really talented."

"Don't change the subject." Tempest's fear zigzagged around Leona. "Don't you play with this bastard, Leona Fiona. If he could do that at eight, even with help, he's had years of practice now and—"

Leona couldn't prevent a bit of her violence from escaping. "And I think he killed Joel, too. Claire lost her baby five years ago, and that was when Joel died. That's too much of a coincidence. He was just playing around, getting warmed up, testing us."

Tempest cursed softly. "I'm coming to help."

"Sorry. You've got a baby on board, and you're out of this one, Tempest Best."

"Great," Tempest grumbled. "The big sister orders me yet again. You're off to fight the wizard all by yourself. This isn't any yellow-brick road, you know."

Leona smiled as she lifted her tote's straps to her

shoulder and prepared to leave her house. "Hey. Those three minutes count for a lot of seniority, and I do have ruby red heels."

A little while later, as Leona drove through Lexington's Monday morning traffic, she decided to call Owen. She needed to hear his voice, to explain that she was not only angry with him, but with herself.

Owen wasn't answering.

With Max waiting in the pickup, Owen made his way around to the back of Vernon O'Malley's house.

The handyman wasn't there, and Owen used a credit card to open the back door and get inside. If Vernon was tied up in Robyn's death and had anything to do with Leona's missing scarf around the nurse's throat, Owen wanted details.

From his initial interview with Vernon, Owen understood that the fiftyish handyman and carpenter had once had a steady job with benefits. "Cutbacks" in the hospital maintenance staff had left him without insurance; his wife's terminal disease had taken all of their savings. Vernon had been unable to secure anything but part-time work. After her death, he'd settled into the freelance home-repair business. That was quite profitable since the area's historic, elegant plantation-style homes needed constant servicing and updating.

On an old residential street, Vernon's tiny house was neat, but reeked of alcohol. Empty whiskey bottles and beer cans filled a trash can. Paperwork lay scattered across the kitchen table. A shoe box filled with medications made out to Lucille O'Malley sat next to a stack of bills. Some of the vials were empty; pills lay scattered on the table. A book of drug definitions lay opened to a page of heavy-duty painkillers. An assortment of over-the-counter medicines was stacked nearby.

Owen studied the pills and the prescriptions written on the vials; he remembered the pills in Robyn's and Janice's prescription bottles. They were a match.

Fingering through the stack of envelopes, he noted the bills and payments to hospitals and doctors. Vernon apparently had set up payment schedules, but he was now far overdue. A telephone disconnect notice lay beneath the other bills.

Owen picked up the telephone, but there was no dial tone. He went back to the table, collected a business card from a box of newly printed ones, and used his cell phone to dial that number. Vernon's usual recording came on. "I'm busy. Leave a message."

"Vernon, I need to get an estimate on central air-conditioning. I was wondering if you could recommend someone." Well established with other workmen, Vernon had recommended different services to Owen. The call was only an excuse to pinpoint the handyman's whereabouts. It hadn't worked.

As he left the house, Owen placed a small tape over the back screen door. If anyone visited this house, the tape would be disturbed.

As soon as he opened his pickup door, Max leaped out onto the ground, barking wildly.

"Max. Be quiet, boy."

At Owen's order, the dog stopped barking. His hackles raised, the dog's legs were spread defensively as he growled at the house. It was the same way he had growled in the direction of the Kentucky River.

Owen calmed Max and got him back into the pickup. "Well, from what you said, Max, old boy, whoever was at my house and by the pond and in the field, has something to do with Vernon. We need to find out just what, don't we?"

Max stared at the house and bared his teeth.

"I'll take that as a 'yes.'"

When his cell phone rang, Owen didn't glance at the caller's number. "Shaw here."

The silence at the end of the line seemed to pulse at him. He glanced at the caller's number, but it didn't matter. The handyman could be using any number, and Owen wasn't in the mood for games. "Vernon, we need to talk."

When the line clicked off, Owen instantly called back. No one answered. He wasn't happy when his cell rang again. He answered without looking at the number. "Don't hang up. I might be able to help you."

This time the silence was followed by Leona's droll, "Okay, if you say so. I do need you to help me, Owen. We've just got time before I open the shop."

Owen stared at Max, who stared back. "I got the impression you weren't exactly happy with me. Where are you?"

"At the shop. I'm going to open late this morning. Don't worry when you see the CLOSED FOR REPAIRS sign on the front door. Just knock on the back one. I'll be waiting."

Fear for Leona leaped into Owen; he started his pickup. The tires squealed as he reversed out of Vernon's driveway and headed toward Leona's shop. *If Vernon had hurt Leona . . .* "Vernon didn't turn up, did he? Are you okay?"

"I'm fine, but I want to talk with him. I've left messages on Vernon's machine and his cell, but he hasn't returned them."

"You called his home?"

"Uh-huh. Several times . . . just about fifteen minutes ago. It sounded like his regular message machine."

Owen's hands gripped the steering wheel until it creaked. *He'd been in Vernon's home fifteen minutes ago. That phone had been disconnected and that meant Vernon had set up camp somewhere else. . . .*

"So we're headed for Sue Ann's house?" Owen said to Leona as he maneuvered the pickup easily through Monday's early-morning traffic.

Leona hadn't said anything about last night, or this morning. Owen decided not to question his good luck at the moment.

"I need to know that she's safe. She's been a good friend for years. I know—I feel that she's terrified. I want to know why. She recommended Vernon, and he could be threatening her. If I find out that he is, I'm not certain what I'll do." She wrapped an arm around Max, who sat between them.

Owen glanced at her. "Take it easy. We can't blow this. There are too many lives at stake."

"I trusted Vernon. He was in my house. He's worked with Sue Ann's husband, Dean, a nice family guy. They have children who could be in danger. Naturally, I'm really afraid for all of them."

"That seems to be the picture. Have you checked with your *friend,* Alex, lately?" Okay, so Owen was a little upset about last night, too. And he was definitely nettled by Leona's attachment to another man.

Leona leveled a look at him. "Yes, Alex is my *friend,* Owen. And I do need to check with him. Robyn's death took most of yesterday. Then you and I discovered we have a little communication problem. I was a bit upset and didn't call him last night, or this morning. But I called the day before, as soon as you flew out with Janice. And I'd seen him the night before. He was bruised but okay."

"That's good. Let's just take this one step at a time. Things are starting to move really quick now. And I agree: We do have a communication problem."

"If you try to pull that commando technique again, things are going to fall apart really quickly between us."

Owen breathed deeply, aware that Leona hadn't cooled down all the way. He was confident he could make her understand that she needed to leave Lexington. After checking out the Celtic design of her jewelry—she usually only wore the brooch—he was certain she was garbed to be the bait. That meant she hadn't changed her mind. "Okay—honey. Anything you say."

There. He'd come up with something that sounded just fine. He'd have to develop another approach to make Leona see things his way. He'd handled tricky real-estate problems; he could handle her. *Or not.* For now, he'd go with the flow. *Women.*

Leona stared at Owen. He seemed pleased with himself, as if he had just passed a very private test. She decided not to question him just yet. Instead, she glanced down at the potted flowers on the floor between her feet. "These are so beautiful. You shouldn't have."

"I thought maybe . . . maybe I'd help you plant them later."

Her senses quivered slightly, and Leona turned to study him fully. Owen's look at her was guarded. "What?" he asked.

"Do these daisies have a special meaning for you?"

Sunlight stroked his stoic profile, those long lashes making shadows on his high cheekbones. The lines around his lips deepened. "Maybe."

Following her instinct to probe deeper, Leona closed her eyes and focused on the daisies, imprinting them over Owen's image. He'd helped his mother pick daisies once. As a boy, Owen had stood with his mother in Montana's fields of daisies. His harsh father had ridiculed him for "doing girl play," but it had been a precious moment in his life. The memory was private and tender, and Leona let it fly gently away from her grasp.

"My father was a harsh man. He was raised that way, laying down the law to my mother. He was wrong to treat her that way. I'm finding that out by my relationship with you." It wasn't an outright apology, but clearly Owen was considering an adjustment to the Shaw-male attitude.

He glanced at Leona, then down at the wolf's-head brooch on her blouse. Aware that Owen studied her, trying to get a fix on their relationship, Leona decided to be quiet.

After a night of missing Owen, she had surprised herself by her response to him when she saw him in the pickup this morning. When he'd smiled tentatively at Leona, she simply bent down to kiss him briefly. It felt very natural and easy, as if she'd never been angry with him. "Good morning. Thanks for coming," she'd said.

After that, Owen had been wary. Maybe he had a right to be uneasy. Leona wasn't exactly certain of herself right now—except that she needed Owen at her side and that she was hunting. She smiled, mocking herself. Last night, Owen was only doing what came naturally—he wanted to protect her. Who better to have at her side now, than a protector from an ancient Viking bloodline—with the name "Wolf"?

The breeze from the pickup's open window played in her hair and gently flipped the silver disks at her ears. The woven Celtic design matched the ring she wore. When Leona lifted her hand to smooth her hair, the silver runes tinkled against the wide cuff bracelet. She felt very sensual, very womanly and desired. It was a nice feeling and she settled in to enjoy the momentary respite from danger. From his glance at her, she could see Owen was taking in the changes. "Nice getup. Unique jewelry."

She lifted her wrist and studied the rune bracelet Tempest had created. "She—Aisling—didn't need runes, but she laid them out for show, to disguise how powerful she really was."

"Interesting design on the cuff bracelet. The ends of the designs seem to be two snakes, facing each other, mouths open. Does that mean anything special?"

Leona nodded and considered the bracelet. "Interpretations vary. Some say it represents the battle between paganism and Christianity. But the snakes can be defined as almost everything in opposition. Tempest likes to think that it is our battle with what we don't want—the inheritance from Aisling and Thorgood. Or it could be good against evil, I guess. Depends on how you want to think of it."

"That jewelry is intended as bait and you know it. If this . . . vampire . . . has a grudge against your family, and he knows about your ancestors, flashing that stuff is sure to shake him up."

"Oh? I had no idea. Really?" Leona asked too innocently, as the pickup turned on Man O' War Boulevard.

As if resigned, Owen sighed deeply.

As they drove through Lexington's streets, Leona handed Owen a traveling thermos cup. "I found a tea shop you might like—a little more unique blend than what's in grocery stores. I brewed some while I was waiting. I hope it's okay."

"Mm. Nice. Thanks." He sipped the tea and this time, his sigh was in appreciation. "Chai without milk . . . peppery, spicy, perfect."

"You seem to be a spicy sort of guy." Leona spoke automatically, her mind on their mission.

Owen smiled confidently. "Glad you think so."

Leona took in that supremely pleased masculine tone. "I wasn't thinking about *that*."

"I *like* to think about it."

"Well, stop."

Owen sent her a sidelong look. "You're snagging something from me, aren't you?"

She turned to view traffic, successfully hiding her blush. Owen's body was humming sensually, and hers was responding. "I don't know what you're talking about," she lied.

"I'm sorry last night didn't end well," he stated grimly.

"That was last night."

"You're not holding a grudge, are you?" he asked, glancing cautiously at her.

"Could you just focus on driving? Are you someone who needs a replay?"

"Since you're snippy, I can only take that to mean that you're not happy with how we ended last night, either. I try not to let that get out of control, but you—with you, it's different."

Leona knew exactly what Owen meant. She glanced away from the slight teeth mark she'd left on his throat. Guilt took her into a brooding silence. Lovemaking with Joel had been gentle and sweet and reassuring. With Owen, it had been like a firestorm.

"I'm doing this, Owen."

"I get the picture." He sounded resigned as he braked for a driver who had passed them too recklessly. He glanced at a traffic wreck at the other side of the boulevard where an officer was taking notes. "We may need to involve the police."

"Sure. Try explaining dreams of foreboding, ancient curses, and psychics. Turn left at the next stop light."

Owen turned off Man O' War Boulevard and onto the street Leona had indicated; they continued driving north and west. "Tell me what you'd do if you caught this creep . . . if he sees you all decked out to play and he goes berserk."

"Incapacitate him somehow. Make certain he never hurts anyone again."

"You haven't thought that far, have you?"

"Frankly, no." Leona looked out the window as they passed a lush field. "Janice will love the events at the Kentucky Horse Park and Keeneland. What's your pick of the two-year-olds?"

"Stop trying to change the subject." Owen handed the thermal cup back to her. "That was good. Thanks."

Leona studied the cup and wondered if the woman in Owen's past had served him tea. Did Leona remind Owen of that love? "Tell me about the woman you loved."

Acres of bluegrass spread gently out around them, as Leona directed Owen to the turnoff to Sue Ann's home.

"She was married. I didn't know. It got messy," he stated curtly.

Leona sensed that his scars were too deep to open easily. She placed her hand on Owen's, linked her fingers with his, and sent a soft, gentle pulse to him.

Owen didn't look at her, but he smiled. The tension within him seemed to ease, a sign that he had accepted the psychic caress. "Nice. Thanks. I could use more of that later."

She had to tell him. "Owen, every time I reach out and explore, it gets stronger. I don't know the limits of what I can do."

"Maybe it doesn't have limits. You'll figure it out."

She stared at him. "Just like that? That easy?"

"Just like that."

As they drove, Leona looked at the elegant horse barns, the parallel black-board fences, and the bluegrass fields. "I remember her—my grandmother. I've been thinking a lot about her lately. She terrified me, and she was always focused on me. 'You've got to stop him, Leona,' she said. I never knew what she meant. Now I do. She wasn't delusional, or anything else. At that moment, she was just terrified. Then she changed so quickly, as if someone had changed her, just as Janice and the others were affected. My grandmother was very strong, despite denying her gifts—her blood curse. I think she may have been vulnerable somehow. And someone understood just how to use her weak points. . . . Turn here," she added, indicating the next corner.

Was she strong enough to stop Borg's descendant from harming her, or her family? That uncertainty quivered in her mind as she placed her hand on Owen's thigh. He put his hand over hers. "You're not your grandmother. You can do whatever you have to."

"You believe in me?"

"Sure. Just believe in yourself." Owen's fingers pressed hers before he pulled into a residential section. Leona directed him to Sue Ann's tree-lined street. Her van was in the driveway of her home, children's toys in the fenced yard. The air was sweet with freshly mowed lawns as Leona and Owen stood on the Marshfields' front porch.

A curtain moved in a window beside the front door, and Sue Ann opened the door slightly. Her eyes rounded with fear, her voice hushed. "Why are you here?"

She glanced over Leona's shoulder to Owen. "Who is he?"

"Owen Shaw. Owen, meet Sue Ann. He knows that we're good friends, Sue Ann, and that I'm worried about you. If you're afraid, let me help you. Owen can help, too."

Sue Ann glanced behind her and then quickly turned to Leona. "I'm not afraid. I just don't want to work for you anymore. I'm going to start a catering business."

"That's great. . . . Is someone inside, Sue Ann? Is Vernon here?"

"My husband worked late last night, and he's sleeping now. I haven't seen Vernon since he redid your office. He's been keeping to himself. He's been working at your place, hasn't he?"

"He started my closet, but it isn't finished yet." Leona didn't want to upset Sue Ann further by telling her about Vernon's possible connection to Robyn's death.

"Oh. Well, he's been busy at the Balleau estate. Billy is supposed to come back from tour pretty soon. Vernon is working on one of those old historic homes for some retired guy. And sometimes Vernon gets busy down at Tom's Salvage." Sue Ann glanced uneasily at Owen as if she were suspicious of him. "Vernon has a lot of part-time jobs."

Being suspicious wasn't usual for Sue Ann. But there was nothing usual about the way she was acting.

"I know something is wrong. We can help." Leona said quietly. She glanced at Owen and hoped he understood: Sue Ann might open up about the problem without his presence.

Taking the hint, he said, "Nice to meet you, Sue Ann. I'll wait in the pickup, Leona." Then he walked back to the pickup and let Max out, fastening a leash to the dog's collar. Instantly Max started barking, his hackles raised. Owen leveled a look at Leona, who understood. Max's keen senses had caught a specific psychic residue of someone threatening and evil. The man Leona wanted to catch had definitely visited Sue Ann's.

"If you see Vernon, let us know, okay? I miss you, Sue Ann." Leona touched the other woman's hand. Icy, fearful shivers immediately ran up her own. Images flashed, tumbling through her mind. Acting instinctively, she sent out tiny spirals, sticky as a spiderweb to catch fragments of Sue Ann's life. "I didn't know Vernon was your husband's cousin. Dean has been seeing him quite a bit, hasn't he?"

Sue Ann's eyes rounded. "Did someone tell you that?

Vernon is a cousin, but so far removed that no one thinks of it anymore. Yes, they work together sometimes."

"And drink together, too? Sometimes all night?"

For a heartbeat, Sue Ann stared blankly at Leona. "No one knows about that either."

"Trust me, Sue Ann. I do know." Leona gently squeezed Sue Ann's hand and focused on clearing a mental path. Then she placed images of the good times they'd shared as friends into the other woman's mind.

"Oh, Leona . . ." Sue Ann's fearful cry trembled in the fragrant morning air: her words seemed to tumble from her. "Dean has changed since he's been going down to the salvage yard to help Vernon at nights. They take the good parts out of wrecked cars, then Vernon crushes the cars. I don't know what's happened to Dean since he's been spending so much time with Vernon."

"I have some idea."

"When I said I wouldn't spy on you, Dean got real mad. I was afraid of what might happen. I have to go now. Go away, Leona, I don't want him to start up again. The kids are at my mother's until we get over this bad patch." Sue Ann's lips parted as if she had something more to say. Instead, she shook her head and started to close the door.

Her husband jerked it open again. Dean's appearance momentarily shocked Leona. Usually clean-cut and cheerful, Dean looked as if he'd slept in his clothes. His eyes were bloodshot as he glared at Leona. "Get the hell off my property. Shut that barking dog up, or I will."

Owen immediately put Max into the cab and closed the door. He leaned back against the pickup and spoke quietly to the dog, who wouldn't stop barking.

"Hey, you!" Dean yelled, and hurried toward Owen. "Are you going to stop that dog, or am I?"

"Dean! Don't!" Sue Ann's fearful cry didn't stop her husband from advancing on Owen.

When Leona started down the steps, Owen's eyes locked onto her. His quiet order seemed to vibrate in the morning air. "Stay back, Leona. Or get in the cab with Max."

"Come with me, Sue Ann." Leona wrapped her arms around Sue Ann and held her trembling body. Obviously set for a confrontation, Dean started yelling at Owen, who seemed unaffected.

"He's never hurt me or the kids," Sue Ann whispered. "I love him, Leona. I can't leave him. Dean isn't like this. I don't know what happened. He's just worried about his job and making house payments. We got married awfully young, you know. He missed a lot of what other men did, and maybe he just needs to—"

A woman in love, Sue Ann had found excuses for her husband's behavior. "Then at least let me take you to your parents'. Just until Dean has a chance to think clearly, and you can talk things through. Sometimes people just need a little space and time to think, to resolve what's going on."

Leona placed her forehead against the other woman's and focused. *Come with us, before you're hurt. Think of your children. They need you. And they need Dean, as the loving father he was, not this man.*

Dean smashed his fist into the pickup's fender. Owen's light eyes narrowed, his body tense. Inside the cab, Max was furious, snarling and barking, leaping at the window as if trying to get out. Owen barely moved as he easily blocked Dean's first punch, then another.

Infuriated, Dean charged him. That was a mistake. With one quick movement, Owen flipped Dean onto his back. Crouching beside the winded man, Owen spoke softly, then stood up and faced the women. His voice was calm, as if the violence had never occurred. "Sue

Ann, it might be better if you'd come with us. He's okay, just resting. He'll feel better in a little while."

Her eyes filled with tears, Sue Ann looked helplessly at Leona. "I love Dean."

"I know. That's why you don't want him to feel badly if he hurts you. He needs to cool down before that happens." Leona smoothed Sue Ann's blond hair away from her face. Concentrating on her friend's wide blue eyes, she tried to calm Sue Ann's fear. She focused on the physical connection with Sue Ann, the streams of their friendship flowing warmly around the other woman. "Please. It's the sensible thing to do."

"Sensible," Sue Ann repeated blankly. "Yes, I think so."

She hurried inside the house and in a short time returned with a small overnight bag. "I'd take our van, but Dean—Dean has done something to it, so I can't go anywhere."

Leona helped her into the pickup's cab with Max. Then she circled to where Dean lay. Owen stepped between her and the fallen man. "I wouldn't trust him now, Leona."

"I do." She met Owen's narrowed eyes, that firm set of his jaw. "He's a good man, Owen. None of this is his fault. It's mine."

He considered that thought for a moment, then nodded and stepped back slightly. Leona sensed his alert body near hers, at the ready as she crouched beside the fallen man. Dean groaned slightly and she smoothed his hair back from his face, his blue eyes opened slowly.

"Leona . . ." Owen warned.

Dean had been a wonderful loving husband and father; she had to save him. "Dean, listen to me. This is only temporary. I want you to stop seeing Vernon and stop drinking. If you're taking any drugs, you've got to stop. Sue Ann loves you, Dean. You don't really want to frighten her, do you?"

"No. . . ." Dean whispered unevenly. "I don't know why I do some of the things I do. They just boil out of me for no reason. It's like I'm someone else."

"None of those things are your fault, but you have got to trust me. Dean, you must do as I say."

When he nodded, Leona continued, "You love Sue Ann and your children. This is going to work out. You have to believe me."

Tears streamed down his cheeks, and his hand clasped hers. "Thank you."

Leona continued soothing his forehead. "You are to take very good care of yourself, Dean. Get control. Do not communicate with Vernon. Do not see him. But do call me if he makes contact. Understand?"

"Tell my wife I love her, will you? And that I'm sorry?"

"I will."

Leona glanced up at Owen, who had just placed his hand on her shoulder. He indicated Sue Ann in the pickup's cab; she looked as if she'd shatter at any moment and change her mind. "We should go," Leona said., "Give me a call, Dean, if you want to talk. I'm a good listener."

After saying a humble "Thanks," Dean eased himself up into sitting position and wrapped his arms around his folded knees. He waved at Sue Ann and tried to smile. "It's okay, baby. Don't worry. I'm really sorry. Love you," he called unevenly.

In the pickup, Sue Ann sat huddled in Leona's arms. Closing her eyes, Leona focused her energy on soothing the other woman. On the other side of Sue Ann, Owen was silent as he drove through Lexington.

"Yes, I think you're right, Leona," Sue Ann stated suddenly as she sat upright and dried her tears. "I think this is best and that we both just need a little break. I'm not going to see Dean again until we've talked calmly on the telephone, and he stops seeing Vernon. But Vernon wasn't like that before, either. He's always been such a good-hearted family man, but he has missed his wife terribly. He was away for a while, and he'd changed when he came back—he even looked different, but somehow the same. That's when he started coming over here and got Dean to help him at the salvage yard."

"Just let us know if you hear from Vernon," Owen stated quietly, as he handed Sue Ann his business card. "Everything will work out fine."

"Really?"

"I said so, didn't I?" Owen's reply was just right—confident, supportive, and certain. "Sometimes men just need a little space to figure things out. You're giving it to him. You'll laugh about this while you and Dean are sitting on your old-age rocking chairs and watching your grandkids play. You're doing the right thing. He'll realize that you couldn't have done anything else but what you needed to do. Just recently, I've found that to be true myself."

Leona stared at Owen. *Was this really the man who had demanded that she leave Lexington?*

Owen's smile at her was too bland and too innocent.

Twelve

"NICE WORK," OWEN STATED, AFTER THEY HAD SETTLED Sue Ann with her parents and driven to Tom's Salvage.

In the early morning, the junkyard was already busy. The sound of cars being crushed caused Leona to shiver. She closed her eyes as one dark blue sedan was pressed flat; it wasn't difficult to imagine how she might feel in that same car.

Leona held Owen's hand as they questioned the manager, who hadn't seen Vernon for some time. Once back in the car, Owen suddenly decided to shop for tea. Leona sensed that was a diversion to calm her and didn't protest.

When Owen drove into the strip mall's parking lot, he was obviously very alert to potential danger. He held the door for Leona as they entered Tea-Mart 4 U, a specialty tea shop with custom blends. "I guess that's why I got invited to Sue Ann's? Because Dean might be dangerous?"

"I thought I could manage Dean. I just didn't know about Vernon, had he been there."

"I don't blame you. So then, you do need me, right? You trust me at your back, don't you?"

"I appreciate your help," Leona stated carefully. She

trusted Owen with her life. But she wasn't ready, just yet, to admit that she loved him. She sensed that Owen was pleased with himself. Her feminine senses had been sending big flashing warning signs since they'd left the salvage yard. They weren't spine-tingling, fearsome sensations, but the kind that said Owen was carefully strategizing how he treated her. And those methods had everything to do with his feelings for her.

She remembered how serious Owen had seemed when he'd crouched beside Dean and spoke quietly. Leona had understood that Owen was introducing himself as Sue Ann and the children's protector for the time being.

Protector. If things kept going the way they were, one day Leona might have to explain that label to him. Her sisters had bonded with men who had protected them. It was a unique lifetime blend of love, passion, respect, and friendship.

The Protector label also could be applied to any of Thorgood-the-Wolf's men, who had pledged to protect his and the seer's bloodline through time. Owen definitely qualified as a potential descendant of one of the warriors; his tendencies were the same, despite the veneer of civilization. His "Wolf" name definitely indicated a relationship, and his light eyes and Native American heritage gave him the potential to have visions like a shaman might. *Owen hadn't said anything about visions. Did he have them?*

While standing in the loose-tea section of the shop, Owen talked quietly with the curvaceous salesgirl. She was obviously flirting with him. Leona held her breath while the blonde—who wore a name tag of MISSY—explained the different blends of tea to Owen. Talking quietly, they wandered over to the tulsi-tea section, leaving Leona to stand by herself. Owen seemed to be in a good mood, more friendly than usual, smiling and taking in everything that Missy said. And she had plenty to say.

As Leona stepped out of the shop to answer calls from her family, she heard Owen's rich chuckle. She turned to see him flashing a brilliant grin down at the woman. Though the shop's window, she noted the blonde's hand touching Owen's chest, arm, and hand frequently—when she wasn't licking her lips and toying with her long blonde hair. At one point, he seemed to be laughing at something she'd said.

It was all very disgusting. . . .

Tempest wasn't letting that tidbit get away from her grasp, without teasing Leona. "Jealous, huh?"

Leona thought about breaking the blonde's arms. Then Missy would have a hard time roaming her hands all over Owen! "Not a chance. I'm not the jealous type."

"Oh, I don't know," Tempest singsonged. "You seem pretty hot and upset to me."

"Lay off. He's enjoying himself, you know."

"Yes, men do that. Every once in a while you have to reel them back in. You know, I'm not one for pondering, but it seems to me that you and Mom are having definite problems of a male-species kind. Kenneth has got her on the run . . . she's acting frazzled. But then, she's worried about you, too, so the wave frequencies from her are bouncing all over the place. Yours are just hot and bothered. Relax and enjoy the quirks of the male species."

Tempest spoke with the age-old wisdom of a newly married who had her man in hand. "I'll tell Claire that you're having a little relationship-adjustment problem. This is a reverse play, isn't it? Our cool, calm, poised sister chomping at the bit and ready to pour tea leaves all over that snazzy blonde. Uh-huh . . . uh-huh. I know that's what you want to do, Leona Fiona."

"Lay off and stop teasing me. Owen is free to do as he wants." Leona quickly shifted into business mode and updated her sister on Vernon's connections in the dangerous tangle. Once she finished, she said, "I've got to go."

She was uncomfortable with the reverse roles, her sisters clearly enjoying her relationship with Owen. However, Leona had successfully managed to block them from information about the missing revolver.

Inside the tea shop, the blonde leaned close to Owen as she flipped her long hair yet again. Owen's smile at Leona was brief and bland, as if he'd just remembered her. *That* would have to change. "Are you finished? We really should go. It's too hot for Max in the pickup."

Owen looked at the blonde as he spoke to Leona. "We've only been in here five minutes, and the windows are down. There's a nice cool morning breeze."

The blonde batted her lashes up at him. "I can read tea leaves and tell your fortune, if you like. Or I read palms as well." Missy picked up Owen's hand and held it in both of hers. Turning it over to look at his palm, she ran her fingertip over his calluses. "Oh, I just love a man who has big hands. It usually means he's very good with them."

Leona glanced at Max, and hoped the dog would show signs of being uncomfortable. Behind the pickup's windshield, Max seemed to be grinning. Leona glanced at Owen, whose smile at her also seemed a bit wolfish. Those odd little tingles hit her again, a clear warning that Owen's game plan involved something about her. But she couldn't worry about that at the moment, and nothing felt cool from her viewpoint.

"*I* want to go," Leona stated. She maneuvered her body between Owen and the salesgirl, effectively detaching their hands. She pointed to the glass canisters of green, black chai, and tulsi-chai tea. "We'll take that and that and that. He can compare at home."

Who was this woman she'd become? Leona wondered desperately. *Where had the old Leona gone?* She stared at Owen as if seeing him differently. *Where Owen was concerned, she was definitely possessive. Obviously she needed to protect her territorial rights.*

Owen still wore one of those bland, innocent smiles. "Okay, honey. Anything you say."

He was definitely too docile. She didn't trust that act. Owen was definitely one of those starkly masculine, assertive males. *He had some sort of a game plan concerning her!*

Apparently thwarted in her flirtation, the salesgirl glanced at Owen, who shrugged. He looked amused as he paid for the tea. As they got back into the pickup, he seemed almost jovial. His hand stroked Leona's thigh and cupped her knee. " 'Home' sounds good. Whose?"

The question quivered around Leona, the meaning much deeper than the actual words. She looked down at his hand—one Missy believed to be quite capable. Leona thought about the salesgirl's flirtations with Owen, the way he'd responded so easily, and said, "Mine. I've decided to take the day off. But I'd like to check on the shop first."

"We could pick up some takeout and stop at a park . . . let Max walk a bit. It would be a great day for it."

"No. We are going to *my* house." Her flat statement seemed to please Owen immensely, his grin flashing unexpectedly at her.

At Timeless Vintage, while Max sniffed around the display room, Leona hurried to turn on her radio. Owen set to work, checking for hidden cameras.

Glancing around her shop's display room, Leona saw that Jasmine was elegant as always. As if on center stage, the mannequin commanded attention in her elegant "Derby" outfit. "Date Night" bags gleaming red and black beads caught Leona's attention, and she knew what she had to do. Her family thought she was stronger. Now was her chance to test that.

Walking straight for the handbag, she gripped it tightly, letting herself open to the streams of psychic residue. First, she dismissed the energy-fluff she felt from the customers who had handed the bag and narrowed down to her sisters' touches. Claire, who had created the bag, Tempest, who had held it, and someone else—

Leona almost tossed the bag away as a biting, angry, vengeful sensation slithered up her arms. She held tight and waited until the sensation eased. The test proved that she was definitely stronger. She replaced the bag carefully.

Owen came to stand beside her. "I couldn't find any equipment. What's wrong?"

"I need to know him better if I'm going to take him down. That's what my sister, Tempest, does. Without her gloves, when she feels the history of an object, who held it. I'm not that good, but I got there. I didn't know I could—"

"*We're* going to take him down," Owen corrected, as his arm circled and drew Leona to him.

"Then maybe you should know that Vernon wasn't exactly reasonable when I saw him last. I was at Alex's house when he stopped by. Apparently, they share a widower's grief and a friendship. I'm certain that if Alex hadn't appeared when he did—"

Owen gripped her arms and held her away to study her face. "Has Vernon threatened you?"

His expression frightened Leona. If ever she saw a man who might kill if pushed too far, it was Owen. On the other hand, Vernon was big and powerful, and Owen could get hurt. "I—"

"Okay, he has . . . if not in words, then in deed. And you didn't say anything. You could have told me."

"Look Owen, all that is past and we need to focus on

the present. I have a lot on my mind right now and that's never good for a psychic." Dropping her gaze, Leona studied the silver runes on her bracelet, remembering what she had just learned about her gift. She'd deliberately imprinted Sue Ann with her thoughts—by focusing her energy she'd broken through the other woman's fear and love and brought her to reason. Her extrasensories were growing too quickly, and she didn't understand the limits. This time, to protect her friend, it had worked. What if the next time, she did something wrong and harmed someone?

"I think I want to bake a coconut cream pie and plant those daisies," she said suddenly. The balance between fear and anger had unsettled her. She knew instinctively she needed to balance the unreality of what was happening to her with everyday tasks, as if nothing had changed.

Owen's stare swung from Max to Leona. "Okay, you could do that," he said cautiously. "Any particular reason why you want to do that now?"

When she looked up at Owen, she realized, too, that her jealously had unbalanced her as well. Owen had seemed so blatantly interested in the curvy salesgirl at the tea shop. There was no way Leona's lean body could compare with the blonde's voluptuous one. But instead of voicing her fears, Leona tried for an innocent expression. "No."

Then she glanced at Max, who had sniffed a path to her shop's stairway and started moving upstairs; his huffing and sniffing noises indicated he was tracking a scent. "You won't let Max tear anything up, will you?"

"Max is too proud to go sniffing ladies underwear, and he's been walked. Give the dog some dignity, Leona. You really don't want to face this, do you? Max was all lit up at Sue Ann's. That creep had been there, the same one that Max had sensed at the farm. Maybe we should bring in the police. If that revolver turns up—I guess I'd better report it as missing, huh?"

"That might be a good idea. Max is barking again."

Owen was already taking the stairs, two at a time. Leona followed. Upstairs, they found the dog poised for battle and snarling, his hackles raised.

"I thought you said you had claustrophobia," Owen murmured as he stepped into the crowded office, making it seem even smaller. He moved around the office, checked out the furniture and the ceiling, then quickly inspected everything else. "No camera. No sound equipment. So you are claustrophobic? This doesn't bother you?"

"Vernon miscalculated the distance the shelves would take up and—" Leona tried to breathe and couldn't; her hand went to her chest.

"That would be one way he's trying to turn up the pressure on you . . . by making the space smaller. . . ." Owen turned suddenly and frowned as he saw her. Instantly, his arms went around her, one hand tucking her face against his throat. "Feel me, Leona. Come on, honey, breathe. . . ."

"He's been in here, since I was. He's—I can feel his energy, taking mine. It's sucking—that's what powerful psychic vampires can do, suck away energy and make it theirs. They feed on the vulnerable and weak—apparently, I'm both right now."

"He isn't taking anything," Owen stated grimly. "You're too strong. Fight back, honey. Do what you do, protect yourself. Tell me how this works."

Instinctively, Leona knew just what had happened. She ran her finger along the arm of her desk chair, and it burned her. She rubbed her hands together. "He's imprinted his energy on everything. I think—I think he came in here, retrieved his electronic stuff, and deliberately set about touching absolutely everything."

"Then clean it up."

"Sure. That sounds good. Just take disinfectant and scrub the place down. . . . How?"

"You're not completely afraid. You've still got that kiss-my-butt attitude. Speaking of your curves . . ." Owen studied her for just that instant. The next moment he tugged Leona into his arms and eased her feet apart. His knee nudged between hers, his muscled thigh pressing intimately against her. "Here's how you might imprint both of our energies over this place."

Instantly his heat and energy replaced the evil she'd felt; Leona's breath came more quickly now, but for a different reason. She was already damp and soft and ready—and Owen's intense expression said he felt her heat, too. His deep growl of pleasure and the bulge against her leg increased the low throb within her. She would soon get Owen into her bed. A little old-fashioned cave-woman therapy would definitely help.

"You know, I don't feel his energy here anymore," Leona stated lightly. She leaned in to nibble a trail across Owen's jaw up to his ear. When she bit his ear and licked it, he tensed, heat pouring from his skin. His low growl of pleasure caused Leona to smile. "Owen? Maybe we should go home and imprint my bed."

Owen's hands slowly roamed over her body, his thumbs toying with her breasts. "Hey. Now, that's a good idea."

Rolf replaced the telephone in its cradle. The report hadn't pleased him; one of his "helpers" had been taken out by Leona and Owen. Apparently, Leona had been able to override Rolf's work with Dean. "Leona isn't going to die easily. But nothing will be left of her mind when she finally does."

He'd underestimated Leona. That was a mistake he wouldn't make again. She was developing, getting stronger, but that only made his prey more interesting. During their previous brief meetings, he'd been able to block her. That might change. According to his father's information, the Aisling women were unreliable, their talent able to leap out of their control—and the person trying to control them. His father would know . . . he'd caused the triplets' grandmother, Stella Mornay, to go mad.

Rolf settled back to look at himself in his workshop's mirror. Years of study had perfected this disguise as Vernon O'Malley. He eased off his wig, the net cap containing his long black hair. He winnowed his fingers through the strands. "Ah, that feels good."

Slowly he removed the padding around his face and admired his reflection. He was really very talented, a chameleon, able to move into different social circles easily. Identity theft had always been so easy, and money was practically falling into his hands. Killing had also been very easy, and necessary as he assumed his prey's identity. Vernon had also been chosen carefully, not only for his vulnerabilities, but because of his body build— somewhat near Rolf's. Disguised as Vernon, Rolf could move easily through many lives.

Peeling off a bit of the silicone's adhesive from his face, he angled his face to study it. He swiftly fastened the long hair beside his face into narrow braids, then bound the ends with leather strips. *He was the image of the ancestor in his dreams.* "I do look like you, Borg."

He leaned closer to the mirror, fascinated with his own compelling, hypnotic eyes. That day in her shop, he'd snagged a psychic particle of Leona's, and he'd made it his. But then, she'd caught something of his, too, just as Greer had.

"Aisling, the queen seer who started it all . . . I'll take

Greer down at the last. She needs to know how really good I am. Better than she *thinks* she is. Before I take Greer down, I just might have that repeat performance at the 'Psychic Minds'. Only next time, she'll play the fool."

Only Rolf's father had come close to destroying the Aislings. Rolf smiled smugly. "I am the one to do the job. I've always known it."

With care, Rolf opened a portable thermal-and-humidity-controlled chest. It had taken years to reproduce the artifacts he'd seen in his mind—flashes of ancient times. As he slowly dressed in Viking costume, he relished how he appeared in the full-length mirror, which had been custom-made to accommodate his height and body. Once done, he posed, admiring his reflection. "Leona should see me like this. She will, eventually."

He considered the sheathed weapons at his side, exact replicas of Borg's. Rolf had seen them in his dreams and knew that they'd drawn blood. He considered what he should use to finish Owen Shaw, a short dagger or the heavier one? Or the sword?

As he let his fingers glide sensuously along the three-foot blade of the custom-made replica of a Viking sword, he read the angular characters on the grip. "Borg, the greatest of all Vikings. Strongest in battle, his sword tasting all who would withstand him, their blood red on his blade. His eyes see what others cannot."

For an instant, other visions flashed at Rolf, scenes he didn't want in his mind. Thorgood's second-in-command, a hunter with some seer talent, had cautioned the chieftain about Borg. The hunter had used his gift to track Borg and kill him. . . .

Rolf shoved that vision-flash away. It didn't please him. He preferred to think of possessing Thorgood-the-Wolf's brooch and building his revenge.

The powerful psychic bloodline of Borg and Aisling could have ruled the world. . . .

As he studied his reflection, he remembered the shame Greer had caused him. "She thought I was a fake, one of lower ability. All that is going to change, Greer. I'll have your peers laughing at *you*—not me."

Rolf closed his eyes, letting the fantasy of Leona's pale, naked, bound body appear in his mind, as it often did. She had interfered with his plans yet again. She would pay for that. "Nothing can stop me once I have that brooch."

He glanced at the yellow, mixed-breed dog in the cage behind him. She was coming into heat, perfect to attract Shaw's animal, to draw him away. Rolf had noticed the German shepherd's keen senses were too alert to his own presence and psychic residue. The dog had evidently bonded with the man and was protective of Owen and of Leona.

Odd that animals never bonded with him. As a boy, Rolf had wanted a pet, but they never seemed to survive; there was always that need to hurt them.

Last night, Rolf had planned to visit Leona—in disguise, of course. But the dog had started barking. Leona had come to the window, peering out into the night. He'd stood on the street corner, letting her see him, just enough to make her uneasy. "*Leona.* . . . " he'd whispered into the night air.

The dog's barking and antics had distracted her; Leona's senses had locked on to the animal and closed the link.

He glanced at Shaw's revolver on the countertop littered with theatrical makeup, wigs, and padding. "If the female dog doesn't work, there are always other ways. And that handgun still has Owen's prints on the grip, perfect for a murder charge. I could always have someone in prison kill him there, but then I'd be missing the fun."

He stood back and admired himself. Rolf's features perfectly matched his ancestor Borg's. "Aisling really should have chosen him."

Images flipped through his mind, like a stream that wouldn't stop. With the Celt village destroyed and burning behind her, Aisling had faced Thorgood and his Viking raiders. Unafraid, she spoke to Thorgood. "Take me, I am worth more than anything you will ever have. Leave my people alone."

In the next heartbeat, she'd turned slowly to Borg. Her green eyes had locked with his. She'd sensed his energy immediately and hadn't liked it. Borg had caught the thunderbolt of her power, tempered with a feminine softness. His senses reeled with lust for the woman who could make his own seer powers even stronger. With her in his hand, doing his bidding, he would have everything that Thorgood would ever dream of possessing. Aisling was the prize he had to have in his bed and under his power. "I challenge you for the woman," Borg had called impetuously to the famed chieftain.

Thorgood had turned to him slowly. "Do you, Borg?" he asked coolly, his hand already resting on his sword.

The seer's small pale hand had rested on Thorgood's muscled shoulder, staying him. "I would have you safe, my lord."

"Stand back. This is not for a woman, let alone a captive woman, to decide. You will have to learn to obey me, pet."

"Oh, go play your silly game then. But if you are hurt, I will not be happy."

Incensed at the developing intimacy between Thorgood and the seer, Borg moved to quickly unsheathe his sword. Blades clashed, the metallic sound echoing off

Rolf's basement workshop. Men grunted and sweated and fought brutally, then Borg lay on the ground.

Rolf inhaled abruptly, disgusted by the image of his ancestor, defeated. . . . He'd envisioned that scene so many times. Aisling's clear green eyes had stared directly at Rolf, as if he were Borg. She seemed to peer into his mind at the cruelties, the lust, and the greed. Then she'd raised her head to look straight into the eyes of Thorgood's guard, tall, hardened warriors who would give their blood for their chieftain and the woman he had claimed as his own.

Rolf tapped the sword's honed blade on the countertop next to Owen Shaw's revolver. "He may not have won the seer, but Borg did know how to lay a good curse on the Aislings."

In the mirror, the compelling eyes of his ancestor pinned Rolf. Along that sharp face, thin braids swung like snakes. Lifting his blade to the thunderous sky, he shouted his curse upon the Aisling-Thorgood line.

Then he repeated Aisling's words. They echoed eerily in his underground workroom.

"Men of Thorgood-the-Wolf," she had called. A small woman, Aisling faced a band of warriors much taller than she, their blades red with the blood of her people. Touching the wolf's-head brooch at Thorgood's shoulder, she lifted her head as she spoke to the warriors. Borg knew that Aisling would replace him as counsel to the chieftain and others. Borg's power would be torn away, shredded, by this little red-haired witch who declared, "I give myself freely to Thorgood. You will protect our line as if it were your own."

Thorgood had laughed outright, amused that a mere woman could tell his men to protect their children, as yet unborn. At the same time, Borg's vision had revealed the seer's womb rounding, with red-haired, green-eyed girls, one after another, flowing through time. . . . Aisling's power would pass to those resembling her. And through time, the warriors' descendants would protect the women of the Aisling-and-Thorgood line.

"Damn them all," Rolf cursed violently as he sank the blade into the wooden countertop. He fought to control the temper that was his one weakness, then surveyed the photographs pasted around his well-lit mirror.

The Aisling triplets and Greer stared back at him. His finger caressed the photographs, one by one. Rolf issued his father's familiar chant. "Take one down, weaken the link, take them all down, get the brooch, get the power."

"So this is what psychics do for a comedown."

Leona looked up at him, a smile on her lips as she said, "It beats making pies."

Still tangled with Leona in her guest-room bed, Owen smiled against her hair, letting himself float in the aftermath of their lovemaking. Leona's lips traced a path to Owen's nipple and nibbled gently. Her breasts snuggled against his side, and her thigh lay between his. His hands roamed her naked, soft, warm curves. At the moment, life was good for Owen Shaw.

This time, he had been determined to keep their lovemaking controlled.

Leona did not have the same determination.

In the brief ride to her home, the looks she'd given him had a sexual charge that had him aching. When she'd licked her lips, Owen could almost feel her pulsing around him. He'd kept his mind on bills to keep himself from pulling over and shocking Lexington's residents. Inside her home, Owen had thoroughly searched the house. He'd wanted no interruptions or filming of the sexual marathon he had planned with Leona.

Meanwhile, Leona had gone straight to the kitchen

to make a pot of tea. He'd realized that Leona's tea-making had begun to be a habit, especially when she was stressed. It seemed to give her thinking space. Max had prowled the house, sniffing for any harmful residue of psychic energy. With a sudden huff of approval, he had plopped down on a rug and lapped the water from his bowl. Leona had given Max a bonemeal-and-grain doggie cookie from the tea shop, and Owen had tilted his head to study her curved backside. When she straightened and turned, Leona had caught him looking at her.

"I'm afraid your tea might be a little cool, by the time you get to drink it," Leona had said as she moved toward him. She'd dropped her clothing in front of him, then held up her rune bracelet for him to unclasp. She had that hot, determined look, as if nothing could keep her from him. The nice thing about the lady was that she knew how to make a point, Owen had decided. She'd unbuttoned his jeans and slid his zipper down, cradling the fullness of him in her hands. By the time they reached the guest room, neither of them was dressed.

With her body lying soft against him now, Owen caressed her breast. He'd been sizzled well and good, but he was hoping for more than just helping Leona find escape from her stresses. He needed reassurance that Leona was his—to keep. "That was a great tea shop," he murmured just to jump-start his plan.

Her hand roamed his chest, and she snuggled closer, toying with his nipple and licking it, sending hard jolts straight southward. "Mm. There are others in town. We should try them, too."

Owen rubbed a strand of her hair across his lips. He enjoyed the scent—exotic, fresh. At Tea-Mart 4 U, Leona hadn't liked the other woman's flirtations. Her eyes had turned that dark gold color, which Owen took to be a good sign. Part of good plan was to make certain that the other party involved recognized the advantages of playing one-on-one. "This is nice. Monday noon, and you and I are in bed."

"It's already been a long day," she murmured drowsily against his throat. "I really should get back to the shop and start going over applications."

"Your briefcase and laptop are here. You could do that here, couldn't you?"

She stretched out on her back, and arched her body, pale and curved in the shadowy room, the September day bright and warm outside. "I suppose. Right now, I can't move."

Owen kicked aside his undershorts, still tangled around one ankle. He turned on his side and looked at her. Those soft green eyes were half-closed, her breasts peaking against his caressing hand. "Your claustrophobia is why you don't want to be pinned down, isn't it?"

Her eyes flickered as if an unpleasant memory had crossed her mind. "Uh-huh. I'm really sorry, Owen."

"I'm not complaining."

He traced her nipple, then bent to kiss and flick his tongue over it. Owen noted her slight gasp, the way her hips arched as his hand smoothed a path down her belly. Her hips lifted to the slow rhythm of his fingers and she closed her eyes and sighed. "There's something big, hot, and hard against my hip."

He nudged her slightly and grinned. "Can't think of what that might be."

Carefully easing his leg between hers, he moved very slowly. As his arms moved to either side of her to brace himself, her lashes fluttered slightly, her gaze on him as he moved fully over her. His instincts told him to pin her securely. But he wouldn't. The choice to accept him in this position was hers. "Scared? Tell me, if you are."

"I will," she whispered so softly that the shadows almost swallowed the sound.

His body trembling with the need to thrust into hers, Owen waited and watched for signs of her fear. Did Leona trust him enough to put fear aside?

Her body seemed to be a slow hot wave, rippling beneath him, her legs easing slightly open, allowing him closer. "I know what you're doing. You're making a point, aren't you?"

Owen forced his desire down, concentrating instead on holding Leona's trust. "Something like that."

Her arches cruised his calves slowly, allowing just the tip of him to enter her. Then her feet slid over his ankles, firmly trapping him. One of her hands slid from his shoulder down between their bodies as Leona met his slow, soft kiss. He wanted to give her gentleness and understanding, but his body raged on. He closed his eyes and tried to breathe, then raised slightly to look down where her hand gloved him.

"Owen . . ." Her voice seemed to ache, her need echoing his, building his.

Braced above her, Owen's body trembled with the desire to possess her quickly. As he entered her slowly, Leona seemed to melt beneath him, her lips parted, her uneven breath stroking his face.

"Owen," she whispered again as her hands raised to his back, her fingers pressing deeply. "Owen . . ."

Fully gloved within her tight body, he braced his weight away from her. "All right?"

"I don't know," she whispered unevenly. "I can't trust myself like this."

"Then trust me." He moved slightly, taking the thrust deeper, and she closed her eyes. Then he eased away and thrust again, moving very slowly and watching Leona's expression for signs of fear.

There was only the waiting within her, her senses prowling around her body, testing herself. "It feels good. Your weight, this closeness."

He hadn't rested fully upon her, but it was enough for now. But as he began to ease to his side, her arms and legs gripped him. "More."

Taking a deep breath, Owen braced himself over her again. Leona began to move beneath him, an experimental lifting of her hips and taking him deeper. He strained against the intimate squeeze of her body, his blood pounding hot through his veins, every muscle tense and waiting for release. "Ah—I don't know if I can—"

"Oh, you can. . . ." Leona moved her breasts against him, side to side, her hips lifting and falling, her lips against his throat. "You feel so good. . . ."

Her body started clenching, and he had to have her—

In the aftermath of the sudden storm, Leona held Owen, soothing him as their heartbeats slowed—together. "You needed that, didn't you? What is it, some primitive, possessive-man thing? You were making a point, weren't you? You're smirking, by the way. I can feel it."

"True." Owen smiled against her throat. Leona's trust spelled pure commitment. He'd really felt it, earthquake-jarring, mind-blasting, bone-melting felt it. *This fabulous woman was his; she trusted him with her body, and that had to mean a whole lot of commitment on her part.*

He'd claimed all rights. Leona was his.

Thirteen

LEONA SMILED CONTENTEDLY AS SHE SAT IN HER LIVING room, a notebook on her lap. Owen sat at her desk, working on his new laptop, the muscles of his back prominent beneath all that smooth bronzed skin. As she watched the evening sunlight shimmer on his bare shoulders, she wanted even more of him.

Their afternoon had served as a badly needed respite from the danger stalking her. The sensual blend of an almost primitive male-female clash with that of more tender and gentle moments had seemed almost magical. As Leona remembered him moving over her, a wave of desire caused her belly to clench with the need to go to him. She wanted to slide her fingernails down his back, or kiss his ear and watch those gunmetal gray eyes heat. *Owen Shaw was hers. She'd taken him. . . . He'd changed her life in their short time together.*

Leona hadn't thought of herself as primitive, but the need to mark Owen as her own had surprised her; the shock waves still lingered, blending with softening layers of feminine completion. Her family must have sensed her satisfaction, because no one had called.

Frowning, she tried to focus on work, too, studying the notes she'd been taking on the women she'd just in-

terviewed over the telephone. The prospects ranged
from "big ideas to help improve the customer base" to
"Oh, I can't work those hours" to a hopeful "I could
learn to sew."

One woman, Charlotte Franklin, seemed too desperate
to "do anything needed—clean or hand out sales pam-
phlets on the street, or anything." Leona had felt a trickle
of unease at Charlotte's fearful tone, and she intended to
speak with the woman in person. Charlotte had not heard
the radio ad Leona had placed, and she was reluctant to
explain how she'd known about the vacancies.

Her gaze roamed to Owen again. After surprisingly
easy, companionable afternoon hours, Owen's shoulders and arms bunched with tension as he worked; the
sensation came at Leona in waves. Earlier he had made
short work of finishing Vernon's closet job. An experienced carpenter, he was familiar with Vernon's tools.
Referring to the plans she'd drawn up several times,
he'd put the individual wooden storage spaces together
quickly. Leona's offer of help had been quickly dismissed, which irritated slightly. His mild, "Get out of
the way, honey. Why don't you go bake that pie?" had
followed a few of her minor suggestions.

Leona had thought better of arguing; she'd made the
pie and settled in to her own work. Vernon's whereabouts were still unknown, but they'd decided that they
needed to go about their business and hopefully draw
out Leona's stalker by living as if they weren't on guard.
Of course, the only reason Owen agreed to the plan
was because he was by her side. A woman with a strong-
hunter-type man and his wolf-type dog in tow couldn't
be much safer. Leona studied her emotions, the ease
within her mind, body and spirit was a balm she'd
needed badly, perhaps for all her lifetime.

But Owen hadn't relaxed entirely between his efforts
to finish her shelving and his work at her desk. Leona

had that well-satisfied sense that she had her man in her cave and he was definitely making himself at home.

Owen had seemed to be working out their plan as he worked methodically to create the closet's separate sections. When the shelving had been completed, he'd put all of Vernon's tools in his pickup bed. "He might come to get them. If he does, Max will hear him, and I'll be waiting."

After his shower and their dinner of grilled chicken, pasta, and salad, Owen had sat at her desk. He'd opened his laptop and started pricing serious updates for the farmhouse while Leona had curled up in her easy chair to return the interview calls. She'd been mildly surprised by herself; for hours now, she'd been sharing her "space" with Owen, after years of living alone.

Leona sensed this was the calm before the storm in which someone would die.

Closing his laptop, Owen turned to her. Sprawled back against her desk chair, he finished the coconut pie she'd sliced for him earlier and placed the dish aside. "Good. Thank you."

He took in her ME-WOMAN T-shirt, worn jeans, and bare feet. The giant claw-clip at the top of her head was doing nothing to control her hair. Uneasy with what she sensed he might say, Leona blew a wisp away from her face. She was in her own home; she'd been thoroughly "sexorcised," as Tempest was fond of saying, and she probably wasn't looking her best. "Are we going to have a chat?" she asked crisply.

"Don't give me attitude. It may work with others, but not with me. I suspect you ran a few guys off with that act. But I'm still here, aren't I?"

She closed her notebook and placed it aside, picking up her cup of tulsi tea. She sipped the lukewarm brew to give herself time to think. There was nothing like a head-on argument brewing in her living room to send up big warning signs. "You've been thinking about whatever you're going to say since—"

"Since you agreed to being committed—to our relationship."

Owen's use of "committed" and "relationship" obviously referred to her acceptance of the missionary position. Leona decided not to disagree; she trusted him with her body as well as everything else. It hadn't been long since they'd met, but she was certain they had more than a "relationship."

He seemed to be laying the groundwork for a serious discussion. If he intended to "lay down the law" again, then *she* would make her point that a relationship is an equal partnership. She correctly anticipated Owen's statement: "I don't want you to go out to the farm again."

When her eyebrows lifted in warning, Owen breathed deep and added, "I know you want to come out with me tonight and check on the farm. I'd *prefer* that you didn't go to the farm again. It's too dangerous. I'd *prefer* that you stayed here with Max. He needs the rest."

"Oh, he does, does he?"

Max lifted his head, his ears alert. He did that huffing-questioning noise, then tilted his head as if sensing trouble between the humans. He sensed right. Leona fought back that shimmer of anger closing in on her. "Dangerous? For me? Or for this creep who has been stalking my family? You're not expecting me to back away from this, are you, *honey*?"

Owen leaned forward and braced his forearms on his thighs. He clasped his hands in a gesture that said he was settling in to make his point. "You didn't need to flash those bracelets to let this guy know exactly who you are and what your bloodline is. He knows already. He'll get teed off and reckless and—"

"Show himself, naturally. That's what we want, isn't it?"

"If you're not around, then he'll probably come after—"

"You," she finished. "You really can't expect me to back down from this guy, not now. He's done too much."

"That's exactly what I want you to do. Stop baiting him. If he can adapt himself to look like anyone, he could be anywhere. That's why I want Max to stay with you anytime I'm not with you. And there's one more thing: *If you're not leaving Lexington*—and it doesn't sound like you are—then I think we should live together . . . for your protection."

Leona understood that more was going on beneath the layers of Owen's obvious wariness. "So that would mean that you would live here, right?"

"I'd like that . . . yes. I could work at the farm during the day. I'm putting it up for sale as soon as possible. Neither Janice or you should be anywhere near that triangle of water. It's too dangerous for you. When I'm gone, Max will stay with you at the shop or here. That's the only way I'm leaving you alone. Every night and sometimes during the day, I'll be with you. Well, until your family comes. It's your call how to handle that situation."

"*My family? Here?*"

Owen took a deep breath, obviously bracing himself to continue. "The way I understand this psychic family connection is that when you're all together, you're safe. With racing right here, all sorts of horse shows going on, and different events in the area, it should be an interesting draw for your family. From what you said, Marcus and Neil have never been here, and it might make a nice family vacation."

Leona sank back in her chair and folded her arms.

"You evidently haven't met Marcus. He likes to take over things—including my life. It's been a job to hold him off."

"What about Neil?"

"He just plain thinks I need help and protection."

Owen's smile seemed wolfish. "Yes, well, now you have me for that job, don't you? And Marcus has his father on guard, helping keep Janice safe, which I appreciate. I'd say we have all bases covered. And I get the idea you like sparring with your brothers-in-law."

"So, this is man's work?" Leona asked very carefully. "Protecting the helpless females?"

"And they're worth every minute." Owen stood and extended his hand down to her. "Come on, Red. Before you get too fired up, let's walk the dog and you can cool down."

Leona detested the nickname, but let it slide. At the moment, she had bigger issues. Owen had no idea what could happen when her entire family gathered. She did. "You haven't really invited them, have you?"

"No, not yet, but I just wanted to see what you'd say. I get the feeling that I'm not the problem."

"Did you think you were?"

When Owen shrugged and went into his closed, defensive mode, Leona stared at him. *Why would he worry that her family would object to him? Were his scars with the other woman that deep?*

"No, of course you're not 'the problem.' It's more like—well, not many people can withstand a whole roomful of us. We're all restless now, and it's worse. Claire and Tempest are both pregnant. Every time I talk to them, I get the feeling I'm leaping between cars on a mood train. *They* definitely can't be in the same room, not without some leveler. That can't be Mom. She's got a little problem of her own—it's really kind of cute. Marcus and Neil are not feeling exactly tiptop. And that would leave me to do the leveling—Why on earth would you think that I would *not* want you to meet them?"

A shadow crossed Owen's hard face, and his eyes flickered away from her; he was shielding something from her. "I have my reasons."

So much for the trusting relationship.... Leona stood. Ignoring Owen's extended hand, she placed her hands on her hips. "Okay. Explain. And *never* call me 'Red' again."

"Some other time. Let's take that walk. Come on, Max." Leona searched his tight, closed expression. She decided that whatever Owen had to say, he needed to choose his own time.

With Max on guard at Leona's, Owen decided to check on the horses at the farm. At nine o'clock on a Monday evening, Lexington was subdued, the city's traffic light.

As a hunter, every instinct in Owen told him that this was the chilling, calm moment before danger struck. They'd both needed the quieter day they'd had; Leona's panic in her office had terrified him. She appeared more in control and rested, though they'd definitely been very busy. If he hadn't left, they would be back in bed, and Leona wouldn't get the additional rest she needed.

Owen smiled briefly. That missionary-position event didn't need to happen again, so far as he was concerned. He'd needed that one time to confirm what he already sensed: Leona trusted him. That she had definitely accepted their relationship on all levels.

As he paused at a stop light, he realized he probably shouldn't have pushed for that. Maybe he was insecure. Leona shouldn't pay for his scars.

When the light turned green, and he accelerated, Owen's body tightened as he thought about her lying beneath him, moving with him and accepting him.

He had only been gone a few minutes, but already Owen anticipated his return to Leona. Her good-bye kiss had been followed by, "I'd like to try that again. Hurry back."

She'd patted his butt as he walked out the door. Owen had stopped in midstride and turned to her. "You're sort of cute, when you look shocked, Mr. Shaw."

"That's the first time I've ever been called cute."

"Don't get all snarly, honey. I really like your butt. It's firm and—"

Owen had forced himself to turn and walk away. He hadn't expected Leona's playful mood, but he intended to explore it.

Tightening his hands on the steering wheel, he fought returning to her now. First he wanted to have a very private chat with Vernon . . . without Leona.

He parked two blocks from Vernon's place. To neighbors, Owen would look like any man taking a walk in the evening. If that tiny strip of tape on the screen door had been torn away, it would signal activity.

At Vernon's house now, Owen noted that the mailbox by the front door was still stuffed with mail. He dipped into the shadows and circled to the back. A quick check revealed that the tape had been torn away at one end; someone had been in the house. When he entered the house, he found that the pills and containers were gone.

Replacing the tape, he returned to his pickup. The handyman was apparently still around but not returning calls.

As Owen drove to the farm, he answered his sister's call. "Yes, I'm going out to check on the horses now. Don't worry about them."

He decided that he wouldn't tell Janice about Robyn, or the tapes, just now. Owen listened carefully to Janice's tone, rather than to the words. Her speech pattern had taken on a contemporary phrasing. She seemed lighter, freer . . . and he intended for her to stay that way. "I'm learning so much about myself, Owen. I limit myself to only so many hours on the computer, then I try to balance my thoughts and concentration with meditation. I'm learning different forms of finding an inner peace, and I think I'm stronger that way, like all the storms are sweeping away and leaving me clean. . . . Greer is wonderful. I understand so much about myself that I didn't before. Oh, Owen, you were right. I wasn't bad and undeserving. I was struggling with life, like anyone else."

Janice was expressing everything Owen had prayed would happen for her. "You're going to be fine."

Her tone shifted to excitement. "I may try a few graphic jobs, freelance stuff, but I'm not overloading like before. Greer says balance is important. . . . Owen, our parents were too . . ."

"Harsh? Old-fashioned? Afraid for us?" Owen supplied gently. He was learning more about the shell he'd built around himself at an early age—and his father's harsh advice about keeping women in their place was wrong. Owen realized that in her childhood, Janice had probably been subjected to their father's attitude that a female was of lesser worth. Janice had badly needed the Aislings' encouragement and warmth, which was lacking in the Shaw family. He thought of how his mother had called Janice, "a little bird," proof that she had known how delicate and sensitive she was, even at an early age. "They came from the old ways, Janice. They did the best they could. They loved us."

"I remember. Dad was strict with you, always wanting more from you, and it was never enough for him."

"He wanted the best for me, not for himself."

"He was afraid of your light eyes, of what it could

mean, how different you could be. And you were, Owen. But he didn't understand."

"No, he didn't. Few people understand." Since boyhood, Owen had locked away his visions, so foreign to his family's culture. Did they still hover, waiting for him to release them?

"I . . . love you," Janice stated hesitantly, surprising him. The Shaw family had never expressed endearments, but Janice's felt good and true. They were words Owen needed to learn, to say, too; he knew he needed to bring the words inside him out into the ears of others. He should have given them to Janice long ago.

Janice spoke quietly, as if she sensed he needed comfort. "You gave me everything, Owen. You did everything just right."

"I see the horses now," Owen stated abruptly. "They're standing at the fence."

Janice laughed delightedly. "That's your usual automatic defense. You're uncomfortable with expressing your emotions. But you feel them. I know you do. You need to tell Leona how you feel."

"And you need to mind your own business, little sister." He'd told Leona with his body, but the words were difficult. When they had been by Robyn's car, and Leona had feared for him, Owen had caught her message; it was crystal-clear even though she didn't actually speak. *Leona had wanted to tell him she loved him . . . that he was the other part of her soul and her heartbeat.* Had Leona understood how *he* felt? Without words?

After the call ended and Owen had checked the horses, he stood to overlook the field, leading down to the pond. At twilight, the rustic scene was peaceful, a contrast with the danger lurking nearby.

Janice had been right: Their father had always been wary of Owen's potential though he'd loved his son.

"I wonder," Owen murmured as he started walking

to that triangle of natural water. Before he returned to Leona's, Owen had only a short time to experiment.

Leona had only a short time to check on Alex. As soon as Owen left, she'd called him, but he hadn't returned her message.

Earlier, that evening walk with Max was not ordinary. Owen and Max had moved together, and they had seemed to be patrolling Leona's neighborhood. Owen had stood very still as if letting his senses stretch out to feel the evening. "No rain tonight. That's good."

Leona knew why Owen was reassured. Rain could mean mist. Owen understood how she could be affected; she would become too vulnerable to the psychic stalking her.

She also knew exactly how Owen would react if he discovered she'd left the house with danger prowling around her. *If he found out.* Good thing Max wasn't talking.

She called Alex again from the car, and this time he answered. He didn't object when Leona said she was coming. On the way to his house, Leona thought about how weary Alex's voice had sounded; a weakened psyche was just what a predator needed.

When she arrived, the handyman's pickup was not in Alex's driveway. Seated beside her, Max snarled at the old plantation-style home.

"I know. He's been here, and you know it, too, don't you, boy? Stay here. I just want to warn Alex that Vernon may be dangerous."

Alex answered the door with a sheepish smile. As always, the light in his home was very dim. His gray hair seemed mussed, and he straightened his glasses as he spoke, "I'm sorry I didn't return the call. I've been busy. Please come in, Leona.

Over a slice of her coconut pie, Leona tentatively suggested that Alex should get another handyman.

Alex seemed shaken and fearful. "I don't know why. Vernon is very competent. You know how hard it is to get good handymen for these old houses—the antique molding, the difficult plumbing, the effort needed to preserve the old glass windows. All the things necessary to preserve the integrity of a house such as this take real skill and love. All the rest of the carpenters want that bright light when they work. You know how it bothers my eyes. Did he finish your closet?"

"No, someone else did. Vernon isn't answering my calls. I was wrong to recommend Vernon. I think . . . I think he may be dangerous."

"He's lost his wife. I know how he feels, to lose a loved one. We talked about our grief, right here, at this kitchen table. He cried, Leona. So did I. . . . You're wearing rather unusual jewelry for you, aren't you? It looks Celtic, and there's a lot of it. Any special reason?"

Leona held up her wrist, the silver runes and cuff bracelet gleaming in the shadowy kitchen light. "My sister created these. I've been thinking of her lately." She looked at Alex. "I know you miss your wife, like he does, but Vernon has disappeared. And he was very surly when I last spoke to him."

"He's grieving, Leona. You know how that feels. It's hard to let go, and more difficult to move on. His talks have meant so much to me." Clearly, Vernon had established a sympathetic friend in Alex, a tie that could be used against Alex.

"Alex, I really think Vernon is someone who might be dangerous now. Are you . . . are you finding anything unusual on your computer?"

Startled by the question, Alex blinked owlishly behind his thick lenses. "Unusual? I have online retirement investments that need constant tending. I've been pricing renovation costs and furniture. I've been spending a lot of time on it but other than that, nothing unusual."

She touched his hand. Instantly, a shot of unease zigzagged up her arm, setting off alarms. Leona sensed that same evil as that day in the shop. But she was stronger now and more sensitive. She was certain that Alex had been affected by the predator stalking her family and friends. "Alex, has anything out of the ordinary appeared on your screen?"

He shook his head and seemed puzzled. "No, but—Leona, where are you going?" he asked as she got up abruptly.

She had to know if Alex's computer had been infected. She hurried to the front room where Alex had set up his office. In the cozy shadowy area, lined with empty bookshelves, his laptop was closed. Leona placed her open hand on it. Closing her eyes, she focused on her senses, opening . . .

Suddenly that sharp edgy face snarled at her. His hateful tone snaked around her: *Leona didn't love her husband or she wouldn't be bedding another man now. She has to pay. . . .*

Leona jerked her hand free and rubbed the psychic burn with her other hand. A fiery need for revenge had sizzled around her, laced with hatred, lust, and greed. Those piercing black eyes had locked directly on to her and she'd seen a red-haired woman with terrified green eyes looking at her—her grandmother. Stella Mornay had committed suicide, *because she had to . . . .*

Because she had been told to?

The thought terrified Leona, but she couldn't let her psychic barometer get out of control. She focused on her inner calm. She mentally draped a white protective sheet over her, and the images disappeared. Bracing herself, she turned to find Alex's tall, gentle form hunched in the doorway. From the dark energy on the laptop, Alex had probably gotten the same image as she had moments ago. "I loved Joel," she stated firmly.

"Oh, really?" Alex challenged, his eyes hard and accusing behind his lenses.

His crisp, bitter tone shocked Leona. "Alex, listen to me. It's important that you call me if Vernon makes contact. And you really need to—"

Alex was on her in that moment, clasping his arms around her. His lips pressed hard against hers, his tongue forced into her mouth.

Stunned for just that heartbeat, Leona didn't react. All her senses quivered, scarlet threads circling her, squeezing the breath from her. . . .

Fear caused her to react and her knee jerked into his groin. Alex staggered back, his hand catching her rune bracelet, taking it with him. Shaken, Leona struggled to push her breath back into her lungs. "Alex!"

Doubled over in pain, Alex had tumbled back into an antique sofa. "I'm sorry . . . I'm sorry . . . you're my friend. I don't know what made me do that . . . I don't."

Leona shook her head, trying to clear it. Sue Ann's husband had acted out of character, too. And Vernon was the link between them. The psychic loved to play games with people's lives, tormenting them, and now Alex was infected. "I do know why."

She went to kneel beside him and focused on making him understand. "Alex, you've got to get out of here. You've got to get rid of that laptop."

"But all my information, my retirement funds, my inheritance from my mother—it's all on there." When Alex shook his head, his glasses glinted in the dim light. That hard, slightly crazed look remained.

"You can replace it. You have to, Alex. Believe me."

His brown eyes widened behind his glasses. "Tell me why you would even suggest such a thing."

"Vernon may be a bad influence. Please believe me, Alex. You need to leave here as soon as possible."

"But I've just moved here." Alex stared at her blankly. Then in his soft, gentle tones, he said, "Leona, I do apologize for wanting you so desperately. Perhaps I expressed myself in the wrong way, but you are a lovely, lovely woman. You seemed so desirable tonight. I've never seen you so . . . You're flushed and warm and wearing so much jewelry that I thought you'd dressed for me. It's been so long since I—"

Had a woman? she finished silently. The concept that he thought of making love to her startled Leona. "Alex, we're just good friends," she stated gently.

He stood and faced the street outside, his back to Leona. "I'm sorry for what must have seemed like an attack. But I really think that what you've just said about Vernon—and I know him well—may be a sign that you are paranoid and perhaps need psychiatric help. Sometimes these things travel in families. Perhaps you'd better research yours."

Alex turned to toss her bracelet to her. "I didn't know you were involved in witchcraft. It seems I don't know you at all."

Shaken, Leona made her way out of the house and back to her car. She tried to calm herself as she sat, gripping the steering wheel, and replaying the scene with Alex. Max huffed and tilted his head, his beautiful eyes questioning her.

"Max, old boy, I think we have a definite problem. Alex has definitely been psyched, as we say in laymen's terms," Leona observed as she started the car. "Let's go see what we can do about it."

Rubbing her wrist where she'd reattached the rune bracelet. She noticed a red mark burned into her pale skin. When she touched one of the runes, it seemed hot.

She held her wrist out to Max and watched his response.

Max sniffed her bracelet. Then he stared at the white pillars and spacious porch of the plantation-style house and let out a series of warning barks.

"That's what I thought, too. That bastard has definitely gotten to Alex."

Owen rubbed his hand across his bare chest. Crows perched in the lightning-struck tree near him. He'd been preparing himself, opening his mind to the past and nature around him. He'd gone into his heartbeat and become one with it, flowing along the river of his experiences. He'd come full circle from his boyhood to the man really inside him. He opened the door to forgotten memories and dreams.

Two hours had skipped by as he'd stood or crouched, focusing on that triangle of water. Perched high on the stark branches, defined by moonlight, the crows seemed like a suitable audience for the uneasy, eerie task he faced now.

"Let's see if what the old ones say about gray eyes is true," Owen murmured. In the dim light, he noted the pond's surface, almost like a rippling, restless strip of silver. If he stood in that triangle of natural water, would he feel what Leona had felt? Would the fog come after him? "If you can sense me, you bastard, let's play."

Owen wanted nothing to distract him. He'd removed all of his clothing except a pair of special moccasins he'd kept in his truck. The delicate beadwork designs reflected his Blackfoot heritage. His mother had meticulously created them with love; she'd given the moccasins to him on his twenty-fifth birthday. "Some day, you'll need to walk a difficult path. Wear these and keep safe, Owen Wolf Shaw—Shaman," she had corrected, and her eyes had filled with tears.

At the time, he'd treasured the gift—because it was from his mother.

"Now would be the time to try them out, Mother, to see what I really am." He lifted one of the sweetgrass braids he'd tucked inside the moccasins and brought it to his nose. The scent reminded him of his boyhood in Montana, when he and a friend burned small, smoky fires. They'd wafted the aromatic smoke over them and dreamed of the warriors they would be. To burn sweetgrass now suited Owen's mood.

The oral history of "the gray eyes" in Owen's family was unique: They fought differently, lived apart, fiercely protecting their loved ones. They carved images, angular sticks, then some woven designs, of strange longboats led by fierce beasts.

The stories were old and no doubt embellished, but the connection to the Vikings could exist. Leona's two brothers-in-law all came from Nordic stock. Perhaps they had light eyes. The Aisling women had chosen men of that bloodline. . . . *Was that link true? Or was it an accident?*

Owen hadn't understood his childhood dreams, the clashing of blades, the water that did not end. He hadn't understood the large ships led by "dragons," the bright red sails billowing with wind. He'd dreamed of a wolf and its mate, and tall warriors with metal shields. When he was eight, a wisewoman had called him aside, and whispered, "Gray eyes. They see things others can't. They see in the night, through the rain and mist. Do you? Do they let you hunt like the wolf, when others cannot see?"

As a boy, Owen hadn't wanted to be different and had closed the door to the dreams, refusing them. Janice was sensitive in other ways. And someone had used her emotional wounds and their primitive bloodline against her.

Owen lifted his face to the clean air and swore aloud, "I will dig this monster out and kill him."

Slowly he walked to the pond, studying the black water overlaid by shimmering moonlight. Then he circled the pond until he stood in that dangerous triangle of pond, stream, and river. As he slowly circled the pond three times, Owen visualized the water flowing over him. He gave himself to the stream and the river, and they became his. Their secrets flowed through him, though he didn't seek to understand their meanings. Crouching beside the pond, he scooped its water into both hands, so it would know him and become his friend. "You're not to blame, old friend. May you have the peace you need, the fresh air and the rain to purify you. May your waters feed the animals and let the birds swim upon you in peace."

When his small fire of sweetgrass died and turned to smoke, Owen used his open hands to wash the familiar smell against his face. As he inhaled it, he looked up at the crows. He listened with his instincts, letting his hunter's blood open to the sounds of the night—the deer rustling in the brush, going down to the river. On the knoll behind him, Moon Shadow nickered softly. The bluegrass moved to the call of the slight wind hissing through it.

But Owen focused inward, where the darkness was still and waiting, holding its secrets. The September night was damp and crisp on his body, smelling of leaves and grass and earth, light wind lifting his hair and playing around his nude body as made himself one with nature. The waiting stillness he'd once rejected began to waken, to bloom and envelop him. He accepted the earth, air, and water elements into his body and spirit, and he became one with them.

Suddenly, a soft hiss sounded inside his mind. Piercing black eyes appeared and a mass of rippling black hair. Thin braids swung around a furious, malevolent face—the same face as in Janice's sketch.

Caught by surprise, Owen stepped back and braced himself to fight. When he opened his eyes, full night blanketed the field, a star or two in the sky. There was nothing around him, only the sounds of the night and of his quickened breath and pounding heartbeat. "Come back, you bastard. This time in the flesh."

Closing his eyes again, he let his senses stretch out into the night. In his mind, the image of a yard-long, slender blade appeared; it raised for a deathblow, and Owen went still. At the last moment, he moved aside. A sudden gust of cold wind brushed against his shoulder. Mist circled his nude body, chilling him; it was almost as if a man circled him. Big, powerful, furious, the man seemed to be gauging Owen's strength.

The image of the blade rose again, and Owen crouched to grip and raise a fallen branch to shield himself. The branch cracked as if struck. "She's mine! The red-haired witch is mine" the man shrieked.

"What kind of man preys on women?" Owen asked, his mind hazy from the blow, the sound of his voice echoing clearly in the night.

A furious scream sounded again. "You can't keep her from me. She's mine, so is the brooch."

In Owen's mind, the image of a brooch appeared, a wolf's head in the center. Words flowed into his mind, and he repeated them softly, "House of the Wolf, Thorgood the Great, whose mighty hand holds his people safe, who will kill those who defy him. His line will be long and powerful, reigning after him, for he who holds the wolf, holds the power. . . ."

Owen Wolf . . . Wolf . . . a man of the gray-eyed people, the band of warriors surrounding the small red-haired seer, protecting her. . . . And her name was Aisling. . . .

The family name had been taken from clan of the Wolf, from Thorgood-the-Wolf's men. His warriors had worn the wolf emblem upon their shields, upon their chests.

Distracted by the vision within his mind, Owen wasn't prepared for the swift blow to his head. Dazed, he sank to his knees and the earth seemed to shift beneath him. His hand tried to brush away the blood flowing from his wound, but it blinded him.

Suddenly, the hot burn at his back caused him to arch in pain, and he struggled to his feet.

He heard a gun go off, bracing herself for the hit, which never came.

"Man of Borg," Owen whispered fiercely, the name of his attacker flowing in his mind. He caught it and freed it from his lips again, "Borg. I smell your blood, and soon the air will smell of it, too. No matter where you go, I'll follow, because I have your scent now. I'm going to kill you, you son of a bitch."

When Owen opened his eyes again, the moon was rising and the evil presence was gone; he knew that the time to hunt would come again.

The shadow-spirit had tested him, and now they knew the blood-scent of each other. . . .

Fourteen

"DEAR MR. BORG. F.Y.I. YOU ARE NOT ALONE IN YOUR NEED for revenge. I want my share. My grandmother's and Joel's death weren't accidents, but I have no absolute proof."

With Max at her feet, Leona traced the bracelet's charms, as they lay spread on the kitchen table before her. She arranged the candles nearby. Candlelight suited the night; it flickered on the rectangular silver runes.

At eleven o'clock, Owen had called to check on her. After seeing to Leona's safety, he said he would be delayed. A leak in the kitchen plumbing had caused the floor to flood; the water could damage the flooring and had to be mopped up. Owen's tone was rough, but then Leona suspected he wasn't happy about water damage. In that area, the cell-phone reception wasn't the best either, and Owen had cut the call short.

Meanwhile, Leona had worked off her frustration with Alex's behavior by furiously painting the closet's wood shelving. Then she'd opened the windows in the bedroom. A fan hummed quietly and blew most of the fumes out into the night. A towel at the base of the bedroom door blocked the rest. Max had watched with interest as she'd struggled to put a dresser in front of the door. Otherwise, she wouldn't feel comfortable leaving the window open in a room she couldn't lock. The dresser wasn't a lock, but could act as a brief deterrent.

Confident that Max would alert her to any prowler, Leona had changed into a long, dark teal-and-turquoise lounging shift. Then she'd settled down to circle who she was—an Aisling with relatively untapped psychic powers but ones that were definitely growing.

Today's package from her mother lay opened on the table, the contents spread before Leona. Greer had created a duplicate set of her own index cards for Leona. Each individual in the Aisling family or dangerous incident that had happened to them was represented by a card.

Leona ran her fingertip over a new card that she had written: Joel's "accidental death." Each card in her sisters' lives listed an event harmful to them—Claire's sensory overload when she'd miscarried. The doctor and nurse's handling of Claire had been suspicious. Then both had died immediately after Claire left their care. Later, Claire had been attacked by a man who had committed suicide.

Tempest had been kidnapped by a youth who had committed suicide. Robyn had either killed herself, or someone had done it for her, and that blue-green scarf around her neck had been a warning to Leona. Alex was definitely affected, or rather "infected." Dean—if he stayed away from Vernon—would hopefully recover.

"Committed suicide . . ." The phrase circled Leona. She reached for her own set of index cards and wrote, "Stella Mornay—Grams."

Grams . . . He's coming . . . you've got to stop him, Leona. . . . Was it possible that someone from the Borg bloodline had caused Stella Mornay to lose her control? To spiral her into suicide? If so, why hadn't Greer, a powerful extrasensory, caught the threat to her own mother?

Vernon's whereabouts were still unknown, and he could be the final missing piece of this puzzle.

Leona tapped a blank card. All of the people known to have attempted harm to the Aisling-Bartel triplets were dead. Was it possible Vernon was dead, too?

Leona studied the row of three cards: one for Tempest's husband Marcus and one for Claire's husband, Neil. The third was for Owen. Greer had written "Protector" on each card.

Then she considered each silver rune, each cut with an angular character. Tempest, a sculptor, had always been comfortable using the Aislings' Viking heritage in her art. Leona wondered why Alex grabbed her bracelet in particular—not her wrist. She wondered if the bracelet meant anything to the Borg-descendant who has obviously connected with Alex.

Instinctively, Leona understood that now she needed any items that might help her to bring forth more of her grandmother's plight. She placed the replica of Thorgood's brooch on the table and studied it. Then she hurried to get a cherished handkerchief. It had been embroidered by her grandmother and was a tie to the past. After laying the handkerchief on the table, she placed her open hand on the linen square and focused. Closing her eyes, she put herself back into the time her grandmother had given it to her. Even a child could notice the uneven stitches, which were so unlike her grandmother's previous work. There had been terror in her grandmother's eyes as she'd leaned close. "You won't understand now, but someday you will. I loved your grandfather, but there was another man. . . ."

An image resembling the Borg-descendant slid into Leona's mind, and now she understood. The change in

Stella Mornay was because of an extramarital affair; the man had deliberately used her guilt to drive her mad.... *He's coming...you've got to stop him, Leona....*

Leona gasped and jerked herself back from the images. Closing her eyes again, she gripped the bracelet. The psychic burn hurt immediately, but she focused on each rune, her fingertips circling them slowly as she concentrated on pushing away that dark, consuming, crackling energy and replacing it with her own.

Max growled softly, then issued a sharp warning bark. His hackles raised, he braced all four legs apart as he faced the table.

"Leona?" the uneven masculine whisper hissed around the room as the candlelight flickered. *"Leona?"*

She recognized the masculine energy immediately, and it wasn't Owen's. This energy belonged to the man who had whispered her name in the mist—harsh, dark, cruel, arrogant, manipulative....She'd actually reached out and touched the Borg-descendant's energy! Then Max swung back to face Leona, his head tilted with a question she couldn't answer. Or could she?

"He is strong enough to make a link by locking on to a person's vulnerabilities and making an imprint, Max," Leona whispered. "I think I hear him, but I don't. He took something from me that day in the shop and out in Owen's field. Now I've got something of his. Let's see if I can do this, okay? It would have had to pass through Alex's energy. I want to see through Alex, to the mind of who has affected him."

Leona closed her eyes and focused on her pulse. She used it as a winding stream to take her through Alex to someone else, someone evil. She wound around passages, followed worn steps down into a candlelit cave....

On a cluttered table lay a long blade, the sword's grip and pommel ornate in the Viking style. "Man of Borg's blood," she whispered, "I have you now."

The image began to break apart, a long, zagged tear slowly opening it to reveal another image inside. Long, black, rippling hair swirled around a sharp masculine face. The mesmerizing black eyes of her dreams and Janice's sketch stared back at her. This time they were surprised and fearful. Leona liked the fearful part; she intended to use it.

"I have you, Borg," she repeated softly, as the psychic energy inside her powered on. It fed on his fear and grew stronger. "I know you now. You cannot escape me."

The image snapped shut suddenly. Leona realized she'd been holding her breath. Fighting for air, her head light for lack of oxygen, she breathed deeply. This time her blood burned her veins, hot with anger and frustration. "You bastard. If I'd had that sword in my hand, I would have swung it at you. I'm not letting you go now. I'm not afraid. I'm just mad."

Leona hurried to clasp the bracelet back to her wrist. Hoping to reconnect with the image, she pressed the rune charms against her flesh. The energy-burn was gone. She held her breath, testing one rune again. The silver ran smooth and feminine beneath her fingertip. "I've cleaned away his energy," she breathed in disbelief.

The tingling of her senses indicated a call Leona should have expected. She reached for the telephone, and Tempest's voice exploded. "What the hell do you think you're doing? Claire just called. She's afraid for you. You're not into that witchcraft bunk, are you? We promised that none of us would ever do that. You swore a blood oath on that. I've got the scar right here, on my thumb. *You* made us swear. Remember? Out in Mom's garden, beneath the midnight moon? We were just twelve, and trying to balance our lives. We swore,

Leona Fiona, and you led the pack. Jeez, I can feel the impact here in Michigan. The hair on my head almost stood straight up."

"I made contact," Leona managed unsteadily. "I *think* I made contact . . . with Borg's descendant. I got him!"

"What the hell for? Don't you know this thing can boomerang back on you? That this creep can suck the energy out of you? Where is Owen? I want to talk with Owen. Right now."

To block Tempest, Leona focused on Max: His brown eyes were beautiful. They reminded her of Egyptian eyes, lined in kohl. His ears were pointed and soft beneath her fingers. "Owen isn't here."

"Okay, I just got another psychic door slammed in my face. Tell me just where Owen is. Oh, hell, there's Claire on the other line. Marcus just picked it up."

"Keep her out of this, Tempest. It could hurt her now. *I* could hurt her."

"You're right. Marcus, tell Claire I'll call her back. Leona, you just tapped into this creep's energy. Damn. You're wearing it, aren't you? That rune bracelet—he touched it somehow. How?"

"I'm stronger," Leona said unsteadily. "Your *'read'* is wrong. His energy was on the bracelet, and now it isn't. I cleaned it. *I cleaned it, Tempest Best.*"

Tempest cursed lightly, then the line was silent. "You always did like a good fight, Leona Fiona."

"Tempest?"

"If there's much more to this, Marcus and I are coming down to Kentucky and cleaning this guy's clock."

"Listen carefully. I don't think Gram's insanity and suicide—"

"Oh no, don't tell me. I'm getting Grams's image from you, right now. Dad's and Joel's, too. Leona, what's up? What about Grams?"

"I . . . I think she was seduced into an affair—with a Borg descendant. She couldn't forgive herself, and that left her vulnerable to him. She did things she shouldn't have done."

"What makes you think that?"

Leona didn't want her sister to know about their grandmother's handkerchief. Tempest was the most curious of the triplets; she would surely want to hold the handkerchief in her bare hands. The images it would reveal in her naked hands were intimate and shocking. Leona explained partially: "Him. I got it from him, from the connection in my shop. Something taken, something given."

"I bet you did. I don't doubt it for a minute, so don't think I do. We shouldn't tell Mom."

"She may have some idea already. You've got a job to do, Tempest. That's keeping Claire out of this and being careful when you talk to Mom. And keep that husband of yours out of this. This isn't something Marcus can ramrod."

Tempest whistled lightly. "Grams . . . Dad . . . Joel. . . . Okay, what else is there?"

Leona spoke very carefully. Sometimes the sisters didn't need words, but this time they were necessary. "Owen has light eyes."

"Yeah, so? Mom noticed right away. He's a Protector, same as Neil and Marcus. We knew that. He's not letting anything happen to you. He'll guard you with his life."

"His middle name is Wolf. . . ." Leona took a deep breath and steadied herself before continuing, "And Shaw is from shaman. Owen . . . Wolf . . . Shaman."

After a long silence, in which Leona could sense her sister's racing heartbeat, her excitement, Tempest spoke unevenly. "The blend of his ancestry, his blood . . . He could be really powerful, descended from two different backgrounds. One could open the doorway of the other. Does he know what that means?"

"Some. But not all. I don't think he wants to."

"You need to get the Borg-descendant for closure, don't you? For Joel, Grams, and for Dad?"

"And for the others."

When the call ended, Leona rose to walk to the mirror. Max was immediately on his paws, close at her side. "I know. You're a protector, too. It's a wolf thing, isn't it? You and Owen, the alpha male and his right guard? I did it, Max. I was able to make contact with this creep. I can clean his energy. I should have known I could when Dean settled down after I soothed him. I should have known it when I was able to help Janice or when Sue Ann followed my directions. It was there all the time. What else don't I know about myself?"

Leona's image stared back at her from the mirror. The candlelight framed her hair with a fiery tint, her eyes mysterious in her pale face. "I have to tell my mother that I suspect her mother's insanity and her suicide was because of a Borg descendant. I have to tell her that even at eight years old, one of them was strong enough—with help—to imprint our father. That image caused his death."

Leona considered her reflection. Owen had been right: She was outfitting herself for a fight. Tonight, she'd worn more: an upper-arm circlet decorated with a woven Celtic design and a wide cuff bracelet; the headband that Claire had just sent circled her head. It was a *diadem*, and very old, one Tempest had found when searching for the brooch. *She had gathered her power around her . . .*

Leona looked down at Max who had just huffed. His tail wagged as he hurried to the front door.

"I guess we know who's home, don't we, Wolfie? I'd better put the teakettle on."

"That little witch did it! Leona actually reached me, pulsed right through a mind-stream and saw me! She actually grabbed a part of my energy, and now she's using it!"

Rolf Erling gripped the sword he'd used earlier to mark Owen Shaw; he slashed it across one burning candle to expertly kill the flame. A big, powerful man, Rolf hefted the weighty replica easily. Smiling coldly, he remembered bringing the heavy pommel down on Shaw's head. Shaw had been stunned for a moment, and it was enough to mark him with a Borg blade.

Fresh from marking a man he would kill after toying with him, Rolf had been elated and secure in his underground sanctuary. Then Leona had pulsed through his safety. He'd seen her at the last minute, stunned that she would appear in his mind. Her mind-stream had curled around him. Those green eyes had appeared in a pale face, gently lit by flame. She resembled the Aisling seer he'd seen in his dreams, complete with a *diadem* in that flame-lit hair. The psychic lock had startled Rolf before he could push everything into closing the door to her. Her words still circled him eerily. *Man of Borg's blood . . . I have you, Borg. I know you now. You cannot escape me.*

Rolf looked into his mirror, met his own burning, mesmerizing eyes, and cursed. "Leona has gathered her power around her, the essence of her blood's inheritance. She's getting stronger, but not smarter. If she had gotten smarter, she never would have tried to reach me that way. I could have fried her—I have done it to others and left them as drooling vegetables."

The remaining candles flickered against the walls and on the three-foot custom-made blade. "Man, woman, and wolf-dog . . . they're strong together, the same as Leona's sisters and their men. I've got to separate them."

He looked at the female dog in her cage, and murmured, "You're not ready yet. They told me you would be. Don't take much longer, or you won't be of any use to me."

The yellow bitch snarled at him and showed her fangs.

A familiar chill caused him to turn back to the mirror. The ancestor who should have possessed Aisling stared back at him. Borg's masses of black rippling hair whipped around his head as if he stood in a storm at sea. *"I cursed the seer and Thorgood's line. You know what they did to me. Now finish it, or be finished! You play too much when you should have killed her protector. You know what he is, one of them, one of Thorgood's men, sworn to protect the Aisling line. This one is different, his blood makes him more powerful than the rest. Get rid of him."*

"In my own time. I've marked him."

Marked him? You should have killed him then, you fool. Stop playing. Now is the time . . .

"Now is the time." Rolf closed his eyes. Deep inside, he knew that as the last and most powerful descendant of Borg, he couldn't fail.

The penalty would be his own death. His own father had failed, because Stella Mornay had eventually committed suicide to save her family. Then it was his father's turn to pay the penalty, just as his father before him. Failure meant suicide, a family tradition.

Rolf placed the sword's tip on the large photograph of the artifact he needed—after killing the Aislings or just taking their minds. Since his birth, the brooch had been described to him—a wolf's-head design, circled with Thorgood's boast and stones set into the design.

The photograph left on Leona's desk was of the aged relic, without the stones. The photograph held Greer Aisling's energy residue, Shaw's, and Leona's.

The Aislings' brooches looked similar, but with a softer Celtic design circling the wolf. When she'd dared enter his privacy, Leona had been wearing her brooch as well as the rune bracelet he'd marked with his energy to disturb her. The little psychic tracer had been intended to signal him if she were nearby, either in the flesh or in her senses. It had failed, an indication that her energy had wiped his away. Rolf's father had been right: the Aisling women were undependable. Their gifts could leap and grow when least expected.

Rolf fought his temper. "I've always liked challenges. They make the game so much more fun, Leona."

Glancing at the clock, he anticipated the long night ahead. With a woman too happy to obey him, it would be sexually exhausting. Rolf's need of her was also in other, crueler ways. For him, she'd dyed her hair red and wore green-tinted contacts. "Mm. I'd better get ready for my date. I need her tonight, to take off the edge."

Leona opened her front door before Owen reached it.

Her excitement over reaching the Borg-descendant quickly died. Owen's chest was bare; he braced one hand against the door frame, the other held a blood-soaked washcloth to his forehead.

"You're bleeding!"

Owen stared at her for a moment, as if he wasn't certain who she was. Then he nodded slowly, and a trickle of blood ran down his cheek. The area around his mouth was pale and tight with pain.

Wrapping her arm around him, she drew him inside. She pushed the door closed, and Owen reached behind him to lock the dead bolt. "I think I made a mess of my truck seat. I need to go clean that up."

"You will not." Leona's fingers trembled as she eased the cloth away from his forehead. The inch-long wound topped a large, swelling bruise. "What happened?"

The warm sticky dampness beneath her other hand caused her to draw away. She held her breath as she looked down at the red stain on her hand. Circling Owen, she looked at his back. Dried blood covered his skin; fresh blood welled from a long gash on his shoulder. "Owen!"

He started to sway, and Leona quickly hurried him from the living room to a kitchen chair. "This is bad. You need attention. The light is better here. What happened?" she repeated.

Owen sprawled into the chair and shook his head as if to clear it. Closing his eyes; he seemed to pale beneath his dark skin. "Ah . . . Could you get me a bag of ice for my head?"

Leona hurried to place ice cubes into a plastic bag. She eased it onto his forehead, taking care not to touch the wound. In another heartbeat, she placed a glass of ice water in his hand. "Drink this."

Owen sighed wearily. He eased his head against her breast, as if he'd found the perfect pillow he'd needed forever. "It's been a long day, honey. I'm beat."

Filled with emotions, fear for him and love mixing equally, Leona held him close for a moment. "Damn you. I love you, Owen Shaw," she whispered unsteadily. "I didn't want to, but I do."

He nuzzled her breast and sighed. "Yeah. I know. Love you, too, honey. Wait . . . I can say it better, but just not now. Women need the words . . . showing you with my body isn't enough. Dad was wrong. . . . But your breasts really are the shade of those calla lilies, your nipples like roses. I wanted to say something about how they taste like honey, but can't think right now. The stallion and mare image fits us sometimes. . . . I like the soft times, too. You're real cuddly, Leona."

Leona lifted his chin; Owen didn't sound like himself. Panic raced through her. Owen could have a concussion. He could be delirious. "How did you know I loved you—exactly?"

"At the pond. I got that from you somehow. You spoke to me. I heard your voice."

Leona remembered her fear for him; Owen had picked up her love for him. *And he'd kept that tidbit to himself.*

They would talk later—definitely. She steadied herself with the reminder that he was safe in her arms. Then she blotted damp paper towels over his back, circling the gash on his shoulder. It was long, if not deep. "Owen, I think we should go to the emergency room."

"Get the envelope out of my pocket." His hand moved weakly toward his jeans.

Owen's curt order caused Leona to move quickly. Reaching in the pocket of his jeans she pulled out a rumpled envelope, gave it to him, then continued gently to pat the dried blood away from the gash. More blood welled up into the cut. "Owen, let's go to the emergency room . . . Please."

He lifted his head and sniffed slightly. "Fresh paint?"

Blinking owlishly at her, he rose unsteadily to his feet. He braced his hand against the wall as he walked to the hallway. When Leona hurried to support him, he stared at the chest of drawers in front of the bedroom door and groaned. He moved slowly back to the kitchen. "Don't tell me."

"You need to sit down. . . . You said you were working on the plumbing, and I had to do something—"

Owen turned to her, and this time his eyes were sharp and steely. He glanced at her grandmother's handkerchief and at the candles, then at Leona. "Like what?"

"Never mind that right now," she answered, guiding him back to the chair.

Owen sat down and rubbed Max's head as if glad for a friend. "He used the microtape in the envelope. He edited my voice into what he needed. I played bits of it, before I left. I didn't call you. . . . Ah, is that the tea-kettle whistling, or just the buzzing in my head?"

"Are we going to the emergency room or not?" Leona demanded as she tended the kettle.

"I don't need it."

"Owen—"

"No. I'd just as soon not explain what happened . . . not after finding a dead woman in my pond and my re-volver is missing. I may be facing questions I don't want to answer—and neither do you. Get me some aspirin, will you? And tell me what you've got in your medicine cabinet in the way of bandages and antiseptics."

Leona hurried to gather every supply possible and returned to see Owen studying that tiny cassette tape. She set to work cleaning his back. The four-inch-long gash had ripped the outer skin. It seemed unusual, the cut almost in a V, down, then back up. "You didn't re-port that gun as missing, did you? Why not?"

"Circumstances. It could lead to a death years ago. I'd rather the details weren't refreshed just now, but I didn't do it," he said, and retrieved a slug from his jeans pocket. He tossed it on the table. "I dug this out of the barn door. That cut on my back wasn't caused by a bul-let . . . try a three-foot-long sword blade. He sliced me once, then used the sword butt on my head. I couldn't see through the blood. The shot came later, when I got up. He didn't want to hit me—I'd have been an easy target. He just wanted me to know he had something I cherished—my father's gun."

Leona sucked in her breath. Images of how Owen

had nearly been killed tumbled around her like shards of ice. Owen glanced at her. "What?"

She thought better of telling him just what she'd seen in that mind-stream, the connection with Borg's descendant. "Nothing."

As she reached for the antiseptic, Owen frowned and caught her wrist. He turned it slowly and eased aside the rune bracelet to study her skin. "Did you burn yourself?"

"It was an accident."

"You're going to tell me about it when you stitch me up."

"Stitch you up?"

Owen smiled sheepishly. "Just kidding. That's what they did in the Old West, wasn't it? Poured whiskey over it and used a needle and thread? But a few butterfly bandages should do it, honey."

"This is an odd time to start making jokes, Owen."

Those gray eyes pinned her again. "Going to tell me what you've been doing since I last saw you? Other than painting that closet? And why you're dressed like that, with that headband, and burning candles?"

He touched the stack of index cards. "And about those? Explain. More details. You're leaving something out."

Leona was hiding something.

At four o'clock in the morning, Owen left Leona sleeping in her guest room. It wasn't his bed, and that grated. The instinct to have *his* woman, in *his* bed, ate at Owen. The bruise on his head and the V-shaped gash on his back hurt, despite the pain pill Leona had given him and he couldn't sleep. The last he remembered before dozing off was Leona bending over him to smooth his hair. On his stomach, Owen had given himself to those soft hands roaming his back, her lips trailing a few soft kisses on his skin, the silky wisps of her hair across his shoulders, and had floated off into darkness. . . .

He'd known Leona was easing and healing him. Even Max understood something was happening and had come to look at him, then had padded off. Owen had drowsily sensed that the dog would stand guard during the night. The shadows he'd glimpsed beneath Leona's eyes said she'd also stayed awake to rouse him periodically, to ask his name and other details, checking him for a concussion.

Owen tentatively rolled his aching shoulder. The skin was tight and healing unbelievably fast. Those shadows on Leona's pale skin probably had more to do with her using healing powers than actual loss of sleep. *She didn't yet know her capabilities, and that frightened Owen; he feared what she could step into. . . .*

As he eased out of the bedroom, he patted Max. The dog plopped down at the bedroom doorway. "Good dog. Stay with her."

As if he understood perfectly, Max padded to the bed and leaped up beside Leona. He lay close against her body. "Huh. Looks like you've done that before. Just don't get used to it."

Owen took a couple of aspirin, made a turkey, lettuce, and tomato sandwich, and poured a glass of milk. He checked his messages on his cell: another five-acre farm had just come on the market, the price reasonable, and a couple of older cottages perfect for starter or retirement homes. A farmer had returned Owen's query about the price of winter hay, and the lumberyard clerk needed to schedule delivery of the farmhouse's new thermal windows. Owen smiled slightly at the next message: an invitation to one of the thoroughbred farms, the payoff for stepping into the town's business and society circles.

The final message gripped Owen: Jonas Saber, an old friend with ties to Montana's law enforcement had received Owen's fax, a copy of Janice's sketch. Owen had sent the sketch to Jonas, knowing that if there was a connection between what happened to Janice and to Leona's sister, Claire, Jonas would find it. Jonas might also be able to methodically pinpoint and date the guy's every location and move.

Greer's index cards and the jewelry Leona had worn were still on the table. Leona had explained a little about the cards, but not enough. Owen sat down to eat and to compare them.

Spreading the cards out, he tapped Janice's, then aligned "Montana" with the "Montana" on Claire's card. The connection jarred him. "Protector" had been written on his card, and matched the other men's labels. Three men, three "Protectors."

Two cards weren't in Greer's handwriting. Leona had written "Grams" on one and "Dad" on another.

The triplets' father had died in an accident when the triplets were four. Their grandmother had gone mad and years later, she'd committed suicide. How did Leona connect them to the other cards? What else was she doing when Owen had arrived? The candlelight could have been romantic, but Leona was doing something else—she was definitely hunting. *It took one to know one.*

Had she found anything? If she had, she wasn't talking, and that ran to the issue of trust. Maybe she feared him still. Maybe she feared herself and her power.

Owen picked up the bracelet and studied the silver runes. He could almost see Leona laying them in flickering candlelight, a seer at work. The runes warmed Owen's fingers, almost as if he'd known them from another time.

He traced the angular Viking characters as he remembered last night. The slight injury on Leona's wrist wasn't an accidental cooking burn. She was hiding the real cause, and Owen sensed that she was protecting him—or someone else.

He smiled tightly; Leona had definitely acted as if she trusted him. She had hesitated only slightly when he'd mentioned the revolver could be traced to a death, but she hadn't asked questions. She hadn't asked about that blade either. Mention of a three-foot sword should have caused some remark and definitely questions. But Leona acted as if she already knew exactly whose sword he was talking about.

Unused to taking orders, he'd actually liked Leona's earlier. Her care for him seemed possessive, another indication that he was very special to her. He'd practice that "I love you" thing, so it wouldn't come out wrong.

After taking a sip of milk, he picked up the gold band that had been around Leona's head, running his thumb around it. It was obviously very old. When Leona had opened the door, he'd been slightly dazed and in pain. Her long dark teal-and-turquoise gown, the gold head-band around her red hair, those green eyes in that pale face, and the ethnic jewelry could have been Aisling's, Leona's ancestor.

A long time ago, he'd seen someone else who looked like Leona and had dressed like her. The image flirted with Owen, then slipped from his grasp. He traced the angular characters with his fingertip; he recognized them yet they weren't from anything he'd read or actually seen.

Rubbing his forehead, he tried to remember. Blurred images danced beyond his grasp. . . . He'd seen another woman who looked like Leona, but with long red hair, tossed by the wind. He'd taken an oath to protect her children with his life. He'd seen a sword like the one to-night before. He'd hunted a man with a sword like that, tracked his scent. . . .

Owen looked at the runes and the candle. The white cloth the jewelry had been lying upon was linen and bordered with a woven Celtic design. The combination of the elements and Leona's outfit tonight seemed as if she were exploring who and what she was. If she was, Leona was playing with fire, opening doors to her gifts. What had she found?

When Max's claws sounded on the hardwood floor, Owen looked up to see Leona coming toward the kitchen area. She looked exhausted. Leaning forward he waited until she came close to check the gauze bandage over his back. Then he caught her wrist, drawing her down to his lap. He rested his head against Leona's shoulder; she felt like home, peaceful and sweet and a little bit like his future. "Don't move, honey. We wouldn't want those cuts to open again, would we?"

"No, we don't. You seem better."

"I am." Leona stroked his hair and kissed his forehead, and Owen let himself drift softly. "Thanks," he said simply.

"You're welcome."

"A healer, huh? I've heard it could happen."

"I had no idea. I just knew that you were responding to me, and that nothing could happen to you. How are you feeling?"

Owen arranged her to straddle him, sliding his hand up beneath her gown to find her bare and sweetly curved. He nuzzled her breasts, found her peaked nipples beneath the fabric, and suckled them gently. Leona's uneven breath, her body warming and moistening to his prowling fingers, caused him to smile. "I'm feeling like this," he whispered against her ear.

An hour later, Owen lay watching Leona sleep.

Early dawn lightened the shadows of the room. Her hand looked pale and slender as it rested across his chest. Lifting her hand, he kissed it and studied the mark on her wrist.

Leona shifted slightly, her leg stroking his, her fingers smoothing his chest. "Mm?"

"He didn't intend to kill me, Leona. He wanted something else."

Her tone changed to uneasy. "Uh-huh?"

"He didn't want to kill me last night, Leona. He's good with that sword, or he could have killed me. It takes practice to use a blade like that. He wanted to mark me, and that's what happened to your wrist, isn't it? He's marking his kills, Leona. He's testing me for the real thing—and then it won't be a game. You need to tell me everything you know, before he comes back to finish the job."

When Leona tensed and tried to pull her hand away, Owen held it momentarily. He wanted her to know that he wouldn't give up getting answers easily. "You know something about that sword, too. I want to know what."

Fifteen

"I'M IN THIS JIGSAW PUZZLE. TO PLAY THIS GAME, I NEED TO know how all the pieces fit . . . including Joel, your father, and grandmother."

Owen leaned against the kitchen counter, a cup of freshly made black chai in his hand. A strand of that sleek, blue-black hair crossed the white bandage on his forehead and those brooding, smoky eyes followed Leona. Lines cut deep at the sides of his mouth and between those dark eyebrows, and morning stubble darkened his jaw. Wearing only jeans, Owen looked tough and ready to fight.

Leona's hand trembled as she buttered halves of two toasted bagels. She lifted a jar of strawberry jam and silently questioned Owen. He nodded. "That looks homemade."

She spread the jam. "It is. It's one of the things I like to do for my family, putting jam in jars, sealing them."

"Everything all nice and neat and sealed away, huh?"

She dismissed his comment. It concerned more than jam; it concerned her life. "Sit down. I need to check your shoulder."

"Then we'll talk." Owen sat down in front of the plate of scrambled eggs, hash browns, and bacon, and dug in.

"I didn't know how you liked your eggs." Leona sat down to pour milk in her chai. As she stirred circles into the dark spicy brew, she compared it to her life. It changed by the minute—Owen's life blending with hers, the circles of life tightening around them.

"Scrambled are fine. You could have asked," he said.

"You didn't seem to be receptive earlier. You were brooding."

Owen munched on a piece of bacon and stared at her. "Do you blame me?"

"Small talk makes big stuff easier. It oils the way, so to speak," Leona stated quietly. Her chai was rich brown now and mellower. Her tea was very different from Owen's dark brew . . . just as she was different from him. As a woman, definitely. As a person who wanted revenge for crimes committed against her family, she was the same. At times he seemed to move on instinct, and she had that in common with him at times, surprising herself. And there were moments when her dark and primitive elements also matched Owen's.

Owen's body tensed slightly, his eyes averted to his plate. "I never learned small talk. Is that what you did with Joel?"

Leona looked at the morning sunshine passing through the window; her life with Joel seemed centuries ago, not just five years. "We talked about our dreams as well as everyday things! the children we wanted, my shop, what kind of grass to plant, his work as a medical supplies salesman—incomes, budgets, that sort of thing. He was a very gentle person."

Owen took a deep breath and his fork pushed though the hash browns. "These are good."

His mind clearly wasn't on food. Just yesterday, Leona had wanted to see Owen sitting just like this, talking with her. But now shadows slithered between them, and Owen was obviously comparing himself to

Joel, the fit uneasy. Leaning back in his chair, his fingers toying with her rune bracelet, he finally spoke. "I loved her . . . my first love. I didn't know she was married . . . to a rich man. My family didn't have money. She wanted to meet in secret. I believed everything she said, that she wanted to be certain of what we had, before going public. When I found out she was married and faced her with it, she laughed. She said I wasn't good enough to show off to her friends."

"Then she wasn't good enough for you," Leona stated firmly. Owen had finally opened a deep emotional wound to her; when wounds were opened, they could be healed. She leaned forward to brush his bottom lip, taking the tiny bit of jam to her own lips. Owen sucked in his breath and a jolt of sensuality hit low in her stomach. An image of him, carrying her off to bed, flickered through her mind: Owen over her, possessive, his hands staking hers to the bed, claiming her in hard, hungry thrusts. *He'd been perfect for her own hunger. She'd bound him close with her body; she'd captured him as he claimed her, confident that he would see to her pleasure. She'd known that he would come gently into her arms after that storm. . . .*

"You never made love with him like that, did you?" Owen asked suddenly, an indication that he'd also had that image of their lovemaking. He shifted uncomfortably, and in a quick show of her possession, Leona stroked his thigh. Hard muscle leaped at her touch, and pleasure rippled through her. *Perfect . . . primitive . . . she could be as free as she wanted with him—or as soft and tender and feminine. . . .*

"No. I knew I could trust Joel in certain ways. But he wouldn't have understood a certain part of me that I'd always known existed. I think he may have been too frightened if I'd opened—and he never would have been comfortable with me again. But he did love me."

She'd never told Joel of Aisling's image, the image that haunted her every time she looked in the mirror. Everything in Joel's world had been logical. He wouldn't have understood.

Leona looked down at her hand on Owen's thigh, her pale fingers pressing deep into the denim and hard muscle. She knew the feel of that skin against her own, the intimate—

"Stop that hand, lady. You're playing with fire."

"With you, yes," she admitted. Nothing pleasured her more than setting Owen off. *Love you, babe . . .*

Owen stilled and turned her hand to hold it. He was clearly set to tell her everything. "She didn't really care, but that didn't stop her husband from coming after me. I almost killed him, but a friend—Jonas Saber—stopped it. But I think she *did* kill her husband, with my dad's revolver—the one that's missing now. I'd taken it to show off for her—and she asked to borrow it, for target practice. They tracked the gun to Dad. I was in Wyoming when her husband died so I had an alibi. Dad lied for me and said he'd loaned it to her because she'd heard prowlers when her husband was gone. When the police questioned her she claimed the gun had misfired when her husband was cleaning it. They believed her, though I've always questioned that. Then Jonas pulled some strings and got the revolver back for my father."

Determined to put his dark past away, Owen slowly eased the charm bracelet around Leona's wrist. His hand stayed to stroke her skin. "I don't want anything to happen to you."

"It won't. You won't let it." Leona understood exactly how safe Tempest and Claire felt with their husbands, men with whom they had bonded; she sensed the same safety and unity with Owen.

She also understood how difficult it was for Owen to come the emotional distance, to express himself in words. Grateful to him for sharing his past with her, she hoped to reassure him. Lacing their fingers, she let her feminine softness blend with the harshness of his past. "My relationship with you is entirely different from mine with Joel's."

"Sometimes it's hard to tell. You hide what's going on with you."

"You're a still-waters-run-deep, yourself. I trusted Joel with all my heart. But somehow, I knew—"

Owen stared at her. "Knew what?"

"That you would come into my life, and it would change. . . . With you, *I* would change."

"Good or bad?"

Leona considered the woman she had been and the woman she was with Owen. "Depends. I'm different. Stronger, more alive. I'm not certain if I like how I feel at times—a little savage, a little primitive."

"I like it when you let go. Or when you don't." Owen smiled slightly as he studied the contrast of their skin, the size and shape of their hands. "You're doing it again. Healing me. I felt it last night . . . like flower petals falling all over me, a warm stream of them. . . . " He studied her expression. "You're opening the store today, aren't you? I wish you wouldn't."

"I'll be careful. We can't stop our lives because of fear. Rather, I will not stop mine. Or ask you to stop what you have to do. Janice is depending on you."

Owen's gaze locked with Leona's as he brought her hand to his lips; then he drew her to his lap and rocked her with his body. "You have to tell Greer whatever you suspect about Joel, your father, and her mother. You can tell me when you're ready."

"The question is: Why doesn't she already know everything?"

"Maybe she doesn't want to know."

"That could be. She could be strong enough to block

herself. I don't know how that works. I only know that this Borg-descendant got close enough to me and I didn't always sense him. He's good at blocking his real identity—or disguising it."

The tingle at the back of her neck wasn't going to go away. "It's Claire. She's worried. I need to talk with her."

As she stood, Owen patted her bottom, then his hand stayed for a slow caress as he also stood. His lips brushed hers, his tongue flicking a bit into her mouth. "I'll take Max out to the backyard. Then you can tell me about what really happened to your wrist."

He picked up his cup of chai and patted her bottom again, a definite proprietary gesture, a man who considered a woman to be his.

Leona liked that feeling.

She smiled as she answered Claire's call. "What's up?"

"You're glowing, that's what. Where's Owen? What's going on, and why did you tell Tempest to keep me out of this?" Claire demanded.

Leona's quiet, gentle sister had definitely changed, and her husband had everything to do with it. Leona looked out the kitchen window to see Max chasing a stick Owen had thrown. The play led into a rougher one, which ended up with Owen stretched out on the lawn, laughing as Max frisked about him. He seemed oblivious to the wound on his back. Struggling to focus on Owen and not her youngest sister, Leona hoped to keep her sister safe from her concerns. "I don't know what you mean."

Gentle, peaceful Claire was set to argue. "Don't you dare block me, Leona Fiona. You're getting too good at it. What's going on? If you don't tell me, Neil and I are headed down there."

That swung Leona's attention fully to Claire. "You can't. It's too dangerous."

She hadn't had time to rephrase her thoughts. To prevent Claire from learning more, Leona concentrated on the rune characters.

Claire wasn't to be detoured. "Have you been wearing Tempest's jewelry, the Celtic stuff? You have, haven't you? I can feel it pulsing around you! You're experimenting with what you can do, aren't you? My gosh, Leona, you're setting yourself up as a target, as bait, aren't you? You are actually going to take this beast on!"

"If he's out there, I'm getting him." Leona rubbed the smooth surface of the *eolh* rune, one that served as a protective charm. In reverse position, it signaled a warning: that whoever asked the runes for answers could be duped in the future, or the ones around them misled.

"That doesn't answer my question. I know that guy is out there, but something new has happened. I want to know what . . . other than you're obviously getting stronger. . . ." Claire cursed softly, for the first time that Leona had ever known. The phrase she used was definitely masculine. But then Claire was learning all sorts of things from Neil, a good-natured man who easily let Claire explore anything the empath wanted—as long as it wasn't dangerous to her. Overly curious, his wife was probably very busy exploring everything about her husband, fulfilling her own need to free that little fighting strand of Viking blood within her.

"I have a little problem, Claire Bear. Maybe you can help me." Leona explained the vision of that eight-year-old boy imprinting Daniel Bartel with that deadly image. "I think I snagged a bit of the Borg-descendant's grown-up energy that day he came into the shop."

She waited for the shock waves coming from Claire to settle into a furious hum. Then Leona spoke carefully. "Five years ago, you were in that hospital, almost the same day that Joel died. Claire, I thought my dreams lately of being crushed were because of how Joel had died in that snow avalanche, but they weren't. I think this monster—a Borg-descendant—took some of my energy when I visited Tempest in July, and definitely when he came into the shop."

"Damn him. That's what we thought! That jerk was playing, just getting warmed up. He was testing himself and us."

Neil's indistinct rumble preceded his order. "Give me that phone, Claire. You're getting upset."

Claire answered him, attempting unsuccessfully to muffle the conversation. "I will not. Leona has him, Neil. She's getting close."

Neil Olafson wasn't one to waste time. "I'm going down there to take care of that bastard, once and for all. Tell Leona to wait for me. I'll just take a little something for my upset stomach, and I'll be fine."

"Dammit, back off, Neil," Claire replied, "Go eat a cracker or something. I think there's something else Leona wants to say. I feel her uneasy hum. She doesn't know whether she should tell me or not. . . . Leona, tell me everything, or I swear, the both of us will come down there."

Faced with Claire's threat and the fear that her unborn baby could suffer from the trauma of a psychic encounter, Leona obliged. "Sit down, Claire. Put Neil on the line, in another room. You're picking up his anger . . . I can't deal with you and overlaps of his anger at the same time."

Neil picked up the extension. He was munching on a cracker. "Husband and protector here."

"You are not to let Claire get upset, Neil. I want you to hear, too. You need to understand how serious this is for Claire. . . . Ready? Okay, Claire, here goes. First of all, you have to keep Mom from discovering that Dad's death was planned. Secondly, she absolutely cannot know what really happened with Grams until I can speak with her personally."

Leona briefly described her grandmother's urgent warning, her guilt over an extramarital affair. Stella Mornay's deep guilt had been used to drive her mad and eventually to suicide.

Claire exploded instantly. "Grams believed her affair was why Grandpa died of heart failure. And that beast wouldn't ever let her go, driving her on. She couldn't force herself to explain to Mom."

"Back then, Mom had all she could handle with us. Grams didn't want her burdened even more. Grams never wanted what she was and had always pushed it away. She punished Mom as a child for telling lies . . . but she just wanted Mom to be—normal. Grams felt guilty and afraid, and she was terrified, too. And she loved us. All those emotions acted against her. She couldn't bear to be an instrument, a doorway into what could happen to Mom or to us."

"Poor Grams. Mom would have understood."

"Grams didn't. She never understood why she began that affair. I think I know. Listen closely, Claire. I actually saw this Borg-descendant, and he didn't like it. I surprised him. I just concentrated and followed a mind-stream, and a thin film tore open, exposing him. Black hair, those braids beside his face, those piercing eyes, those sharp features. He's gotten to a good friend and changed him. Through my friend, and another man I helped 'clean,' I must have picked up more of his energy, enough to track him down. His energy had transferred to the bracelet Tempest made, the runes. One of his victims—my friend—tore it off me. But my friend came to his senses and gave it back."

Leona took a deep breath and continued, "Claire, I

cleaned that bracelet! I did it! I removed his energy.
I didn't know I could, but last night—Owen thinks that
he's marking his kills—he just cut Owen's back when he
could have killed him. I saw him! He's in a cave somewhere, and I saw a sword that looks like it's Viking
judging from the designs on the grip."

As warning prickles circled her body, Leona turned
to see Owen standing at the kitchen door, his arms
crossed over his chest. His hard expression said he'd
heard everything; those gunmetal gray eyes pinned her.
Leona hurried to end the call; she didn't want Owen to
hear more. She feared what he would do with the information "Oh, that's nice, Claire. Good-bye."

"Wait—"

Leona replaced the receiver and braced herself to face
Owen. The phone rang again, and if it was Claire—Leona
read the digital number; it was the wrong moment for
Alex to call. She had to cut him off before he apologized
on the message machine—and Owen could hear what
he said.

She picked up the line, and Alex hurried to apologize.
"I don't know what got into me, Leona. I'm so
sorry. . . ."

"Could we talk later? I'm in the middle of something
right now."

"You're really mad, aren't you? I need to talk with
you."

Leona glanced at Owen, who had come into the kitchen
and now stood at the sink, rinsing his cup. His tense
shoulders reflected his mood; she could feel the prickles
coming off him like small spears. Oh, he was really, really
angry. "I'm afraid now isn't a good time. We'll talk later.
Good-bye."

"Want to tell me about it now?" Owen asked too
coolly, when she hung up.

"I think you heard about everything. I just haven't had time to tell you." She wasn't certain how to handle Owen, his temper bristling around him.

"You've had plenty of time. Let me know when you're ready to talk. I'm going out to check on the horses, and you're not coming along. I want you here and safe. Call me if Vernon turns up, or anything else happens. Just do it, Leona." Owen picked up his moccasins and glanced at Max. "Stay with her."

His crisp order grated, but Leona understood the wisdom of it. In a nasty mood, Vernon could easily overtake her. She had to do something to protect Owen—if he was right, he'd been marked for the kill. Her fear spiked, her stomach turned. "If you have to go out—without me—I want you to wear something for good luck."

He looked wary, but Leona moved quickly to unlatch the small *eolh* charm from her bracelet. She asked for one of his moccasins. As she took it in her hands, the soft touch of a loving woman spread over her. "Your mother's work."

Owen nodded and watched her remove the laces, fashioning a leather cord. Leona slid the charm onto the leather thong, then tied it around his neck. "I'll find you something else to use for laces. Wear this for me," she whispered as she framed Owen's face with her hands. "Yes, I love you, and I don't want anything to happen to you."

Suddenly, Owen pushed her hands away. "Don't try that on me. Don't try to soothe me. Not now. You'd better answer your cell when I call, or I'm coming after you. *I'll always come after you, and you know it.* Just make it easier on the both of us for once, will you?"

Leona closed her eyes and locked into the energy pulsing from him. "You're really going hunting for him, aren't you?"

"You bet. Now I know what I'm looking for . . . one hell of a coward who lives in a cave. All I have to do is find the right cave. I saw him last night . . . or maybe just the imprint of Janice's sketch came at me. But someone put that blade to my skin and shot my revolver. I'd recognize the slug and the sound of Dad's revolver anywhere. He's real flesh and blood, and he can bleed as well. I'm really going to enjoy seeing that."

Leona hadn't told Owen about her vision, how she'd seen the man of her nightmares in his lair. "How do you know he lives in a cave?"

Owen patted her cheek lightly; he was definitely angry. "Why, honey, I just found out. I heard what you said to Claire on the phone. And you've seen that sword. You should have trusted me enough to tell me about everything but you didn't."

Leona realized that Owen wasn't only angry; she'd hurt him. "I'm sorry, Owen."

When he turned away and didn't answer, Leona understood he'd closed an emotional door to her.

She could only hope his mood was temporary.

Throughout the day, Owen's calls to Leona at Timeless Vintage had been brief. The code words and responses they'd prearranged to let each other know they were safe gave her some small sense of security. Even without her psychic senses on the rise, Leona would have understood the vibrations coming across the line; she couldn't miss Owen's impatience and frustration. *You should have trusted me enough to tell me. . . .*

When Leona had entered her shop that morning, she'd been very careful to stop inside the back door. Momentarily, she wished for Max to be at her side. However, because some of her customers were allergic to animals, she'd left him at home. Owen wouldn't be happy about that—if he found out.

Leona had cautiously opened her senses, letting them flow up the stairs to her office and into the dressing area. She sensed no immediate presence.

But in the display room, Jasmine had been pushed down, her body broken and trashed. The mannequin had been the only thing touched in the shop. Leona understood the warning—Vernon, or Borg's descendant, who could be the same, intended to do the same to her.

"If you're listening, freak . . . you'll have a hard time doing the same to me, sword or not."

Jasmine had become almost like a dear friend. It hurt to see the mannequin broken and scarred. But it also demonstrated that her stalker had an unreasonable temper, and Leona could use that against him. *And she had better learn how very quickly.*

Now, after another hard day of waiting on customers and trying to find a clerk and someone for alterations, Leona called Charlotte Franklin. Uneasy about her initial conversation with the young woman, Leona wanted a personal chat. She planned to open herself to every vibration and discover if Charlotte had been seduced into serving Borg's descendant.

On her way to turn the CLOSED sign in the front door, Leona turned to her image in the mirror. Shadows circled her eyes, her hair was slightly mussed from demonstrating to her last customer how a large-brimmed hat should be worn. Her wide cuff bracelet and the silver runes flashed as she lifted her hand to smooth her hair. "Hello, Aisling. You're very close to me now aren't you? Well, I'm worried, too," she said, then felt her palms grow warm.

Leona's heart seemed to slow. Suddenly she was looking at blood on her palms, flowing hotly through her fingers. Images slid through her mind: Max's bared teeth . . . blood. . . . Visions could be interpreted wrong, could be misleading, but Leona understood: Blood would flow. *But whose blood? Owen's? Hers?*

Tires screeched and Leona glanced outside to see a familiar pickup pull into the shop's parking space. Vernon pushed out of the truck, his expression furious as he charged through her front door. Leona backed up, bracing herself as he paused, glanced up at the bell that had just tinkled, and reached for it. A tug and the bell came down, tossed to the floor. There was blood on his leg, his overalls and shirt torn.

If he'd hurt Owen . . . Could Owen already be dead, and she not feel the loss instantly? She told herself to be calm. If Owen needed her, she couldn't afford to clog the connection to him with her fear. "Hello, Vernon. I've been calling you. We need to talk."

He pointed to her, and she noted the towel, spotted with blood, wrapped around his wrist. "You! I went to your house to work and all my tools are gone . . . everything. Someone finished that closet, and it's painted. . . . Then this killer guard dog attacked me."

Leona leaned back against the counter, forcing herself to appear relaxed and confident. It wasn't easy with fear spiking wildly in her. She crossed her arms, one hand gripping her brooch. "If you'd answered my calls, you would have known that there was a dog in the house."

"Not any dog, either. This one is an attack dog. He could have killed me," he answered sullenly. "You owe me for work and for personal damages."

She noted how Vernon's face had changed since she'd met him. The lines were deeper, harsher. *Was it possible that the man who wanted to kill her, to destroy her family, stood so close?* "I'll send a check."

"Pay now . . . cash. I'm behind in my bills, and they're

threatening to take my house. It's all I've got left of my wife. I know you've got money in the till."

"No, I don't. My clientele usually prefers credit cards or monthly billing."

"Fancy pansy," he taunted in a surly tone as he came to stand over her. Vernon smelled of alcohol. He hadn't shaved, his ball cap was pulled down over hair that was greasy and untended.

Leona pushed herself back from fear; she became very quiet, almost an observer to her own reality. The energy pulsing from Vernon was the same as she had cleaned from the runes; his usually kind eyes had changed from dark whiskey brown into a hollow black. *Was this Borg's descendant, beneath layers of disguise? Or had she been blocked from seeing the real image of him somehow?*

Was it possible that she believed what she wanted to see?

There was one way to find out: "Vernon, do you know a man with a sword? Someone with long black hair and black eyes?"

"That's a dumb question. Civil war swords—sabers—are big around here, and lots of hippies wear their hair like that. You cost me a good job with Cheslav, and Dean won't see me anymore. We were good friends. I'm losing everything because of you. It's that boyfriend of yours, isn't it? He's been trying to find me. He's put strange ideas in your head, hasn't he?"

When she refused to answer, Vernon leered at her. "Shaw is in your bed and in your blood, isn't he? That would be a fine time to give you crazy ideas, wouldn't it? I heard he's giving other women ideas, too."

Leona dismissed that charge as a drunk man's revenge; he was striking out at her with anything that might hurt. Vernon might attack Alex, a gentle man next. Her heart pounded as she asked, "Did you talk to Alex in person, or on the telephone?"

"I don't see how it matters, but I saw him just a while ago. Your boyfriend had just been there, and Alex looked scared. He was shaking and packing to 'take a little trip.' My foot—Alex was running because he's scared. He's not the kind to stand up for himself and make trouble by calling the police. Shaw left word with Alex that he has my tools. I ought to press charges on Shaw. But I won't, unless I have to. I'm not like Alex—I like to settle things myself, so they get settled *right,* if you know what I mean. I called Shaw's place to tell him off. He's keeping my stuff there. He said I'd have to come get my tools in person. I may just do that, then one of us is going to pay big-time. Shaw needs a few lessons, the hard way. No, I don't want police to deal with him. I want to do it myself—no one treats Vernon O'Malley like dirt."

"So you haven't seen Owen yet?"

"If I had, I would have dealt with him."

Relieved that Owen hadn't been hurt, Leona relaxed slightly. Once Vernon left, she'd warn Owen. While Leona feared for him, Owen had already demonstrated he was a skilled fighter against an enraged man. Alex however, was another matter.

Leona knew Owen had decided that Alex needed to be warned off. Alex had called just after she'd opened the shop. He'd sounded shaken. "Shaw is a primitive, Leona. I'm really sorry about yesterday, and I tried to tell him that it was an accident. Would you please tell him? He seems like such a bully."

She had reasured Alex, though she wondered how Owen knew about Alex's attack. *You should have trusted me enough to tell me*—He'd found out anyway. Maybe he'd sensed it.

Since Alex's morning call to her, he hadn't answered hers. Leona had to know if he was all right. "Vernon, did you hurt Alex?"

"No, he's been good to me. But I could see he was scared out of his skin by Shaw. Alex wouldn't let him in the house. Shaw stopped short of forcing his way in. He broke a window on Alex's door, that special-glass window. I'll make Shaw pay for that, too. And breaking into my house and going through my things."

Leona couldn't imagine Owen destroying the lily-of-the-valley art piece. But right now, she had to know: "Did you kill Robyn White, Vernon?"

Ignoring her question, he frowned suddenly and began to survey her shop. "It seems different in here. There's more room somehow."

"My mannequin was destroyed. *Someone* broke her to bits. I think that shows that *someone* can't control their temper, don't you?"

Vernon pivoted and glowered down at her. "You accusing me?"

"I know you gave Robyn pills that she gave to Janice Shaw. Did . . . you . . . kill Robyn?" Leona repeated.

"You don't know anything. Even if you did, there's no proof." Vernon's smirk sent cold chills through her. "Why don't you ask your boyfriend about how he gets his kicks? And the next time I see that dog, I'll kill him."

After he stormed out of the shop, Leona took a deep breath. She didn't doubt that Vernon was in a killing mood.

Owen was on his list, and he wasn't answering her call. . . .

"I understand you have something important to tell me. I want to talk with you, too," Greer stated over Leona's cell phone. "I'm between planes in Denver now, and I'll be there late tonight. It's just for overnight, unless you need me for longer. Kenneth will stay with Janice."

After leaving a message on Owen's cell, Leona quickly closed the shop. Now she drove through Lexington on her way to Owen's. She still hadn't heard from him.

"You need me, don't you, Leona Fiona? You need me to come to you?" Greer asked unevenly over the wireless connection. Her uncertainty marked the barrier that Leona had placed between them long ago.

"I think this . . . situation calls for someone stronger than I," Leona admitted cautiously.

"You're stronger than you think, Leona," Greer stated. "I feel it."

"I . . . I owe you an apology. I'd like to do that in person. I've been wrong about so many things."

"We're not an easy lot to understand. I love you, Leona. Truly I do."

For the first time in years, Leona was able to answer with certainty, "Love you, too. Truly I do."

Stopping home to pick up Max, Leona tried Owen's phone again. He still wasn't answering. A traffic accident at a Man O' War intersection seemed to take forever to clear. By the time she got to the Shaws' farm, it was nine o'clock and the old farmhouse was partially lit. Owen's pickup was parked in front, and so was a nifty little red sports car.

As Leona walked by that sports car, Max started barking at the mixed-breed dog inside. He leaped at the car, scratching the gleaming finish before Leona could stop him. Inside the car, the other dog leaped from front seat to backseat, paws pounding at the window.

When Leona finally was able to grip Max's collar and tug him away, the muscled, seventy-pound dog strained against her. She hauled a reluctant Max up the steps. On the porch, Leona glanced around, hoping that Owen would appear to help her.

He didn't.

When she managed to maneuver Max inside the house, Leona heard the shower running.

A woman wearing only a man's white T-shirt leaned against the doorway leading into the hallway. Her face was flushed and her long hair—a shade of unnaturally bright red—was tousled. "If you're looking for Owen, he'll be out in a minute."

Sixteen

"AND YOU ARE?"

Leona held Max's collar, restraining him as he continued to bark at the woman as she pulled on a pair of jeans that had been tossed—seemingly in a hurry—on the floor. Leona recognized that bark: Max was reacting to the scent of evil. Something about the intimate scene didn't feel true to her. And the woman seemed familiar somehow. *Had this woman hurt him?* Leona braced herself against a fierce need to physically protect Owen.

That thought stunned her. Obviously, Owen could protect himself. Leona's emotions had more to do with claiming him back from another woman.

Once dressed, the woman cowered against the wall, her brilliant green eyes lit with fear. "Don't let that dog go."

Suddenly, Owen appeared behind the woman, wearing only his jeans. He looked just as he had that morning in Leona's kitchen *after they'd made love.* His expression puzzled, he glanced at the woman, then at Leona. "I thought I heard voices out here."

Moving quickly toward the front door, the woman, grabbed a big croco-leather handbag from a table on her way. "Well, so long. Had a great time, Owen. Call me."

Owen frowned, confused. "Wait a minute—"

"Now, honey," the other woman said. "I told you I didn't have all day."

Owen's wary glance at Leona questioned her belief in him. Acting quickly, she moved Max to block the woman's exit. As the dog bared his teeth, the woman stopped. "Owen told you to wait. Do it," Leona ordered. Then she narrowed her eyes at the woman. "You seem familiar. Who are you?"

The woman glanced at Owen, then stared down at Max. Fear glittered in her eyes. "Please don't let him go."

Leona smiled coolly. She knew this women's face but she couldn't place it. Her coloring wasn't the same. She obviously was wearing tinted contacts and had dyed her hair. "Well, then. Maybe you'd better tell us who you are. You look very familiar."

"Ah . . . ah . . . Missy Franklin. We met at the Tea Mart?"

Something clicked in Leona's mind and she realized Missy's voice was familiar, too. "Isn't it Charlotte Franklin? You called me to interview for work?"

"I—yes. Missy doesn't sound professional enough for your place, so I used my middle name. Can I go now?"

"No. Exactly what are you doing here?"

Missy seemed stunned. "Isn't it obvious?"

"Did someone tell you to come here, to make it *appear* as if you'd had sex with Owen?"

"I—I thought he might be attracted to me. I *knew* he was. But nothing happened here." Her confused expressed supported her next statement, "I was supposed to bring a dog. I don't know why."

"I have some idea why you don't know." Leona moved Max aside and opened the door. The woman ran out of the house, and, a moment later, her car raced down the driveway.

As Leona turned slightly, an image flashed in the window glass. A man's hands locked around Missy's throat, her eyes pleading with him. Stunned, she turned to Owen, caught his stricken expression, and the image clicked shut.

Leona told herself the vision had come because of her anger. Finding another woman in an obviously intimate situation wasn't easy to ignore—even if Leona understood the setup. Those were probably her hands on Missy's throat. It was nothing more than jealousy that prompted the vision. "You look cute like that—guilty," she managed as she tried to bank her temper. "Helpless and guilty."

"Your eyes just got that dark gold color. I swear I didn't ask her to come here. I locked the door before—" Max started barking furiously, leaping at the front door. "She's gone now, Max. Stop that barking."

When the dog wouldn't stop, Owen sighed and let Max out. The dog took off at a run. Owen watched from the doorway, then quickly slid on his moccasins and followed.

Max chased the other dog—the yellow one, that had been in the sports car—straight across the field. Both dogs headed toward the river, with Owen running after them. Leona hurried to follow.

Owen's harsh order cut through the air. "Max. . . . Hold. . . . Max. No."

In the field, Max had caught the other dog by the throat. The German shepherd's hackles were raised, the powerful dog poised to kill. As he reached the dogs, Owen quickly gripped Max's collar. "Leona, hurry. Take her collar and hold tight. Max. . . . No. . . ."

As Leona moved into position and gripped the yellow dog's collar, Owen crouched to soothe Max. He glanced at Leona. "She's in heat."

"Shouldn't he be—"

"That's the point. He isn't. He's acting the same way

as he did at Sue Ann's. This isn't about mating. Max wants to kill. I think he's picked up the scent of the man we're hunting. That means that creep is close, and he's afraid of Max. They may have already tangled. The female was meant to get Max out in the open. She's wearing a generic collar and doesn't have a name tag. If she's wearing a 'pound' locator chip, I doubt that it matters. She could have been picked up from anyone."

Owen scanned the wooded area nearby. "If he's out there somewhere, he's close enough to shoot Max. That would be his style—the mark of a coward. We're getting to know quite a bit about this creep. No, Max. Stay. . . . Ease her away, Leona, but do not let her go. Watch out. She'll try to bite you."

As Leona held the dog's collar and forced her back from Max, her senses prickled with the psychic residue on the dog; Owen was right about the plan to distract Max. "Missy Charlotte Franklin. . . . Owen, she sounded strange on the telephone interview. I wanted to make arrangements to meet her away from other customers in my shop—I guess I just did meet her."

"Leona, she's telling the truth. I didn't—we didn't . . . I didn't know she was here until I got out of the shower. I heard you both talking," Owen stated urgently.

Leona trusted Owen completely, but someone wanted the depth of that trust shattered. Jealousy wasn't an emotion she'd liked experiencing, even if there was no reason. Struggling to hold the terrified female dog, she asked tightly, "Would you mind if we hashed this over later?"

"You're probably too tired to talk after your flight, Mom. We could call it an early night," Leona said, as her mother and she settled into the living room to talk.

"It may be eleven o'clock here, but it's only eight on the West Coast. But if you're tired, we could wait until the morning. No matter what it is, Leona Fiona, it is never too much for us to handle." Greer's green eyes were too perceptive, and Leona felt as though every nerve in her body was transparent.

She also sensed that Greer had something very important to tell her.

How could Leona tell her mother that Daniel Bartel's death had been intended? Or that Grams's suicide had been the result of a planned affair?

Leona's senses tingled slightly. She suddenly realized she was sensing Owen's call. She must be as strongly connected to Owen now as she was to her sisters and her mother. "I need to take a call. It's Owen. After he dropped off the stray dog at the animal shelter, he's been hunting Vernon and Missy. Missy hasn't returned calls, and that isn't good. Her life could be in danger. And Owen is worried about what I might think. But I knew it was a setup the moment I saw her."

"He wouldn't betray you. Ever. You've bonded." Smoothing the Celtic design on the sleeves and neckline of her dark green caftan, Greer nodded as though deep in thought. "I have some things to do in my room. Let me know when you're finished talking. It's important to Owen to know that you're safe, Leona. Tell him that nothing will happen while we're together, but he must be on his guard. This beast likes to hunt at night."

Leona frowned; Greer's statement was odd, almost as if she knew the killer. "I think Owen may like to hunt at night, too. He has Max with him."

"This man never liked animals . . . they instinctively know that he hurts."

"Owen loves animals. They take to him right away."

"I wasn't talking about Owen."

Another strange comment, almost as if Greer knew the predator. As her mother left the room, Leona answered the telephone. "Owen?"

His voice dragged as if he were too tired. "Vernon has dropped out of sight. I can't find Missy, either. Her friends say she goes out to bars at night. So far, she hasn't turned up at her favorites. She just got fired and divorced, after having an affair with her boss. She's having a hard time paying off her credit cards. She can't make her rent for much longer. Missy is the same type of vulnerable personality that a predator would find easy to destroy. . . . I know you don't want to talk about earlier—at my house, do you? Nothing happened with Missy, Leona, believe me."

"Oh, I do. But I want to know why you went to bully Alex Cheslav."

The silence at the end of the line said that Owen was considering his answer. "That mark on your wrist. . . . You said a friend, a 'he.' I asked Sue Ann about who that might be. By the way, she and the kids are settled into her parents' and it looks promising where Dean is concerned. Anyway, she told me that the friend was probably Alex."

Leona rubbed the slight mark on her wrist. "Alex never intended to hurt me. That was an accident, Owen."

"Sure." His dark tone said he didn't believe her.

"You had no reason to try to destroy that beautiful stained-glass window. I helped pick that out. Lily-of-the-valley was his wife's favorite flower."

"I wanted to reach inside and pull him out, because he wouldn't come out to talk with me. But I did not break a window at his house." Owen's tone said he regretted not being able to get close to Alex.

"And if he had come out? You might have hurt him. He was wise to stay in the house. He's gone now, by the way. You've terrified him. He's a gentle man." She took a breath. "Owen, my mother is here. We're coming out to the farm first thing in the morning, if that's okay?

She wants to stand in that triangle. She's not the strongest away from the ocean—"

"Is she strong enough to protect you?" Owen demanded. "Maybe I should come over there tonight."

"I was just going to see if you would drop by. I want to check those bandages."

"On my way. How about some late night Chinese takeout?"

She wanted Owen safe—with her. "Just come. I'll fix something."

Owen finished the hearty potato soup and tuna sandwich, then sat back from the kitchen table to drink his tea.

As much as he appreciated the hot black chai and the ice cream melting over a still-warm piece of chocolate cake, Owen couldn't relax. After a hard, emotionally draining day, the circumstances of the last few hours didn't make for relaxing. Missy Franklin had disappeared, so had Vernon. "If this creep follows his pattern, Missy is likely to wind up dead."

He studied the two women before him; the midnight hour seemed to suit both Greer and Leona. Leona had inherited her mother's classic bone structure and those mysterious green eyes, as well as that frame of dark red hair around her pale face.

Owen rolled his shoulders slowly, his skin slightly tight and uncomfortable. But then, anyone would feel disturbed in a room with two such women; a river of vibrations seemed to run between them, a definite communication. Owen sensed that some change had taken place in Leona's emotions regarding her mother. They were softer, more understanding.

"Owen, you're staying here tonight, of course," Greer murmured, her voice as cool and calm as Leona's sometimes was.

Leona instantly averted her face and didn't extend an overnight invitation. Though gracious despite how drawn and tired she was, Leona was too calm. He wondered if she really believed the Missy Franklin setup.

And then there was the danger lurking nearby. There was no need to frighten the women, but Owen had noted the layers of fog around the cul-de-sac when he'd arrived. He'd even spotted the black SUV gleaming softly beneath a streetlight.

Owen had decided not to give chase. Instead he intended to sleep in his pickup, just outside Leona's house. His pickup would serve notice that he was on guard. So was Max.

As if picking up his thoughts, Leona said, "You might as well get comfortable and bring in your change of clothes. We'll put away things while you shower."

The look in her eyes reminded him of the earlier scene at his house. If Leona believed him, she trusted him. If she didn't believe him . . . "Bring in your things, Owen," she murmured. "I've picked up men's soap and a few things for you."

He stood to dig out his wallet. "You didn't need to do that. I'll repay you—"

Leona stood beside him. "Of course, you won't. You're doing enough. And I wanted to. Make yourself comfortable and we'll talk later."

Leona wanted him with her. That went a long way to proving she didn't believe Missy's setup. Owen relaxed and realized he'd been very concerned about Leona's real take. He was so happy now he thought he might be floating. But then, with two powerful women psychics nearby, maybe he was. Glancing down at his feet, he saw that they were firmly on the ground and his relationship-love with Leona was right on target. He realized he was grinning.

"Hi," he whispered to Leona. That seemed silly when

he'd already been with her for an hour, but this moment was new and special. Her whispered "hi" was intimate and husky, the perfect response. Everything was okay.

Greer smiled up at him. "We both know you're not going anywhere tonight. You won't leave Leona—or me. It's misty outside, and we're all uneasy. We might as well make the best of the time we have together. We have a lot to talk about and only a few hours to do so. I'm weaker within only a few hours away from the ocean—"

Leona pivoted to Greer. "Is that why you didn't know they were going to raid our house all those years ago? Why you didn't know, or feel, something was going to happen, that we were basically kidnapped?"

"Yes. But then, your grandmother had been calling me constantly. She was ailing terribly at that point. Signals can get mixed. I knew there was something horrible going to happen. I thought the signals were coming from my mother. She'd already talked about not wanting to live. I've never understood what had happened to her. I really tried to help, but she wouldn't tell me. A 'read' was impossible."

Greer's eyes shimmered with tears. "But I should have known, should have expected the researchers would try to find some means to test my daughters. I'd been keeping the scientists at bay for years."

"I didn't know. You were torn between Grams and us. I thought you put work ahead of our safety, and that as a clairvoyant, you must have known—"

"I should have. But I didn't. I am so sorry, Leona. Sometimes we can't tap into those who are closest to us, or our own futures."

Leona's hand reached out to her mother's. "Do you think a Borg descendant had anything to do with that nightmare?"

Owen instantly slid his arm around Leona and drew

her close to whisper, "If you are going to get into details about Borg, put on some music to block your voices. Sound equipment could be outside. Play something. I'll be back in a few minutes."

Alarmed, Leona dug her fingers into his wrist. "Don't go farther than your car. I don't want anything to happen to you."

Owen's fierce expression softened momentarily. "Don't worry, honey. I'll take care and be right back. Max, stay here."

After Leona locked the door after Owen, she went to the window and watched him disappear into the night. She quickly moved to turn on her sound system. The whiteout sound of the ocean's waves, the cry of seagulls, floated over the room. Greer immediately seemed more relaxed, and Leona said, "I noticed that in Tempest and Claire, too. Our affinity to water, the colors, the sounds. It's because of the Viking seafaring blood, isn't it?"

"Probably. It would take someone like you to notice. Owen had to go, you know. He's on the hunt."

"I know, but he'd better come back. I'm only giving him a few minutes. I should be out there with him." Leona shivered slightly as she noticed that the mist had started to bead on her window.

"He wouldn't hear of it, and you know it. You gave him a rune to protect him. He'll be safe. The man we seek is a coward . . . he won't let Owen get close to him if he can help it."

"That's what Owen said. He's a coward. I'd thought of him as a predator and our family as being stalked. But now, I believe he is a coward, and that's very empowering to me. I'm learning about the balance of power and what I can do."

"The woman, Missy, is already dead. You feel that, don't you?"

"I knew—later, when I separated my emotions from that image. When I remembered her image, I saw a big man strangling her. There was just no time to warn her—and then, I was pretty angry, too. I'm not exactly certain how to separate precognitive scenes from my own emotions as a woman."

"Practice. And quickly. You've already started, Leona," Greer said firmly.

Max huffed, wagged his tail and hurried to the door. But Leona had already moved to quickly open it. Owen stood in the doorway, and she reached to draw him inside. "I didn't knock," he murmured.

"Get in here. . . . I could feel you nearby. It's a good feeling. A safe one."

"That black SUV was around, but now it's gone." Inside Leona's house, Owen touched her cheek. It was also a good feeling to come home to his woman. He smoothed her hair, and tenderness flowed between them. He bent to kiss her lightly. Leona was doing her thing, her soft essence moving in to calm him. Peace settled over Owen as gently as spring rain. It eased away all the bristling anger and frustration.

However, the need to kill whoever was stalking her simmered in Owen and could reawaken in a heartbeat. "I'd better take that shower."

When Owen returned a short while later to the candlelit living room, he noted the soothing ocean sounds filling the room. Seated on the sofa, Greer and Leona were talking quietly, their hands joined and their eyes filled with tears. Uncertain about interrupting an obviously emotional feminine and family moment, Owen hesitated.

"Come sit down," Greer invited. "We need to talk. We've waited for you. Leona has something she wants to say to me. For that, she needs you with her."

Owen eased into Leona's easy chair. To his surprise,

Leona moved to sit on his lap. It wasn't a sensual gesture, but he sensed she needed contact with him. He held her hand and waited.

"Tell me about Daniel, Leona," Greer said suddenly. "You let images stream from you when I held your hand just now. I caught them, but I . . . my emotions are too strong. I don't want to accept the sight of that boy running in front of Daniel's car. I need the words. It . . . it can't be true, can it? Your father is in your mind, Leona. Why now?"

Leona held Owen's hand tightly as she softly explained her vision. An eight-year-old boy had imprinted a scene in Daniel Bartel's mind, and it had led to his death.

Greer closed her eyes and leaned her head back against the sofa. Her voice was thick with emotion when she whispered unevenly, "So he was strong even then, a child born in revenge and hatred. Instead of playing with toys, he used the lives of others to amuse himself."

"He had help. Someone was holding his hand, joining his strength and coaching the boy. I suspect—sense—it was someone of the same bloodline, and probably his father."

Greer seemed to take a deep steadying breath. Suddenly, she stood, her arms crossed over her chest. "And there's more. I caught more, Leona. But I need the words. Joel and Claire, for some reason they're tied together in this ugly curse-package."

Leona glanced at Owen and he nodded slowly. Owen understood perfectly. Leona must explain other disastrous events. "Five years ago—"

Greer's eyes flashed at Leona. "Five years ago, Claire miscarried. She'd walked into a robbery in progress. The emotions of the frightened crowd in the bank had caused her to overload and faint. She was taken to the hospital, the wrong thing for a delicate empath who is disabled and can't protect herself. I used my gifts to unravel some of this ugly story. According to what I learned from the staff later, the doctor and nurse who treated her had changed dramatically. Their personalities had become irrational at times. They angered quickly, they stole things, and there was even a report of quick sex in a storage room. Then there was the improper diagnosis and the incomplete paperwork. Even their signatures had changed. Unable to protect herself, Claire would have been surrounded by their greed, lust, hatred . . . every conceivable evil emotion known to mankind. On maximum overload, she lost her baby and almost her mind."

Greer's fierce expression softened slightly. "Your husband's accident was also five years ago, too. I got the image that someone invited him to go for that snowmobile ride."

"A man with sharp features and black eyes. He was very busy five years ago."

"And getting stronger."

Leona looked at Owen for reassurance. The next death would be even worse to explain. Owen nodded and gently eased Leona from his lap. "Do it."

She moved to Greer, framed her mother's face with her hands. With her forehead against her mother's, Leona focused on images of her maternal grandmother, the kind ones drawing a tender smile from Greer. Then Leona began opening the doors to the darkness slowly, letting the winding streams of red encircle a face with familiar features, slightly different from that of Janice's sketch. Wine poured in glasses, firelight shimmering in the glasses, turning the wine bloodred. A masculine hand raised, and a silky powder was poured into one drink. The wineglass raised to the woman's lips. . . .

Focused entirely on the scene, Leona felt her mother's

mind slide into the stream of blue and green, tendrils of red circling them, binding mother and daughter as they coursed together. Greer trembled, but her fingers locked on to Leona's wrists.

The powder swirled in the glass, and a woman with green eyes and long, red hair raised it to her lips once more.

"Mother . . ." Greer whispered unevenly, and her eyes opened. "She had an affair. It began with a drugged interlude, then she was blackmailed into more rendezvous. My father died of a heart attack a year later, and she never forgave herself. That's why . . ."

Greer held Leona's face now, looking deeply into her eyes. "How did you know? Don't tell me you communicated with the dead. How could you know she went mad because of that affair? *I* didn't even know."

"She took her life, not because of her gifts, but because of that affair. She couldn't live with her betrayal of Grandpa and the probability that she had caused his heart failure. When Dad died, she came to stay with us for a while. Her mind was already slipping, but she tried to keep herself stronger for you—you were so fragile then. She managed for a while, but the timing was so awful. She did try to tell you, but couldn't. Then she committed suicide to protect us, to end the weakened connection."

Greer's hand went to her heart, her expression stunned. "When she stayed with us after Daniel died, you were less than five years old. I was—"

"Vulnerable. She told me I had to be strong for you, and that I had to get my sisters to do the same. We had to see you through, because she knew she was getting weaker. Those images must have been lying in wait for me all these years, until I was a woman and could better understand."

Leona glanced at Owen, seated in the shadows. His

light eyes caught the candlelight, his finger and thumb smoothed that silver rune at his throat.

"Finish it. Tell her the rest." Owen ordered roughly, his deep voice pulsing around Leona. When she hesitated, Owen leaned forward, his voice sharp and commanding. "Now, Leona. Finish it now."

Greer's wide eyes stared at Leona in disbelief. "I always knew you held Aisling closer than any of our family. I need to know. Do what Owen says, finish it."

"For years, I'd been troubled by what I thought was only Grams's ramblings. But—Let me do it this way." Leona placed her forehead against her mother's and called back the image of her grandmother leaning close to Leona as a child.

Grams's fingers had gripped Leona's thin arms tightly as she'd whispered urgently, "He's coming for all of you. He has someone now who is getting strong and evil enough. He's already killed. He'll be an adult before he comes after you and the object he must have. . . . I won't be here. You and your sisters have to be strong for your mother. You have to protect all of them. I'm so sorry, Leona. I can't do this. *He's coming . . . you've got to stop him, Leona.*"

"Oh my God. . . . My mother held on for another five years—she died just after that so-called gang of medical researchers took you and your sisters. . . ." Greer suddenly pushed back from Leona, her body doubled as if in pain. She sagged back onto the sofa, her arms wrapped around herself.

Leona hurried to her mother, but Owen rose to draw her away. "You're too filled with the past now, Leona. She can't take more. I'll do it."

He sat beside Greer and drew her against him. "Listen to the sound of the ocean, Greer. Listen, see the ocean and your home and your daughters, and close out everything else."

Exhausted by pushing herself far beyond the limits she understood, Leona leaned against a wall. She covered her face with her hands and tried to separate herself from that traumatic memory.

"I know exactly who he is, in the flesh," Greer murmured. She bent down to hold her face in her hands. "I should have known all along."

Rolf Erling smoothed a cloth over the well-polished sword blade. He held it up to the firelight. He thought of how Owen Shaw's blood would soon coat the tip. Like a scarlet ribbon, Shaw's blood would flow down the long center indentation and drip from the ornate guard.

Missy's neck had snapped so easily in his hands. But then, he'd been practicing since his preteens and had become quite the expert. Alex Cheslav's scrawny neck had been almost as easy to break as Missy's.

Missy Franklin had been simply another tool that Rolf had needed. And she had performed badly. Rolf had explained very carefully why she had to die. "It's not my fault that you failed to get close to Leona or to destroy her bond with Shaw. He wouldn't be there, in that house with her mother now, if you'd been successful. You were supposed to separate Shaw and Leona emotionally and get that guard dog out into the open where I could kill him."

The image of the bitch-in-heat running from the German shepherd flitted through the shadows of Rolf's underground sanctuary. The bitch had drawn the German shepherd out into the field, but Shaw had quickly stopped the German shepherd from engaging with her. Shaw and Leona couldn't be hit by Rolf's high-powered rifle. Gunshot wasn't how they should be destroyed, else he could have killed Shaw earlier with his own father's revolver. Rolf lifted the sword to the candlelight and studied it; he preferred the tried-and-true, hands-on method.

"No wonder Shaw and Leona get along so well with that dog. Its ancestry traces back to the wolf, the standard of Thorgood, the man who took everything from my family."

Rolf ran his thumb along the honed blade, created by a master craftsman. He'd boasted that it was his best work, and Rolf had instantly decided that the craftsman would not forge another as fine. The man's death was the blade's first taste of blood—it seemed only fitting. "Greer can't stay forever. She's too smart for that. She knows she gets weaker the longer she is away from the ocean. I've never had a functioning problem with geography. All I need are people to feed my energy. When she leaves, it's back to business as usual."

He placed the tip of the blade on his mirrored image. In his mind, tiny cracks radiated from that silvery surface. The cracks spidered out, and the mirror seemed to drip away, revealing a familiar, ancient scene: Borg raged at Thorgood, furious that the seer, Aisling, had chosen the Viking chieftain instead of him. A seer in his own right, but one who used mind-altering herbs and dark spells, and fed off the minds of others, Borg had yelled his curse on the witch and the chieftain's line. Then out of the transparent mist on the mirror, Viking warriors took shape, each fiercely pledged to protect the line he had cursed. *When Borg had sought safety, the hunter, a minor seer, had led the pack to him. His own brotherhood had turned against him, led by that man named Hunter, despite the fact that Borg's visions had kept them safe through crossings and raids. And now Thorgood had replaced him with the red-haired witch. . . .*

With Aisling's unlimited gifts, Borg could have ruled the world—instead, he was left with nothing.

Rolf had learned much from his father, from the oral generation-to-generation history. Each man of the Borg bloodline was bred to carry out the curse. For centuries, they'd studied the strange vulnerabilities of the mind, those little triggers that could link one incident to another like images brought about by the mist.

Claire and Tempest had responded nicely to his psychic calling; that sailboat tipping when the triplets were three gave them a fear of water that had made them vulnerable. Leona was equally vulnerable and receptive. The findings of the parapsychologists' tests had been only too easy for Rolf's father to acquire; the institute's janitor had easy access to everything about the famous triplets.

In fact, through Stella Mornay, Rolf's father knew quite a bit about Greer and her triplets. He'd known exactly when Greer would be gone and when was the best time to contact the parapsychologists. Greer Aisling had already refused their attempts to test the triplets, and they instantly initiated suspected neglect and abuse charges.

"Thanks, dear old dad." Rolf savored the hatred running through his blood; it made him strong. He was even more powerful than his father, who had ruined the triplets' grandmother forever.

Rolf's father had meticulously described each step: He'd weakened Stella Mornay and turned her energy back on herself. He'd given Stella time to weigh how really bad she was before deepening that guilt. Overwhelming guilt—with no release—had taken her to another place, where all her visions had collided into a nonreality.

With Rolf's father as a teacher, and his father before him, the Borg-descendants had learned well. Each improved the technique of using water and mist to call forth that Viking sailing blood—blood the Aislings shared.

That day in the shop, taking a part of Leona's energy had been easy. But Rolf hadn't expected her to snatch that bit of his.

"But then, that could prove useful, a bit of me—in Leona," Rolf mused, and added, "We're linked now. I can use that. It's time to get everything back that Thorgood took away from us. It's time to repay Greer for my own personal humiliation."

Rolf ran the tip of the blade lightly over the glossy photograph of Thorgood's brooch, which was taped to the mirror. Leona had been so busy that she hadn't missed it. "You'll be mine soon. So will every power you hold."

Seventeen

"**MOTHER IS TRYING TO REST. SHE'S HAD ENOUGH FOR ONE** night," Leona said as she settled onto the sofa with Owen. "She wants to go out to the farm before daylight. The earth and air will be fresh and damp. She'd be the strongest then."

Owen drew her into his arms. Greer had been badly shaken by the actual cause of Daniel Bartel's death, a young psychic-in-training.

The boy's trainer? Most likely his father, who transferred his hatred, desire for revenge, and obsession with the cursed brooch to his son.

Owen had recognized the pure rage in Greer's and Leona's dark gold eyes. If psychics could combine their gifts to become stronger, the women could have started a storm *inside the house*.

"She wants to go before daylight . . . that's only five hours from now." Owen's thumb stroked the soft, outer curve of Leona's breast as she snuggled against him. Strange, how a woman's softness and warmth could comfort him without the need for sex. "Did Greer tell you who she thinks he is?"

"No. She's dealing with a fresh grief now—and her

anger. She's always been cautious to shield us from her own emotional trauma."

Owen lay back on the sofa and drew Leona's head to his chest. "The vibrations are zinging all over this house. I can feel them. You've both got to get control. We have to move very carefully now. One wrong move, and this guy can go underground again. We're too close now, Leona."

"I'd buried that scene with Grams. Owen, a part of me still can't believe she committed suicide. But every other person who had been used, their energies siphoned off, has done the same thing. Grams' case was different. Her extrasensories were unwanted, but strong. She didn't want her insanity to be used as a weapon against us."

"She must have loved you all very much."

"Enough to die for us. I swear, I will kill this new monster, Owen."

"Settle down. We'll get this creep. But right now, you need to rest." Owen stroked her hair and watched the fiery highlights play through his fingers. Just holding Leona, knowing that she was safe, eased him. Max had started pacing, making the rounds of the house. Owen understood—the dog wanted to hunt, just as he did. But tonight, it was better to stay near and safeguard the women. "Don't think about that. Is there anything that you can do to help your mother rest?"

"Other than finding that creep and letting her at him? No, I don't think so. She asked me to leave her alone. That's what she does when she needs to calm herself and refocus. My mood now isn't helping her. She wants me to reassure my sisters." Leona tensed slightly and glanced at the telephone. "That's Tempest."

Owen didn't question Leona but reached for the telephone and handed it to her. A man's voice rumbled and Owen listened carefully. If the late-night caller was the killer, Owen didn't want Leona talking to him. When Leona began to speak, he took the telephone. "Owen Shaw here. You'll have to deal with me."

On the other end of the line, a woman yelled, "Damn you, Marcus! Give me back that phone."

"She's yelling at Marcus, so you're right—it is Tempest," Owen whispered to Leona.

For the first time that night, Leona seemed amused as a man's voice rumbled over the line. Instead of taking the receiver from him, she got up and moved into the kitchen.

Owen glanced at her as he listened to the slight crunching sound on the other end of the line. Then Leona's brother-in-law spoke crisply. "Marcus Greystone here. What are you doing, Shaw? Running interference? My wife knows something is wrong and wanted to call Leona. It's hell controlling Tempest when she thinks one of her family is in danger. I had to take the phone from her. I'd prefer she didn't get so excited just now. Where are we in this thing? Is Greer okay? Tempest says she can feel the vibrations from here. Neil just called. Claire is upset, and both our women are ready to come down there. All I can tell you is that this red-haired bunch can be pretty excitable, and it's difficult keeping a lid on the situation. Neil and I haven't been having fun in the mornings, you know. The idea of travel and air currents, landing . . ."

Marcus's voice trailed off, then hardened into a masculine clip as he explained. "It's our wives, you know. Morning sickness. We have to be careful of them now. . . . My God, they've got a lot of energy. I'm so tired lately."

Owen smiled briefly, then quickly filled Marcus in on the details. When he heard three clicks on the telephone line, he turned to the kitchen and saw Leona holding the other phone. "It's my wife," Marcus sighed. "She's on the extension. From the sound of it on your end, so is Leona, and just maybe Greer."

"Hello, Marcus. How are you?" Greer asked calmly, as if she'd never experienced the trauma of a short time ago. "I'd like to remind you that your father is *not*, repeat *not* telling me that I can or cannot go anywhere—especially if I want to visit my own daughters. The moment I get back, I am evicting him from the premises."

"Well, Greer, I'm sure you'll handle my father," Marcus stated in a tone that suggested he was grinning. "By the way, he just told me that he thinks you're a beautiful woman."

Greer's silence preceeded a cool, "Good night, Marcus. Give my love to Tempest."

Tempest's hoot of laughter sounded on the line, then Greer sighed. "Good night, *everyone*."

Instantly, there were three disconnect clicks, and Leona came to sit beside Owen. She stared at him, one eyebrow lifted, as if mocking the man-to-man conversation.

"You think you've got a line on this guy, Owen?" Marcus asked, his tone deadly serious.

Owen held the phone away as Leona reached for it. She looked as if she were ready to argue with Marcus. "I'm working on it. We're close."

"It's damned difficult keeping out of this situation," Marcus muttered. "Keep us posted."

When Owen hung up the line, Leona stood and stared coolly down at him. Owen expected a lecture, but instead she held out her hand to him. "Let's go to bed. We only have a few hours to rest."

Owen hesitated just slightly, uncertain of Greer in the next room. Then Leona added, "You and Marcus and Neil can't help yourself. For that matter, Kenneth Ragnar can't either. It's a male thing, bred into you. Only it's ten times worse than regular men, because you're all bred to be Viking cowboys, circling the wagons, protecting the women."

Taking her hand, he rose and followed Leona into her bedroom. "Just give me a sword and a shield."

"I've heard that one before."

"From Marcus?"

"And Neil. They seem to complement each other—Neil as the lighter temperament, Marcus as head-on. I've enjoyed jousting with both of them, but there comes a time when the big-brother act grates. It's been hell without my very own sword-and-shield man."

For a few heartbeats, Owen wallowed in his new position, an accepted mate for his woman. She was taking him to her bed. It was his right to lie beside Leona and comfort her in the trying hours. *She needed him as a woman needs a man.*

He looked down at Max, who had followed them, then pointed to the opposite bedroom. Greer might need the comfort of the dog in the next restless hours. Obediently, Max padded to the Greer's room and huffed a few times. The door opened, and he padded inside.

Leona and Owen knew that sleep was probably not on their agenda tonight as they settled into Leona's bed. When Owen's hands ran lightly over her body, Leona understood his need to reassure himself that she was safe.

He looked at where Joel's portrait had hung. "It's gone."

"But not forgotten. He was a kind, good man, and it's time to put him to rest." She stroked Owen's cheek, her fingers winnowing through his hair. "I should call Claire. Hold me while I talk to her. She'll understand more about you then."

As Leona folded her body back against him, spoon fashion, Owen focused on the calm center within him.

Leona needed him to help her. She had to tell her sister, and Claire was far too sensitive. Sensing his support as she waited for Claire to answer, she turned slightly to look up at him. "Thank you."

As Leona spoke quietly to Claire, Owen let himself float easily into the softness of her voice. He followed the stream until he found an opening, then gently slid his heartbeat's steady pulse through it.

Leona tensed in his arms and turned to him, her eyes wide and surprised. "Yes, that was Owen. He's feeling his way around, but he knows there are passages in which he is stronger. . . . Instincts? A natural hunter? Maybe. But we know it's something more, don't we? I need to go, Claire. We're going to find this bastard, and we're very close. It's just a matter of putting the pieces together. . . . Yes, truly I love you, I do. Tomorrow then. . . . Good night."

Owen found a dark passage. Years ago, he and Jonas Saber had sought their vision-quests in the same manner. He followed the scarlet streams into another, and another. Another stream flowed from a side passage, winding around him. It was softer, yet it made him stronger, and he could see more clearly. He'd gotten that scene from Leona earlier: candlelight flickering on rocks that had been painted white, steps that were sagging and worn. . . . This time, a dark, cold, bottomless pool flowed around him, and sucked at his body. A long blade struck through it, and he raised his own. . . . A crash of metal against metal, and blood flowed down the blades. . . .

"Exactly who is Jonas Saber?" Leona asked too quietly. "You said he was a friend?"

She'd been in that dark stream with him, and she'd snagged Jonas's energy. . . . Owen decided that he needed a better time to explain what he suspected. He patted her bottom, caressed it a little, and snuggled her close in his arms. "My friend from Montana, the one who saw that my father's gun was returned. He's interested in buying a two-year-old thoroughbred at one of the farms. I said I'd show him around. We talk sometimes. Let's get some sleep, honey."

Leona turned to him, wrapped her arm and leg around his body. She nestled her face against his throat, and whispered drowsily, "Liar."

With her warm and soft against him, Owen stared at the ceiling. With Max on guard in Greer's room, and Leona in his arms, the women were safe for a few hours.

Dawn could change that.

They stood by the pond, exactly in the center of the triangle of natural water.

In the dim light of predawn, the water was slightly warmer than September's cool air. Layers of mist settled over the pond as Greer and Leona began to walk toward it. Owen followed closely, his eyes watchful. Max stayed near, circling the humans as if on guard; he stopped periodically to sniff at the lush grass, bent with dew.

The women stopped in front of a small tree where the dew glistened on a delicate spiderweb, the fine, perfectly created web sagging beneath the weight.

"He's like that spider, casting his web out for victims, drawing them in," Leona murmured. She sensed that Greer would take her own time in giving the name they needed.

"The coward is in hiding, or the dog would be after him. If I'd had him in my hands last night, I would have—I have always detested that savagery in myself, the part that isn't Aisling but comes from Thorgood. I had to see Owen for myself, how you had bonded with him," Greer murmured. "He's quiet cold steel to your impulsive, curious, and fiery warrior side. He sees the part you hide from the world. You love him, and yet you feel bound to Joel."

"I realize now that I've never given Joel closure. It's probably because on some level I sensed that he'd been murdered and needed to be avenged. I could have stopped him from on that trip. I felt guilty. Is that how you feel about Dad? That you loved him so much you couldn't move on?"

"No, Daniel will always be with me. I see him in my daughters." Greer lifted her face to the clean air. "I can feel that monster's presence . . . he's been here."

"You know his name. Who is he?"

Greer looked up at the crows, their feathers gleaming blue-black in the first rays of sunlight. "I knew his energy, and I'd seen him in dreams—we'd both seen him in dreams. But I didn't put that image together with a man I met years ago—another psychic. Until I started working with Janice, I hadn't made the connection."

Her fingertips dug into her arms. "His name is Rolf Erling. I believe he might be around forty or so now. I met him more than fifteen years ago. I was working a crime scene. A crowd had gathered, but I was locked into my work and ignored them. Then he stepped from the crowd. He called me a fake and wanted me to explain the details of the crime to the crowd right then. I refused to be put on display, but I did the read privately. I gave the victim's last images to the police, who followed them to a murderer. Then came another challenge when I was receiving an award for helping find a serial killer. Erling had gathered a following of lesser gifted. They worshipped him and became his followers, using spider tattoos to mark themselves. His hair had been dyed red then, his complexion lightened—he was already an expert at disguise. But the eyes were compelling—black, bottomless, lifeless. I felt evil in him from the first. I just didn't know how much."

Greer drew her dark green woolen shawl closer around her body, the cold, damp morning penetrating her warm sweater and slacks. "I knew then that he wouldn't stop trying to best me. That's sometimes common for those who are driven to prove themselves. Erling came to challenge me again, this time among my collegues. It was at the World Convention of Psychic Minds ten years ago."

As she stroked the wolf's-head brooch at her shoulder, Greer's eyes changed into dark gold. "I was the keynote speaker. He challenged me from the floor. By that time, I'd had enough and invited him up to the stage. I was determined to stop Erling's insinuations and challenges once and for all. The audience was spellbound—to use a witch-word—and we began testing. It was grueling. Later, I was exhausted, but I had my pride. Erling was defeated and furious at every turn. We began with small tests, then invited people to the stage. We probed their pasts, their problems and illnesses. Rolf Erling had some talent. He was good at theatrics. But I finally showed him to be the fake that he really was—at the public display he just had to have—in front of the world's most foremost psychics."

Greer tightened her shawl around her. "Then he went too far, trying to probe inside *me*. He went for my tender spot, my mother's death. Anyone could have discovered that by researching us. Or that's what I thought then. Now I know that he had very *intimate* knowledge of exactly why she committed suicide."

She took a deep breath and narrowed her eyes, as if looking inside to the dark memories. "I blocked him successfully and returned the favor. I should have gone for information about his family, but I considered that beneath me. I only looked into his adult life. Perhaps even then, I sensed I couldn't step too far into his evil. This took over an hour, and an official staff checked the details of my findings. They delivered the results to the crowd. The use of mind-bending drugs, amateur hypnotism, blackmail, and theatrics do not go a long way with my peers. They laughed him out of the auditorium. I went back to my life and family. I'd heard that he'd died in prison some years later. . . . I never thought about him again. I should have."

Greer stopped suddenly and closed her eyes. "He must have been able to block me, or I would have caught visions about my husband and my mother, and possibly my daughters. . . . Perhaps even my father, his fatal heart attack. But I remember Rolf Erling's energy. I feel the residue now. Rolf stood right here. He called to Janice."

Greer held her face in her hands and shivered. "I should have remembered those eyes. How could I forget? They were in my dreams, Borg's eyes. Maybe I didn't want to remember anything so evil. Maybe I didn't want to accept that such evil could actually be alive."

Aware of her mother's struggles, Leona whispered, "Please don't go on. I know what this is costing you."

"No, he has to be stopped. I have to do this." Greer straightened and inhaled the morning air. She spoke as if she had to bring her darkness out into the fresh air to cleanse herself. "I tried to deny that the man in Janice's sketch and in her mind was the same man as in my dreams of Thorgood and Aisling. How could that be possible, after all? But in working with Janice, I've seen his eyes too many times to forget. He'd already connected with her through her computer. He'd told her to 'open' when she saw mist circling the pond. She became very receptive to him, the frequency increasing as he experimented with her . . . the drugs, the subliminal tapes, the trigger words. He already knew of her weaknesses, of her life. He researches well—I give him that. Through Janice, I picked up traces of Rolf. But I had to be certain. Now I am. The Shaws' move here was definitely his doing. But he didn't expect that you would bond so quickly with Owen. He thought you had loved Joel too much. Rolf wants you for himself, an Aisling 'witch,' as his ancestors called my family."

"'Witch'? Makes you wonder about our ancestors at Salem, doesn't it? If the Borg bloodline had anything to do with that? We are all in danger. This has to be finished here and now. There's too much at stake."

"Yes, there is. I feel it." Greer drew in her breath and seemed to brace herself as she looked toward the river. "He stood nearby the river that day, calling to you. Yes, it's the same man. His father was strong—damn him. Rolf has had a lifetime of learning how to feed off other's energies. Revenge and hatred run through his blood. He's worse than the rest of his family because he can control his temper—to a degree. Sometimes it slips from his grasp, and that is the time he's the most vulnerable. He has no conscience. That's the first thing I sensed about him, that he had killed and ruined lives. I should have gone after him."

Greer stroked her shawl slowly, thoughtfully. "He got stronger each time, building his hatred for us each day. He's consumed with the need for revenge. He's empty inside, that black, burning, unfed hole eating him. Getting Thorgood's brooch won't cure that. He'll always want more."

She looked at Owen, who stood back a few feet, his eyes skimming the area, his body alert. "You knew Rolf was here. You know him. Rather, you know something of him, from your bloodline and from something else."

Owen nodded solemnly. "Maybe. This is new to me.

I'm uneasy, but then, I'm afraid for Leona . . . for all of you, and for Janice."

The dew seemed like tiny jewels on the spiderweb, red and green and purple colors trembling within them. Then a chill prickled Leona's skin, followed by a furious masculine pulse—she'd recognize those particular vibrations anywhere. She turned to Owen. "You know who he really is, too, don't you?"

At one o'clock that afternoon, Leona stood alone and watched Greer's jet take off into the clear blue day. Greer had been reluctant to leave, but Owen and Leona had convinced her. Rolf Erling would merely bide his time and resurface when he chose.

Before departing, Greer had held Leona's hands and advised, "Block out everything but that tight tunnel focused on him. Know that you are stronger and that his will belongs to you. Know that your sisters and I are with you. Together we form a much stronger bond than he can tear apart. See Thorgood's brooch in your mind. Know that you are the one to wear it, that Rolf's evil makes him unworthy. Find his weakest spot. I suspect it's his temper and his ego—and search until you find one tiny opening. Make it bigger in your mind. See a river of energy flow from him. See it flow into you. Feel it making you stronger. Take some energy now—from me."

They'd held hands and suddenly a warm familiar pulse flowed from Greer to Leona. "Take it," Greer had whispered softly. "You're going to need it. Get him, Leona. I should have gone after him and fought him, taken everything from him, and I didn't."

"You know I love you," Leona had managed unevenly; she'd only seen Greer's uncontrolled anger once before, when retrieving her ten-year-old triplets from the institute. Leona had the uneasy sensation that if Greer wanted to, she could "fry" an opponent. If it were true that Leona could match Greer in power, could she also strip the mind of another?

She might have to. . . .

Once Greer's plane was out of sight, Leona moved quickly.

Owen was to meet her later. He'd been called to the police department; a detective wanted to know more about the revolver found in Robyn White's apartment.

The bright day outside the airport had almost blinded Leona, the maple trees would soon be tipped with autumn orange. A slight wind lifted her hair, and she knew death would call soon.

"Be careful how deep you go into Rolf's mind," Greer had warned. "There's a borderline, and once passed, that darkness can become your own. I stopped there, and admit my fear. If I'd gone past that, I might have seen what had happened to Daniel and my mother."

Her mind on her mother's warnings, Leona glanced at a tomato-red car in the short-term garage. Missy's car had been that color. Then she saw another red car, darker, more like wine, the color of a bloodstain, and another. They seemed to be like blood droplets, leading to an open wound.

Owen and Greer had had a private chat without her. Leona didn't doubt it was filled with instructions to call. But when Greer had reached for Owen, and he had lowered to place her forehead against hers, Leona had become uneasy. And Owen wasn't answering her questions.

She recognized the chilling stillness before the image flipped into her mind. . . . She saw her image in a windshield, her face pale, the wind churning her hair into a storm of fire. Owen's face appeared, a sword tip at his throat. Her hair turned long and black, and her face wasn't her own. Black, bottomless eyes turned to stare at her.

Leona began to run. She had to see Owen and quickly. Nothing could happen to him.

While they'd stood in the Shaws' field, Owen revealed the names of two men he suspected: Vernon and Alex. He'd made Leona promise not to see either one of them until he was with her.

"That's impossible," she'd said immediately. "I've dined with Alex, in his home. I've helped him look for furniture," she'd argued. "He isn't anything like the man in my shop that day."

Owen had glanced uneasily at Greer. "According to Jonas Saber, Alex Cheslav was never married. He lived with his mother in Utah. When she died, and Cheslav had retired, he sold everything and moved here. I'll ask Jonas to check out Rolf Erling's death in prison. Someone else probably took Erling's place in the grave. He'd need a body build—height and weight similar to his. From talking to your Alex through that closed door, I sensed that he was a tall, fit man, not the seventy-year-old, retired office worker you described. I almost did break down that door."

"I don't know. . . . Jonas Saber? How will he be able to help us?"

"He ranches a little, hunts a lot—people, mostly. And an investigator of sorts."

Leona had stared at him blankly, and Owen had shrugged lightly. "Pays to have friends. Jonas and I—we have something in common—that old gray-eyes thing."

Before he'd said good-bye to Greer and Leona, Owen had promised not to confront either Alex or Vernon—until Leona was with him.

Her mind on everything that had happened, Leona hurried to her car to return home and collect Max.

She was just about to unlock the door when she sensed someone behind her. "Hello, Leona. I've been waiting for you," a man's voice crooned softly as the needle slid into her arm.

Through the haze quickly weighing her down into darkness, Leona saw the flat, black eyes of a killer.

They were the same as she'd seen in that windshield. She should have paid attention to her extrasensory perceptions.

"That will have to change," she heard a woman slur, and recognized the voice as her own.

"We've got a little problem, Shaw."

Across the police department's table from Owen, the detective nodded toward the revolver wrapped in plastic. Tom Roman spoke in the same clipped mode as the deputy coroner. "Ran a check on the prints. It's got your fingerprints on it. We'd like to know how it got in Robyn White's apartment."

"She must have taken it." Owen glanced at the clock on the police department's wall. At two o'clock, Leona would have already put her mother on that homebound jet.

Tom Roman had the stern, seasoned look of a man who had seen everything. Foster, the young woman beside him, was doing her best to look tough and experienced. Clearly Roman didn't like her assignment to him. He seemed irritated when Foster tried to interject. "That revolver has been fired recently."

"I've cleaned it, but I didn't shoot it. I don't know how it got to Robyn's apartment."

It had been fired just after Owen had been marked for the kill. Owen decided it was easier to slant the truth just a bit. "I've been busy trying to get my sister settled, and I had a few emergencies at the house. We've only been here a little over three weeks. I put the revolver away and went on about my business."

"That's no excuse. A loose firearm is everyone's business. When a gun is missing, it gets reported." Roman's stern look at the young woman said he suspected Owen knew more than he was saying. "What I want to know about is your relationship with Missy Franklin. You've been having an affair with her, haven't you?"

"No." Owen thought of that morning when Leona had found Missy in his house, then added, "She came after me. I'm involved with someone else."

"A Ms. Leona Chablis. We ran a license check on your pickup and checked around her neighborhood. Seems your truck was seen at her place late last night. All night, in fact."

"That's right. How did you know I'm seeing Leona?"

When Foster leaned forward, clearly poised to take part in the interview, Roman shot her a dark look. Clearly not happy about his shut-up-and-learn look, she took a deep breath and sat back in her chair. Roman nodded, turned to Owen and continued, "from the coroner's report she was at your house when Robyn White's body was found. And from notes on Missy's desk . . . Ms. Chablis' phone number, the name of her shop. We checked the other shops there. Your pickup showed up on the parking lot's security tapes. Wasn't hard to connect the dots."

The detective sat back in his chair and eyed Owen. "Okay, Shaw. Here's what we've got: Missy Franklin had a thing for you. She wrote that you were sleeping together and that you liked redheads. Not hard to translate a lot of hearts around a man's name. Pretty hard to do two women at one time, isn't it? Some guys take drugs to do that."

"I wasn't involved with Missy, and I've never taken performance drugs."

Roman tapped his pencil on the table. "Funny thing

about you, Shaw. People around you turn up dead. First Robyn White, then Missy Franklin's body is found in the river near your place. Her neck was broken, expertly snapped. The coroner places her death about midnight or so. Where were you at that time?"

"With Leona *and* her mother. I stayed the night. I was with them until you called this morning." Owen explained that Greer was just visiting for overnight, and added a little inventive reason for her brief visit. "Ms. Chablis and myself are planning to get married. Her mother wanted to meet me."

"You work fast. It took me two years to get my wife to agree to an engagement, and another two to get married. I'll need names, addresses, and a check on that, Foster. Get busy. Now back to you, Shaw," Roman said, as the young woman left the room. "There's something strange about this whole mess, including that old six-shooter. Want to tell me about it?"

Owen suspected that the detective would probably run a background on him. If he did, a report on his father's gun would turn up. "A friend borrowed it from my father. She said it misfired while being cleaned and a man died."

Roman shoved a pad at Owen. "Write that part out for me, will you?"

An hour and a half later, Owen stepped out into the bright September sunshine; Tom Roman's "Don't leave town anytime soon" was still fresh in his ears. The detective wanted answers from Leona, too, but she wasn't answering her cell, home, or shop telephones.

Owen drove to Leona's house and found Max alone. He collected the dog and headed for Timeless Vintage. The CLOSED sign was still on the front door, and Owen circled to the back. Owen punched in the security code he'd seen Leona use and went inside. Leona wasn't there.

A drive-through check at the airport's short-term parking revealed her car was still there.

With Max at his side, Owen stepped inside Alex's house.

While Owen searched for Leona, the dog hadn't barked, but his hackles were raised, his body tense. One look in the old overgrown, musty greenhouse had shown it empty. Entry through the back sunporch had been easy. The old house creaked slightly as though protesting the intrusion, and Max growled. A quick pat quieted him as Owen went into the kitchen. He circled the rooms, then moved upstairs. Clearly in the process of renovation, the house was empty.

Owen hurried downstairs and left the house. The garage, an old building needing repair and overgrown with vines, stood near the backyard. Owen noted that the grass running from the garage to the house was pressed flat. It was dying, a path beginning to form. The twin doors in the front of the building had been padlocked. "If Leona is in there . . ."

He picked the lock in the side door. When the door resisted opening, Owen put his shoulder against it. One shove, and he entered the shadows. Max growled again and padded into the garage. He circled the big black shiny SUV while Owen checked the interior. It was empty—except for the high-tech sound gear on the passenger floorboard. A man's ball cap lay on the dashboard, the emblem advertising the local lumberyard; it was a hat like Vernon had worn. In the rear of the SUV was a toolbox, filled with tiny cameras like the one at Leona's. A box of sound gear in the passenger seat proved to be high-tech, able to catch distant sounds.

When he left, Owen was careful to leave everything as he'd found it.

When he returned to his truck, he found Leona's rune bracelet on the seat. Beneath it was a note in her handwriting. Owen studied the script more closely. Someone was very good, but not good enough to imitate her handwriting. The note read: *Go home. Wait for my call. There will be instructions at your house.*

When he let Max sniff the note, the dog's hackles rose, and he bared his teeth. Fear for Leona chilled Owen as he glanced around the street. With his ability to blend into any circumstance, the Aislings' predator could be watching from any of the spacious, well-tended yards and magnificent plantation-style homes. Before Owen and Max could get to him, Erling could kill Leona.

Owen patted Max's head. "That's what I thought. Erling wrote it, not her. It's a trap, we know that, don't we, boy? But for now, I'd better play his game. Leona's life is at stake. Where the hell is she?"

On his way to the ranch, Owen called Sue Ann. She hadn't seen Leona, either.

Eighteen

LEONA FOUGHT THE POUNDING PAIN IN HER BRAIN; SHE forced herself to surface from the black, swirling bog.

The dream she'd just had still wrapped around her. The streaming wisps had seemed too real. His compelling black eyes had been close to hers as he'd crooned her name. A man's hand had laid open on her chest, pressing gently, yet the pain of being crushed was excruciating. . . .

He was playing, testing Leona's pain limits, her reception to his power. . . . She had to fight. . . .

Shaking free of the nightmare, she opened her lids slowly. Her extrasensory nerves jumped; her survival instincts pushed away the cloud in her brain. When light pierced her eyes she closed her lids again. This time, she let her senses prowl.

Cleaning scents mixed with the heavy reek of liquor and the stench of dirty clothing filled her nostrils. A man was singing a country music song in another room, and from the clatter of dishes and his footsteps, he was moving around and cooking.

Leona opened her eyes again and adjusted to the softly lit room. She was lying on an opened recliner, her arms tethered behind her. She moved her hands experimentally and noted metal circling her right wrist, biting into her flesh. Her cuff bracelet was on her left, pressed too tightly to her.

His back to a wall, Vernon sat on a tarp on the hardwood flooring. He appeared unconscious, his bib overalls soiled. Liquor bottles and prescriptions filled the toolbox beside him. On a nearby table was Leona's large monogrammed travel bag. She glimpsed her usual tote stuffed on top.

The room's decor was elegant, a chandelier overhead, surrounded by unlikely acoustical tile to block sound. The walls were covered in tile, and an elaborate mix of drums, guitar cases, and several music keyboards filled one end. Digital and microphone equipment clustered around the music instruments. A bold B.B. had been scrolled on the bass drum. Several contemporary red couches stood in front of the sound equipment. At the opposite end of the room was a large-screen television and heavy-duty exercise equipment, including weights and a bench. The nearby wall was filled with framed photographs, gold records, and a wall clock. A large poster of Billy Balleau and his band dominated the arrangements.

Vernon would have access to Billy Balleau's home while he was on tour. Leona was in the country music star's home! And whoever was in the next room was probably Rolf Erling, the man who wanted to kill her!

The drapes were closed, but the digital wall clock read 8:00 P.M. It had been hours since that needle had sunk into her arm!

Leona struggled against her bonds, but she couldn't move. Flashbacks of being bound as a child hit her in terrifying waves. But she wasn't a child any longer, she was a woman. Leona breathed quietly, forcing back her panic. She focused on Owen, calling out to him with

her senses, willing him to find her. . . . *Owen* . . .
Owen . . .

She wasn't surprised to see the tall, physically fit man
carrying in a silver platter, a tea towel tossed over his
shoulder. "Hello, Leona Fiona," he said cheerfully.

With the air of a man playing host, he placed the
platter loaded with a wine decanter and elegant glasses
on the table beside her. His long hair was damp and
curled around that sharp, cruel face. His thin lips barely
curved in what served as a pleased smile. There was no
mistaking those mesmerizing black eyes. His clothing
was evidently couture: a casual-male style from the best
of the European designers; a light, blue long-sleeve
sweater clung to his powerful muscles, his slacks seemed
to flow with his movements, and he wore his Italian
loafers without stockings.

His continental appearance came second to the vibrations emanating from him. When he'd been in her
shop, disguised as that Nordic blond, Leona had caught
a fragment of those same energies. But now, unwrapped
to reveal this monster's true nature, they were psycho-
pathic and deadly. "Rolf Erling, I presume?"

"At your service. I thought you'd recognize me. I was
right. . . . I'm always right. This room is great, isn't it?
High-tech sound equipment, courtesy of a country
singer now on tour. Vernon was looking in on the place
for Billy Balleau. It's acres from the other estates, so we
won't have to be quiet as we entertain ourselves. It's
quite comfortable, more so than Alex's house."

Rolf poured the wine with elegant movements. "I
hope you like pasta. I'm on a tight schedule tonight, or
we would have had sushi. I learned from a master chef
in Japan."

"Oh, did he live?" Despite her sarcastic tone, every
particle in Leona concentrated on Owen. *Owen? Can*

you hear me? Feel me? Can you see what I see? She looked around the room, willing Owen's psychic antenna to tap into the stream she projected. She focused on the poster of Billy Balleau.

Rolf momentarily seemed to enjoy the memory of the chef. Then he shrugged. "No. The sushi chef didn't live. Neither did the artist who created my sword."

"And Alex?"

"Mm," he mused. "Useful . . . but dead, too, I'm afraid. He was a very lonely man after his mother died."

Leona feared asking the next question, but she managed, "And Owen?"

Rolf picked up a wineglass and studied the contents. "Balleau's wine cellar is stocked . . . regional brands, nothing Australian or French. . . . Oh, Owen is upset, I'm sure. He's to be a good boy, and he knows it. Otherwise, you'll pay."

"I'm going to 'pay' anyway, aren't I? So is Owen?"

"Bills must always be paid, my dear. It's only logical."

Leona focused on a large picture on the wall, the winner's circle at the Kentucky Derby, and a blown-up advertisement for Billy Balleau. *Billy Balleau . . . the initials B.B. . . . she was in the home of Billy Balleau. . . . Owen? Come to me. . . .* "You're afraid of Owen, or you'd meet him, man-to-man. You're afraid of me, or I wouldn't be tied."

A ripple of Rolf's anger burned her. But his only visible anger was how he placed the wineglass too gently on the tray. Studying Leona, he slowly wove one braid beside his face, tied off the end, and fashioned another.

"You're not afraid, are you?" he asked almost clinically, as if he were studying her reactions. "No, you're too angry to be afraid. I can feel it pumping from you, like fire in my veins. That's good. I can use that."

Leona forced herself to calm. She pushed down her

fury, when she actually wanted to attack him physically. "Was Missy afraid?"

"Oh, yes. It was delicious. Robyn gave in too easily. Missy fought a little. It was arousing. I was only sorry it lasted such a short time." He walked to a long drape and eased it aside to reveal an embellished leather sword scabbard. "You've seen this before you surprised me that day. Maybe you'd actually like to feel it. By the way, how do you like the new cuff bracelet you're wearing? A gift from me to you. The cuff will keep the ropes from marking your skin. Have to keep the restraint marks at a minimum, you know."

Rolf studied her as he held the ornate grip of the sword. The deadly slide of three-foot tempered steel from the leather caused Leona's skin to crawl. She forced herself to smile. "That's a pretty toy."

The blade flashed as Rolf brought the tip to her throat. He turned it, using the edge to lift her chin. "You really shouldn't have tried to 'see' me, Leona. I didn't like that."

"This isn't going to work, you know. Owen will find me. He's—"

"One of them," Rolf supplied. "One of Thorgood's warrior-descendants. His faithful men who had promised always to protect the Aisling line, blah-blah-blah. Your sisters bonded with their descendants, too, though Neil and Marcus didn't have what Owen does. You know that old saying, 'save the best for last.' That would be you and Owen Shaw. I needed him to transport the bait, which you nicely took."

"Just exactly how did you know we might connect? This is a big city."

Rolf smiled knowingly. "Robyn suggested your shop to Owen. She thought Janice might need a little feminine pick-me-up. Wasn't that nice of her? And I knew that once Janice held that bag, she'd want to meet you."

"That was very smart of you. What is my travel bag doing here? It's not exactly your style . . . neither is my monogrammed tote."

Rolf glanced at her bag. "You dropped your bag at the airport. I thought it wise to take it with us. I already had the travel bag. Vernon was kind enough to bring your things to me in it. Including the exact outfit you wore when you called me that night—the green gown, the gold headband, the armband. I wanted you to wear them when I finally had you by candlelight. There may be a little blood on the bag . . . his. It seems he tangled with your dog."

Vernon had come to her shop that day after he'd been to her house; Max had attacked him. Owen? Can you hear me? Owen?

Rolf lifted the blade higher and bent down to peer into Leona's face. She focused on her own strength. She focused on Owen's, on the bond she had with her family, and they with her. Rolf's eyes narrowed, his nostrils flared. "Family . . . You call your family to you. The clan gathers to protect their own. . . . How sweet. Just as you and your sisters and your mother always do, protect each other. Red-haired witches, all of you. My ancestors saw that a few of you were burned at the stake. Interesting when that hair—" he lifted a strand of her hair with the blade—"actually catches fire."

"And what you did to my husband? And my sisters? My father and my grandmother? All planned, wasn't it?"

He smiled coldly. "Daddy did such a good job with your grandmother. And your grandfather. Dear old dad was a good teacher, but not as strong as I. I found that out when I did your father. I was only eight, you know. . . . But then, you do know, don't you? All those little images that came more frequently when you opened to help your sisters. I've had those visions ever since I could remember: Thorgood, Aisling, the way the clan ran Borg out into the world, the hunter who tracked him, that brooch and the curse, of course."

Rolf ran that cold deadly blade along Leona's cheek. "Thorgood's brooch is going to be mine, and you could share everything with me. But it isn't your nature, is it? I don't think I could trust you in my bed, Leona. If I drugged you, or took your mind, it just wouldn't be the same. Maybe I could use some other inducement to make you cooperate. You've always been very sensitive to what happens to your family."

Lifting the blade away, he let the light dance along the deadly edge. "You don't actually know who Owen is, do you? Shall I tell you something that neither of you knows? Yes, that would be appropriate since both of you are going to die."

"I'm not going to open for you, Rolf."

"That's too bad. They say a picture is worth a thousand words."

Greer had said there was a certain borderline, after which there would be no return. She'd also said that he had a temper, and Leona decided to push him. "My mother said you're a fake, needing to use drugs and hypnotism, and devices to appear as if you are a psychic talent. But she found you out, didn't she?"

"Not quite. I blocked Greer from reading certain details of our history together. And I blocked you. Neither one of you was strong enough to get past my energies."

"My mother didn't try. She could have fried you if she'd wanted. Instead, she just proved you to be weaker, a fake who had to use gimmicks. The great Rolf Erling, bested by a mere woman. And an Aisling woman, at that."

"You need a lesson, Leona Fiona." Suddenly, Rolf focused those black eyes on hers, and bent close. Opening his hand, he placed it directly on her chest. Leona refused to show fear and braced herself for the impact, for that sense of being crushed. The force pushed at her. She pushed it back, willing herself to be stronger, to lean into his energy and curl herself around it, snatching it back within her. . . .

Rolf's eyes widened, and he jerked back his hand, rubbing it against his thigh.

"Naughty little girl." His open hand crashed against her cheek. The blow snapped her head to one side. She took the pain inside her, took Rolf's angry energy, and fed herself with it; she forged it into one cold, thin shaft. When that shaft was white-hot, Leona opened suddenly and sent out probing tendrils to weave into his mind.

This time, those hard black eyes widened just slightly. Then Rolf smiled grimly. He sat beside her and sipped his wine as he studied her. She shifted her head away from Rolf's hand, but his fingers winnowed through her hair in a caress that caused her skin to crawl. He looked down her body, letting his hand flow over her breast, and squeezed her thigh slightly. "You've got great legs. You should wear dresses more, though these slacks look very nice. You have that classic look."

Rolf wrapped his hand around her ankle and slid his fingers up under the slacks. He took another sip and looked at her lips. "Is this what you like? Sensual? Slow? Is that how you do it with Shaw?"

Owen had heard her silent cry before. Would he now? *Owen, come to me. . . .*

When she didn't answer, Rolf smiled. "You almost had me a moment ago. Sending out those little feelers, but that isn't how it's done. It's more of a seduction, and good ones take time. Seduction is like growing a plant from a tiny seed—feeding it slowly, tending it."

"You prey on the vulnerable. That's the mark of a coward."

"Or superior intelligence. I like the play, moving the

lesser around in their little lives, letting them kill themselves—like my father did with Stella Mornay."

"He drugged her, Rolf. She never would have been unfaithful or gotten in so deep. He was rotten, too, weak, and a blackmailer. Not really someone to be proud of, was he?"

Rolf shrugged and downed the last of the wine quickly. Then he placed both hands on her ankles, caressing them. A sensual heat began at his touch and started warming her skin, crawling upward. Leona jackknifed her legs away and raised both to kick. Rolf quickly caught them, forcing her legs back to the recliner. "It only makes sense to use weaknesses, doesn't it? Everyone is vulnerable, somehow. Why not make use of what is already available? He said your grandmother was very—hot."

Leona's temper spiked, and she forced it back. *Owen.* . . .

Rolf's hands clamped around her ankles, holding her still. "Is this how it felt at the Blair Institute of Parapsychology? When you were lying there, feeling everything your sisters were feeling? Claire's terror as she absorbed every emotion possible and the physical pain of others? Of Tempest's furious anger?"

A wave of claustrophobia hit Leona, swirled around and enveloped her. For just that instant, Leona was that ten-year-old girl, unable to protect her sisters. For just that heartbeat, she was a child again. She almost cried out, furious with herself for not revealing her precognitive dream. . . .

Then Leona glimpsed pleasure in Rolf's black eyes, the eyes of a torturer, a predator who would take his time. She thought of the daisies Owen and his mother had picked together, of the pot of daisies he'd given her. The images calmed her. "I'm over that now. I couldn't have stopped them. I wasn't to blame."

Rolf's fingers bit into her ankles. "I read the reports. You couldn't have gotten over that nightmare so easily."

"You're bluffing. Those reports were destroyed. A court order from my mother—"

"Not all of them. My father had already taken copies—he was quite active in that whole scenario. For years, I studied them, detail by detail." Rolf looked down at his hands and eased his grip. "Your skin is very fair. I must be careful."

He'd been foiled, and a slip of his anger had escaped. Leona snatched the thin angry strand before it could slither back into Rolf's keeping. "They tested you, too, didn't they? In a psychic ward? Let me guess . . . they declared you unsuitable to live within the general population? That 'crazy-as-a-loon' thing?"

His smile didn't reach those cold eyes. "They just didn't understand me. I have needs. I inherited them, just like you did, that old DNA thing. And I can live quite nicely anywhere, as anyone I choose. You didn't ask about Shaw—about what you don't know. Aren't you interested in your lover? You see, I've had the same visions as you, but perhaps with the opposing point of view. Would you like some wine now? Or would you prefer to eat. I'll have to feed you, of course."

"I'd rather not. I get the feeling I'd choke on anything you prepared. I'm a little nauseated by you right now."

"Mm . . . your defiance is so predictable. Later, then."

She had to know. "I thought you had some lie about Owen that you wanted to tell me."

"Ah! The famous Aisling curiosity. I thought you'd never ask. I'm looking forward to meeting Shaw, to see if he's as good as his ancestor. His secret? A special gene, that of a clairvoyant that must have gone back to prehistoric times. I caught the images from Janice, wall paintings on rock, hunting and the usual male-female fertility symbols. She never understood them, but I did and used them. In Owen Shaw's case, the Viking genes dominated, thus the 'gray-eyes,' as men like him have been called for centuries. It's likely that his images—perhaps dreams—ran more to male interests. The combination of primitive and Viking has made him very strong, but he's untrained . . . I'm not."

"You think Owen has visions?" Leona asked unsteadily. She turned to look at the initials on the bass drum and on Billy Balleau's huge poster. *Owen, I need you. . . .*

Rolf caught her chin and turned her face back to him. "I *know* he sees images. Janice told me that Owen and his friend, Jonas Saber, went on secret boyhood 'vision quests'. Their fathers punished them for it. As men, they were talking, and Janice overheard. I tested Owen at the farm, didn't he tell you? Gave him a vision, and he reacted to it. He was busy thinking about that and distracted when I marked him as my kill . . . that little wound on his back I gave him when I could have killed him then. You know about marking, don't you, Leona? Those little bite marks on his throat, scratches on his back, like a cat in heat? That little amulet, the silver rune you gave him?"

"Let me go. Just give me your nice little toy, and I'll be happy to mark you."

Rolf laughed wildly, the sound eerie and hollow in the specially created sound room. "What an attitude! That's the best thing about you, Leona. You've got killer instincts. You're cold and creative. I admire that. You just haven't used your talent yet. I'll miss enjoying that part of you. I'll have to kill you. Or have you commit suicide. Likewise your sisters and your mother, then I'll have Thorgood's brooch. I'm going to enjoy Greer for a time, though. I am going to ruin that witch . . . enjoy it as her so-called peers laugh at her."

That thread of fear Leona had been fighting snaked through her. *She had to protect her family. Owen? Come to me. . . .* "Revenge won't give you what you need. You'll never have enough. What are you going to do with Vernon?"

Rolf turned to consider the man in the stupor. "In a drunken rage, he's going to kill both you and Shaw. He's going to crush you and Owen in a car at the junkyard—I thought crushing would be very suitable for your death. Then our boy Vernon is going to have an unfortunate accident."

"I wouldn't count on it."

At eight o'clock, Owen stood inside that triangle of natural water. If Leona and her family could communicate through that medium, perhaps he could catch some of her energy.

Six hours had passed, and no one had heard from Leona. It was too soon to report her as missing, and that wouldn't be wise anyway. If cornered by the police, Rolf would kill Leona instantly. Leona was out there somewhere, and Owen had to find her.

There were just times when legal means weren't possible, and this was one. Fighting needed to be done on a different plane. Owen closed his eyes, let the earth and sky enfold him, until he became one. He let the visions he'd fought since childhood float into his mind, the ships with the red sails, prows biting into the seas, men straining at oars. . . . Crows gleamed on trees, feathers shining like polished obsidian. Men painted on rock walls hunted deer. . . . Heavy swords and mallets, screams and smoke. . . .

A woman with red hair and green eyes stared at him through the smoke. . . . *Owen. . . . Owen, come to me. . . .*

Ancient tribal drums pounded in Owen's mind. A man with long black hair stood in a cave, the walls painted white, the sword gleaming on a table, reflected in a mirror. Wigs and cosmetics littered the table, chemical bottles lined in a row. Tall white pillars of a plantation home appeared out of the darkness and steps leading downward into darkness. . . .

Owen recognized that home; it was Alex's. Raising his arm, he rubbed the bandage over his back, the mark of the man he wanted.

At his side, Max snarled, his hackles raised. "Okay, you know what we need. Let's go hunting."

The country estate of Billy Balleau wasn't difficult to find.

The initials of B.B. on a bass drum had appeared as Owen had looked down at a white plate on Alex Cheslav's kitchen table. As Owen focused on the plate, the singer's image and a room designed to hold his memorabilia and music equipment slid across the plate. "She's doing it, Max," Owen stated quietly. "Leona is telling us where she's at."

An earlier check had shown that the black SUV was gone. On a second, more thorough search through the house, Max had found the panel in the kitchen that led down to a "hidey-hole," commonly built in homes during the Civil War.

The earlier image that Leona had given Owen of sagging, worn steps, and a stone wall, painted white had been accurate. Only a few bits of furniture and a smashed mirror remained.

Owen had tapped the white plate he'd been holding. Leona was pushing herself, trying to connect with him, and she'd succeeded. "B.B. . . . Billy Balleau's . . . She's there. Let's go."

"No wine? Nothing to eat? I'm sorry you didn't want to share my dinner with me. I would have been so pleased to dine with an Aisling. . . . Well, then, I suppose we'll have to get busy."

Rolf Erling moved to a side table where his sword rested and inserted a needle into a vial. "Just a little something to help you relax, Leona. Vernon, over there, got to really enjoying liquor and pills. When I needed to be Vernon, I simply drugged him. He was the perfect choice to move around your life—the perfect identity. I'm good at assuming other identities. . . . Once you both are in the car, and I'm ready, I'll call your boyfriend. Owen will come and a dart will make him quite pliable. It's a serum I learned while in the Amazon. The subject can feel and hear everything. They just can't move for a time."

Leona's senses had been tingling. A vision of a man moving through the shadows flipped through her mind. He was hunting. A silver rune gleamed at his throat *Owen?*

A dog moved at his side, both hunters sliding quietly through the night.

Rolf tapped the needle and a liquid sprayed into the air. "I'm all packed and ready to leave. I'll be visiting your sisters next—probably Claire. She'll be the most affected, the weakest. Tempest and Greer will be very easy. . . . Too bad Owen won't be able to appreciate my craftsmanship. I would have liked him to watch."

A shadow moved at the doorway, and Owen said, "I'm here now. Why don't you tell *me* about it, Rolf?"

"Owen!" Leona struggled against her bonds but couldn't get free. She kicked her legs, accidently bumping the serving tray. The large silver platter fell to the floor, shards of the wineglasses tumbling around it.

Owen wore the brooch at his throat—the genuine artifact. Tethered by leather thongs, the large rectangular silver-and-alloy brooch gleamed, almost as if it were recharged and ready for battle. A big hunting-knife sheath was at Owen's hip, and he wore beaded moccasins. His eyes were the color of ice.

He moved in a blur, flipping the knife into his hand and crossing to where Leona was strapped to the recliner. One tug at her wrists, and she was free, even as Owen moved in front of her.

Rolf pivoted, both hands expertly gripping the sword in front of him. Waves of masculine emotions chafed Leona, as the two men stared at each other. Owen's anger was cold and deadly; Rolf's was red-hot and crazed. He stared at the brooch. "You are wearing the real brooch."

"House of the Wolf, Thorgood the Great, whose mighty hand holds his people safe, who will kill those who defy him. His line will be long and powerful, reigning after him, for he who holds the wolf, holds the power," Owen softly repeated Thorgood's boast. "And it's mine. The woman of Aisling is mine, too. I have everything you want—the brooch, the woman, and most of all the power. . . . You feel it, don't you, Rolf? That weak curse your ancestor placed on it? You're welcome to try to take it anytime."

Owen's tone sent chills through Leona. He taunted Rolf, and he meant to kill him. "Owen—"

When Rolf lifted his sword to his face in a salute, Owen spoke too quietly. "Leona, stay back. This has to end here. I'm going to finish him. If it doesn't end now, he'll just be back."

"You've got that right, Shaw-shaman." Rolf began closing the distance between them, his blade raised in an expert stance. "I'm going to wear that brooch tonight, and I'm going to have Leona first—before I kill her."

Owen's single word cut through the air. "Try."

When Leona gripped the back of Owen's shirt, he shoved her back. "Keep out of the way."

The force sent her stumbling against the wall. Before

she could catch her breath, a vise clamped around her ankle. Vernon looked up at her, his eyes wild and murderous.

She struggled against his grip. "Vernon, don't do this."

He turned slowly to the two men circling each other, one held a sword, the other with only a hunting knife. "Figures. That's a Bowie. I knew Shaw would have something like that."

"Vernon, I know you didn't want to be any part of this."

"I'm going to kill him," he muttered.

Terrified that the big muscular man would help Rolf, Leona struggled with all her might. "Vernon, let me go."

His other hand raised, clamping on her wrist. He started easing upward until he stood and leaned against the wall. Vernon's gaze remained locked on the two men in the center of the room.

"I'm going to kill him," Vernon repeated as he seemed to try to shake free of his stupor. He drew Leona along the wall, out of the main area. "You stay put."

An expert swordsman, Rolf moved toward Owen, who held only his knife. Owen danced out of the way as the blade swished toward him, then again. The deadly sword came down, slicing into the drums. Cymbals crashed, the bass drum toppled. Owen weaved around the set, and Leona realized he was drawing Rolf away from her. "Vernon, let her go," Owen ordered. "You don't want to hurt her."

Beside Leona, Vernon was breathing hard. He leaned forward, engrossed in the fight, as if he were waiting for his chance to enter it. Leona fought Vernon's grip, but he held tight.

"I marked you, Shaw. And now I'm going to kill you," Rolf said as he continued forcing Owen backward.

"Try." Owen bent quickly as Rolf's blade went over

his head. When Owen came up, he held the large serving tray in his hand.

*Sword and shield, the protector staking his life for an
Aisling.* The thought ricocheted around Leona and in
her mind she saw another battle, the protectors moving
in on Borg and his men, ready to protect Aisling. . . .

"Let her go, Vernon," Owen repeated quietly. "Or
you're next."

Rolf laughed wildly. In that instant, Owen moved in
close and slashed the other man's arm. Blood flowed
over the expensive material, and Rolf looked down in
disbelief. In that instant, Owen's blade swung upward,
skimmed a thin line along Rolf's cheek, then sheared a
braid.

Almost in slow motion, the thin braid arced in the
air. Owen caught it on the flat of his blade and flipped
it toward Leona's tote. "Keep that for me."

Rolf felt for the missing braid as he stared at the blood
running down his arm. He felt his cheek and appeared
stunned at the blood on his fingers. Owen smiled coldly.
"First blood, Rolf. *You're* marked now."

Leona concentrated on that blood, seeing it in her
mind, increasing the flow. She had to weaken Rolf; his
sword was an advantage Owen couldn't afford.

Filled with rage now, Rolf slashed wildly as Owen
danced out of the way. He sailed the silver platter into
Rolf's midsection, almost as if the heavy platter was a
child's toy. Rolf went down to his knees, momentarily
stunned, and Owen moved in quickly, his blade at the
other man's throat. "I've marked you, Erling. You're my
kill now."

Suddenly, Vernon released Leona and pushed from
the wall into the battle. "No, you can't. . . . He's . . ."

Rolf's raised blade caught the onrushing man in the
side, and Vernon fell upon Rolf. "He's mine! Get her

out of here," Vernon yelled, apparently unfazed by the wound.

Owen hesitated, then looked at Leona, who was rushing toward him. He caught her body to him as he ran out of the house and into the night. Taking her hand, he ran down the driveway toward the main gates of the estate. "I want you out of here. Nothing can happen to you."

Breathing hard, Leona managed, "You're not going back in there without me."

From across the shadowy driveway, a big man moved, the three-foot-long blade glinting in the moonlight. He held an automatic in his other hand, aimed at Leona and Owen. "I'm getting that brooch, Shaw," Rolf stated coldly.

"Not tonight. Not ever." Owen glanced at the driveway's front gates. They swung open and headlights bit through the night.

Max appeared in the shadows beside Owen, clearly poised to leap at Rolf, to tear out his throat. "Stay, Max. Leona, if you have to, let Max do what he needs to do."

The rev of a huge motor signaled a large bus approaching at a fast speed, building momentum to climb up the hill to the estate.

"Get out of here! I have to pay back what I've done!" Vernon yelled as he ran, plowing into Rolf.

The momentum took both men into the path of the speeding bus.

Almost as if in slow motion, Billy Balleau's tour bus appeared to hit both men, the heavy weight rolling over them.

In a heartbeat, Owen ran toward the men, the bus's brakelights silhouetting his body. He bent over the crumbled body, then ran back to Leona. "Erling wasn't hit. He's out there somewhere."

He nudged Leona back into the night's shadows. She held Max's collar as the men leaped from the bus circling back to Vernon's crushed body. Highlighted in the brakelights, Billy Balleau yelled, "Damn groupies! Can't ever get away from them! They're everywhere. Hey! Wait a minute. That's my damn house-sitter. What the hell?"

Another man stood looking down at Vernon's body. He pushed back his Western hat. "I wasn't driving that fast. He just jumped out in front of me. But I thought I saw two men."

"Oh, Felix. I told you to get different glasses for driving at night. Now you're seeing double. Call the police. Like I need this."

Owen quietly eased Leona and Max off into the nearby trees. With a nod, Owen indicated a vehicle moving down a back road. Though the headlights were out, in the moonlight he could see it was an SUV. "That's Erling. Let's go."

Nineteen

"OWEN, WHY AREN'T WE FOLLOWING HIM?" LEONA ASKED,
as Owen made no attempt to follow the SUV. Instead,
he drove his pickup in another direction.

"I don't think we have to worry about losing Erling."

"Is that all you have to say? I want it to end, Owen.
We can't let Rolf get away." The dashboard's dim light
did not soften Owen's grim profile. On Leona's other
side, Max sat, his body tense, periodically snarling and
revealing his teeth. Both males were focused and grim.
Both were on the hunt. Both could get killed.

The violence of the past moments quivered around
Leona. "My mother knew exactly what you would do
with that brooch, didn't she?"

"Greer knew I needed this. He'd used Janice as bait,
and this brooch was certain to draw him out. He and
his ancestors have been weaving around yours for centuries. It's time it ended. . . . When we come to this
next intersection, I want you to get out. Take Max with
you—and that purse." Owen glanced at the travel bag
Leona clutched tightly against her. Leona hadn't realized she'd grabbed it on their way out. Terrified and
hurried, she hadn't wanted to leave any part of her life
near Rolf.

Stunned by his order, Leona stared at him. After all that had happened, she couldn't bear being away from Owen. "Where am I going?"

"Anywhere safe. I'll call you as soon as it's finished."

"'As soon as it's finished.'" Leona held her breath; frustration churned in her like fire. "Don't tell me. This is man's work, right?"

Owen didn't look at Leona. "I can't see you in a sword fight, honey. This isn't going to be a mental-break-bones. When it comes down to muscle alone, I'm the best competition. Rolf is mad enough, crazy enough to want flesh and blood, to best himself with that sword."

"I will see this through, Owen Wolf Shaw. I will *not* hide. I claim my right, given to me by my bloodline, just as you claim yours."

"Garbage, and you know it. Nothing will stop him, but death. If anything happens to you and your family—"

"I know exactly what could happen. Rolf made that crystal-clear." Leona tried to hold on to whatever logic was still floating around them. She gripped Max's pelt for comfort. The dog wasn't listening, and neither was Owen. Leona's fear for Owen ran to panic; regardless of danger to himself, he was determined to see Rolf dead. "I love you, Owen."

Owen's reply seemed automatic. "Love you, too." He leaned forward, slowing to stop for a red light. "Get out. Now. Take Max."

He reached across Leona and Max to open the door. "Out."

When the dog didn't move, Leona swung the door closed. "He's not going anywhere, and neither am I. What the hell are we doing, parked here and letting that monster escape? I am not hiding from Rolf. *We* should have followed him."

Leona dug her fingers into Owen's thigh. "This is

idiotic. He has a gun, Owen. He could shoot at us at any time. If I get out, it will be to find him—by myself."

"You would, too. . . . Stubborn woman. Okay, then. We didn't follow him because—" The light turned green, and Owen's pickup surged forward. "That bastard has made a boast. He has to deliver—kill me and get the brooch and you—tonight. His call. I'm just going to make it easy for him. He'll check your place first, then he'll drive to the farm. I intend to be waiting. It's better that a showdown doesn't take place where other people could get hurt. Your neighbors on that cul-de-sac might not know how to handle a sword coming at them."

Owen was primed for a rematch, and Rolf had a gun and that deadly sword; though Leona had seen Owen's skill, she didn't bother to hide the fear in her voice. "We could drive away. You don't have to do this, Owen."

This time, Owen turned to her, his eyes glinting in the shadows. "Sure. You were all decked out, using yourself as bait. What am I doing that is any different?"

Leona gripped the brooch, and a surge of another woman's fear coursed up her arm. Instinctively, she knew that Aisling had feared for Thorgood, a man set on protecting his honor and his love.

"Dammit," she whispered as she stared out at the moonlit night, the peaceful pastures and the rock fences lining the familiar road to the Shaws' farm. "I know. A man has to do what a man has to do."

"You got that right. Erling is a killer, and he won't stop. Prison won't hold him. He'll just be in the wings, waiting to harm your family—and a lot of other people in the process." Owen glanced down at the cuff bracelet Rolf had placed on her. "Take that off. Put on the brooch. If anything happens to me—"

"It won't. Not if I can help it." Leona flung Rolf's bracelet to the floorboard. She would have thrown it out the window, but then someone might find it. No one else should be affected by Rolf's evil.

Owen patted her leg. "Take the brooch off me. Wear it. Right now, I don't have anything to mark you as mine. And right now, that's the closest thing I have. Erling only needed to know that I wore it first—it's a man-thing."

"I'm getting very tired of 'man-things.'" Leona quickly donned the brooch, the metal surprisingly light, despite the large size. When she wrapped her arms around Owen, he glanced at her. His second glance was longer, and he briefly bent to kiss her tears.

"Don't cry, honey. Those little red-haired nieces of yours are going to be just fine. Everyone is." Owen wrapped his arm around her and pressed her close. "I'll be safe. He's not going to use that automatic. He'll want to use that sword. He has to prove himself, to him and to his bloodline, and whatever other garbage goes through his head. I didn't learn how to fight in a pretty gym. Our skirmish will be outside, my advantage. I also see well at night. Erling needed those contact lenses and glasses for a reason."

"Sure. You're having your high noon at nine o'clock at night. You've changed the dynamics from a gunfight to sword and knife. Men have to show up. Men have to die—one or both."

"That's about right."

At the Shaws' farm, Owen parked the pickup. "I want you and Max inside the house. I'll show you how to use a shotgun, just in case. Wait here a moment while I check out the grounds. Let Max out and lock the doors."

Leona waited only seconds after Owen and Max started patrolling, then she got out of the pickup. Owen met her on the front steps. "Okay, I'll ask: What's in the bag? It must be good for you to keep it so close."

"Things. My things. My bag."

"Must be special."

"I didn't want Rolf to have any part of me." She glanced at the thin black braid lying on top of her clothing. "But I guess I have something of his. What made you do that?"

"Instincts. 'Counting coup' is also an age-old tradition. He'll want it back. He's not getting it." Owen glanced around the house and drew his blade; he cautiously advanced into the house. At his nod, Max started hunting through the rooms.

"Stay in. Keep the door shut," Owen ordered Leona when Max returned. Apparently, Max's quick check of the house revealed nothing.

In the darkness, Owen briefly held Leona. "Take it easy. We can do this, Leona."

Leaning away from her, he scanned her face. "You're white and shaking. . . . Don't blame you. If this goes down wrong—but it won't—I want you to let Max go. Rolf will have to deal with him while you get in that pickup and get the hell away. Got it?"

When Leona didn't agree, Owen shook her gently. "Do it."

"Wait here? While you're out there with him? I don't think so."

Owen took a deep breath and shook his head. "About this Thorgood's warrior-descendant thing, add in a little old-fashioned shaman to the bloodline, whatever."

"We know all that."

"Sure. You know everything. Maybe I'd better tell you what *I* know."

Leona crossed her arms and stood back. "Rolf was kind enough to inform me that you have visions. It would have been great if you'd mentioned it earlier. Tell me."

"Okay, I have some—powers, gifts, whatever. I came out here, explored myself, bonded with nature, let some ancestral memories trickle into me. . . . We all knew Borg would do everything in his power to ensure the end of Thorgood and Aisling's bloodline. I knew it. I saw Borg lay his curse on that same brooch. Rather, that vision came to me as I breathed in the scent of Montana's sweetgrass."

" 'Sweetgrass?'"

"I brought some braids with me. I burned one in the way of the old people. I let myself become one with the earth and blood from the ancients, and I saw things."

Owen touched the brooch, then in the same motion, smoothed Leona's hair. "The same shade. The same green eyes."

"Do not tell me you fell in love with Aisling, that you're really another descendant of a disgruntled would-be lover."

Owen's brief smile flashed down at her. "Not quite. Must have been hell communicating with her through the mirror, every time you looked at yourself. Okay, this is what I know, what I saw in my vision. We—the brotherhood, called Men of the Wolf—had to finish Borg and his men. Thorgood had a second-in-command. That was my ancestor—on one side. His name was Hunter. My other ancestor's images were primitive, not like the Viking symbols, but they opened the gate for me to see. They stopped Borg then, and I'll do it now."

Owen's hand moved to caress her. His sensual need throbbed at her, wrapped around and softened her body. "Nice, real nice. Very convenient to remember this now, to give me assurance, I suppose. This last-minute information is no comfort at all. And Owen, I do not know how you can think of sex at a time like this."

"Honey, with you, I'm always thinking about it." Owen smiled briefly and continued describing his dream. "Thorgood was busy. I imagine he was teaching his wife that *sometimes* she needed to listen to him. That left his men to run down Borg, who had been causing problems. My ancestor had a few—powers—he was the tracker, the hunter, a minor seer."

"Great. Just great."

Owen glanced at the windows and inhaled deeply, like a man catching a scent and preparing himself to hunt. "He's hungry tonight. So am I. It's a good night— clear, the air fresh, the moon bright."

He turned to her, and the pure sexual jolt hit Leona, taking away her breath. In that instant, Owen closed the distance, his need igniting hers. His hands ran over her body, claiming her. The caress was hurried and rough, but didn't hurt. Owen wanted to claim what was his by right, the woman who loved him.

Leona recognized that need, that binding possession spiking her own primitive need to bond physically with Owen. She dived into him, hurriedly unhooking his belt and easing down his jeans. Owen cupped her breasts briefly, then slid his hands down her body, shaping her curves as he pushed down her slacks. She clung to him as he eased her back onto the kitchen table, her legs wrapping around him as he entered her quickly, his chest pressing down upon her, his body already thrusting, pushing deeply within her, his hands lifting her to him. Leona dug in for the pleasure and the challenge, hungry for him, tossing away everything but Owen, the pressure building in her. His fingers slid around and touched her, increasing her pleasure, Leona couldn't move as the shock waves vibrated throughout her body.

Owen held her wrists as he stared down at her, his body taut and pouring into hers. She didn't fight the restraint because she understood his need for possession—it matched her own.

Then, as if he'd just realized he'd pinned her wrists, Owen forced his fingers to relax. He rubbed her skin as if trying to erase an injury. "Don't you dare apologize," Leona managed as she wound her arms around him. "There will be other, sweeter times, but not tonight. I wanted this, too."

"Other times. Yes, the soft times a woman should have. I want that for you. You're going to have them—from me."

Owen's shoulders relaxed just slightly, but his heartbeat pounded against her body. Leona held him briefly and smoothed his back. She wrapped her hands in his hair and drew his face close to hers. "Other times. You promised me, Owen. I'll be waiting for those other times," she whispered fiercely.

When Owen eased away and helped her to stand. Leona's legs were weak, her senses dazed as she took in the red marks on his throat. Her breasts still ached from his touch, heightened by his lips and teeth and the hot suction of his mouth, her body vibrating with the need for more.

He quickly dressed Leona, then himself, straightening the brooch at her throat and skimming his fingers lightly over her sensitized breasts. "You were burning the minute I touched you. Are you okay?"

"Of course, I'm okay."

Owen grinned and patted her bottom. "Liar. You're all flushed and ready for more, right now. You'll have to wait."

"Sometimes I could just—" She smoothed her hair in a shaky effort to find calm. It was nowhere around. Owen was right; she moved on instinct, and she'd wanted him desperately, a purely primitive need to claim him.

As she grabbed his shoulders she could feel him moving away from her, priming himself for the battle. After he instructed her on the shotgun, her terror returned. Frightened for him, she whispered desperately, "Please, Owen. Let's leave."

"Too late. I just saw his headlights flash through the trees on the other side of the pond. He's parked on that old side road. . . . Max, stay. Leona, I'd really appreciate it if you didn't distract me from what I have to do. Stay put and remember what I said about Max. If things so wrong, and you need to gain some time to get away, let him go. He knows what to do." Owen swept her to him and kissed her hard. With a solemn nod, he stood back, took off his shirt, and moved out into the night.

She glimpsed the long, red marks on his back, marks of her passion only heartbeats ago.

"Damn you, Owen Wolf Shaw," Leona whispered as she watched him through the window. The moonlight gleamed on his naked shoulders, his lean body quickly closing the distance between the field and the pond.

Beyond the pond, at the trees bordering the field, the moonlight caught on a thin silver line. Leona instantly understood: It was Rolf's deadly sword.

Like Owen, Rolf had come to finish his quest.

Owen moved toward the woods and the gleam of moonlight on that sword. He hurried in order to keep the battle away from the house. If anything happened to him, Leona would need time to get away.

Rolf stood at the edge of the field, his drawn sword a silver vertical line in the moonlight. "Shaw, you have something of mine," he called.

"You'll have to kill me to get it." Closer now, Owen noted the distant beat of music. It grew slightly louder, headlights gliding through the night on the side road. The heavy beat seemed to bounce off the night. Then it stopped near where Rolf had parked.

Rolf had also noticed the vehicle, which began driving away. Suddenly, another set of headlights appeared and followed the first away into the night.

"Maybe you didn't know, Rolf. We have a little problem with car thieves along this road. They're reportedly very good. You can say good-bye to your toy. The next time you see it, it will either be a different color or maybe just a stripped frame. Too bad. And all that nice equipment, too. Wonder what the street value is on those?"

Rolf's long hair flared out around his head as he turned back to Owen. Stepping from the shadows, he raised his sword, gripping it with both hands. "It won't matter. I'll have everything, once you're dead."

"Then let's get on with it." Owen advanced slightly. Rolf had a temper, and Owen knew he had that advantage; Owen had always been as cold as steel in a fight. "Want me to slice off that other pretty braid, Erling?"

The taunt hit home. Rolf charged Owen, who moved easily aside. Owen concentrated on the image of Borg, cornered by Thorgood's warriors. "You know who I am, don't you?" he asked.

"Of course. The hunter, a minor seer, second-in-command on one side, a primitive on the other." Rolf advanced with both hands wielding the sword. As he expertly moved the blade around, the night air filled with the sound of its deadly hiss. "And you're Janice's dear brother. You remember Janice, don't you? Her troubled life?"

Rolf's taunt caused Owen to misstep, and the sword's tip grazed his thigh. Off-balance, he staggered back and went down. His head hit hard, and though momentarily stunned, Owen managed to crouch, his blade raised.

Poised in midair, Rolf's blade gleamed as he stared at the woman standing too close to Owen. "Aisling, my lady," he whispered softly as the honed tip of his sword lowered to trace the brooch at her chest. He tapped it lightly, the metalic ring sounded like a death chime.

"I'll never be yours. Is this what you want, Rolf?"

Dressed in a long gown, Leona could have been Aisling. The slight breeze lifted her hair around her face, the headband gleamed across her forehead, and the silver runes tinkled against her cuff bracelet. She held out her other hand, and Rolf's braid dangled from it.

That deadly, honed blade gleamed in the moonlight as it lifted again to Leona's throat. Owen eased slowly to his feet, aware that one wrong move and Rolf's sword could kill Leona. He glanced around and found no sign of Max. Owen should have known that she'd protect the dog by locking him in the house. Leona wanted this face-to-face with Erling too much to let anything interfere. A challenge was one thing, her death another. Fear riveted Owen, his voice coarse as he ordered quietly, "Move away, Leona."

Neither Leona or Rolf seemed aware of him, their stares locked. The air seemed to vibrate around Owen, the extrasensories challenging each other's strength.

"I'm stronger," Rolf stated firmly, his eyes pinning Leona. He glanced at Owen, as if just noticing him. "Move, and I'll kill her, Shaw. I will anyway. Shaw has had you just now, hasn't he, Leona? You look like a woman who's been used recently. I can feel you now, you're hot—vibrating with sex. You're really very primitive, aren't you?"

Leona ignored the naked hunger in Rolf's expression; Owen didn't. He tensed, ready to spring. With enough luck, he could knock Rolf—and the sword—away from Leona. At this moment, this heartbeat, Owen let his savage instincts rule him. Civilization would make him pay later, but not tonight. His blade would taste Erling's blood, moving through his heart and across his throat. "Leave us, Leona."

"This is my right," she stated firmly.

Rolf's thin lips lifted in a smile. "Throw down the blade, Shaw, or I'll run her through right here."

Owen didn't hesitate. He threw his blade, point deep, into the bluegrass. "Let her go. Fight me, man-to-man. You can use the sword."

"I'd be a fool to try to fight a primitive without my weapon, wouldn't I?" Rolf glanced at Owen's knife, then kicked it aside. The tip of the sword lifted slightly to prick Leona's pale throat, and a droplet of blood appeared. "That's a good boy. Don't try to match me, Leona. You'll lose. You're weaker here."

"Wrong. My family is with me, and Owen. *Owen?*" Her voice sounded the same as when she had called to him earlier, seeking an opening into his senses.

Owen focused on Leona and their senses linked and became one. Rolf's head went back as if taking a blow. One hand left the sword to hold his head.

"How does it feel, Rolf? Put . . . down . . . that . . . sword," Leona ordered softly. Her eyes seem to glow in the night as she leaned forward, pressing her skin against the blade. "Obey me. I hold the power of Thorgood and Aisling. You will do as I say."

Rolf shook his head as if trying to free himself. "Give the brooch to me."

While Leona held Rolf's attention, Owen cautiously rose and eased to stand beside her; that blade was too close to her throat for him to do more.

"Give you everything? I don't think so," Leona said. "You'll have to take the brooch, Rolf. Owen isn't going to let you do that. Neither am I."

"You're only a woman. I'll have Shaw's blood to-night."

"Don't be so sure."

Owen glanced at her. Leona had that fighting look, and she wouldn't·stop. She began backing toward the bluff overlooking the Kentucky River. Owen stayed close to her, with Rolf advancing on them, weaving that deadly blade. Ready to defend his love, Owen began to inch in front of her.

Then suddenly, Leona pivoted and ran toward the river. Surprised, Owen turned slightly, leaving himself open to Rolf's charge. The body blow knocked the wind from him, but he stayed on his feet, following Rolf as he chased Leona.

She stopped on the edge of the rocky cliff overlooking the river for a moment. The next moment, the silver brooch sailed in a high arc toward the river.

Catching up to her, Rolf cursed. "You'll pay for that. Shaw, go after it."

As Owen came to a stop beside them, he recognized a dark shape in the field; Max moved silently toward them. Rolf's eyes widened as he turned toward Max's low warning growl. He began to back away, fear quivering in his voice. "Call off that dog."

Rolf and Leona stood at the very edge of the cliff now, and Max was crouching, gathering his muscles to spring. His teeth glistened in the moonlight as he continued to growl softly. If Rolf went over that deadly cliff, he could take Leona with him. . . .

"He'll go for your throat, Erling," Owen stated. "He'll rip it out."

"Call him off!" Rolf took one step backward. His eyes widened as the earth gave way beneath his feet. He swept out an arm to catch Leona, but instead just brushed her shoulder, sending her off-balance.

Owen caught Leona's wrist just as she lost her footing. He tugged her into his arms as Rolf's wild, surprised cry echoed in the night.

As Owen stood, holding Leona tight against him, the sickening sound of Rolf's body hitting the rocks echoed in the night. Moonlight caught on Rolf's blade as his sword flew high, then straight down into the center of the river.

A loud splash sounded, and Leona and Owen peered down to the river. The current had caught Rolf's body, sweeping it along.

Startled by the noise, deer leaped from the brush and across the field. An owl swept across the night sky, and Leona listened to the solid heavy beat of Owen's heart beneath her cheek. Max lifted his head, and his eerie howl echoed against the rocky bluffs and slid over the quiet river.

"You could have been killed," Owen whispered huskily as he gathered her closer.

Leona couldn't speak. She trembled as she wrapped her arms around Owen.

Rolf's body floated into the shadows, and suddenly Owen and Max were gone. They were only shadows in the night as they moved into the woods bordering the river.

Leona hurried after them. "Owen!"

It seemed like an eternity as she picked her way through the shadowy trees, the thick brush. Suddenly, Max and Owen appeared, startling her. He took Leona's hand, leading her from the woods into the field. "I had to make certain he was really dead."

"Did you . . . ?"

"No. Years of hate and madness killed him. When things quiet down, I'll see what I can do about retrieving Thorgood's brooch."

"I threw Tempest's replica. He didn't die for the real one. It's in my pocket."

"Smart girl." Owen grinned as she withdrew the brooch and placed it back on his chest.

Then she grasped the ancient relic and drew him down to her face. "That's my mark, and you're mine. Got it?"

"Got it."

Epilogue

"IT'S BEEN A HELL OF A LONG NIGHT. I JUST STOPPED BY TO let you know that you can relax. We think we have Missy Franklin's killer and the owner of that SUV. He turned up dead. Fisherman found him at dawn. Looks like he got too close to the cliffs lining the river and lost his balance. Pretty beat-up by rocks."

At eight o'clock in the morning, Tom Roman glanced at Leona and Owen as they sat at her kitchen table.

"Is that right?" Owen asked. Beneath the table, his hand pressed Leona's. It had been a long night for them, too. "I have been concerned about that murder. My sister is due back soon, and I wouldn't want a killer lurking around."

"We found that SUV with the tire tracks matching those we found at your place, Shaw . . . the ones taken after that Missy Franklin was killed. We did a sting operation on that gang of car thieves roaming this area. Found the SUV in an old tobacco barn we've been watching. It was loaded with high-tech equipment and gear for making disguises, wigs, and such. Plenty of cash in it, and the suitcases were filled with high-class clothes that would fit the weirdo with the long hair. Since it didn't seem that the country boys would be using that stuff, we ran some prints. . . . Seems like the dead body washed up down river from your place was the owner of the SUV. He was a man who was supposed to have died in prison years ago . . . name was Rolf Erling, real bad guy."

Only Owen seemed to notice that Leona's hand trembled slightly as she lifted the teapot. This time, Rolf Erling wasn't coming back to life, or taking someone else's identity or mind. Owen had seen Erling's body and had found no heartbeat.

Leona's voice was a little more husky than usual and her face pale, but she managed to appear natural. "More tea, Detective?"

"No, thanks. Been drinking coffee all night. . . . Since this Erling-guy was seen on that same farm road earlier, and those boys didn't have the know-how to use that equipment, we think they're tied together somehow. We found a picture of Missy Franklin on the SUV's sunvisor. It's just a matter of putting the pieces together. Shaw, that farm you bought has been sitting empty for a while. So Erling and his gang could pretty well do what they wanted on the property. You just turned up at the wrong time, so your revolver will be returned shortly."

The detective yawned and wiped his eyes. "Excuse me. Like I said, it was a long night. Got a call last night to go out to Billy Balleau's. He just came home after a tour, and your carpenter, Vernon O'Malley ran out in front of the bus—it killed him. The bus driver saw everything. He just couldn't stop in time. O'Malley smelled to high heaven of alcohol. Balleau says his best wines are gone. O'Malley was house-sitting, and reports say he'd been acting strangely. If you have any information on O'Malley, we need it. Looks like O'Malley went on a drinking binge and trashed Billy's sound and entertainment room. Left a real mess in the kitchen. Balleau is mad as hell."

Roman picked up his teacup and sniffed lightly. "Good stuff. Have to get the wife to get some, better than that green stuff she's so high on. Chai, you say? I'm not fond of adding milk, though. . . . Too bad about O'Malley. We need good repairmen around these old plantation-style houses. Takes a handcrafter's experience to fix 'em."

He scratched Max's ears, and the dog leaned into the luxury; he seemed to be grinning. "Good boy. Friendly kind of mutt, isn't he?"

Leona remembered the way Max's powerful body had tensed, poised to tear out Rolf's throat. "Not always, but he seems to like you."

"I'm a likable guy. . . . Funny thing about this weirdo. He was creepy-looking with all that black hair. Looks like he had just cut off one of two little braids beside his head. And he was packing a shoulder holster. The automatic traces back to a Utah owner, a Mrs. Ted Cheslav. She's deceased, and her son, Alex, bought a place in Lexington. He hasn't returned our calls."

"Oh, Alex? I know Alex Cheslav," Leona stated, to anticipate any questions that might be asked later.

Leona glanced at Owen, who looked relaxed as he sipped his tea. She knew he wasn't; his tense, angry vibrations hadn't stopped hitting her since last night. Owen hadn't been able to take Rolf's blood, and that violent need still ran deep.

"She dated him, before me," Owen stated, as if he'd picked up her purpose. His dark tone suited the part.

"I did not *date* him. He was retired and a good many years older than I. He came into the shop one day and seemed lonesome so we had dinner a few times. He was very nice. I haven't seen him for a while." No one else would be seeing Alex either; Rolf had admitted killing him and taking his identity. But Leona was certain the police would uncover those facts soon enough without involving her or Owen.

The detective flipped through his notebook and stood up. "I'd better be going. We'll question him later. This creep probably stole the gun from Cheslav. We've got Cheslav's address, but no report of a stolen gun."

He took another sip of his tea, and continued, "The problem is, Vernon O'Malley seems tied up in everything that has happened, and he's had a real hard-luck streak—wife dying, bills unpaid. Maybe he was tied up with this Erling fellow. O'Malley got around town . . . he would have been a good connection for a criminal mind. We found some paperwork in his pocket that said Cheslav had him working on his house. O'Malley had plumbing supplies delivered at Cheslav's house, same as the both of yours. Real expensive sound and camera equipment in that SUV. An odd thing was there, too—a fancy scabbard for a long sword. We're tracking down the sales of those now. O'Malley was hard up. He could have been involved in a car-theft ring. Don't go anywhere until I wrap this up. We may need you for more questions."

When the detective left, Leona closed the door against the morning sunlight. She turned to Owen beside her. Max looked up at her, then at Owen, and apparently decided that he didn't want to be involved in this particular discussion. Padding to his rug, he yawned and sank into a big, furry heap.

Owen yawned, too; he looked wary, as if he wanted to escape the same way. Leona wasn't letting that happen. He had questions to answer. Last night, they had been badly shaken and had returned to her home. They'd spent a sleepless night, holding each other close, the embrace reaffirming to each other that they were alive.

"You are *never, ever* to play at duels again," Leona

stated quietly before she rounded on Owen. She didn't waste time. Grabbing a fistful of Owen's shirt, she tugged him closer. When he resisted, she took the *eolh* rune at his throat and eased him down to her eye level. She glanced at the silver rectangle in her hand; the good-luck piece had protected them well—rather Owen had. "Okay, Shaw. Let's have it. I want *more* answers. Now. What else did my mother tell you, before she left?"

Owen reached both hands around to cup her bottom. Caressing her slowly, he eased her closer to him and bent to nuzzle her throat. "Things," he murmured against her skin. "Just things."

The sizzling need for Owen slid through Leona's veins, her body already melting, preparing for his. "I'm going to find out everything, you know," she said, as Owen lifted her into his arms. "You're going to tell me."

Owen smiled down at her. "Uh-uh."

"You're blocking me."

"Uh-huh." His kiss lingered and played and heated.

"I could distract you, then have my way with you."

"Really looking forward to that, lady."

The late-September morning remained bright and warm in Lexington. It had been a full week since Rolf Erling's death.

Owen and Leona had met Janice, Greer, and Kenneth Ragnar at the airport. Claire and Neil's flight would arrive later. Tempest and Marcus were driving and would arrive in the late afternoon. The Aislings badly needed the week to spend together and comfort each other.

Janice had changed dramatically. In jeans and a long-sleeve maroon sweater, and wearing a Celtic protection pendant at her throat, she was radiant. She ran to Owen and leaped into his arms, placing tiny eager kisses all over his face. Astounded, Owen held his sister close, and when he looked at Leona, his eyes filled with tears. She understood his deep emotions; his sister was finally free and safe.

"Big old softy," Janice whispered as she playfully waggled his head, then hurried to hug Leona. "This is going to be great."

She flung open her arms, and said, "Lexington, here I am. Watch out."

Owen said little as they collected the baggage and drove to the farm, where Janice had to see her horses. Kenneth seemed uneasy, but Janice had evidently adopted him and insisted that he visit with them. Greer was pleasant to him, but edgy, especially when she caught Kenneth looking at her.

They watched as Janice played with Moon Shadow and Willow.

"Nice place," Kenneth stated as he looked around the farm. "These old places have more character than the new. You said you've been making improvements, but you know, Owen, with Neil and Marcus here, we could tackle this place and have it shipshape in no time."

Greer's sigh was audible. "He's always fixing everything. Please give him something to do while we're here."

Kenneth nodded and grinned. "Will work for food. Greer is a really good cook."

Greer sighed again, but before she turned away, Leona caught her mother's bright eyes and blush.

A man who had always worked alone, Owen hesitated. "I don't know if we're going to stay here. It might not be the best place for Leona or Janice. I thought I'd finish the current renovations, then put it up for sale."

"I think it's a perfect place. Now." Leona nudged him. "It's a family-thing, Owen, helping each other. Take it and shut up. Your turn to help them will come soon enough."

" 'Family?' " His gray eyes narrowed down at her. "You mean, you and I, as in a 'family?' Wedding rings, all that?"

"You're pushing, Shaw." Leona understood Owen's need for her to wear his mark—it was primitive and dated, and somehow oddly sweet. This time, it was her turn to look away, heat rushing through her body, the thought of Owen as her love, a man with whom she'd begin a new life.

"You need pushing sometimes, honey . . . now excuse me. I need to talk with Janice."

"Okay if I look around the house, Owen?" Kenneth asked, clearly anxious to start work.

"Fine."

Greer and Leona watched as Owen walked to Janice. He took her hand, and together, they walked toward the pond. There, he took something from his pocket and handed it to her.

Next Owen built a small fire and he and Janice crouched beside it. "It's Rolf's braid," Leona explained. "Janice has chosen to burn it. The next time she comes back here, she'll be clean of the past."

Turning to Greer, she took her hands. "It is a time to clean up the past. Nothing could have changed Aisling's gift to us, and I was a fool to try."

With tears in her eyes, Greer gathered Leona close. A warm soft energy enfolded Leona, sparkling like a waterfall, with flashes of joy and relief. Leona held her mother very tightly, "Are we really done with that curse?"

"I believe so. If we're not, we can handle anything—as a family."

Leona breathed the warm September air. It was fresh and clean, and in less than two weeks, the hillsides would be brushed crisp and bright in fiery fall colors. Nature's cycles would begin anew, without the past's shadows over the Aislings.

When Owen looked at Leona, the impact hit her low and soft and hungry. She forced herself to breathe as images of him moving over her, claiming her fiercely, pounded at her.

She threw an image back at him. In it, she wore nothing, her arms outstretched to him.

In her hallway mirror, Leona studied her reflection. That night, her family had settled into the living room, their conversations a low, pleasant hum. Owen came to stand behind her, his hands on her waist. "Everything okay?"

Leona leaned back against him. "I just see myself, not Aisling. What do you see?"

Owen's gray eyes studied their reflection. "Us. Nothing more."

Three days later, the picnic table had been set in front of the farmhouse. The Aisling women stood near the table and added the finishing touches to the evening meal.

They watched the men walk from the farmhouse toward them. Owen, Marcus, Neil, and Kenneth each wore a carpenter's tool belt around their hips, plenty of dust on their shirts and jeans, and big grins on their dirty faces.

"Thorgood's men," Greer murmured, her tone filled with humor. "Coming back from battle, ready to feast. They've done well, and they know it."

"Just look at all that swaggering, macho testosterone. They couldn't be happier, swinging hammers, walking across the roof, tearing out walls, hiking up two-by-fours on their shoulders," Tempest said. "Then at night, they're all busy with their powwows on investment and thoroughbreds. Janice is checking on a two-year-old for them right now. They're going to keep her busy, just running down leads."

"We're the 'fetchers.' 'Drive into town for this and that,' and 'get me that.' It's a good thing they're enjoying themselves," Claire stated. "It's almost a relief to take turns working in your shop, Leona. I think your new employee is going to work out just fine. With Owen in your life, you'll need more time off—men need to be handled with care . . . or so Neil tells me. . . . They'd better do well on this one if they're going to build the addition onto our house."

Tempest sat down and began eating. "I'm hungry all the time now. Marcus still gets sick sometimes when he looks at food. Sorry, I'd wait, but—sorry, I can't," she stated cheerfully around a mouthful of potato salad. "They can help us move into that adjoining horse farm that Marcus just bought. Janice has agreed to run it for him. But he's thinking we might move here. I wouldn't mind if I had a studio. It would be like having a built-in babysitter with Leona nearby. And Mom could stay with us when she wants."

"Neil says there is plenty of opportunity to expand his business here, too. We'll see," Claire said.

Leona couldn't concentrate on what her family was saying. She was too busy staring at Owen as he walked toward her. There was no mistaking that look in his gray eyes.

"In another minute, she'll be drooling," Tempest murmured in an aside.

"Wait until she hears that they're going to redo her office."

Leona considered the four men walking toward them. Descendants of Thorgood's men, they'd protected the Aislings, just as their ancestors had protected the Celtic seer with their lives. All these contemporary men needed was a sword and a shield.

"You know, I don't understand a couple of things," Leona said suddenly. "We've all been together pretty consistently for three days. Why aren't we mixing each other's emotions and thoughts? We seem to be functioning pretty normally . . . for us."

Greer nodded to the hungry men approaching the filled picnic table. "Because of them. You've bonded with them, and that's settled the restless part of you."

Leona studied the men, each wearing a grin. Like Western gunfighters, they unstrapped their tool belts, tossed them into a heap, and set about cleaning up with the soap, towels, and water on the pickup's tailgate.

After washing, Owen walked straight to her. "Hi, green-eyes. Miss me?"

"No," Leona lied, as he took her in his arms.

"I'll have to work on that," he whispered against her ear.

Tempest looked up into the sky. "Look. The crows are flying away."

"Always three crows," Claire said softly. "I wonder why."

Owen's gray eyes caught the evening light. "There are all kinds of legends about crows. But I think they are the watchers. Three crows, three women. Their job is done now."

Leona stared at him. With Native American shaman and Viking blood, Owen was capable of—"Owen, did you have any kind of a vision about them?"

"Now that would be telling, wouldn't it?"